ENDREACH

KEVIN PINES

DARK VALLEY PRESS

For Erin
Without you, I never would have finished this book.

PART I

THE VILLAGE IN THE VALLEY

1

The fog was lighter than usual for the time of year, hanging in thin wisps about the cluster of cottages that sat at the center of the valley. Gently sloping hills rose on all sides, covered in bright-green foliage. A dense wood loomed at the crest of the westernmost hill, shrouded in a fog far denser than that which hung over the valley. Far in the distance, beyond the woods, mountains rose up to meet the sky.

The homes at the base of the hills were sensible, clean dwellings fashioned almost entirely of wood. The walls were composed of huge logs, felled from the woods above, neatly lain atop one another and joined at the corners. The smooth wooden shingles of each roof were well oiled, without a trace of rot to be seen. At a glance, every building appeared to be identical, until one got closer in and noticed the little personal touches each resident had made. Several of the homes boasted well-kept flower gardens, while another displayed a detailed wooden carving of a bird, perched atop the front door's lintel.

At one of the westernmost cottages, deep red curtains

hung in the windows. They were the favorite possession of Mateya Longshear, Endreach's best tailor. Though she'd made countless similar draperies for the other residents of the village, she'd taken extra time and care with her own. Not a stitch was crooked or out of place, and no matter the dampness in the air, they always hung voluminously. The detailed embroidery around their edges showed scenes of birds in flight, interspersed with roses, Mateya's favorite flower.

Jendar Longshear glanced at them yet again as his eyes made another roving trek around the tiny, sparsely furnished room. The curtains looked almost out of place—elegance among simplicity. He glanced at the bare wood floors and up to the rafters of the ceiling above. He gazed out the bedroom door, into the cottage's main living area. He looked everywhere but at the large bed that sat beneath the window, upon which a small form lay.

Looking would have been too painful. Seeing the face of his mother Mateya—her skin sickly gray, her mouth twisted in a grimace—wasn't something he relished. He looked instead at his younger brother, Mathias, who knelt by their mother's bedside, softly stroking her graying hair.

Those two are so much alike, thought Jendar. Mathias always had been the stouter of the two young men, sporting his mother's figure as well as wavy hair that was the same brownish shade their mother's had been in earlier years. Mathias also had their mother's broad, flat nose and her square jaw. She'd often laughed that she would have looked better as a man and had always nodded her head at Mathias, as if to prove it. Though not the most handsome man in the village, he looked good enough to be a favorite among some of the young women.

Jendar, on the other hand, took after their father. His

hair was as vibrantly blond as it had been as when he was a boy, even though he was now twenty years old. Lean and sinewy, he possessed his father's sharp nose and piercing green eyes, as well as his height. As much as Mathias always liked to good-naturedly boast about his superior build, at least Jendar could always take satisfaction in the fact that he was taller.

"How is she?" he said softly.

Mathias grunted. "Not well. They took a lot from her this time. Too much."

Jendar stepped forward and gently placed his hand on his brother's shoulder. The rough weave of Mathias's brown woolen shirt—the type commonly worn by most of the villagers—tickled his palm. "You've been in here all morning. You should take a break."

Mathias hesitated, then nodded, pushing himself to his feet and leaving the house.

Jendar knelt by his mother's bedside, forcing himself to stare at what he didn't want to see. Her features were sallow. She appeared wasted, deathly. He shuddered as he placed a hand on her back.

"I'm here," he whispered, knowing she couldn't hear him. "Mathias went out for a bit, but he'll be back."

Like his brother, he reached out and stroked her hair. One of his fingertips brushed a rough spot on her neck, and he cringed, jerking his hand back involuntarily. He cursed himself silently for such a foolish reaction. He pushed his mother's hair to the side and forced himself to look at what had provoked his revulsion. A single red puncture wound stood like an angry hill on her neck.

It still hasn't healed. You know what that means.

A single tear slid down Jendar's cheek and splashed against a floorboard.

Just like Father, he thought. *Pretty soon it'll just be Mathias and me.*

He sat beside her for a while longer, listening to her quiet breathing. He stood only when Mathias came back inside.

"Still the same?" Mathias asked, though he almost certainly knew what the answer would be.

Jendar nodded as he stood and walked out into the cottage's main chamber. "We have today. That's probably it. You remember how fast Father went when he reached this point." It wasn't a question.

Mathias sat heavily on one of the sturdy benches beside the rough wooden table in the center of the room. "Just us," he breathed. "It'll be just us. First Father, now Mother."

Jendar sat down next to him. "We both knew this time would come eventually."

Mathias's breath hitched, and he wiped at his eyes. "It doesn't make it any easier."

"No, it doesn't."

"And one day...one day...it'll be our turn." Mathias's tears flowed freely, and he fought to speak through them. "One day...when we're older...the lord and lady will finish us...and leave our children without *their* parents."

Jendar put an arm around his brother's shoulders and squeezed him tightly. "We'll need to petition the lord and lady for marriage," said Jendar. "And have children of our own. At least that way we'll live a little longer."

Jendar tried to speak confidently, to instill hope in his brother.

If only he knew how I really feel.

Mathias had a lustful eye for many of the young women of the village, and would regularly confide his desires to Jendar. Jendar would always smile and nod in agreement, though he never admitted that it was the *men* of the village that interested him.

If the lord and lady knew...

He shuddered.

"I don't know if I'm ready for marriage yet," Mathias said tightly. "Who knows who they'd choose for me?"

"It might not be that bad," said Jendar. "Mother and Father were always happy."

Mathias sighed. "They were lucky. Plenty aren't. They'll probably match me up with ox-faced Juliana Woodwright. I swear that girl had a bull for a father."

Jendar chuckled. "It won't be so bad, no matter who they pick for you. Besides, it's better than the alternative."

Mathias grunted. "Only if we have children. If not..."

Jendar felt no need to finish his brother's thought. Everyone knew what happened to the childless among their village.

"I need some air," said Jendar. "Will you be all right?"

Mathias nodded then blew his nose into a handkerchief.

Outside the cottage, Jendar gazed idly at his surroundings. Nearly identical buildings marched off in the opposite direction, met in the center by an intersecting row of the same. To the north of the cottages lay the fields, to the south the workshops. Everything the villagers needed they produced themselves. Livestock for meat, grain for bread and vegetables for stew. No barter system existed among the villagers, nor did currency of any kind. Everyone was expected to work, and everyone got a fair ration of whatever they needed, whether clothes, food or tools. The village's immense well provided an abundance of fresh water—more than enough to support the five hundred or so people who lived there. The only things the lord and lady provided were the occasional cart of iron ore, delivered twice yearly, and

intermittent permission to log at the very edge of the
western wood, on the Nobles' side of the Line of
Demarcation.

Jendar's gaze traveled north, up the gentle slope that led
to the fields and beyond. It settled on the crest of the north-
ernmost hill, where an unnatural darkness clung to the
hilltop like a brooding storm cloud. It was always dark up
there, even when the sun was bright and hot. Deep within
the gloom, he could just make out the outlines of a black
fortress. He'd never gotten close enough to get a good look
at the structure, and he'd never met anyone else who had
either.

When people journeyed too far north of the fields, they
tended to disappear.

He looked to the south and saw the same thing mirrored
on the opposite hilltop: darkness and a massive black
building.

The lord and lady didn't venture out often. To Jendar's
knowledge, the only time they did was to feed. Though he
could count on one hand the times he had seen either of
them, they weren't easy to forget. They looked eerily similar,
even though they were of the opposite sex. Their skin was
pale and waxy, and their noses were sharp, almost beak like,
jutting severely above their overfull, rose-colored lips.
Though they were strange to behold, it was their eyes that
made Jendar cringe; pale and yellow, they glowed dimly in
the darkness, and featured prominently in his nightmares.

Very little was known about them, except that they were
immortal and terrifyingly powerful. It was said they had
lived in their castles—the lady in hers, the lord in his—since
the beginning of time, surviving even the Great Sickness
that had ravaged the countryside in olden times. Most
people spoke of them as gods.

Though Jendar wasn't entirely convinced of their godliness (they had to eat just like everyone else, and what kind of god needed food?) he knew one thing surrounding their lore was true: there had been a cataclysm some time long ago, and though many people had died, the lord and lady had somehow survived. Indeed, Jendar firmly believed the reason the western woods were so strenuously forbidden, and so often prowled by the Nobles' slavering thralls, was to keep the people in the village from knowing just how vast their civilization had once been.

This revelation had come to him as a boy, when his parents' admonitions that he must never, under any circumstances, venture into the western woods had filled him with such curiosity that, as young boys tend to do, he had disobeyed them at his first opportunity. His first two visits to the woods had been brief; several of the Nobles' malforms had been foraging nearby on both occasions, forcing him to quietly and hastily retreat.

The third time, however, he'd gotten lucky. None of the creatures were prowling the woods that day, at least not near where he had journeyed. He had managed to get a good way in before the sinking sun had forced him back the way he had come. Each time he visited the woods, he journeyed a bit farther. The malforms had only spotted him twice, occasions that Jendar remembered vividly. Fortunately for him, the ones that had attempted to run him down had been great lumbering brutes, ill-suited to moving quickly through the woods. Both times, Jendar had arrived back at the village breathless and terrified, vowing never again to venture too far in.

But his curiosity always seemed to get the better of his common sense, and back he'd go, pushing his journeys ever farther. Jendar had learned to be cautious, to listen, and to move with stealth. He had spotted the malforms on many more occasions, but they never again saw him.

One day, after sneaking away from the village particularly early, he had managed to push all the way through to the other side. That was a day he'd never forget.

The woods had begun to thin out gradually some time before disappearing completely, lush foliage slowly giving way to scraggly brush and stunted, half-dead trees. The farther along Jendar crept, the less alive the landscape appeared. Although the slope of the land began to rise, he pressed on, sweating from the effort of climbing up the steepening hill. Dirt cascaded down behind him with every step, with no roots of any kind to hold it in place. He looked back the way he had come and saw the woods standing proudly at the edge of the festering earth around him, seeming to eschew the barren rock on which he stood. Jendar went back to his climb, mounting the last ridge before the hill's apex.

Immediately, he noticed the shapes.

Squat, dull gray and half the height of a man, they thrust up through the soil like cairns in seemingly every direction. Slowly he approached one, placing his hand on it, feeling its perfect smoothness beneath his fingertips.

Metal. This is some kind of metal.

Jendar rubbed at the shape, clearing away layers of grime, and was shocked at how much it shone.

Not a trace of rust anywhere.

The best iron rusted easily if left out in the rain for just a single night, but the metal before him seemed perfect, as if it had just come from the forge.

He gazed at the other shapes for a while longer, counting them.

Ten. Fifteen. Twenty.

They were everywhere, in every direction, all the way up to the top of the hill. He continued the climb, slower this time, counting each new shape as it came into sight.

As he reached the top of the hill, and his eyes fell upon the valley below, his concentration shattered. All thoughts of counting the shapes fled, and for a moment, his lungs couldn't get enough air.

The valley was immense—five or six times the size of the relatively tiny impression in which the village of Endreach sat. The hills on the far horizon were visible only as small humps, rolling off into the distance. It wasn't the valley's size, however, that made Jendar's eyes widen and his muscles go slack.

The valley was full of *things*.

The dull metal humps had been a mere foreshadowing of what the valley held. Massive objects of the same metallic sheen as the shapes he'd seen stood in perfect rows, side by side, flanking wide, jet-black strips that crisscrossed the entire valley floor.

The objects varied widely in size and shape. Some were short and wide, with fluidic, twisting lines that befuddled Jendar's perceptions. Others were impossibly tall, impeccably straight, reaching so high they were nearly at the same level as where he stood at the very highest point at the edge of the valley. Each one was unique, and all seemed so artfully delicate as to crumble at the slightest touch, yet bold and strong enough to survive an inferno.

Their majesty was marred by the silence that pervaded the valley like the pause before a scream, and the haze of dust and filth that choked every corner of the valley floor lay heavily upon them. The gleaming objects, however, were mesmerizing in their unparalleled craftsmanship; breathtaking in size; and utterly dumfounding in their sheer

number, yet there was a sadness to them, a sense of loneliness made more profound by the heavy silence of the place,
and the lack of any living thing.

No birds. No animals. No plant life. Nothing here moves. Not
even a breath of wind.

As Jendar stared and the silence of the place began to
grow oppressive, he was suddenly struck with a revelation
that made his legs give out. His backside hit the ground
hard, but he barely noticed.

A village. I'm looking at a village.

Though the construction was completely foreign and on
a scale that was practically unimaginable, there was no
mistaking the layout. What Jendar saw could only be some
kind of immense *village*, built to a scale that defied compre-
hension. The black swaths that spanned the valley floor and
met each other at evenly spaced right angles could only be
roads, while titanic shapes jutting upward beside them like
hogbeast spines bore the unmistakable hallmark of
buildings.

The more he stared, the more he began to notice details
that he hadn't seen right away. The roads, though straight
and true, were littered with debris. The buildings, though
breathtaking, bore unmistakable signs of age. In fact, some
of what he'd originally taken for squat, jagged structures
were in fact buildings that had toppled at some point. One
such stubby, forlorn shape sat at the foot of a perfectly
linear patch of destruction that spanned nearly the entire
valley floor. The remnants of the part of the building that
had fallen lay in eternal repose among the shattered
remains of its crushed fellows.

Jendar couldn't imagine how old this village must be. In
his mind, anything constructed from a metal that scoffed at
the elements should have the power to exist forever. The

state of some of the buildings, however, seemed to suggest otherwise.

After gazing incredulously for a while longer, he wondered who had built this village. Immediately his thoughts went to the lord and lady. Surely this must have been their handiwork, created long ago for some unknown purpose. No man or woman would have been capable of conceiving a village of such massive proportions.

It wasn't until months later, when Jendar had worked up the courage to explore the ruins, that he realized the massive expanse had once been the dwelling place of humans. As he cautiously picked his way through one of the abandoned buildings, he came upon a room that was stacked floor to ceiling with artwork. Paintings and sculptures of astounding workmanship crammed the room from end to end, preserved in clear cases of varying shapes and sizes. Every piece of art depicted humans in one fashion or another, from grisly scenes of epic battles to beautiful renderings of mothers and children.

In all of it, Jendar saw not a single depiction of anyone who looked like the lord or lady.

As the years went on and his explorations of the ruins grew bolder and more prolonged, he discovered hidden caches of strange and wondrous artifacts, inventions from a forgotten time that put the best work of his fellow villagers to shame. Many of the items he found no longer functioned, but once in a great while, he stumbled upon something that did.

Unbeknownst to anyone but his brother Mathias— whom he had finally taken into his confidence after Mathias had pinned his arms behind his back and demanded to know where he had snuck off to so often—Jendar had managed to gradually smuggle a number of artifacts into their home. They lay concealed under a loose floorboard, behind the ladder to the loft where he and Mathias slept.

Initially, Mathias hadn't approved of Jendar's exploits and had insisted he never make the trip again. What if the Great Sickness still lurked among the ruins? Even worse, what if the Nobles found out? Everyone knew they had the uncanny ability to discern exactly what went on in the village. Surely, they knew about Jendar's visits to the forbidden wood and were waiting for an appropriate time to punish him. Mathias was shocked to learn that Jendar had been making his trips into the ancient village for a little more than a year and hadn't been punished yet.

Eventually he had convinced Mathias to go with him. Ever since, the two of them had made each journey together, smuggling back what they could. Each time that they beheld the ruins of the magnificent village, they reminded themselves of the danger involved in traveling there. Though Jendar and Mathias hadn't yet suffered any form of reprisal for their actions, they had seen others subjected to punishments for similar offenses.

Just last season, Rett Woodcutter had loudly boasted that he and his sons had killed a malform in the woods after logging a good distance beyond the Line of Demarcation. The weathered flaying post that stood on a raised platform in the middle of town did nothing to dissuade him. He'd always been a proud man; perhaps his pride had given him the illusion that the Nobles were somehow incapable of punishing him.

The next day, Rett found himself tied to that very post, before the entire town. When the malforms had finished canvassing Endreach's homes and workhouses to ensure that everyone was present, his offense had been declared before the assembled townsfolk.

The crier, as he was known, was a malform who stood mostly upright and had alarmingly human features. His gnarled arms and legs were much straighter than most, and his teeth were square, not sharp. Still, he was unmistakably monstrous. The creature was as grossly muscular as the rest of his kind, and his patchy scalp leaped with lice. A severe overbite made him drool almost constantly, and his speech, though comprehensible, was hopelessly slurred. Unlike the other malforms, he wore what passed for clothing—a ragged, stained set of gray trousers and a frayed vest, open at the chest.

Once the offense had been made known, another malform, brutish and more typical of the race, had begun to deftly carve the skin from Rett's thrashing frame. To this day, Jendar could still hear his screams, and the screams of every one of his fellow villagers he had witnessed being punished in the same manner. A sight like that was something one never forgot.

He and Mathias were both well aware of the risks involved in traveling to the ruins and had long ago vowed never to share their journeys with anyone, not even their parents.

I wouldn't even chance telling old Bershon about this, he thought now, as he gazed at the two dark, foreboding castles.

A stoop-shouldered oak of a man, Bershon Oresmith, at fifty-five years, was old enough to be nearing the end of his days. He was widely regarded as somewhat of a recluse and a bit of an eccentric, and since he and his apprentices were only required to work the forge twice a year when the ore carts were delivered, he had a great deal of idle time on his hands. He spent much of this time either drinking or targeting rats and blackjays with his sling and bag of stones, items he never seemed to be without.

Though he'd gone after vermin for as long as Jendar could remember, the drinking hadn't started until Bershon had lost his two young sons, Josha and Verdan, in the fire that had consumed the original forge. No one in the village ever commented on the old man's drinking, and as strange as he was, people appreciated him not only for the fact that he made all the village's iron tools but also because he was most likely the reason the village had virtually no rats.

Though he avoided most of the other villagers, he had always been close with Jendar's family, and had been a confidant of Jendar's since he was a boy. He was slow to judge and always lent a sympathetic ear. Whenever Jendar broke something or otherwise violated his parents' rules, Bershon always had been there to help soften the blow. The man had been a friend of Jendar's father, Olef; they'd been close since before Jendar was born, and Bershon had taken it especially hard when the lord and lady had decided that Olef had lived long enough. Bershon had been there the day they'd lit Olef's pyre and had visited the family twice already since Mateya had fallen ill.

Soon it'll probably be Bershon's time too, Jendar thought. *The lord and lady don't often allow people to grow as old has he has.*

He felt a pang at the thought of losing him. He'd always been like an uncle to Jendar and Mathias and always had a joke at the ready for Mateya. His wife, Bella, had been just like him—stout of body and mind, with a quick wit and a pleasant, rosy face.

The Nobles had taken her two years ago.

Jendar kicked at the dirt and turned back to the door. The wind must have shifted, as he could just make out the ripe scent of the eastern bog in the air. Inside, a freshly kindled fire greeted him. Mathias had ignited some tinder and was gradually adding larger logs.

"Can't say I'm really all that hungry," Jendar said, as he plopped down on the wooden bench.

"I'm not either," said Mathias, his voice strained. "But we need to eat."

Jendar left Mathias to his task and checked Mateya again. Though she hadn't moved an inch, her chest gently rose and fell.

For a moment, Jendar wildly entertained the hope that his mother would pull through, that the Nobles' excessive feeding hadn't overwhelmed her. Perhaps, if she recovered enough, they could make the journey to the ancient village together. Maybe, if they ran far enough, the lord and lady wouldn't find them. They could live among the ruins, together, safe from the predations of their overlords.

Then what? said a voice in the back of his mind. *Where would you farm? How would you take cattle through the woods undetected? What if the malforms found you? Or the Nobles themselves?*

"We could run farther," he whispered to himself. "Beyond the ruins. Take enough supplies to get us through. We could keep running, until...until..."

"What did you say?"

Mathias turned to look at Jendar. "Nothing. Just muttering to myself. Thinking about how crazy it would be to just take Mother through the woods, to the ancient village, where the lord and lady can't find her."

Mathias paused, his eyes narrowed. "I don't think that's crazy at all," he said slowly. "I think it just might work. We could take turns carrying her on our backs. We could bring food, water. They'd never find us there. The ancient village is too big for them to search the entire place."

Jendar shook his head. "No, Mathias. It would never work."

"Why not?" Mathias shot back. "Think about it! We could bring seed. We could farm beside the ancient village, where there's open land. We could steal a few calves from the pasture, start our own herd, and..."

"Mathias."

"...we could dig a well. Start a new village, a new life. Maybe we could even take some of the others with us! I'd bet my prized shears that Mathilda Thatcher would go. That girl is the most beautiful in the village, and we could get married—"

"Mathias!"

Mathias stopped mid sentence.

"It would never work," Jendar said. "Think about what you're saying. Do you know how much we'd need to bring? How many cattle for milk and meat? And what about tools? Shovels for digging the well. Ploughs for the fields. Hammers and nails to build fences for the cattle and saws to cut timber. Do you really think we'd carry all that through the woods without someone—or *something*—noticing? Besides, if we went missing, the Nobles would find out."

Mathias shrugged. "But how would they know what happened to us? For all anyone would know, we fell into the bog. It's happened before."

"To an entire family, at the same time? With two or three cows and a host of supplies missing? Think about what you're saying. No one would believe that. They would know we ran away."

Mathias opened his mouth, as if to argue. Then his shoulders slumped. "There's really no way, is there?"

Jendar moved to where Mathias stood and embraced him. His brother hugged him back.

"It'll be all right, Mathias. We pulled through when they took Father. We'll pull through again."

Mathias said nothing in reply.

"Why don't we get dinner started?" Jendar asked. "You're right—we need to eat."

2

Between the two of them, they were able to get dinner together relatively quickly. Some crushed grain from their stores and a few hastily chopped vegetables from the garden out back made a hearty pottage, which the brothers devoured. Jendar took a bowl in to Mateya and set it by her bedside in case she should come to, but she remained motionless, barely breathing.

They'd nearly finished when a sharp rap on the door interrupted them.

"Ho, there!" came a gruff, slightly slurred voice from the other side. "You boys home?"

Jendar smiled as he opened the door to the stooped figure of Bershon Oresmith. Like most of the other villagers, he wore a brown, woolen shirt and matching trousers, though he also sported a rough leather vest that looked as if he'd fashioned it himself. From the smell of the man, he'd been in his cups again.

"Bershon! Good to see you. Won't you come in? We've some dinner left if you're hungry."

Bershon nodded graciously. He entered with his characteristic uneven gait and seated himself at the table. Mathias stood, fetched a fresh bowl, and ladled a couple of scoops of pottage into it.

"Thank you, my boy," the old man said, helping himself to a large spoonful. His meaty hand, bearing its fair share of burns and scars from hard work at the forge, virtually eclipsed the spoon as he grasped it. He brushed a stray wisp of thin, graying hair off his forehead, then scratched at the graying stubble on his rounded jaw.

"How's your mother?" he said between bites.

"The same," said Jendar.

Bershon grunted. "Lovely woman, Mateya. Shame it's come to this again. She had a lot of years left in her. We all do, in the end."

Jendar and Mathias remained silent.

"Brings me right back to when they took Bella. People say the pain of loss goes away with time. But it doesn't. You just learn to live with it, or it eats you alive." He took another large bite, chewing slowly. "So many taken before their time. So many lives cut short. The thought of it is enough to drive a man mad."

Mathias nodded dejectedly. "Mother...was strong. Full of life."

Bershon nodded. "Most are, when they're taken. Strength doesn't mean anything. When you're old enough... well. My time's about here too, I'd reckon. Won't be long before those bastards show up to bleed me dry."

"I think you have some time left, yet," said Mathias hopefully. "Maybe more than you—"

Bershon waved his comment away with a gentle motion. "That simply isn't true," he said softly, "and you and I both know it."

He fixed Mathias with a penetrating gaze. His bright-blue eyes, sharp as ever, made Mathias squirm uncomfortably. He turned to Jendar. "Your father, Olef, and I went back a long way. A *long* way. He was the first friend I remember having, in days so far back I can't remember much. When our parents' time came, we looked out for each other. And we vowed that one day, when we had little ones of our own, whoever was left would watch out for them. And that's what I intend to do."

He spoke those words with such a sense of finality that there was no arguing with him.

Bershon finished his pottage and declined the offer of a second bowl. He stood, reaching into the rough leather pouch that always hung at his side. He uncoiled his sling, which he had wrapped neatly around his weathered tan belt. Silently he opened the door and poked his head outside. Suddenly he grew very still, then slowly lifted a stone from the pouch and fit it to the sling's cup. Then, in one motion, he was out the door, the sling whirling. Eyebrows raised, Mathias glanced at his brother. Jendar shrugged and mouthed, "No idea." Jendar heard the light slap of leather as Bershon released the stone, followed by a brief cry as the stone struck something.

Nodding with satisfaction, Bershon reentered the cottage and shut the door behind him.

"Noticed that one on my way over," he whispered.

He glanced under the table then poked around the cabinets beneath the window. He made a quick circuit around the room, pausing briefly at the door to Mateya's bedroom. He glanced back at Jendar.

"Mind if I have a look under the bed? I swear on my life, I won't disturb her."

"Uh, yes, I guess," Jendar stammered. "But why?"

Before he'd managed to fully form the question,

Bershon had disappeared into the bedroom. Moments later he was back in the main room, heading up the ladder to the loft where Jendar and Mathias slept.

"You boys notice any rat droppings around here?"

Mathias frowned. "We keep a clean home, Bershon. Trust me, there are no rats here."

He nodded but continued up the ladder anyway.

"Well," he said on his way back down. "You don't lie. This house is spotless. Not a sign of vermin anywhere."

Finally Jendar found his voice. "Bershon, I mean no disrespect, but what on earth are you up to?"

The man again seated himself at the table, tucking his sling back into his belt. "The blackjay outside," he began. "The one I took down a moment ago. It wasn't *right*. Blackjays are finicky. They never stay in one place for long, unless they're nesting. Or mating. But that one...it just sat there. Staring. At this house. It hadn't moved a muscle since I came in. Now I'm not perfect, and I could have been wrong, but I'd bet all the drink in the ale hall that the blackjay outside was a thrall of the Nobles."

The skin on the back of Jendar's neck prickled, and he shivered.

Mathias frowned. "What do you mean, 'a thrall of the Nobles'? It's not a malform, Bershon. It's just a bird."

"Aye. No doubt it was a bird. But it wasn't *just* a bird." Bershon dropped his voice even further, and the brothers had to lean in to hear him. "Ever wonder how the lord and lady always seem to know what goes on in the village? How they know who steps out of line, who to punish? It's the blackjays. And the rats.

"I'm not claiming that every single rat or blackjay is worrisome. Most of them behave normally enough. But sometimes there are one or two that don't do what you'd expect rats or blackjays to do. They sit still. They don't forage or run from people. They *listen*. The Nobles use them as their eyes and ears."

Jendar wasn't sure what to make of Bershon's odd statements. Yes, the man often made strange comments, like the time he'd loudly announced—in the middle of the village square—that he'd work no more iron after dusk because he didn't like the way hot iron glowed in the dark, but the assertion that rats and blackjays were in the employ of the Nobles seemed ludicrous, even for him.

"What do you mean, they listen?" Mathias asked softly. He met Bershon's eyes with a gaze that was every bit intent as the old man's.

"The lord and lady have a lot of strange abilities. One thing they can do involves animals—only certain animals, mind you. They can...*inhabit* them somehow. Use them to see and hear things, even when they're far away. Why do you think I carry this sling? I kill every rat and blackjay I see that doesn't act normal. And more than a few of the normal ones too, just to keep the Nobles' eyes off me. Less suspicious that way."

"So you're saying the blackjay outside was...was really the lord or the lady?" Mathias asked. "Watching our house?"

Bershon shook his head. "No, no, not a Noble in the flesh. But the eyes of a Noble, yes. And yes as well to it watching your house. Mateya has been chosen to die. To my knowledge, one or two other people in this village who have gotten up in years have been chosen as well. And you know what? Every single one of their houses—*every one*—has a blackjay on a neighboring roof, staring at it."

Mathias's skin turned a shade of gray, and he looked ill. "Are you certain, Bershon? Why have we never heard of this before?"

"You've never heard of it because no one knows. And the Nobles don't want us to know. I'm the only one who's on to their secret."

"Why tell us then?" said Jendar.

Bershon's tone grew even more serious. "Because I swore to Olef I'd look out for you boys. As you know, your mother doesn't have much time left, so I'm going to teach you everything I know about the Nobles. How to keep your heads down. Avoid notice. How to live as long as you can. You just have to swear one thing to me: tell no one else. What I know...it's dangerous. People have been killed for far less than passing this type of knowledge around."

Jendar glanced about nervously, considering Bershon's words. Were they the ramblings of a half-drunk, half-mad man, or did Bershon really have information that could help them? If he did possess such knowledge, what kind of danger would Jendar be putting himself and Mathias in if he let Bershon tell them?

Before he had a chance to voice any of his concerns, Mathias spoke up. "What do you know? Tell us everything."

Jendar shot him an agitated glance, which his brother ignored.

Bershon smiled lightly. "The bit about the spies, you know. Never trust a rat or a blackjay."

"What about cattle? Or sheep?" Mathias asked, leaning forward.

"They're fine. Nobles don't seem to like using them. *Can't* use them, more than likely. Their magic favors scavengers. Carrion eaters. Creatures of the dusk."

"What about bats?" the boy pressed.

Bershon shook his head. "Too stupid. The animal has to be clever for the Nobles to use it, and there ain't a bird or rodent that's cleverer than a rat or a blackjay. They need to be small and inconspicuous. I've heard of them using wolves before, but what good would that do them here? They need something the villagers don't see as a threat."

"How about dogs or cats?" asked Mathias.

"Too domesticated. Maybe a wild dog or cat would work but not one that's being cared for by a human."

Jendar brought his hand down on the table—not hard, but enough to put a jarring halt to the conversation.

"Bershon," he said, favoring the man with an expression he hoped was mild, despite his clenching guts. "I'm the eldest, so I speak for our family." He turned his gaze upon Mathias. "You need to remember that as well, brother."

Ashamed, Mathias looked down the table.

"These things you want to tell us..." Jendar said. "I worry about them. Please don't misinterpret what I'm saying—I love you like family, Bershon, and I appreciate any help you're willing to offer. And I know Mathias does too. But what you're saying...such words are dangerous. If you're right, and the Nobles' eyes and ears really are everywhere, what's to stop them from overhearing us right now? And punishing us for our knowledge?"

"Jendar," said Mathias, "you of all people should know that the lord and lady don't see and hear everything. How long have *we* remained safe from their punishments?"

Jendar was about to argue but stopped himself. Mathias was right, of course. They'd been journeying to the ancient village for years, returning home with artifacts that undoubtedly would earn the Nobles' ire if they learned of them.

"All I'm saying is this," Mathias continued, "if Bershon knows something that can help us live a little longer, wouldn't we be fools not to hear him out?"

Jendar gave what his brother had said a moment's

thought before nodding. "I might be older," he said slowly, "but I guess I'm not the only one with a bit of wisdom on my side."

Mathias practically swelled with pride.

"If you don't mind my asking," said Bershon, with an amused twinkle in his eyes, "just what have you two boys been up to that might earn you a death sentence?"

Jendar decided that anything he was willing to share with Mathias, he could share with Bershon. The man was obviously willing to put his own life at risk to help them. The least he could do was show him a degree of trust.

"We've been beyond the western wood, Bershon. Many times. We've been making the journey for years now."

Bershon leaned back in his chair. "So you've seen the old village."

Jendar's mouth practically fell open, and Mathias's eyes grew wide. "You...you know of it?" Jendar said.

The man grinned widely, revealing a couple of missing teeth. "Of course. Been going there since I was younger than you. Haven't been there in years, on account of my back, but I'd imagine it hasn't changed a bit. It never does."

"But...I thought..." Jendar stammered, unable to finish his thought. His knowledge of the village, and what it contained, had given him a feeling of isolation over the years. True, having Mathias as a confidant helped, but that didn't change the fact that what he experienced there—and what he learned of the ancient people who had lived there —were extraordinary things he'd thought he'd forever be forced to keep buried within his soul.

"I've been there," Bershon repeated softly, resting a rough hand on Jendar's forearm, as if he knew exactly how the younger man felt. "I've explored it many times, and I still haven't scratched the surface."

"Have you...found anything there?" asked Jendar.

Bershon nodded. "Wondrous things. Ancient devices. Light-makers, lifters and spinners—gadgets of all kinds. Most of them still worked when I found them, though only a few still do now. Others seemed to be in good shape, but I never could figure out what they were for."

"Lifters and spinners? What are they?" asked Jendar.

"Lifters are little rectangles that, well, lift things. Point a lifter at a heavy object, and you can move it without laying a hand on it. Spinners spin. Really fast. Not exactly sure what they're meant to do, though. They are fun to watch, at least."

"We've found a lot there too," said Jendar. "We have a few light-makers ourselves. No one but Mathias knows. Not even Mother. I can show you some of the things we've brought back, if you want."

Bershon nodded. "Please do. I've always loved the ancients' inventions. Hard to believe there were ever people capable of building such things." He let out a sigh laced with sadness. "How far we've fallen."

Jendar stood up from the table and walked back behind the ladder that led up to the loft. Kneeling, he pulled a small, flat piece of metal from his pocket. He inserted it between two of the boards and, with a quick motion, pried one of them up. Beneath the board was a long, narrow pit, roughly four hands deep. The bottom and sides were lined with an oiled piece of hide, perfectly contoured to fit inside. Arranged atop the hide was an assortment of neatly stacked metallic objects. One side of the hole was dominated with shiny metal cylinders, about a half hand tall, stacked in three neat rows. The other bore a stack of devices of various shapes and sizes—some were rectangular; a few were square; some were spherical. One was a smooth disk with rounded edges, about a quarter-hand deep and as wide across as a dinner plate. The disk's surface was pristinely smooth and flat, save for a cylindrical indentation at its center.

Jendar moved to the side as he heard Bershon and Mathias shuffle up behind him. Bershon let out a low whistle.

"Quite a collection you've got there. And in such good condition! I recognize that"—he pointed to the disk—"and those," he said, gesturing to the rows of cylinders. "I have one as well and plenty of cylinders to boot. Mine was never in the best shape—pretty banged up, but it worked for a while." He hunched down next to Jendar. "Some of these I recognize, too," he said, pointing at the rest of the devices. "Any idea what they are or what they do?"

Jendar shrugged. "I've gotten a few of them to do... things. Some of them don't appear to do anything. Either they don't work, or I simply have no clue how to use them. Generally, if I find something intact, I bring it here, whether or not it's in working order. It just...doesn't seem right to leave them there, in that forgotten village. They're treasures, and they should be preserved."

Bershon nodded. "One or two of these are actually pretty useful, once you know how to use them. Some of the others, I'm not familiar with. That sphere," he said, pointing. "What does it do? Does it work?"

Jendar nodded. He reached down and gently lifted one of the devices from the hole. It was a perfect sphere, black as onyx, bearing a small cone that protruded from it like a tiny nose. Jendar shook it, and three colored glyphs appeared on the surface opposite the cone. One was red, one green, one blue.

Gently, Jendar balanced the sphere on the cone. He steadied it with one hand then touched the blue glyph. He removed his hand, but the sphere remained upright, balanced perfectly. It began to spin, slowly at first but rapidly gaining speed. When its speed was such that the three glyphs blurred together into a single, multicolored ring, the sphere slowly rose off the floor. It emitted a soft melody, bearing intonations completely different from those produced by any instrument Jendar had ever heard. When it reached a height of about three hands, it stopped rising and glowed a resonant blue from within. Its color gently shifted from blue to orange, then to a deep red. The melody continued to play the entire time. The three of them watched, mesmerized. Mathias's lips bore a small smile, as did Jendar's. The sphere was incredibly soothing to behold. He had brought it out on more than one occasion since his mother had fallen ill.

"Beautiful," Bershon breathed.

After a while, the melody began to fade; its spinning slowed; and it lowered itself back to the floor. It balanced on its point until the spinning stopped. Then, all at once, the glyphs blinked out, and the sphere fell gently on its side.

"Only the blue symbol works," Jendar said. "The others don't seem to do anything."

Carefully, Jendar put it back with the rest of his trove.

"I've never seen anything like that before," said Bershon. "I can only guess at its original purpose. A music device, no doubt, but something more than that. I felt...very relaxed when I watched it."

Jendar nodded. "It's one of my favorites."

"One of these days," Bershon said, "I'd like it if you would come by, if my back isn't hurting too much, and take a look at what I've managed to find over the years. I think the two of you would enjoy it."

"We would, and thank you for the invitation," said Mathias.

Bershon nodded. "The disk. May I see it?"

Jendar nodded, and Bershon reached down and gently removed the device.

Carefully, the old man turned it over in his hands. "Perfect. Not so much as a scratch on it. Where did you manage to find one in such good condition?"

"Some years ago, when Mathias and I were exploring one of the old buildings, we found a room on one of the lower levels. A lot of what was in the building was as you'd expect—dust, decrepit bits of who knows what, broken doors. Well, the doors to this one room were in nearly perfect shape. Closed tightly. Of course, we were intrigued. The seam down the middle of the door was just wide enough to insert the tip of a metal bar we found lying around. Between the two of us, we were able to work the bar in and pry the doors open."

"Bershon, the room was perfect," Jendar continued, smiling. "No dust. No debris. It looked like whoever was in charge of the place might have stepped out just moments before we walked in. And the cylinders...hundreds. Thousands. Rows upon rows of them, on shiny metal shelves, covering three of the four walls, stacked so high the light barely reached the topmost ones. All in perfect shape, near as we could tell. Now, at that time, I had no idea what they were. To me, they were just pretty objects, decorations of some kind.

"It wasn't until I found that"—he gestured to the device Bershon held—"that Mathias and I figured out what they were. The disk sat on a smooth, black table, at the foot of the only wall in the room that didn't have those shelves. There was a single chair at the table, made out of an identical material. I moved it to the side to get closer in and get a better look at the disk. One of the cylinders was already in it, and there were a few more arranged neatly next to it. When I went to pick it up, I accidentally brushed the part of the disk right next to the cylinder holder—the part that starts the thing up. As you can imagine, we had no idea what to expect. I don't know how either of us went without dying of fright when the room around us disappeared, and we found ourselves...somewhere else. There was open sky above us. Trees, grass. The scent of fresh air. And there were people there—gathered together, laughing and talking. It seemed so *real*."

"I think the only thing that kept me sane," said Mathias, "was that I could still see you."

Jendar laughed. "Agreed. You and I seemed to be the only things left of the room we'd just been standing in. Except for the doorway, of course."

Bershon nodded. "I remember my first time with one of them. Nearly scared me to death. As soon as I saw that door, I jumped right back through it. Left the disk where it was, didn't dare go back for it for quite some time."

"We did pretty much the same thing," Jendar said. "The door was behind us, as it always is. We could still see the room through it. It wasn't far from where we stood, but getting to it seemed to take a lifetime. When we were through, our new surroundings vanished. Mathias and I were right back where we'd started, in the exact same positions we'd been in before we left.

"Both of us just stood there, staring at each other, too terrified to move. We thought we'd just been magically whisked away to some other place. It wasn't until we worked up the courage to fiddle with the disk again that we realized none of it was real."

"So," said Bershon with a grin, "how did you finally figure it out?"

"We tried talking to the people we encountered," said Mathias. "We went back in to the same cylinder. Back to the open grassy area, with the people nearby. They were having some sort of party. A little pavilion had been set up, where more people sat and spoke with one another. And all of them spoke so strangely; we couldn't understand a word of it. And the way they dressed...I've never seen anything like it. I have no idea what material their clothes were made of— definitely not wool. The colors they wore were more vivid than anything I've seen, like rainbows on fabric. When they ignored us, I thought they either couldn't understand us either, or they were just being rude. I reached out to touch one of them, and my hand...passed through him. That's when I noticed our feet—they weren't exactly touching the ground, but they weren't elevated. It was like they were suspended in something that wasn't really there. Our footing was sound enough, but it wasn't exactly firm. It's a feeling I still haven't gotten used to."

"Of course," said Jendar, "we both know now that we hadn't really gone anywhere at all. At least not physically. But it took us a long time to figure out what was happening. Close as we can tell, when you use the disk, your body stays put, but somehow your mind goes into the cylinder, seeing whatever's there."

Bershon nodded thoughtfully. "Never thought of it that way. To me, it always seemed like what was in the cylinder came into my head, rather than the other way around. Either way you look at it, it's probably the most incredible thing I've ever experienced. So...how many of them have you seen?"

"Lots," said Jendar. "We've seen almost every one of the

ones under those boards. We look at them all here, to minimize the amount of time we actually spend in the ruins. Usually at night, when Mother goes to sleep. The interesting ones we keep. The ones that don't make any sense, we take back to the room."

"I've seen a few of them myself," said Bershon. "There never seemed to be any rhyme or reason to what was in them. Sometimes it seemed like just a random collection of events from someone's life. Others, it was like a play, but played out in real life. Stories of action and drama, in places with red skies and purple plants—things you wouldn't imagine. Even though I couldn't understand a word of it, there was no mistaking it. Like the performances in the commons but much more vivid."

"We've seen a few like that, too," said Mathias.

"And," said Bershon, suddenly growing serious, "I've seen one that had all the action but none of the drama. Real-life events, captured as they occurred. That's how I know what happened. What happened to the people in that village."

"It was the Great Sickness, wasn't it?" Jendar said quietly.

Bershon sighed heavily. "Yes. But the sickness isn't what you think. That's all I'll say until you actually watch the cylinder."

Jendar and Mathias grew silent. Neither of them had ever encountered a cylinder that documented any true-to-life events of any seriousness; all of them seemed to be the type of live-action drama that Bershon had described or innocuous gatherings of random people and places.

"There's a reason," he began, "that the lord and lady keep us on such a tight leash. A reason we're not permitted to go far, and a reason they give us that damn 'health serum' every year come springtime. Part of it has to do with the Sickness. But not all."

The health-serum injections had been a fact of life since Jendar was born and, to his knowledge, had been carried out for as long as anyone in the village had been alive, and even before that. Each spring, a dozen or so emissaries—less-unpleasant malforms, dubbed jokingly by Mateya as 'the only somewhat normal-looking beasts the Nobles own'—descended upon the village. Everyone lined up in the commons to hear the same monotone speech, delivered from the twisted mouth of a creature probably never meant to utter human words, about how the health and safety of the villagers was their lord and lady's *top* priority, and about how important the health serum was in staving off the Great Sickness. Then half the malforms would administer injections, given from stubby, pointed tubes made of a metal that looked suspiciously similar to the material the devices in the ancient village were made of. The other half would go house to house, building to building, looking for anyone who hadn't shown up to receive their injection.

It was common knowledge that Serum Day was an event not to be missed. There was no excuse, from injury to mourning, that would suffice to appease the malforms. Once or twice in Jendar's lifetime, they had found an unfortunate soul who, for whatever reason, hadn't been in the commons at the appointed time.

The truants were bound and forcibly removed from the village. What happened to them once the malforms had hauled them back to the Nobles' fortresses...well, no one could say. The only thing anyone knew was that no one who had been taken away ever came back.

"There's a cylinder you boys need to experience," Bershon said, moving to the table and taking a seat. The boys joined him. "I still have it, even though my disk doesn't work. If you'd oblige me, I'd like to bring it by. Maybe… things will make a bit more sense to you once you see it."

"What do you mean?" Mathias asked.

"There's a lot about us, about our people, that you don't know. No one does, really. To my knowledge, I'm the only one in the village who's seen what's in the cylinder. The only one who knows what happened, all those years ago."

Jendar raised his eyebrows. "The Great Sickness? But we all know about that."

Bershon shook his head. "We haven't been told everything. We were never told how it started, or why. We've never had the chance to question why we live in this valley, with our simple tools, and not in a grand village like the one beyond the woods, with all the marvelous inventions and roadways and buildings."

Jendar and Mathias stared unblinkingly at Bershon.

He grinned. "I take it I've piqued your curiosity?"

"Yes…you have indeed," said Jendar slowly.

"What's on it?" blurted Mathias. "What did you see?"

"In due time," said Bershon. "Best for you just to see it for yourselves." He gazed off into space for a moment, his bright-blue eyes seeing something invisible to Jendar and Mathias. "And now," he said, standing, "I think I've troubled you boys enough for one night. I'm off to home for a drink, then to bed."

"A moment, if you would," said Jendar. He went over to his hiding spot, placed the sphere and the disk back inside, and carefully fitted the board back in place. "You never know who—or what—might be trying to see in."

Bershon nodded. "A wise precaution."

Mathias opened the door for their guest, and they saw

him off with a pair of hugs and a few more goodbyes. Mathias had barely closed the door when he exclaimed, "Can you believe it? He's been there too! Who would have thought old Bershon was prowling around that village, the same as us?"

"*Quiet*," Jendar hissed, pulling the curtain back and peering out. "Remember what he said about the blackjays... and the rats."

Mathias nodded, dropping his voice. "I wonder how many others have been out there as well? How is it that we've never heard of this before?"

"Probably the same reason no one knows we've been there. It isn't something you exactly talk about openly."

"You know what else I wonder? How not a single rat or blackjay ever saw us. The forest has got to be full of them. We're lucky. *Very* lucky."

Jendar nodded. "You're right about that. Luck or no, you'd better believe I'm going to be keeping a much closer lookout for those types of creatures, now that I know how the Nobles use them. The last thing we need is to be discovered creeping off into the woods."

Mathias grunted his agreement as he moved to the fireplace. "It's getting late," he said. "Going to bank the embers, then I'm off to bed."

Jendar yawned, as if in agreement. "Let me check on Mother, and then I'll be right behind you."

As Jendar crept into Mateya's bedroom, his mind whirled, trying to process everything he had learned from Bershon. Most of all, his thoughts kept going back to what the old man had said about his cylinder and what it contained.

Maybe there's something there...something Bershon missed. If it explains in any way just how we came to be where we are, there has to be hope for us. Maybe we won't have to live like this anymore. Maybe there's a way to escape the lord and lady.

He walked softly to his mother's bedside and reached a hand out, gently touching her face. He gasped in shock as he felt the coldness of her skin.

Mateya was dead.

3

Jendar and Mathias spent most of the night in mourning, trying their best to comfort each other, sharing stories of Mateya and their father from younger days. Even when they'd both grown exhausted in the late-night hours and finally had lain down, neither of them slept very well. When the skies began to lighten on the eastern horizon, Jendar sat up in bed, wiping a pair of red-rimmed eyes.

He nudged his brother awake. "I need to go down to the workshops. I've got to pick up a black sash from Jone Weaver. People will need to know we're in mourning. We also need to have the pyre builders send a cart..." He couldn't finish the sentence.

Mathias pushed back his covers and slowly stood. "I'll go with you."

After cleaning themselves up, they made the trek down the neat cobblestone road that led through town, nodding at those they passed on their way to Joan Weaver's shop.

Like their parents, Jendar and Mathias were tailors, apprenticed to their mother and father. Now their family's workshop—and all the responsibilities that came with running it—was theirs. The family was responsible for manufacturing, mending, and altering garments for all the residents in the village's northwest quadrant, and they were never short of work. A black sash tied through the shop door's handle would notify villagers that Jendar and Mathias were in mourning and the shop would be closed for three days—the standard mourning period.

Jone Weaver's shop sat among a cluster of buildings on the eastern side of the workshop district. Among the other businesses nearby were the tailors, weavers, and dyers that were all responsible for supplying their designated portions of the village with clothing. Many of the shop workers were already getting started; the days always began early in the village.

Jendar approached one of the large buildings, indistinguishable from the others save for the painted wooden sign above the door. It depicted a bolt of blue cloth and a loom. Jendar tried the handle and found the door open. Hearing the sounds of the looms working in the back, he and Mathias approached the counter, manned by a boy of perhaps twelve years old.

"What'll you be needing?" he asked the brothers.

"Mourning cloth," Mathias practically whispered.

The boy bowed his head slightly. "Very sorry for your loss, sirs. Give me just a moment."

The boy ducked through the doorway that led to the work area, and true to his word, he returned but moments later with a length of black cloth. He handed it to Jendar, who received it with a courteous nod.

"Thank you kindly," he said, heading for the door.

The Longshear family's workshop was two buildings over. Jendar glanced for a moment at the sign on the door—

a spool of thread with a pair of tailor's shears—before tying the black sash through the handle.

Hard to believe the entire place is going to be ours, he thought. *It's going to be so empty without Mother.*

"I suppose we'll need to petition the Nobles for an apprentice...or two," said Mathias, wiping a bloodshot eye. "We had trouble enough keeping up with the orders once Father died; I don't know how we'll do it ourselves now that Mother is gone."

"We will," said Jendar, "once we've finished mourning."

Though it was typical for children to follow their parents' trade, there were instances when there were simply too many of one type of worker already. To keep the pool of available workers where it needed to be, all apprenticeships, even those of family members, had to be cleared with the Nobles. The vast majority of times, a child who wished to follow in his or her parents' trade had little trouble securing an apprenticeship at their family's shop, as someone would be needed to replace each parent when their time came. In the instances when children couldn't work with their families for one reason or another, they were assigned to a petitioner by the lord and lady.

"And," said Mathias glumly, "we might need even more apprentices, depending on what the Nobles decide when we marry."

Jendar pursed his lips. Yet another decision made by the damn Nobles—which spouse's profession the new family would follow. There was a chance that either of them might have to learn a whole new trade when they married, depending on what the lord and lady deemed necessary for the village.

"I don't want to think about that now," said Jendar. "Let's

just get to the pyre field and have old Karmen send us a cart."

The two of them walked to the field, which lay just south of the workshops, in silence, trying their best to be polite to those they passed. It wasn't long before they reached their destination.

The field looked like any other: patches of dirt interspersed with greenery, dotted here and there with the occasional cluster of wildflowers. It was the pyres, however, that made the fields stand out—great stacks of brush and logs, upon which the villagers placed their dead. There were always fresh pyres at the ready, for death was ever present. Four stood ready to light, with a fifth a little more than a pile of blackened, still smoldering ashes.

At the edge of the field nearest to town was a small hut, next to which stood a horse and wooden cart. The horse chewed idly at its feed bag, not giving the brothers the slightest acknowledgment as they approached. Jendar rapped twice on the solid planks of the hut's front door; moments later, the boys were greeted by a tall, thin man with a blunt nose; hollow cheeks; and hair that was beginning gray at the temples.

"Karmen," said Jendar, nodding. The man returned the courtesy.

"I'd say I was glad to see you boys, but the fact that you're here means...Mateya?"

Neither Jendar nor Mathias said a word. Their silence was answer enough.

"So sorry for your loss," Karmen said with a bow of his head. "I'll get the cart at once. "Astra," he called, leaning back into the hut. Moments later, a spry young boy with curly hair and huge brown eyes emerged. "Get Zacharias ready. We leave immediately."

Jendar, Mathias, and Astra had to walk quickly to keep up with the horse, even though Karmen kept him to a slow walk, and it wasn't long before they arrived back at their house. Bershon stood outside the door, leaning against the house. When he saw the cart and horse, his face fell.

"Boys," he said as they arrived, "I was wondering where you were. So," he said, his voice quavering, "that's it then. She's gone." He sniffed, wiping at his eyes. "My condolences. She was an extraordinary woman. Made everyone who knew her happy."

"She did," said Mathias. "We knew she was going when the Nobles decided to take her...but...this isn't easy," he barely managed.

Jendar put an arm around his brother's shoulder. "She's at peace, Mathias. She suffers no more."

Mathias nodded, wiping his eyes.

"Would it be all right with you boys—*men*—if I came along?" Bershon asked quietly.

"Of course," said Jendar. "We consider you family. No need to even ask."

Most of the villagers had regarded Bershon's presence at their father's pyre lighting as strange, and Jendar figured it would be no different this time. Pyre lightings were intensely personal experiences, rarely attended by anyone other than the deceased's immediate family. Nevertheless, Jendar knew how close the man had been to his parents, and he refused to turn him away.

After instructing Karmen and Astra where his mother could be found, Jendar and Mathias waited outside. The two pyre builders entered the home, Karmen with a thick white shroud in his arms. As the two of them attended to their business, Jendar's eyes flitted about the homes across the street. When they settled on the roof of the building directly across from theirs, a queasy sensation rolled through his gut.

A blackjay, perfectly motionless, was perched atop the roof's peak. It stared directly at them, so still it seemed it wasn't even breathing. Jendar swallowed to moisten his throat, which had suddenly gone very dry, and forced himself to look elsewhere. He glanced instead at his brother and Bershon. Mathias stared at the ground, kicking idly at a pebble in the road. Bershon fiddled with his hands. Neither of them had apparently noticed the bird, and Jendar chose to keep quiet about it.

Before long, Karmen and Astra emerged, carrying Mateya's shrouded figure with them. Gently they placed her body on the cart.

"We can begin the lighting straightaway," said Karmen, mounting his horse. "There are no others this morning."

A flick of the reins got his horse moving, and the group followed behind. Before long, they arrived at the pyre field. Karmen dismounted, and he and Astra carefully lifted Mateya from the cart. Reverently, they placed her horizontally atop one of the pyres. They stood back in silence, heads bowed, while Astra walked back to the shack to fetch a torch.

When he returned, lit torch in hand, Karmen spoke softly. "Mateya Longshear, we thus return you to the earth, in the presence of your family. May your eternal rest be peaceful." He handed the torch to Jendar—the eldest living relative—who leaned forward and touched it to the lowest logs of the pyre. The logs had been prepared with pitch earlier and roared to life with little coaxing.

Karmen turned to Bershon and the boys. "I'll leave you to your thoughts," he said. With a deep nod that was nearly a bow, he departed.

Jendar, Mathias, and Bershon stood silently, watching as the flames of the pyre grew. Before long Mateya's burial shroud was engulfed, and the three men could just make out the outline of her face beneath the flames as her features slowly turned to ash. The thick smoke of the pitch-soaked logs was thankfully strong enough to eliminate the smell of cooking flesh that Jendar knew must be present. Soon the blaze had obscured their view of Mateya's form entirely. Mathias sobbed openly, while Jendar did his best to comfort him while blinking through his own flow of tears. Bershon stood a little apart from them, wiping his own eyes.

"Mother," Jendar said, his voice hoarse, "you were always kind and understanding. You raised us well. We will honor your memory by being the best men we can be."

They stood in silence the rest of the time, no one able to speak, even as the flames died down. By that point, little remained of the pyre except a heap of blackened logs and ash.

"We should be getting back," Jendar managed. "I really need to sit down."

Mathias and Bershon said nothing as they nodded. The three men plodded back the way they had come, silent for the most part, save to offer a courtesy to a fellow villager. Back at the house, Bershon hesitated at the front door.

"I should be going...wouldn't want to intrude. You two need time to mourn."

"Nonsense," Jendar said. "Please come in, Bershon. I told you—you're as good as family here."

Nodding gratefully, the older man stepped inside, closing the door behind him. The three sat down at the table in the main room. Mathias prepared a fire for pottage, while Jendar went out to the stores to gather some grain.

When Jendar returned, Bershon cleared his throat. "I

came by this morning to try to catch the two of you before you went to work. I had no idea she'd passed in the night."

"It's all right, Bershon," said Mathias. "Who would have known this would happen? Besides, one of us would have told you anyway."

"What I mean to say is," Bershon continued, "the real reason I came by this morning was to give you something. But I don't think the time is right for that now."

"What did you want to give us?" asked Jendar.

"I realize now isn't really the time for this," he repeated, "but I brought this by, as promised." He reached into a pocket and produced a shiny metal cylinder, identical to the ones concealed beneath the floorboard. "Things being how they are, I think there will be a better time to see what's in it. You don't need any more emotional shocks right now."

"It's really that bad?" Jendar asked, his brow knitted.

Bershon nodded. "Horrendous. But necessary."

As he began to put the cylinder away, Jendar stopped him. "Nothing could make today any worse than it already is," he said. "*Nothing*. If what's in this cylinder is as important as you say, I'd rather see it sooner than later. Do you agree, brother?"

Mathias hesitated then nodded.

Jendar did his best to push all thoughts of his mother from his head. The cylinder, no matter how disturbing, would provide a much-needed distraction. He stood and walked over to the floorboard that concealed his cache. He pried it open and retrieved the disk.

"You're sure about this?" Bershon asked, as Jendar placed the disk on the table.

Jendar nodded. "Anything to take our minds off Mother."

Bershon handed him the cylinder, and Jendar placed it

in the indentation. Instantly, three yellow glyphs appeared on the device, not far from where the cylinder sat. Bershon stretched out his hand, where it hovered over the central glyph. He hesitated just a moment before pressing down lightly.

4

Instantly the room, the cottage, their entire village, was gone. Their surroundings had been replaced by a narrow, unfathomably long room. The ceiling, significantly higher than the tallest building in the village, bore brightly glowing orbs, suspended on thin chains and bathing the room in sunny brilliance. The room stretched off in either direction, far enough that the people who darted back and forth at the far ends looked to be no larger than insects. A row of beds lined each of the longer walls of the chamber. Every bed was occupied, many with people who writhed and moaned, filling the room with a sound that made Jendar ill. Bizarre-looking creatures, bright white from head to toe, hustled from bed to bed. The creatures were around Jendar's height but bulky and coated in saggy, almost shiny skin. Their heads were devoid of hair, and their faces were oddly distorted, shiny like their skin yet translucent. In strangely rounded hands, each creature carried the same blunt instruments used by the malforms on Serum Day.

Jendar took an involuntary step back.

"What are they?" hissed Mathias.

"Don't be alarmed," said Bershon. "Go on—take a closer look."

Though Jendar knew the creatures couldn't harm him, he approached the nearest one with tense footsteps. It stood beside the bed of a groaning man, probably somewhere between Jendar and Bershon in age. As it gently pressed the tool into the man's arm, Jendar leaned in closely and got a good look at the thing's face.

What he saw staring back at him was the face of an ordinary woman, concealed behind some type of thin, clear substance. As the figure stood, he realized he wasn't looking at the skin of some wild creature but exceedingly strange clothing. The outfit completely covered the person who wore it—indeed, the only inkling Jendar had that a person lay beneath it was the fact that he saw a woman's face peering back at him.

"What is it?" Mathias repeated.

"They're...people," said Jendar. "Go ahead. Have a look for yourself."

Mathias did, cautiously. "Their clothing," he said at last, "I've never seen anything so odd. Not even the lord or lady dress so strangely."

"Their manner of dress is off-putting," said Bershon, "but it's by no means the strangest thing you'll see."

Suddenly a stream of bright-red symbols appeared in midair, directly in front of Jendar. They scrolled sideways, seeming to disappear into the air as more symbols replaced them.

Mathias reached out and pawed at the air in front of him. "What are they?" he asked, turning to Bershon. "Can you see them?"

"I can," Bershon replied, "though the ones I see are

directly in front of me, at eye level. I can't see what's in front of you, but I'd imagine it's the same thing. Red symbols? Moving?"

Mathias nodded.

"I see them too," said Jendar.

"No idea what they mean," said Bershon shrugging, "but I'd imagine it's some kind of writing."

"Writing?" asked Mathias, wide eyed. "In the air?"

Bershon nodded.

Writing of any kind in the village was exceedingly rare. There were very few who knew how to read or write, and they did so only because their trade demanded it. The scribes, as they were called, were tasked with penning petitions to the Nobles and, on the rare occasions when any responses weren't delivered by an emissary, reciting the Nobles' responses in the town square. Their craft was considered highly secretive. Learning to read or write if one wasn't a scribe's apprentice was a punishable offense.

Jendar shook his head. "This makes no sense..." He trailed off as a crisp, staccato voice rose up all around them. Although the voice wasn't all that loud, it demanded attention. Its syllables and intonations were utterly foreign; though Jendar imagined he was hearing some attempt at speech, the words were nothing more than gibberish.

"Far as I can tell," said Bershon, "we're seeing a...proclamation of sorts. The entire cylinder is like this—that voice, the writing, the scenes...well, you'll see. It all ties together. Now just watch."

Jendar returned his attention to the man who lay in the bed next to him. A thin white sheet covered his body from the waist up. He was shirtless, olive skinned, and coated in bright-red, oozing sores. They were everywhere—across his chest, down his arms, and all over his face and neck. One of his eyes was swollen shut, pushed upward by an angry red lesion that had broken open high on his cheek. Jendar grimaced and stepped back. He turned around and looked at the next bed. In it was a woman, slightly older than the man but with the same affliction: lesions covering every inch of visible skin.

Mathias, peering at a bedded figure on the other side of the room, looked as if he'd turned a shade of gray. "What's wrong with them?" he asked.

"I've had a long time to think about that," said Bershon, "and the more you see of this cylinder, the more you'll probably agree with me. We're seeing the Great Sickness."

Abruptly the scene changed. The long room vanished, along with the beds and their diseased inhabitants. The trio now stood outside, in the center of a black roadway. The street was lined with buildings that Jendar found quite familiar—only these were intact, and they were mind-bendingly tall, taller than even he could have imagined, high enough to touch the clouds. He and Mathias stared up in openmouthed awe at the resplendent line of huge metallic structures that marched endlessly off into the horizon in each direction. Whatever ancient village the brothers now beheld, it was even larger and more magnificent than the ruins they had visited so often in the past.

Although the red symbols continued to pass in front of Jendar's field of vision, he ignored them, unable to tear his gaze away from the sights before him. He almost didn't notice the shapeless piles that lay at the foot of each building and the puffy, white-clad figures that walked between them, sometimes bearing large burdens to lay atop the heaps.

Jendar moved closer and retched when he saw that the piles that endlessly lined the roadway in each direction consisted of men, women, and children. Some were fully clothed, while others were half naked; all were covered in the same red sores that had afflicted the people in the beds.

"What...what's happening?" Mathias said breathlessly. "Are they all...dead?"

Bershon nodded. "Every one of them."

"So many," Jendar said, exhaling loudly. He tried counting the deceased but gave up.

It's endless, he thought. *Endless piles, endless dead. Too many to count. Far too many.*

"This one street..." said Mathias. "There are more dead people here than all the people in Endreach."

The indecipherable voice in the background prattled on, but Jendar had tuned it out. "Bershon," he said quietly, "this is what you meant, isn't it? What you said earlier—about how terrible the cylinder is?"

"Yes," he said grimly. "But even worse than what you're seeing, is why you're seeing it. I think *we* did this. To ourselves."

Jendar frowned, and noticed a similar expression on Mathias's face.

"What do you mean by that?" asked Mathias.

"Watch," said Bershon.

Almost on cue, the scene changed again. Now they stood before a shiny, high-walled complex. Though they couldn't see much of what lay beyond the walls, they made out the tops of squat buildings, much shorter than the ones they'd just seen, peeping over the wall like frightened children. The walls themselves were perfectly smooth, as far as Jendar could tell, and were topped with a vicious line of barbed spikes.

Turning, Jendar immediately noticed that a large number of people stood on a large black patch of roadway before them. Without warning, Jendar, Mathias, and Bershon gently began to rise.

"What the...?" Mathias spluttered.

"Relax," said Bershon. "Remember, we aren't really here. Nothing here can harm us."

Mathias nodded, albeit with a hint of uncertainty.

The three continued to rise a bit more, until they clearly saw all the people arrayed before them. Again, there were too many to count. Though Jendar didn't think the number came anywhere close to the number of deceased individuals in the ancient village, he still guessed they outnumbered the people in Endreach by a healthy margin.

The people were arranged in neat, square-shaped formations. Each of them wore a matching outfit—though Jendar was a good distance away, he saw that the clothing was tight fitting, midnight black, and covered every bit of the people's bodies except their heads. Though he was too far away to tell for certain, it looked like the hair on all their heads had been shorn to the skin.

Each person faced the same direction, where a large platform stood. Atop the platform a tiny figure perched. As Jendar squinted to get a better look, a rectangular image suddenly appeared in the upper left of his field of vision, above the scrolling red text. The image depicted a man standing rigidly at a podium. He was taller than Jendar and clean-shaven. His clothes differed from the people who stood before him—they were looser, more of a darker brown than black, and bore four small but bright gold medallions, attached at the left breast. His head had an even mix of black and gray hair, and deep creases spread outward from the corners of his eyes. He was old—probably Bershon's age, perhaps a bit older. Every part of his body was still, except his head, which bobbed frenetically, thrusting forward with each syllable that burst forth from his wildly animated lips. The words he spoke were suddenly audible to Jendar, and though he couldn't discern their meaning, he felt their vehemence.

Another image, the same size as the first, opened to the upper right of the symbols. It depicted a cluster of four strange devices, each one as large as their cottage. Like almost every contraption Jendar had seen of the old world, these objects had been fashioned from shiny, smooth metal. They were dome shaped, and each had three cylindrical protrusions extending from the very apex of its dome. Tiny figures—people—stood beside them, touching specks of blue light that shone from the surfaces of the devices. Suddenly a series of rapid, bright-green flashes erupted from the protrusions atop the domes. The entire scene was bathed in a chaos of madly flashing green light; the effect was so dizzying that Jendar had no choice but to shut his eyes, lest he become ill.

When he opened them, another scene had taken its place. In it, Jendar saw the black street of another village, very similar to the first. However, this village teemed with life. Innumerable people walked along the sides of the streets, close to the buildings. They seemed to come from all walks of life: some light skinned, some dark; some young, others old; some with extravagant hairstyles of blue or vivid pink, others with no hair at all; some with outfits of brilliant material, others with simple brown or black clothing. Together they displayed an incredibly vibrant tapestry of human life, one that quite literally took Jendar's breath away.

In the center of the roadways, strange devices sped along in either direction beside the people. Shaped like oblong disks, they were roughly half as high as Jendar at their centers, but tapered thinner at their edges. They hovered just above the ground and moved of their own accord, not pulled by oxen or people.

As Jendar marveled at the wondrous sight of the ancient village, the street was suddenly bathed in a quick succession of searing green flashes, so bright that they overwhelmed his vision. After a few moments, when the flashes had abated and Jendar could see once again, he noticed that every person was lying on the ground. Some writhed weakly, while others wretched soundlessly, and still others screamed. All of them clawed at their throats as if they'd just swallowed nails. Instantly the scene changed, focusing close in on a group that had collapsed near the corner of a building. The exposed skin on their faces and hands burst open in several places, oozing a thick green substance.

Jendar was certain that if he'd been there in the flesh, he would have emptied his stomach. He glanced at Mathias. One of his hands was pressed to his mouth, the other to his belly. His eyes practically bulged from their sockets.

The scene changed again. The scrolling glyphs, as well as the moving images to the upper left and right of Jendar's field of vision, disappeared. Jendar, Mathias, and Bershon found themselves in a room filled with harried-looking people. Everyone appeared disheveled, as if they hadn't bathed in weeks. Only a single light source hung overhead, its brilliance failing to reach the farthest corners of the space the trio now occupied. The walls were decorated with bright-blue banners, hung at regular intervals and stretching from the floor to ceiling. Each banner depicted a white eagle in flight, encircled by what looked to be stylized stars, also in white. At the head of the room, hunched over a podium, stood a bedraggled-looking man. His wiry hair was completely white and stood out from his head in every direction. He had a bulbous nose and weak chin, as well as dark circles under his eyes. In his right hand, he held a cloth that he repeatedly used to mop at his brow, which dripped with sweat. He addressed the crowd in a tone that suggested he was attempting to calm his audience, yet he couldn't prevent his own panic from creeping into his voice. The man stopped speaking for a moment, appeared to swallow a lump in his throat, then attempted to continue. All that emerged, however, was a hoarse croak. A shaky hand slowly moved to his throat, which he massaged. Once again he tried to speak, and once again he failed. All at once, he fell to his knees, his mouth open in a silent scream. Pustules burst forth from his hands and face, spewing droplets of green fluid onto the podium and surrounding floor. The room erupted in chaos as people trampled one another, vying for the exits. One by one, the room's inhabitants began to fall, struck down by the same affliction that had just claimed their leader. Before long, everyone was on the floor, covered in festering lesions, moaning and clawing at their throats.

Abruptly their surroundings vanished, and they found themselves back in the Longshear home, seated at the table. The glyphs on the disk remained illuminated for a moment more, then winked out.

5

No one said a word. Mathias looked like he might vomit, while Jendar kept replaying in his mind what he'd just witnessed.

Finally, Bershon spoke. "I know that wasn't easy, but you had a right to know."

Mathias at last found his voice. "But what did we see? What did it all mean? Those people...those flashes..." his voice trailed off.

Bershon sighed. "When I first saw what was on that cylinder, I was just as perplexed as you two. But I've had years to mull it over. *Years*. And I have a few sound ideas about what it all means. First, the people. Like I said earlier, I believe they were afflicted with the Great Sickness. And it's a lot worse than I ever imagined. Everyone got sick. *Everyone*. Every person who lived, everywhere. And most of them—almost everyone alive—died from it."

"What about those things with the green flashes? What are those?" Mathias asked.

Bershon shrugged his shoulders. "That, I can only guess at. But the way the cylinder was put together, showing those things, then right away showing those huge green bursts of light in that village...well, it makes me think that somehow those devices were responsible for the Sickness. And if you'll remember, the devices went off after those people touched them. So..."

"So the people who touched them did this. Whatever killed the people in the village, it started with those people and those devices," Jendar said.

"You're a smart one," Bershon said with a melancholy grin. "Aye, that's what I'm getting at. Those people, whoever they were, unleashed something that killed everyone."

"But...why would they do that?" asked Mathias. "Why would anyone want to hurt or kill so many people? There were children there."

"I can't see any logic or reason for it. Makes no sense to me at all. But the evidence is there—humans killed humans. In great numbers. Entire villages dead, all at once. We know there was a Sickness, but...what we didn't know is that *we're the ones who caused it.*"

Neither Jendar nor Mathias said anything. Jendar could think of nothing *to* say. No word or phrase could describe his feelings toward the idea of so much death and suffering, apparently wrought from the hands of people who, presumably, also wound up dead in the end.

Bershon broke the silence. "Did you notice the tools those white-clad people used? Same as the ones the malforms use on us, come Serum Day."

Mathias nodded slowly. "They use them to fight the Sickness. So...it's still around. It can still kill us."

"Maybe," said Bershon. "But one thing's for sure: if the Nobles lived through that, they certainly wouldn't want it to happen again."

"But why..." Jendar's voice trailed off.

Bershon looked Jendar squarely in the eye. "What would you do if all the village's cattle became ill and all the crops withered?" he said. "You'd panic. You'd know that if everything you depended on for nourishment died, you'd die too. You'd do your best to try to minimize the damage, find the cause, stop it if you could, and by all means, salvage whatever food was left.

"And once you had secured a food supply, gotten your cattle together, made sure they weren't sick and dying, what would you do then? You'd care for them. Feed them. Breed them. Slaughter and eat them, when the time came. Keep the herd at a respectable size—not so big that they'd be too tough to manage but not so small that you'd risk running out of food. You'd cull out the troublemakers—the ones who are too aggressive, who are sterile or barren. You'd keep track of which animals breed with which, keep track of their children, keep interbreeding to a minimum so the bloodlines stay clean and trouble free. And *that*," he said, slapping his hand on the table, "is exactly what's been done with *us*."

Jendar's eyes grew wide, and Mathias's mouth slowly fell open.

Bershon nodded again, a self-satisfied smirk twisting the edges of his mouth.

"It explains...everything," Jendar finally managed. "The petitions for marriage. The ones they choose to kill or take. This valley!" He stood abruptly, bumping into the table. Mathias winced. "It's...it's a corral! Think about it," he said, fixing his eyes on his brother. "No way out to the north or south. Get too close to either fortress and—poof!—you're gone. The bog to the east—treacherous, impossible to cross. The western wood—forbidden. We're penned in! Penned in like meat!"

Bershon snorted. "We *are* meat."

Jendar sank back down. "Our purpose in life, our whole existence, means nothing. *Nothing*. We're just food. Food for the Nobles."

"What...what can we do?" whispered Mathias. "Is it really so bleak? Do we have to live our lives like this?"

"Not much choice, is there?" said Bershon.

"There's always a choice," Jendar said, narrowing his eyes. "Maybe it's time we chose to do something different."

Bershon placed a hand on his shoulder. "I didn't teach you all this so you'd run off with a head full of crazy ideas. I taught you what I know because I owe that much to your father. I showed you the cylinder so you can have a better under-standing of who we really are. So you can know, deep down, we're more than just food for the lord and lady. We have the power to shape our own destinies. It wasn't the Nobles and their power that brought us so low—we did this to ourselves."

"But if we have that kind of power over our own destinies, why live like this?" asked Jendar. "Why can't we take back what we once had?"

Bershon massaged his temples. "That's not what I meant at all. I meant you can shape your own life in the context of living *here*. You can one day die knowing that your race is greater than you ever realized. I showed you all this to give you a sense of who you really are. The way things are, well... there's unfortunately no way to change any of it. You'd need to convince every last villager—in secret, no less—that there's hope of a better life. But what could you possibly say to convince them? And even if you did, how could you hope to stand against beings as powerful as the Nobles?"

Jendar had no response for that. "Did father know about this?" he said instead.

Bershon nodded. "Of course. I showed him the cylinder

years ago. Never could convince him to go to the ruins with me, though."

"And what did he make of all this?"

"He told me to forget what I'd seen," Bershon said with a sigh. "Said that such knowledge was dangerous. Begged me to destroy the cylinder—and the disk—or at least put it back in the ruins where I'd found it. I disagreed, and we argued. In the end, my decision to show him the cylinder nearly ended our friendship."

"So Father wouldn't have approved of you telling us all this," said Mathias.

"I'd imagine not. But I told Olef I'd look out for you. You two are the only family I've got left. Before my children, Josha and Verdan, died, I showed them the cylinder. You had a right to see it too."

"I'm going to need some time," said Jendar, "to sort through all this. Time to think about what it all means. What it means about us, about our place in this world. Everything I thought I knew—it just changed. All of it."

"It did," said Mathias, "but...I don't think that's a bad thing. I think Bershon is right; we needed to see it."

"I don't know what I—" Jendar began. His breath caught in his throat as something from the back corner of their home caught his eye, in the shadows beneath the loft where the sunlight from the tiny front windows didn't reach. Yellow orbs, head height from the ground, glowed softly in the darkness. Jendar could just make out the outline of a shadowy figure, barely illuminated by the orbs' pale yellow glow.

Bile rose in his throat as he sought frantically to warn the others. Nothing emerged from his mouth except a few hopeless gasps.

"You all right?" Mathias asked, giving him a sound slap on the back.

Jendar coughed, spluttered again, then leapt to his feet. As he did so, the figure quickly faded back into the shadows.

"Noble!" he finally managed, pointing frantically at the shadows. "Noble! There!"

Bershon spun about, nearly upending the table as he jumped to his feet. Mathias sat where he was, unmoving, his mouth agape.

"A *Noble?*" asked Bershon. "Which one? Where?"

"Beneath the loft! I couldn't tell if it was the lord or lady. I just saw its eyes. It's gone now. But it was there a moment ago!"

"You're sure you saw it?" Bershon asked. All traces of color had drained from his face.

"Yes! It was there, in the darkness. Staring right at us!"

"There's no telling how much it saw or heard," Bershon said. "My guess is it didn't hear much; otherwise we wouldn't still be here. Put everything away. *Now.*"

Jendar snatched the disk and cylinder from the table. He hurried toward his hiding place, never taking his eyes from the darkness beneath the loft. He knelt and secreted his items away, his hands shaking so badly he could barely get the floorboard back in place.

"You saw the lord or lady? *Here?*" Mathias said, finding his voice at last.

"Unusual that one of them would allow itself to be seen so openly," said Bershon, his voice trembling. "And in daylight hours, no less. *Very* unusual. But they do know this place. Mateya...well, they might have been coming back for more."

Jendar shook his head. "This morning, when the pyre lighters came—there was a blackjay. On the rooftop across the way. It just stood there, still as stone, staring at us. I'll bet it was one of theirs. And if it was, they already know she's dead. They'll have moved on to someone else."

"Then why was one of them here?" asked Mathias.

"No idea," said Bershon. He opened the front door just wide enough to stick his head out. After a few furtive glances up and down the street, he closed it tightly. "No commotion outside. No malforms. If they knew about the cylinders, the disk, and everything else, we'd have been taken away by now. Or worse."

Jendar backed quickly away from the darkness, toward the front of the house. He knocked into the table in the process, nearly losing his balance.

"I don't think I've ever heard of one coming out in the daytime," said Mathias, his voice quavering.

"Most likely they can't," said Bershon. "They probably stay out of the sunlight for a reason. Hurts them somehow or weakens their powers. Look at their fortresses: black as night on both hilltops, no matter the time of day."

"Suddenly I have the urge to find a sunny spot and stay there," said Jendar.

"Well, whatever you do, make sure you don't look too far out of the ordinary," said Bershon. "The less conspicuous you act, the better. That Noble wasn't here for any of us; otherwise we'd all be dead. I have no idea what it wanted, but the fact that it didn't stay is definitely a good thing."

Jendar slowly sat back down, still not taking his eyes off the back corner of the cottage. "I need to keep calm," he said, trying to control his trembling voice. "It's not like they haven't been here before."

"But then...at least we didn't see them," said Mathias.

Bershon grunted. "Like rats. You rarely see 'em, but you can sure see the damage they do overnight."

6

It took a great deal of time for everyone's nerves to settle, but when it finally seemed as if Jendar's heart would no longer explode, Bershon took his leave and headed home. Mathias and Jendar remained in their cottage, seated at the table in the main room, in surroundings that were far too silent. Gone was the playful banter between their mother and father, and the sounds of activity that usually never ceased until bedtime. The back room sat empty, its bed no longer bearing the burden of death.

I can't believe they're both gone, Jendar thought. *Our family. Our life.*

Mathias interrupted his thoughts. "I want to go back."

Jendar gazed at him, his brow creased. "Back where?"

"To the ruins," he said. "After seeing what was in that cylinder, I want to see more. I want to see everything. I want to know why. Why did we kill ourselves? Why did humans unleash the Great Sickness? I want to learn everything I can. That room, with all the cylinders—there's so much there we haven't seen."

Jendar nodded noncommittally. "Someday soon, we'll go back."

"I'm going today," said Mathias, "and I want you to come with me."

"I don't know if I'm up for that right now. It's been quite a morning already."

"That's exactly why we should go," said Mathias.

He headed toward the back of the cottage and up the ladder to the loft. The brothers kept their packs, water skins, and a few other belongings up near their bedrolls. It was only a couple of minutes before Mathias was downstairs with their gear.

"I told you," said Jendar. "I'm not up for it."

Mathias thrust his pack at him. "You'll be glad once you get out of here." When Jendar didn't respond, Mathias whispered, "Please. *Please*. I need this. I can't sit in this house, in this village even, or I'll go crazy. Mother, that cylinder, it's all too much. I need to get out. Besides, this is the best time to go. The shop will be closed for the next three days, and things are going to get very busy after that. Who knows when we'll have another chance?"

Jendar hesitated a moment longer before he sighed, taking his pack and skin from Mathias.

"I suppose I'll manage," he said.

It didn't take them long to fill their packs and skins, and they were out the door soon after. The village was nearly deserted; pretty much everyone was working, either in the fields, the pastures, or the workshops. Nonetheless, Jendar and Mathias took their usual precautions when leaving the village. They headed north, where a copse blocked the view of their route to the woods from much of the village. They traveled quickly, and soon they were within the western wood.

The forest was quiet that day, the only sounds coming from the two brothers' footfalls as they made their way through the underbrush, along with the occasional birdsong.

No blackjays, I hope, thought Jendar, keeping a close eye on the trees.

"We should have plenty of daylight to get in a good day's exploration and still be back before nightfall," said Mathias.

Neither of them had ever been in the western woods after dark, and Jendar certainly wanted to keep it that way. Though the malforms foraged to an extent during the day, they were extremely active at night.

"Everything looks to be quiet at least," Jendar said softly. "Only birds. Nothing...larger."

Mathias nodded.

The two of them continued on, moving deftly through the foliage, quick and nearly silent. They tended not to converse very much on their treks through the woods. It made it that much easier to focus on their surroundings and kept the chances of them stumbling into a pack of malforms to a minimum.

Finally, they arrived at the Line of Demarcation.

The line was exactly that—a line, red as blood, roughly two hands wide, that ran on the ground the entire length of the woods. It was hard and smooth to the touch, perfectly straight on its edges, and flanked on either side by a half hand or so of plain brown dirt. Nothing, not even the most tenacious weed or creeper, ever grew in that soil.

The two of them paused at the line as they always did and grasped hands.

"For luck," they whispered, and stepped over the line as one, right foot first. The old superstition to enter a place of danger right foot first had always been a tradition in Endreach. Jendar had always found it a bit silly, but even he had to admit it was always best to be on the safe side.

On the other side of the line, they continued their journey as they had up to that moment. They moved swiftly but not to the point where they'd be forced to breathe more heavily than usual. The malforms that lived in the wild weren't known for their intelligence, but they had ears and knew how to use them.

As the woods grew denser, the light filtering through the boughs above dimmed, giving the surrounding forest an almost dusky appearance. Here and there, a bird chirped, and occasionally the underbrush rustled as the brothers frightened a small animal from cover. Aside from that, the only sounds were those made by Jendar and Mathias as they headed farther into the woods.

Jendar felt a light touch on his shoulder. Eyes wide, he turned to his brother. Mathias had stopped moving and held a finger to his lips. When he jerked his head toward the woods behind them, Jendar turned to look.

He saw nothing, but...wait. There was movement behind them, slow and methodical. Too big to be a squirrel or chipmunk, too deliberate for a deer. Instinctively he crouched, as did Mathais. The underbrush around them was fairly thick, making for a decent screen. As they listened, the movements paused for a moment, then continued, growing closer.

Sweat beaded on Jendar's forehead as he squinted into the brush. Whatever it was, it was far enough back that it didn't disturb any of the nearby foliage. Mathias nudged him with an elbow and pointed to their left. The same deliberate rustling had started up from that direction. Perspiration dripped from Mathias's brow, and he wiped it with one of his sleeves. He raised his eyebrows, and Jendar shook his head in return.

As they sat concealed, more sounds came from behind them, then from the left and the right. Noises of stealthy shapes moving through the brush filled their ears, breaking through the otherwise completely silent forest like screams in the night.

Mathias gripped his brother's arm, his look almost pleading. Jendar made a calming gesture with hands, which he hoped weren't shaking too visibly.

They haven't seen us yet, whatever they are, Jendar thought. *Stay calm. Don't move. Don't speak.*

They remained motionless, peering as far behind them as their cover allowed. Then Jendar spotted movement among the foliage, near where the sounds had originated. Something was creeping through the brush, low to the ground. Though Jendar couldn't see what it was, he had a pretty good guess.

Malforms. He mouthed the word to Mathias, who nodded quickly.

Slowly, quietly, the brothers edged away. If they stayed where they were, the encroaching predators would surely discover them. Their best bet was to reach an area with better cover and stay there until the danger passed.

Suddenly the rustling behind them came to a stop. As Jendar and Mathias continued to move away, the noises continued again, now louder, more earnest.

Closer.

It hears us. It hears us, and it's following us.

Never before had Jendar encountered a malform that was this adept at tracking. More often than not, a bit of stealth and a willingness to lie low for several minutes was all it took to avoid them.

Not this time. Skies above, not this time.

As the brothers picked up their pace, the sounds behind them grew closer still.

Now Jendar heard it breathing and grunting as it clawed its way through the leaves. As he glanced behind them, he saw the leaves not ten spans back part as the malform rose on its hind legs, sniffing the air.

Its hide was tan and rough, hairless for the most part except for a coarse black patch that covered its chest. Its head was oddly elongated, pointed like that of a rat and tipped with a moist snout that twitched as it tested the air. Its mouth was a rictus of jagged yellow teeth. Its eyes were slits on either side of its head, so thin that Jendar wondered if it could even use them. Two tufted ears thrust up through the oily mass of long, tangled black hair atop the thing's head.

It stood higher, ears twitching. It cocked its head then stood perfectly still. Jendar and Mathias kept moving low to the ground, as quietly as they could.

The malform tilted its head back and emitted a strange, guttural whistling sound. It was answered by more of the same, from seemingly every direction. Jendar's heart raced, and his legs threatened to buckle.

Surrounded. They have us surrounded.

"*Run!*" Jendar spat.

As Mathias and Jendar broke cover, the woods around them exploded with the mad thrashings of malforms clawing and trampling their way through the underbrush. There was no hiding now. Speed was their only hope.

They ran deeper into the woods, both well aware that their route back to the village had been cut off. The boys were fast, easily leaping and dodging scrub and deadwood, yet the frenetic sounds of a four-legged creature, sprinting heavily, rapidly closed behind them.

Jendar didn't dare to turn and look, lest he miss something in front of him that might send him sprawling. He glanced wildly about, hoping to find a tree with branches low enough to climb, but he saw nothing.

The sound of the creature's wild panting seemed to come from but a hand's breadth behind him, and he ran with renewed vigor, keeping pace with Mathias.

He heard the beast grunt as it lunged, heard the clumps of dirt it kicked up skitter away in every direction. The creature slammed into him from behind, knocking him off his feet. He landed on his stomach, and the malform landed on top of him. In an instant, it twined its powerful arms around him, crushing the breath from his lungs. The thing stank worse than a rotting corpse, and Jendar retched as he tried to get some air. Just within his field of vision, he spotted another shape careen through the air, and Mathias went down, screaming.

As the malform stood, wrenching Jendar from the ground, he fought with utter desperation to free himself. Kicking his legs frantically, he reached behind him, hoping to find something, anything, to grab on to. He managed to get a grip on a hunk of scaly hide, pulling and wrenching it as hard as he could. If his efforts caused the creature any pain, it didn't let on.

In front of him, another of the malforms had Mathias in its grasp. Like Jendar, he'd been hoisted from the ground and sat suspended in the arms of a creature identical to the one attacking his brother. Somehow, through the sound of their screams and the blood rushing through his ears, Jendar heard more of them approach.

One of their group circled in front of him, grabbing at

his legs. He kicked it, hard, and his captor rewarded him with a powerful squeeze. His screams were cut off. His ribs strained, and his pack dug painfully into his back. Surely, this would be the end of him. It wouldn't be long before his bones snapped under the pressure.

A sudden concussion rocked them from behind. The malform shrieked, dropping him heavily. Jendar pulled in breath after breath of sweet air, scampering along the ground, trying to put as much distance as he could between himself and his former captor.

Before long, he noticed the threat had effectively doubled. A second group of malforms had arrived. They were more typical of the type Jendar had come across in the woods before: incredibly broad, hairless, stoop-shouldered brutes with jutting chins and shelflike brows. Their backs were lined with sharp, bony spines, and each creature bore a single horn in the center of its head.

These beasts fell upon the first group of malforms with a savagery that made a hunting wolf pack look like toddlers at play. They wielded their oversize arms like clubs, bashing their smaller brethren, howling at a volume that made Jendar's ears ring. Every blow drew a fleshy explosion of gore and the dull, meaty crunch of bone. The smaller malforms fought desperately, raking their aggressors with claws and teeth, tearing ribbons of flesh from their enemies even as their own bones and flesh were pulped by fists the size of small boulders.

Wrenching his eyes away from the massacre, Jendar spotted Mathias. His brother was staring, mouth agape, at the gut-wrenching spectacle of a dozen or so nightmarish monsters tearing one another to shreds.

"Run!" Jendar shrieked, staggering to his feet.

He pawed at his brother on his way past and nearly

stopped to let out a sigh of relief as Mathias's trance broke
and he found his feet. They sprinted from the melee with a
speed born of reckless terror. They kept running well after
the sounds of combat had faded and disappeared. They
didn't stop until they had broken through the edge of the
woods, where the ancient village lay before them.

They collapsed to the earth, coughing and gasping.
Jendar clutched his sides, certain that if he didn't, his lungs
would explode. Mathias wasn't faring much better. He
vomited, emptying his breakfast on the ground in front of
him before falling to his side, panting.

Some time passed before either of them managed to
catch his breath enough to speak.

"I thought...we were done for," gasped Jendar.

Still breathing heavily, Mathias rolled himself into a
sitting position. He turned his head and spat.

"Lucky for us..." he began. A sudden coughing fit interrupted him. He cleared his throat and spat again. "Lucky for
us...those first ones...had some competition."

Jendar also sat, willing his breathing to return to normal.
After several minutes, he was able to speak again. "I'd like to
know how that first group found us. And more important,
where they came from."

Mathias shook his head. "They've never managed to
sneak up on us like that before. Never. They had to have
been lying in wait for us. Which means they knew we were
coming."

A ball of ice formed in the pit of Jendar's stomach.

"You don't suppose," Mathias continued, "that the lord
or lady sent them after us, do you?"

Jendar swallowed hard. "I hope not."

"If they sent them, there'll be more," said Mathias in a
small voice, "and they won't stop until we're dead. How can

we go home? If the Nobles intend to bring us down, we can never go back to Endreach. They'll know we're there. They'll find us, and kill us."

"We have no idea if running into that pack was a coincidence," said Jendar, "or if the lord and lady really were behind it. Besides, if the Nobles wanted us dead, why didn't they simply do it in the village and make examples of us? Why wait until now? It isn't like them to punish secretly or quietly."

"No," Mathias said, "I suppose it isn't."

"At any rate," said Jendar, standing, "We're here now. Let's make the best of it."

Mathias stood as well. Miraculously, neither of them had lost their packs in their frantic scramble to get away. Mathias dove into his, withdrew his water skin, and drank deeply; Jendar did the same.

When they'd sufficiently refreshed themselves, they headed down toward the village.

"I'd like to get back to the room with all the cylinders," said Mathias. "Seeing the one that Bershon brought has gotten me very curious. What else might we find there? We haven't even begun to get through everything in that room."

"Agreed," said Jendar. "And I propose a different strategy —rather than try to go section by section, let's take a fair-size sample from multiple places around the room. Maybe they're organized in some way. We might have missed a lot simply because we've only taken cylinders from the same set of shelves so far."

Mathias nodded. "Sounds like a good plan."

They'd been to the cylinder room on enough occasions that they both had the route memorized. They entered the village on the same ruined street as always. The familiar shapes of empty and toppled buildings reared up on either side. On previous visits, they'd been inside nearly every intact building along their route; the only ones they hadn't entered were the structures with no visibly marked entrances. These buildings were smooth the whole way around, and Jendar often wondered how one might gain access and what might be inside.

"There's still so much of this place we haven't seen," said Mathias.

"It would take a lifetime to explore it all. Perhaps two."

The boys remained mostly quiet for the rest of their journey. Though they'd never before seen malforms in this ancient village, their recent experience had shaken them both so much that anything less than absolute caution was unthinkable.

Before long, they arrived at a massive structure, several times as wider than many of the other buildings in the immediate area. The structure had six entrances: three in the front, two in the back, and a smaller entrance on the right side. The side entrance was where they headed. Of all the entryways, only the one on the side had been ajar when they'd first discovered the building. All attempts to force open the other doors, even from the inside, had failed.

As always, the sliding metal doors that made up the entryway stood just far enough apart that they could squeeze through sideways. On the other side, Jendar and Mathias saw complete blackness.

They removed their packs and rummaged through them. Each produced a stubby metallic wand, two hands in length, tipped with a crystalline sphere—souvenirs of one of their treks into the village. They had several more at home among their cache, in case the ones they held should ever malfunction.

Jendar clutched his wand in his right hand, flattened his

left, and firmly struck the butt end of the device. Radiance burst forth from the sphere, bright enough that it pained one's eyes to look at it directly. After Mathias did the same, they slipped through the doorway.

They stood in room that was as large as the entire inside of their cottage. Great heaps of damaged furniture and other debris lay piled against the walls. A thick layer of dust and grime coated the floor, disrupted by countless sets of the boys' footprints.

The light from their wands struck every corner of the room, dispelling nearly all shadows. At the far end lay an open entryway that led to a vast corridor running the entire length of the building. Jendar and Mathias entered that corridor, light wands held aloft. The hall's ceiling was relatively high, perhaps a span or two higher than the tip of their cottage's roof. Globes that were nearly identical to those on their light wands, though quite a bit larger, hung suspended on thin chains at regular intervals. Though the boys always had suspected that the globes produced light, they'd never figured out how to activate them.

The smooth, straight walls of the corridor were interrupted every so often by large entryways that led to other hallways. Jendar and Mathias had explored them all as far as they could. Many of them ended in sealed doors they'd never managed to pry open.

The brothers continued until they reached the center of the hall. On either wall, an identical entryway opened up to corridors that ran perpendicular to the one in which they stood. They took the right corridor, and before long, they stood in front of one of the familiar double doors.

This door, unlike the others, was substantially ajar. On the floor beside the door lay the metal bar they'd initially used to pry the door open. They walked through, single file, with plenty of room to maneuver. Jendar went first, and as soon as he entered, he held his light wand aloft.

The room was three times as large as the room they'd first entered, its ceiling at a height equal to that of the corridor from where they had come. All four walls of the chamber, including the wall through which they'd made their entrance, were lined with metal shelves from floor to ceiling. On each shelf were neatly arranged stacks of cylinders.

The shelves weren't labeled, and they couldn't figure out why the cylinders were arranged the way they were. When they'd first discovered the room, they'd begun by removing cylinders from the bottom shelf, just to the right of the entryway. Their intention was to experience as many of the cylinders on that shelf as they could, then gradually work their way around the room. Up until now, they had gone through only about two-thirds of the cylinders on that first shelf.

Jendar walked over to the shelf, kneeling as he dug through his pack. He produced three cylinders, which he replaced where he'd found them. They'd been largely uninteresting..

He stood, watching Mathias as he slowly paced the room's perimeter, his deep-brown eyes roving the shelves. "Let's really mix it up this time, like you said. Get a good sample from all sides of the room, high and low shelves."

Jendar nodded. He reached a hand out and grasped one of the shelves. He pushed and pulled as hard as he could, but the shelves exhibited no movement. "Sturdy as the day they were built," he said. "We should be able to climb them, no problem."

Mathias, ever the deft climber, quickly scaled to the top. He rummaged about for a moment, toppling a few of the stacks. When he'd gotten hold of a cylinder that felt right—why, he couldn't say—he slid it into his belt pouch. When he was finished, he climbed back down.

They moved together to the back of the room. The table that held the first cylinders they'd ever viewed still stood in its original place, untouched since that day. As they grew closer, Mathias gripped Jendar's arm so tightly it hurt.

"Skies above, Mathias! What on earth—"

"*Look!*" Mathias whispered.

At first, Jendar didn't have a clue what had prompted his brother's reaction. Then he saw, and bile suddenly rose in his throat.

Someone had rearranged the table. Its entire surface had been cleared, save for two things. One was a cylinder. The other was a disk—pristine, identical to the one they'd first taken.

The two objects sat near the front edge of the table, right next to each other. The chair that was beside the table had been moved and was now positioned before the shelves on the table's left-hand side.

"Someone has been here since we were here last," said Mathias.

"But *who*?"

"Bershon perhaps?"

Jendar paused. "No, he said he hasn't been here in years. It must've been someone else."

"If someone else knows, if someone else has seen us come here, maybe there's a reason those malforms were waiting for us after all. Maybe someone tipped off the Nobles that we were coming."

Jendar grimaced. "But who? Who could have followed us here without our knowledge? Our field craft is probably better than anyone else's in Endreach. I can't believe someone could have shadowed us through the woods the whole way to the village without us figuring it out."

"It had to have been Bershon," said Mathias. "*Had* to have been."

Jendar looked again at the objects on the table. "One thing seems fairly certain. Whoever put this cylinder here meant for us to see it. The way these things have been placed—it's too deliberate."

"You might be right," said Mathias. "Maybe there was something else Bershon wanted us to see."

"But why didn't he just show it to us back in Endreach?"

Mathias shrugged. "Who can say? Although he's like family to me, there's no denying he's rather odd."

Jendar couldn't argue with that. Still, something about the situation made him uneasy. "I don't know about this. This all seems wrong. I don't think Bershon would do something like this. He'd tell us flat out that he wanted us to see whatever is on this thing."

"Maybe he would; maybe he wouldn't. Whatever the case, we're meant to see it. There's no denying that."

Jendar pursed his lips, unable to take his eyes from the cylinder and disk.

"Well?" said Mathias. "What are we waiting for?"

He picked up the cylinder and pressed it into the indentation at the disk's center. Immediately the familiar yellow glyphs sprang to life on its surface. He extended a finger, hovering over the one in the center. His hand trembled, and he exhaled audibly. Then he pressed down.

7

Nothing happened. The room remained exactly as it had. The table, the shelves—everything—stayed the same. Perplexed, Jendar turned to look behind him. Then he froze. They were no longer alone. A figure—seemingly male—stood not a half span away, between them and the exit. He was nearly as tall as Jendar and was clothed in a strange outfit: black pants, black shoes, and a tight-fitting black shirt that covered his neck. The figure's close-cropped hair was nearly as dark as his clothing. His skin was as pale as that of a corpse, his lips blood red, while his sharp nose protruded angrily from beneath his smoldering yellow eyes.

Mathias made a small sound in the back of his throat as he backed into the table.

A Noble! And nowhere to run, Jendar thought. *We're cut off!*

"How..." Jendar began. Then, in an instant, he knew.

The disk *was* working. The images on the cylinder had been taken from within the very room in which they stood.

"Mathias, wait," he said. "The cylinder. This is a part of it. The doorway out is there," he said, pointing.

Mathias's eyes remained wide, and he tensed, ready to spring.

"It's all right," Jendar began. He was interrupted when the Noble began to speak.

"Greetings, travelers," he said. His voice was deep, stern, oppressive. He spoke in a very strange accent, and every syllable he uttered sounded flat, as dead as the grave.

"I was quite surprised to learn that someone had discovered this chamber," he said. "I suspected you would return again. It was my hope that you'd find this cylinder and activate it."

Jendar glanced at Mathias. Although he had relaxed a bit, he was still clearly on edge. Jendar moved toward his brother, aware that every muscle in his own body was taut to the point of snapping.

"Though you can undoubtedly see what I am, I must first reassure you that I mean you no harm."

The Noble then paused, as if to let the statement sink in.

No harm? Jendar thought, almost angrily. *Did you mean no harm when you or your companion on the other side of the valley bled our mother dry? Did you mean no harm when you penned our entire village in like animals?*

"It's no doubt strange for you, and perhaps frightening, to see one of my kind address you so openly. I assure you again—I'm not your enemy. I simply want to pass on some information to you, information I believe you'll find useful if you'll continue to hear me out."

"They know we've been here," Mathias whispered. "We'll never be safe again!"

"Keep calm, brother," Jendar said, nearly laughing at the ridiculousness of such a statement coming from someone who was on the verge of a mental collapse. "We're in no immediate danger."

"The fact that you've left your village and, flaunting the rules, journeyed here on a regular basis suggests to me that you can be trusted with this information," the Noble continued. "You clearly don't view your overlords with the same sense of awe as the rest of your people."

Jendar wrinkled his brow. This creature thought it was a *good* thing that he had disobeyed the Nobles' rules?

"Though much differs between us, we share a common enemy: the Nobles who rule over your village."

"*What?*" Jendar blurted. "But isn't…" He trailed off.

"This one's different," said Mathias, tugging on Jendar's sleeve. "Look at his clothes. He doesn't dress like the lord or lady."

How many of them are *there*? Jendar wondered.

"I believe I can help you," the Noble said. "I have knowledge that can aid your people, information that can give you a better life. I offer you freedom."

"Freedom?" whispered Mathias.

Jendar shook his head. He was afraid to speak, lest he miss what the lord would say next.

"What's been done to humanity is nothing short of a travesty. No person should be treated as an animal. What your lord and lady have done to your village—to countless people throughout history—is unforgivable. And they must answer for it."

For the first time in the creature's discourse, Jendar sensed an emotion beneath his deadpan delivery.

Rage.

The lord paused again, staring straight at them, unblinking. His terrifying golden eyes seemed to brighten. "I have knowledge that can help you," he continued. "I'd like to meet with you so I might pass this knowledge on."

Jendar and Mathias stared at each other. Though Jendar

couldn't tell for certain, he imagined his brother's thoughts mirrored his own.

Meet with us? Jendar thought, frowning. *What sort of trickery is this?*

"You undoubtedly have misgivings about this proposition," the Noble continued. "I understand all too well the fear you must feel toward those of my kind. Let me assure you again—I mean you no harm. I know of your journeys here. I can follow your movements, through the woods and through this city. If I ever wished you ill, I could have harmed you at any point.

"Furthermore, as a gesture of goodwill, I give you this gift: free passage through the woods. Come and go as you please, with the knowledge that you won't need to fear any creature of darkness. My servants will be on hand to protect you, should you require their assistance. You don't even need to call for them; they'll act on their own, should anyone attempt to harm you.

"I urge you to agree to this meeting. Your freedom, and your lives, depend upon it. Should you agree to my proposition, please return here tomorrow night, after dark. One of my servants will await you here, in this room, and will lead you to me. I again offer you my assurances that the woods will be safe. No creature will harm you as long as I order my servants to protect you.

"I realize this is a big decision, and you don't have long to ponder it. Time is, however, of the essence, and I must know by then if you're truly interested in helping to secure the freedom of your people. I wish you safe travels and hope to meet you in person soon."

With that, the Noble and the doorway behind it vanished.

Neither of the brothers said anything for some time.

Jendar was trying to sort through the jumble of confusion swirling through his mind. Everything he'd ever known had been turned upside down in less than a day. And now, a seemingly benevolent Noble had addressed them as equals and requested—*requested*—that they meet to discuss knowledge that would allegedly help him, Mathias, and the rest of the villagers. Such behavior was unheard of, and Jendar was at a complete loss as to what it all could mean.

"Play it again," said Mathias.

"What?"

"Play it again. I want to see it again."

Jendar obliged. As the lord spoke again, Jendar tried as hard as he could to detect any trace of hostility or hidden intent. The creature was impossible to read, however, except for the one point in the conversation when he mentioned the other Nobles. After they heard it a second time, there was no mistaking it—fury tinged his voice.

If Jendar were to believe that the Noble didn't intend to turn that fury upon Mathias and him, that belief would have to be forged from pure faith, without a shred of evidence to suggest whether or not the lord had spoken truthfully

When the cylinder had ended again, Mathias regarded Jendar. "What are our plans?"

Jendar shook his head. "I have no idea what to make of this. We need some time to think. Let's bring this cylinder back with us, perhaps play it again."

"I think there's some truth to what he said. If he wanted us dead, or if he wanted to feed on us, he could have easily done so by now. There's more going on here than we realize."

"Even so, I wouldn't easily trust one of them, or take what he said at face value."

"I agree," said Mathias. "Still...I wonder."

Jendar retrieved the cylinder but left the disk where it was. "We should be getting back," he said, "before it gets dark. We can always come back and explore later. I'd like some time to sit and think about what all this could mean."

Mathias didn't argue.

Slowly they walked out of the ancient village—the *city*, as the Noble had called it—and back to the edge of the woods. When they arrived, they stopped and stared into the trees. Though neither of them said it aloud, Jendar was certain they both felt the same thing: mindless fear.

After what had happened earlier, it wouldn't be easy to make the trek back through the forest, even though this new Noble had promised them his protection. Nearly being captured or killed by a pack of malforms wasn't an experience one took lightly or forgot easily.

After a few more moments, Jendar finally spoke. "Let's get this over with."

He started forward, unsure at first if Mathias would follow. He let out a deep sigh when he heard his brother's footfalls behind him.

They moved even more slowly and cautiously than usual through the woods. Regardless of the lord's assurances that they would be protected, Jendar didn't feel the least bit safe. Every rustle of leaves brought the brothers to a dead stop, hearts pounding. Fortunately, their caution was unwarranted, as they encountered no malforms on their way back.

Once they had cleared the woods, it took all of Jendar's restraint to keep himself from racing back to Endreach. He maintained his composure, mindful that a reckless approach could very well end with someone spotting them.

They took their usual route around the copse and, to their knowledge, arrived home with no one the wiser.

The moment Jendar shut the door, Mathias collapsed onto one of the bench seats. Jendar's hands still trembled, and he removed his pack slowly, joining his brother.

"I've been thinking," Mathias said slowly. "I bet those malforms we saw in the woods, the second group, belonged to this new Noble."

Jendar chewed on that for a moment. "It could very well be," he said. "It does seem odd that they would have been on hand at exactly that moment and stranger still that they made no attempt to run us down."

"But that still doesn't explain that first group." Mathias shook his head. "I have a bad feeling about them. It really did seem like they'd laid a trap for us. Like they knew we'd be there."

"I agree," said Jendar, "but that raises its own questions. Why the trap? If the Noble I saw here earlier was behind the attempt on our lives, why didn't he just finish the job when he had the chance?"

Mathias shrugged. "No idea. Something about this whole thing just seems...off."

"Maybe..." Jendar began, trailing off.

Mathias raised his eyebrows. "Maybe what?"

Jendar chewed his lip. "I almost hate to even say this, but maybe this new lord could answer that question."

"So you think we should meet him?"

"I don't know what I think anymore," said Jendar, with a sigh. "The whole proposition still seems crazy. What does he really want with us? The notion of his wanting freedom for our village is hard to swallow."

"It does seem strange," said Mathias. "But you have to admit—there's so much about the lord and lady that we don't know. We have no idea what motivates them, no inkling why they think the way they do. In truth, I never before suspected for a moment that there might be *more* of those forsaken things."

Jendar grunted. "We know so little about what's really out there. We've spent much of our lives knowing only this valley and, more recently, the valley of the ruins. There could be hundreds more Nobles beyond the boundaries of our lands. And what if...*what if* there are more people out there like us as well?"

Mathias gazed off into space, a faraway look in his eyes. "I've never even thought of that."

The two remained silent for a moment longer.

"For all we know," Mathias continued, still seeming to peer off at something only he could see, "there are countless villages. There could be hundreds more. Thousands. Who knows just how far these lands go? All we know about is what we can see up to the horizon. And as far as we know, no one has ventured that far from Endreach."

"Maybe the new lord has those answers as well. Maybe he can tell us what's out there."

Mathias, his eyes dancing, turned his gaze back to Jendar. "We should go back. Tomorrow night. See what he has to say."

"I admit, I'm more than a bit curious at the prospect. But is it safe? What guarantee do we have that he doesn't have something horrible in mind for us?"

"Like what?"

"Well," said Jendar slowly, "the Nobles—the ones in this valley, at least—have been known to take people away who displease them. But why? Why not punish them in the village square, like the others? What do they *do* with people once they have them?"

"I don't know," Mathias said, shaking his head.

"As much as I'd like to believe this new lord has our best interests at heart, I...I don't know if I can. There's still too much that doesn't add up. And now we're expected to decide, almost immediately, whether to grant its request for an audience?" He sighed. "I don't know if I'm ready to trust him so blindly."

"Look," said Mathias, "I have the same reservations you do. But I think it's worth at least considering. Let's not simply dismiss this opportunity out of hand. We have a little time to think on this—until tomorrow night. Turn it over in your mind. Whatever decision you make, I'll stand by you. You're the eldest, and I respect that. But please...please at least consider going and hearing the creature out."

Jendar nodded slowly. "I'll think on it."

8

J endar and Mathias spent the rest of the day taking care of idle tasks. They tidied the house from top to bottom, weeded the garden, and swept the floors. Neither of them spoke of Mateya or of the lord and his offer. In truth, neither of them spoke much at all about anything. Jendar's mind wouldn't stop racing, and he fought madly to regain his of mental composure.

In the midst of it all, he pushed his feelings of grief and loss down as far as they would go. He promised himself that when he'd reached a decision about whether to see the lord, and when he'd followed that decision through to the end, he'd take the time to properly grieve his mother's death.

As the sun grew lower on the horizon and Jendar heard the sounds of their neighbors returning home from work, a burning pain in his stomach overtook the chaos in his mind. He realized he'd barely eaten all day and was surprised at the fact that it had taken him so long to notice his hunger.

"I'm going to put supper on," he announced as Mathias returned from dumping their old wash water.

Mathias absently rubbed his stomach. "Good," he said. "I feel like I could eat an entire cow."

"Speaking of cows, it won't be long before we can replenish our meat rations. It's been nearly a month; we'll be due a fresh supply in a couple of days."

Mathias groaned. "Now you're really making my mouth water. There's only so much vegetable pottage I can take."

Mathias had always had quite a taste for meat, even more so than the rest of the family. Mateya had often set aside a portion of her own ration for him so he'd have extra.

Jendar kindled a fire, filled their cook pot with water, and placed it over the flames. Mathias opened the larder and pulled out a sack filled with what was left of their grain.

"I'm going to dig some gnarlroots from the garden," Jendar said, heading outside.

When he returned, Mathias already had added the grain to the water and was stirring it. Jendar sliced the gnarlroots and added them to the pot. Though it certainly wasn't meat, the pottage still smelled wonderful, and Jendar's stomach growled.

The boys ate in silence, taking little time to devour every last scrap of what they'd made. Just as they had finished cleaning the dishes and banking the fire's embers, a knock came at the door.

When Mathias drew the door open, the brothers were greeted with Bershon's hunched form. Mathias stepped aside to admit him. "You always do seem to come when there's food about," he said with a grin. "Unfortunately we've just finished cleaning up."

"Not to worry," said Bershon. "I already ate."

He heaved himself down atop one of the bench seats.

"How are you two holding up?"

"As well as can be, I suppose," said Jendar, joining him.

"We went back to the ruins today," said Mathias.

Bershon waggled his eyebrows. "So soon? I'd have thought you'd be in mourning all day."

Jendar sighed. "We are. Believe me, Bershon, the sadness of losing her...it's almost unbearable. Mathias and I made the journey to escape. To do something with ourselves for the day, to try to forget what's happened."

"I have some advice for the two of you," Bershon said. "Fight the urge to flee the pain. Running doesn't do a thing. You can take it from me—I learned that lesson the hard way when I lost Josha and Verdan. When those bastards took Bella from me, I used what I had learned. I grieved. I didn't try to lose myself in my work or outrun my feelings. I let the pain fill me. Yes, it was hard. But in the end, it was better."

Neither Jendar or Mathias could respond to that. Maybe they *had* been trying too hard to outrun their grief. Maybe the trip to the ruins had been a mistake.

And now we're stuck in a position where we can't allow our emotions to rule us, Jendar thought. *Not until I decide what to do about this new Noble.*

Jendar debated for a moment whether to tell Bershon about what they'd found. It didn't take him long to conclude that he owed the man that much.

"Truthfully, Bershon," he said, "we no longer have the time to grieve."

He laid everything out for his old friend, from their initial journey through the woods and the thwarted malform attacks, to the strange cylinder featuring the new lord, and the creature's bizarre request. When he had finished, Bershon looked dazed.

"I've never heard of such a thing," he said quietly. "A *third* Noble. Who would have thought there'd be more?"

Mathias shook his head. "We certainly never would have imagined it."

"But think about what it means," said Jendar. "If there are more lords and ladies, perhaps there are more people as well. Maybe more survived the catastrophe that nearly ended our race."

"I suppose it's possible," said Bershon, rubbing his gray stubble. "We know so very little about what's out there, beyond the confines of this stinking valley."

"Maybe this new lord can tell us more," said Mathias. "I'd certainly like to ask him what else is out there."

"Maybe he can tell you more," said Bershon, "or maybe this whole thing is some sort of elaborate deception. I don't pretend to know what motivates the Nobles to do what they do. But I do know this: they aren't to be trusted."

"I agree," said Jendar, "but I have a strange feeling about this whole situation. Something is afoot, Bershon. The first group of malforms in the woods *had* to have known we were coming. How else could they have appeared as they did? And the strangeness of them. They moved like shadows. Mathias and I didn't know they were there until they were almost on top of us. Have you ever seen a malform move so adeptly through the woods?"

Bershon shook his head.

"Then," Jendar continued, "there was the visit from the Noble in the cottage. In broad daylight, in front of all three of us. No attempt to feed, no punishments meted out. It doesn't make sense."

"And you think visiting this creature in the ruins will give you an inkling as to what's been going on?"

Jendar nodded. "A part of me does. That's why I'm glad you're here. I value your advice, Bershon. I'd like to hear what you have to say on the matter."

Bershon exhaled a long sigh. "You say this lord is new, but how do you know for sure?"

Jendar shook his head. Although the new lord had dressed differently than the lord of their valley, other than its clothing, the two looked nearly identical.

"Personally," Mathias said quietly, "I can't. They all look alike to me."

Bershon nodded. "How do you know, then, that it wasn't the lord of this valley?"

"I guess we don't," said Jendar, "but that still leaves an important question: why? Why would he go to such lengths to entice us into a meeting? What could he gain from that?"

"As I said, I can't begin to guess why those creatures behave as they do," said Bershon. "I can see why you'd be curious, but I urge you again: don't let your curiosity overcome good sense. You don't know what this thing's plans are or if he's even who he says he is."

Jendar stared at Bershon for a long moment before responding. "I see the wisdom in your words, Bershon. Still, I think what I'm feeling goes beyond mere curiosity. I can't explain it any better than that. I get the sense that this visit has the chance of yielding something more than just answers. Maybe it'll furnish us with a path."

Bershon leaned forward. "A path to what exactly?"

"Freedom," said Mathias.

Jendar and Bershon turned to look at him.

"That's what the lord said. Freedom. Freedom for our people."

The weight of Mathias's statement pressed down upon them all, and no one seemed able to speak for several long moments.

Finally, Bershon cleared his throat. "A lovely notion, to be sure. But one that isn't guaranteed."

"True," said Jendar, "which is where my reservations lie. Everything you've said has made sense, Bershon. Everything. This won't be an easy decision to make."

"What will happen if we don't go?" Mathias asked quietly.

Jendar rubbed his chin. "What do you mean?"

"I mean what I said. What will happen if we ignore the lord's request?"

"Nothing, I suppose," said Jendar.

"That's exactly it," said Mathias. "Nothing. Nothing will happen. We'll continue to exist as we always have, providing the villagers with clothing, and living in fear. We'll take the apprentices the lord and lady assign us and marry as they see fit. We'll live to be about the same age as mother and father, *and then they'll kill us.*"

Mathias paused, letting his words sink in, before continuing.

"If we don't meet with this new Noble, nothing will change. But if we go, there's a chance for something different. Was the creature being honest? I can't answer that. But what do we have to lose? If his intentions are hostile, so be it. Better to die now than live the next thirty years of our lives like caged animals."

"There's wisdom in what you say as well," Jendar said. "I can see the validity to both of your arguments. Going would be extremely dangerous and carries the risk of death or worse. Doing nothing, on the other hand, is the safer choice. Yet, if we do nothing..."

He let his voice trail off. He glanced toward the back of their cottage, at the doorway that led to what had been their parents' room. He thought of his mother: her laugh, her smile, and how much he loved her. A tear rolled down his cheek, and his throat clenched. He wiped his eyes with the back of his hand.

"I loved her very much, you know," Jendar said. "Mama —that's what I called her as a boy. And I can tell you, I feel very much like a small boy right now. Our parents are dead, and the responsibility of our family is on my shoulders."

He pulled a piece of cloth from one of his pockets and blew his nose.

"Any decision I make could be the end of us. Inaction will lead to us being bled to death before our time. The same fate will befall our children and *their* children. Action might lead to our demise in the ruins at the hand of this self-proclaimed 'ally.' But...it might not." He wiped his eyes again. "One choice is guaranteed to end in death. The other at least has a *chance* of success...and a better life for us all."

Jendar gazed at Bershon, smiling despite his pain. "Old friend, I understand your concerns. You don't want to lose us, especially after losing mother and father so soon. But I now feel almost certain that this meeting must happen."

He glanced over at Mathias, whose eyes were also wet.

Bershon heaved a great sigh. "I can't make you stay. You're a man now, Jendar, and able to find your own way. If you're determined to go, I make only one request: take me with you. I've been going to those ruins a lot longer than you have. If things take a turn for the worse, the odds are better that I'll be able to get us out faster or at least find us a safe place to hide."

"We'd be honored to have you," said Jendar.

9

The following morning, after eating the largest breakfast they could stomach, Jendar and Mathias stuffed their packs full of roots and grain. They each took a small cook pot, a spoon, and a tinderbox and also filled their water skins.

Before he'd left the day before, Bershon had gone through their cache of items from the ruins, and showed them a few useful things. Jendar pried up the loose board, and each grabbed a light stick. Additionally, they took the following: a pair of rectangular objects that supposedly controlled the larger light-spheres that hung from the ceilings of the ruins; a small, circular disc that Bershon swore could open the structures' locked doors; and a metal cube that – when used in the correct room – was supposed to cause fresh water to flow from the wall.

Bershon had told them he'd be there by midday. Restless with anticipation, neither brother spoke much that morning. Each of them tried his best to kill time with idle tasks, but there wasn't much to do—the house was already spotless, the garden had been weeded, and nearly every article of clothing they owned was freshly laundered. When midday finally arrived, Jendar and Mathias prepared enough lunch for three people, in case Bershon hadn't yet eaten.

The boys ate hungrily, each lost in his own fantasy world about what tonight's encounter might be like and what it could mean for Endreach. When they'd finished lunch and washed the dishes, Bershon still hadn't arrived.

"Midday is nearly gone," said Mathias. "Where could he be?"

"It's not unlike our friend to sleep past midday, particularly if there's no work at the forge and if he's been in his cups the night before."

"We should go to him," said Mathias, reaching for his pack.

Jendar gripped his arm gently. "If we travel through town together toward Bershon's home, what will people think? We're carrying enough supplies for a beast of burden. Should someone—or, worse yet—*something* take notice, our departure might be observed."

Mathias relaxed, taking a seat at the table. "You're right. We need to be careful. If one of the Nobles' creatures sees us heading for the woods..."

"Still," said Jendar, "I do wonder what's taking him so long. We need to leave, and soon, if we want to make it to the ruins before nightfall. If he doesn't arrive soon, I'll head to his home, alone, to fetch him."

The brothers waited for another hour. Finally, Jendar couldn't stand it any longer. Shaking his head, he went to the door. "We've waited long enough. I'll be back."

Although he didn't see many people on his way to Bershon's, he tried to move as casually as possible. Though his instinct was to rush over there, he knew such behavior would attract notice. He kept an eye out for rats and black-jays but saw none.

Though the village was fairly quiet, a faint, droning voice carried across the stillness of the afternoon. It grew louder the closer Jendar drew to Bershon's home. As it became more distinct, sweat beaded on his forehead.

It can't be, he thought.

He continued on, hearing the voice more clearly with each step. Though he continued to deny it—to hang on to the hope that what he was imagining what he was hearing —the dire truth became apparent the moment he rounded the corner.

Bershon's street was like all the others in the village, lined on both sides with neat little cottages. The old man's home was near the corner Jendar had just turned, only four houses in. A stooped shape stood in front of his friend's door. It was dressed in soiled, tattered rags that could only be called clothes in the loosest sense of the word. Its arms were longer than most men's, hanging down well past its knees. Its shoulders were broader by far than those of any normal person, and its head sat at a queer angle atop its neck.

The sight of the malform crier was, in and of itself, nearly enough to send Jendar into a panic, but the throaty, lisping syllables it belched out in an endless loop were what threatened to push him completely over the edge.

"Bershon Oresmith has been taken by our masters as punishment for traveling past the Line of Demarcation."

Jendar's mouth fell open, and he staggered, unsure whether he should keep going or run back the way he had come.

The malform turned to look at him, twisting the corners of its cracked lips into a hideous grin as its mouth continued to form the syllables of its announcement. Jendar choked on his own saliva, coughing uncontrollably into his hands.

Get it together! Keep moving! If this creature knows you were here to see Bershon, it'll run you down on the spot!

With tremendous effort, Jendar continued on, trying his best to look as nonchalant as possible despite the vomit that threatened to rise in his throat. He walked past the beast, mindful of its cruel, penetrating gaze, and forced his steps to remain slow and controlled until he reached the end of the street.

When he rounded the corner at the opposite end of the road, he could control himself no longer. Unconcerned about the bewildered glances of rare passersby, he broke into a wild run, not stopping until he reached his cottage. He threw the door open, slammed it shut behind him, and peered out the front window. Thankfully, there was no sign of any commotion on the street.

In an instant, Mathias was on his feet. "What is it? What happened?"

It wasn't until Jendar attempted to respond that he realized just how out of breath he was. "Bershon..." he gasped. "They've...taken him!"

Mathias turned white. "Who's taken him?"

"Nobles. Crier...was there. Outside Bershon's cottage."

Jendar threw himself down on one of the benches, trying to regain control.

Mathias gripped him by the shoulders, leaning down to look him in the face. "What did the crier say? Why was Bershon punished?"

Jendar gazed up into his eyes. "Travel. Beyond the Line of Demarcation."

Mathias hissed as he raced to gather up their gear. "They know. Somehow they know. If they took Bershon, they very well may know about us as well. We need to leave *now*. It's no longer safe for us here."

Jendar nodded, grabbing his pack and water skin from Mathias. "We'll go quickly," he said, getting back some of his wind. "At this point, I don't care how suspicious we look. We can't afford to travel slowly."

Mathias hefted his pack then opened the door and stepped out into the street. Jendar followed, closing the door behind them. Mathias turned left and headed toward the edge of the village. Jendar began to follow when a sudden movement above caught his attention.

It was a blackjay, fluttering down to land on the peak of a roof directly across the street. Once it landed, it didn't move. It stared, unblinking, at Jendar and his brother.

"Blackjay!" Jendar whispered to Mathias. "One of theirs!"

Mathias picked up his pace, nearly to a jog. Jendar kept up with him, glancing behind them every few moments. The blackjay stayed where it was. Still, it stared at them. Jendar tried to put the sight of the bird out of his mind.

All it's doing is watching. There's no danger. Stay calm.

His thoughts unraveled when a chorus of guttural screams resounded from down the street behind them.

"Malforms!" Jendar shouted to Mathias. "*Run!*"

Without a backward glance, Mathias bolted. Jendar matched his pace, even though he was still slightly winded from his earlier run. Before long, they reached the edge of the village.

"Straight for the woods!" Jendar shouted. Taking their usual route around the copse would be suicide; they'd never make it in time. Through the countryside, they ran as fast as their legs could carry them. Even so, the woods seemed impossibly far away.

Glancing back, Jendar spotted four stooped malforms loping from the village, closing fast.

"We'll never make it!" wailed Mathias.

"Dump your gear!" screamed Jendar, unshouldering his pack. He let it fall to the earth, along with his water skin. Instantly, running became much easier. Mathias apparently had heard him, as he also let his supplies fall to the ground.

As soon as Mathias's pack dropped, an eerie howl pierced the air from the direction of the copse. As Jendar turned toward the sound, three malforms exploded from the foliage. They were the same long-faced creatures that had nearly killed them in the woods the previous day. They ran on all fours, with the speed of wolves.

Jendar glanced again at the forest. Though they might have managed to outrun the first group, he realized they'd never get to the trees before the newcomers reached them.

Nevertheless, instinct spurred him on. The cries of the original pack grew fainter, while the wailing of the new malforms increased in volume. Their footfalls shook the ground as they thundered toward their prizes.

Jendar's hope was all but gone, and he wondered how it would feel to be ripped apart and devoured.

"I...I can't go on," Mathias gasped over his shoulder, his pace beginning to slow.

"Faster!" Jendar screamed. "They're almost—"

A new, horrifying sound split the air. In front of them, six massive shapes lumbered from within the trees. Each towering malform was the size of a small outbuilding. They clutched huge wooden clubs that appeared to have been fashioned from the trunks of trees, and they were adorned with crude clothing, made from metal plates, that covered their legs and torsos. Each creature wore a dented metallic helmet.

At first, Jendar reeled in fear, nearly stopping entirely. Mathias had the same reaction, frenziedly trying to slow his pace and reverse course. Then a wild thought occurred to Jendar.

The new lord's servants. Could it be?

"Run toward them!" he shouted, picking up his pace again. He passed Mathias, well aware of his brother's puzzled expression. "They're allies!"

Jendar must have spoken the words with conviction, despite his numerous doubts; when he glanced behind him, his brother was running full speed once again.

Jendar knew that if he was wrong about the newcomers, it would mean death for them both. Yet he also knew death was a near certainty anyway. There was no chance of them outrunning the speediest of their pursuers.

The new malforms sprinted forward, and several of them broke off into a second group. One group headed straight for Jendar and Mathias; the other raced toward their four-legged adversaries. The brothers continued their breakneck pace toward the towering shapes.

Jendar closed his eyes as he grew near. *If the end comes now, please let it come quickly.*

He ran three more steps. Four. The roars of the creatures before him grew deafening.

Then, almost instantly, they were behind him. Jendar faltered and opened his eyes. The only remnants of the malforms from the woods were the furrows their feet had torn in the earth. He glanced behind him and saw them rush toward the first group of pursuers.

It was a bloodbath. The smaller creatures were no match for their armed and armored assailants. With beastly howls, the larger malforms swung their clubs with deadly precision. Each bone-crushing impact sent the smaller creatures flying, rending them into bloody, unrecognizable shapes. In moments the battle was over, and they turned their attention to the four-legged malforms.

They needn't have bothered. The allied malforms that had broken off into a second group had already dealt with them. A lone survivor ran full speed for the horizon, pursued by one of the larger malforms. In moments, it became clear that the pursuit was hopeless, and the larger creature gave up the chase.

Jendar stopped running and bent over, trying to catch his breath. Mathias did the same, never taking his eyes off the newcomers. Abruptly, the six lumbering creatures turned and walked slowly, almost casually, toward them. One of them stooped to pick something up from the ground. With surprise, Jendar noticed that when it stood, it was holding the boys' packs and water skins in a single massive hand.

The huge creatures slowly surrounded them. Weapons lowered, they seemed eerily at ease. The malform that had retrieved their supplies approached them. It extended its arm, holding out their gear. Jendar hesitated, then stepped forward and accepted their packs and skins.

"Thank you," he said, his words a barely audible rasp.

The creature grunted something incomprehensible in return.

One of the malforms gestured toward the woods, uttering syllables that sounded more like growls than speech. Wordlessly, the others walked briskly toward the edge of the forest. Even though every instinct in his body told him to run the other direction, Jendar followed. Moments later, Mathias joined him.

Neither of them spoke. They kept pace with their rescuers, nervous squirrels among proud wolves, following them deeper into the woods. Before long, they reached the Line of Demarcation. The creatures crossed it without hesitation, as did Jendar and Mathias. Jendar saw no reason to adhere to their normal "right-foot first" ritual; their luck already had seemed to run out.

10

The group moved carelessly, stomping foliage, grumbling loudly, and generally making a racket. Clearly their escorts weren't concerned about arousing attention. Jendar continued to move in silence, stealing a glance sideways at the giant who walked beside him. He'd never before been this close to a malform and had seldom been able to get a truly good look at one; even the village crier was often too far away to view with any great amount of detail, and Jendar never had cared to stare at the thing too closely in any case. Now that he was in a position to examine the creature more closely, he noticed something that disturbed him deeply.

It swiveled its head casually back and forth, seeming to gaze into the surrounding woods. Though it never looked directly at him, Jendar had no problem getting a clear view of its eyes. They weren't the eyes of an animal or some other creature.

They were the eyes of a human being.

Those eyes could just as easily be mine, Jendar thought.

Unable to stop his stomach from clenching, he wrenched his gaze away.

Why? Why does this thing have human eyes?

As discreetly as possible, he stared at the others in the group. Their eyes were the same: fully human, with the same colors one would find among the villagers. Brown. Hazel. Blue. Brown again.

Jendar thought he would vomit.

How can we have anything in common with such vile creatures?

He glanced sidelong at his brother. Mathias walked with his eyes downcast, clearly not wishing to see their companions any more than necessary.

As much as Jendar wanted to share this new finding with Mathias, he elected to keep silent. There was no telling how these things would react to his words. He turned his thoughts to something that disturbed him even more: their meeting with the new Noble.

Initially, Jendar had felt fairly confident that he was making the correct decision. Now, faced with the reality of the situation, he was no longer certain. Then a new thought occurred to him.

What will happen after *the meeting?*

His mouth went dry at the thought of what had occurred when he and Mathias were heading out of the village toward the woods.

The malforms knew what we were planning. Somehow they knew, and they tried to stop us. We can never go home again.

The thought of leaving their home behind, forever, made his throat constrict.

I won't cry in front of these beasts. I won't.

The cottage and village where he'd grown up, where all

his earliest, happiest memories had been formed, was now off limits to them.

And Bershon...poor Bershon. They've taken him as well.

He thought of their old friend's laugh, his comfortingly casual demeanor, his quirks. At that moment, he missed the man deeply.

When the Nobles took someone, that person was gone. Forever. No one who had been punished in that manner had ever returned.

Just keep moving. Keep moving, and keep those thoughts at bay.

Pity, whether for himself, or for his family's closest friend, wasn't an option. Jendar needed to stay focused, to keep himself in the moment, if he wished to survive an encounter with a Noble.

Whatever happens afterward...happens.

The resolve he felt after those words echoed through his mind kept him going, step after sluggish step, through the woods, and toward their inevitable destination. The meeting would take place. It *had* to take place. More than ever, he realized that if he and Mathias had any chance of survival, it lay within the grasp of this new Noble.

Before long, Jendar spied the familiar metal husks, thrusting up out of the earth as if trying to escape. Soon the ruined city lay before them. Without hesitation, the malforms took to the downward slope as if they'd done it a hundred times.

They probably have, thought Jendar. *These things undoubtedly have been through the woods, maybe even as far as Endreach.*

The creatures took a different path through the ruins that Jendar was used to, winding through several unfamiliar streets. Each turn brought Jendar a new, breathtaking sight.

Some of the buildings that he'd only seen from the distance of the hillside now towered above him. They were far larger than he'd originally thought, shining orange in the waning daylight.

Finally, the group approached a building that Jendar instantly recognized: a twisted spire, seemingly made entirely of glass, that could clearly be seen from the hill at the edge of the valley.

We've come almost all the way across the city.

A glance at the sky told him it was far later than he'd originally thought. Late-afternoon orange was giving way to red, and the tops of the buildings were the color of blood.

The largest malform of the group, undoubtedly the leader, strode up to the front of the building. After fumbling about in the soiled rags that passed for its clothing, it produced an object too small for Jendar to make out. It waved the object in front of itself, and the two closest panes of glass—each easily twice the height of Jendar and Mathias's cottage—parted down the middle, revealing a dimly lit corridor beyond.

The beast turned and beckoned for the boys to approach. Jendar gripped his brother's arm then released him and walked forward. The malform turned and lumbered into the corridor. The half-dragging, thudding footfalls of the malforms resounded behind Jendar, as well as a much smaller, daintier set. Without looking, he knew Mathias was behind him.

He had expected the soaring, multistory entryway, seemingly an architectural fad of the day in which it was created. What he hadn't expected was to find himself in such immaculate surroundings. Every light sphere in the ceiling was aglow, and though the light they cast was dim, it was enough to see the gleaming stonework beneath their feet, wiped clean of any smudge or trace of dust, and the floor-to-ceiling tapestries in nearly every color of the rainbow, with work of such impeccable quality that they no doubt would put Jone Weaver to shame.

The tapestries depicted fantastical scenes of fierce battles, eerily foreign landscapes, and beasts that defied imagination. One of them depicted a large, white creature with a flowing mane, like a horse, but with a single horn jutting from its forehead. Jendar wished he could have taken more time to admire them, but the group was moving quickly.

At the rear of the entry chamber, two passageways branched off in opposite directions. The leader of the group headed down the one to the right. After traveling a short distance, they entered a circular chamber with a ceiling nearly as high as that of the entryway. The lead malform strode to the far end of the chamber, again waving the small object at what looked to be a large door, perhaps a half story high. Quickly and silently, the door slid open. Beyond it lay a much smaller room, about the size of the common area in Jendar and Mathias's cottage. The malform entered, and Jendar and Mathias followed. Jendar was confused when the rest of the group piled in behind him. There appeared to be no other doorway through which to exit the room, and the space was cramped. As the last creature entered, Jendar found himself pushed flat against one of the side walls, not far from the entrance. He tried not to panic, and for a moment, he entertained the notion of grabbing his brother and making a run for it. He swallowed his fear, closed his eyes, and willed himself to calm down.

Jendar was about to open his mouth and ask just what purpose was served by cramming them all into such a small space, when the leader again brandished its tiny device. To Jendar's horror, the door slid shut.

He glanced at Mathias, who had gone completely white. The stench of the creatures was palpable: a powerful, musky odor that made his eyes water and throat burn. Fighting to keep from screaming, he looked back at the leader. Softly glowing blue glyphs had come to life on the wall to the right of the closed entryway; the creature slowly tapped several of them. They flashed three times then went out. A voice, speaking in a language Jendar didn't understand, suddenly spoke from above. Then he got the unmistakable impression that they were moving upward.

Before long, the door slid open again, and Jendar was shocked to see that their surroundings had completely changed. Gone was the room from which they'd originally entered. A wide hallway, as dimly lit as the rest of the building, stretched before them.

Almost nonchalantly, the leader exited the small room,. Jendar hesitated but was swept out of the tiny space by the exodus of the massive creatures around him. The group started down the hall, and Jendar followed.

He stopped when he felt a sudden, crushing pressure on his arm. He hissed, raising his fist involuntarily, and found himself face-to-face with Mathias. His brother's eyes appeared haunted, and he still hadn't regained his complexion.

"What just happened?" he whispered hoarsely. "How did the room change?"

Jendar wished he had an answer. "I don't know."

He tugged Mathias along, and his brother reluctantly followed. As they walked down the hallway, it gradually widened until it opened into a yawning chamber. At the far end of the chamber was a rectangular door, similar to the one they'd walked through just prior to the drastic changed in their surroundings. Like seemingly every other area of the building, the chamber was dimly lit. The leader turned to regard the men. It raised a massive hand, gesturing to the wall on the far side of the room. The wall was lined with oddly rounded chairs and benches, all seemingly made out of cloth.

"It wants us to sit," whispered Mathias.

Jendar nodded, walking over to the nearest bench. He sat, instantly surprised at how soft and comfortable it was. Mathias took a seat next to him.

"These benches are more like beds," Jendar said.

Mathias opened his mouth to respond but closed it when the lumbering form of the leader approached them. Its crude armor glinted dully in the soft glow of the overhead light orb.

"*Wait.*" The word dragged itself from the creature's throat like a rat from a cesspit. Feeling his face contort in revulsion, Jendar fought to relax his features.

Though he was only partially convinced that he'd understood what the creature had said, he nodded. The malform nodded in return then abruptly turned, heading for the far side of the room. When it reached the rectangular door, it again procured the tiny device, and with a wave of its hand, the door slid open. It stepped into the tiny chamber beyond, and the door slid shut.

The other malforms remained behind. Most of them stood still, staring vacantly. One or two occasionally adjusted its armor or shifted its weapons from hand to hand.

Wolves, returned from the hunt, Jendar thought. *Waiting for their next kill.*

Instantly he wished there were some way to make himself smaller or fade away completely.

Fortunately, their wait wasn't long. The door slid back open, and the leader emerged. The creature regarded Jendar and Mathias and, when it noticed them returning its gaze, beckoned for them to join it. The brothers stood slowly and made their way carefully through the malforms that stood throughout the chamber.

The leader stepped aside to allow them entry into the small room. As soon as Jendar and Mathis were inside, the door slid shut again. When the familiar blue glyphs leapt to life on the wall, the malform touched several of them, one after the other. Again, Jendar felt the strange sensation of movement. Before long, the sensation stopped, and the door slid open.

The space that stretched out before them was similar to the other rooms, with a high ceiling and smooth metallic walls, and nearly as long as the village square. It was far darker than the others, however. Though three large light orbs were positioned in a neat row in the center of the ceiling, they were so dim that they offered only the merest suggestion of illumination.

In the center of the room was a long table with three squat shadows clustered at its far end. As Jendar's eyes adjusted, he realized the shadows were chairs. A dark figure, mostly obscured by the dimness of the room, sat in the chair at the head of the table.

Hearing a quiet, sighing noise from behind them, Jendar turned just in time to see the door to the tiny room slide shut. Jendar and Mathias were greeted with a silence that stretched on for an uncomfortably long period of time.

"Come forward, please."

The voice that carried across the stillness of the

chamber was the same as the one they'd heard on the cylinder. Its depth nearly made the air in the room quiver, and though it carried little emotion, there was a finality to its tone that left no room for argument.

The brothers glanced at each other, neither wanting to take the first step. Jendar's lips pressed together in a thin line. He inhaled deeply then started forward. Mathias followed.

As they approached, the figure's features became clearer. Midnight-black hair. Skin as pale as death. Lips the color of spilled blood. Nose like a dagger. And those eyes...they glowed a soft yellow in the dimness of the room, and though they filled Jendar with revulsion, he couldn't help but stare at them.

When Jendar and Mathias reached the table, they paused. Two high-backed metal chairs stood across the table from each other. The chairs been pulled out, seemingly anticipating the brothers' presence.

"Sit." The Noble gestured to the chairs.

Jendar gently touched Mathias's shoulder. "It'll be all right," he whispered.

Nodding, Mathias walked toward the chair to the right of the table, while Jendar headed for the opposite one. He gripped the back of the chair with a hand that was as wet as if he'd just bathed. Slowly he lowered himself into place beside the lord, not daring to look the creature in the face. He gazed across the table at Mathias. His brother's face was nearly as devoid of color as the lord's.

"Thank you both for coming on such short notice," the Noble said. "Your presence here pleases me. By coming to meet me, you've shown great faith in a world where such a thing scarcely exists."

Jendar opened his mouth but promptly closed it again. His throat had grown tight, and the words wouldn't come.

"Look at me," the creature said softly.

Feeling a sudden, light pressure on his left forearm, Jendar nearly leapt to his feet when he saw that the lord's bloodless hand rested there. He gritted his teeth and took a deep, stuttering breath. With great effort, he turned and met the Noble's gaze.

"I'm not the same as those who rule the valley," he said softly. He turned his eyes upon Mathias, whose arm he also held. "I've summoned you here because I believe I can help you. And I believe that you, in turn, can help me. I have watched your village for quite some time. It didn't take long for me to notice the two of you. You have a sense of bravery and an independent streak that none of the other villagers possess. This is why I've chosen to contact you."

"What do you want of us?" Mathias croaked.

The lord removed his hands from their arms and placed them in his lap. He sighed deeply, as if the weight of creation lay upon his shoulders.

"Before I ask anything more of you," he continued, "it's only fair to tell you about myself, about my kind, and about the events that have brought us all here. You look at me, and you see a beast. Inhuman. Cruel. Predatory. And you're right. I'm driven to feed, whether I want to or not, and the blood of you and your kind sustains me. Such as it is with those who rule over your village.

"The greatest truth I have for you is one that's been hidden from humans for millennia. To possess this knowledge is to cut through the lies the Nobles have used to oppress you for countless years. We aren't gods. We aren't all-powerful, all-knowing beings. We have weaknesses. We can be harmed, even killed. Most important, Nobles were human once. Just like you."

Jendar's mouth fell open. *How can this be? The Nobles... human? What about their power? Their omnipotence?*

As soon as the thought formed, Jendar nodded, understanding seeping in. For quite some time, he had suspected that the lord and lady weren't all that they seemed. This bit of information seemed to prove it.

The lord sat back in his chair. "Each and every one of us Nobles was transformed into what we are, twisted and perverted."

He gazed off into space for a moment before continuing.

"My story spans hundreds of years. It'll take some time to tell. I'll arrange for your accommodations if you'll stay and hear me tell it."

Jendar glanced at Mathias, took a deep breath, then said, "We can't go back to Endreach. Take all the time you need."

The lord nodded. "So my agents have informed me. You can take shelter here, with my servants and me, for as long as you need. I open my home to you."

"Thank you," rasped Mathias.

"There's no worse feeling than knowing you can never return home," the lord said quietly. "I myself am keenly aware of that."

The brothers settled back in their chairs, their curiosity nearly eclipsing their fear.

"My name," he began, "was David Levin."

PART II

DAVID'S STORY

11

As much as I tried to deny it, I knew that one day my job would kill me. That night, so long ago, I was working late. I looked at my watch, making a halfhearted effort to tuck in my shirt.

It was 11:15. I'd be going home earlier than usual.

My team had been on a death march to finish coding a sales management system for a demanding client in – of all places – Moldova. I'd pleaded with management to push back against the project's aggressive timeline, but they'd refused. They were blinded by dollar signs, which was typical of people back in those times.

I slogged through the dimly-lit parking garage, toward my red Volvo S60, which was the only car left at that hour of the night. Even though I felt terrible, I remember smiling. I loved that damn car.

It was far more than a simple means of conveyance. It was the first big purchase my wife Rebecca and I had ever made together. It was the car we had driven to our honeymoon in Florida, the car that had shuttled our newborn daughter home from the hospital five years before. Rebecca had wanted a cheaper car, but I had lobbied hard for the Volvo. In retrospect, she'd probably been right about the car being too expensive, but I was arrogant, and would never admit that.

In spite of my exhaustion, I quickened my pace. The sooner I got home, the better.

Rebecca's most likely in bed by now, I thought, *and Sarah's probably been asleep for hours, but at least—*

Something slammed into me from behind, knocking me to my knees. I Sputtered as I tried to regain my breath, but I did not have the strength to resist as powerful hands dragged me to my feet and pinned me to the side of the car. Something hard dug painfully into the small of my back, and the stink of liquor and cigarettes wafted near the side of my face.

"Your wallet. Your jewelry. I want it all, or you're fucking dead."

I grunted as the man drove the object into my back even harder.

"I got a gun pointed right at your kidney. I'm gonna reach in your pockets and take what I find there. You move, you know what happens."

I tried to control my breathing, my throat constricting as panic threatened to overwhelm me. I felt a hand slide into the back pocket of my slacks, felt my wallet being removed. The man quickly patted my arms down, finding the smart-watch that had been a birthday gift from Rebecca the year before. More deftly than I could have imagined, the man unclasped the watch and pocketed it. Calloused fingers probed my neck, gripping the thin silver chain upon which a Star of David hung.

"Please," I whispered, "that was a gift from my father. He passed away a year ago. Please, let me keep that."

"Man, I don't care who it's from. It's *mine* now."

With a tiny bit of pressure and an audible snap, the chain gave way.

"Nice doing business with you."

I remained frozen in place, pressed up against the Volvo, even as the man's running footfalls echoed off into the distance.

I tried to think quickly. I'd need to call the police immediately, and file a report. Maybe there were surveillance cameras around, and they'd captured the crime. Maybe I'd get my belongings back.

I turned slowly, half expecting to see the man still standing there, aiming a gun at my head. I let out a relieved sigh when I found the garage empty. I ran back the way I'd come, heading for the elevator. I stopped before I'd gone half a dozen steps. Something lay on the ground not far from where I stood, something that shone in the dim light of the garage.

It was my star!

In his haste, the thief must have dropped the piece of jewelry. I hurried forward to pick it up, but stopped dead when gooseflesh rose inexplicably on the back of my neck. I shuddered, suddenly certain that something horrible stood right behind me.

I whirled around, ready to fight to the death, and was shocked to see a strikingly beautiful woman standing before me. Her cheekbones were high and fine, her skin flawless. Her complexion was just on the rosy side of pale, while her lips were full and red. She was about my height, and she possessed a build that was voluptuous yet muscular. She wore a well-tailored black blazer, matching slacks, and crisp white blouse. She looked as if she'd just come from a board meeting.

She smiled, and my skin crawled. Something about her was...wrong. That's the only way I can describe it. I was instantly convinced that some kind of horror hid beneath her apparent beauty, a dark presence that suffused the entire parking garage with a sense of malice. My heart beat faster, and I broke out in a cold sweat.

"So sorry," the woman said. "I didn't mean to startle you."

Her voice carried a very faint accent, one that I couldn't quite place, but that reminded me of Eastern Europe.

"That...that's...okay," I replied, taking another step back. "I...I need...I need to..."

Despite my revulsion, I could not look away from her eyes. They were a deep, resonant brown, nearly the same shade as her long, lustrous hair. I shook my head, blinking, and felt my gaze returning to her eyes again.

"*Look*," she whispered, her vulpine smile never wavering. "*Look at me.*"

Something was there, in my mind, and I felt my eyes grow wide as I got a distinct sense of something *sentient* slithering its way through my consciousness. Clutching myself, I gasped at the invasiveness. I tried to look away but found myself unable to move.

"That's it," she said, so softly I could barely hear her. "*Look.*"

Her eyes...

My vision grew cloudy. Everything was out of focus, except for the woman and those cavernous eyes.

"Don't struggle," she said. "Relax."

Slowly the tension left me, and I exhaled loudly. I vaguely recalled that I'd been terribly upset about something a moment before, but the memory of the event was fuzzy.

"Good," she murmured, "very good. Don't fight. There's nothing to fear. I'm here. *Your mistress has come.*"

Her words echoed through my mind, their force shaking me to my bones. My surroundings grew dim.

"Yes," she said. "That's it. Let yourself go."

I felt my mind slip away, felt my memories coalesce into mush. I again had the nagging sensation that something bad had just happened, something that should have disturbed me deeply.

I could not recall what it was.

"There are no worries, no concerns," the woman said. "There's only me."

She licked her lips, and I vaguely noticed that her tongue was strangely pointed, almost sharp. Part of my subconscious—distant, nearly inaudible—screamed in terror. The feeling was brief, and moments later I wondered if I'd felt anything at all.

She walked deliberately toward me, and gently placed a hand on my face. She tilted my head to the side. I recoiled at her touch, crying out, but a sudden sense of calm washed my fears away. My surroundings grew dim, and my muscles relaxed.

I didn't even feel it when she sank her pointed tongue deep into the flesh of my neck.

12

I awoke in a panic. The recollection of everything—the robbery, the beautiful woman, the parking garage, came crashing down upon me. For an instant, I couldn't breathe. I sat bolt upright, drenched in sweat.

My God, what happened to me? I thought.

I realized at once that I was naked. The darkness of my surroundings was as thick as oil, and I probed about with spastic fingers, hoping I could locate my clothes. Wherever I was sitting, at least it was soft and warm.

I realized that I was in a bed. I reached over to the opposite side but felt only sheets. I tried to remember what had occurred after my encounter with the woman, but my mind was blank. I wondered if I had been drugged.

Unable to locate my clothing in the darkness, I stepped quickly out of bed. The carpet beneath my feet seemed thin, but it was as soft and silky as the sheets. I gripped the bedding with both hands and ripped a blanket free, wrapping myself as best I could. I inched forward, one arm out, trying to find a wall. Before long, my fingers came into contact with something cold and hard. It felt like stone.

Using the wall as a guide, I chose a direction and moved slowly forward. I tried listening for any noise that might tell me where I was or who else might be there, but my pounding heart and the blood rushing in my ears made hearing nearly impossible.

I walked my fingers up and down the surface of the wall as I moved forward, hoping to find a light switch. I felt nothing.

I kept moving, trying to keep my emotions under control. Finally my fingers struck something thin and hard protruding from the wall.

When I flipped the switch, the room filled with light so bright that it hurt my eyes. I shielded them for a moment until they had a chance to adjust.

I stood in an immense, circular, stone-walled chamber with a high, pointed ceiling. A large wrought-iron chandelier hung suspended on a black chain. Though the fixture looked ancient, it blazed with the steady glow of electric light bulbs.

Thick wooden crossbeams met at the ceiling's apex, supporting planks of a deep, rich brown wood. A large, grand-looking bed, made from the same dark wood as the ceiling, loomed not far to my left. The woodworking was astounding; hand-carved designs of leaves and flowers seemed to cover every inch. The rug beneath my feet was impeccably woven, softer than any I'd felt, with a detailed scene of a mountainous countryside spanning it from end to end. Equally impressive tapestries hung on the walls, depicting ancient wars and all manner of fantastical creatures - unicorns, satyrs, many-headed serpents and creatures for which I had no name adorned them from end to end.

The room had two tall, iron-banded doors, with great

metal rings for handles. I walked to the closest one first, and with a mighty tug, I pulled it slowly open. I found the switch and flicked the lights on.

The chamber before me could have been called a bathroom, but *bath* would have been a more accurate term. A dizzying array of mosaic tiles covered the ceiling and walls, depicting the landscape of a vast forest. In the center of the room, a pool of steaming water smelled faintly of rose petals, while a sink and toilet sat at the far end.

I switched the light off, headed back into the main chamber, and moved for the other door. I grasped the handle and pulled, but the door didn't move. I tried pushing. Still nothing.

I hesitated for a moment then made a fist and pounded as hard as I could.

"Hello?" I shouted. *Hello! Is anyone there?"*

There was no response.

I pounded and shouted for a few moments longer but still heard nothing.

Don't panic, I told myself. I shook my hand, which ached fiercely from hammering on the massive door.

There was something else as well, a distant pain that for some reason, I couldn't quite place. Instinctively my hand went to my throat. Though the skin on my neck was smooth and uninjured, it suddenly stung, and I inhaled sharply.

My neck, I thought. *It's my neck. My God...*

A vivid memory of the night before bloomed in my consciousness. A beautiful woman, sinking her sharpened, elongated tongue into my throat.

In an instant, I was across the room and into the bathroom. I flipped the lights on and headed for a small, gilded mirror that hung above the sink. My hair was disheveled beyond belief, and my cheeks were pale and strangely sunken. I ignored my appearance for the moment, tilting my head, examining the area of my neck where the pain had originated.

There were no signs of injury.

Perplexed, I exited the bath, leaving the lights on. Had I imagined what had happened?

That doesn't matter, I thought. *I need to find a way out of here, and I need my clothes.*

I hitched the blanket up around me and scanned the room. The elaborately carved bed was the only piece of furniture. There were no dressers, tables, or anywhere else my clothing could possibly be.

I headed back for the door I couldn't open, intent on kicking it this time, when a metallic clunking echoed through the chamber. The door swung out into an expansive hallway. I prepared to bolt, lowering my shoulder, ready to flatten anyone who stood in my way.

Then I saw her.

My legs seemed to liquefy, and I sat down hard, the blanket falling away from my shoulders. All understanding of my current situation vanished.

There was only her.

She wore the same outfit as before: a black suit and white blouse. She looked as lovely as I remembered, but... there were differences. Her skin was far paler than it had been, her hair was now black. And her eyes...they were no longer the deep, captivating brown they'd been during our first encounter. They now glowed softly yellow, as if lit by an inner fire.

There were others with her, out in the hall, but I couldn't make them out. Their shapes blurred into the rest of the surroundings like spilled ink. The image of the woman was all that remained clear.

She smiled broadly as she entered the room. At a gesture, the door swung quietly shut behind her.

"You're awake," she said, sounding mildly surprised. She knelt beside me and took one of my arms in her hands. She gently raised me to my feet. The blanket completely fell away, but I didn't notice.

"I didn't expect you to arise this soon. You're much more resilient than I'd imagined."

She guided me to the bed. I sat, somehow knowing the woman wanted me to.

"I guess I shouldn't really be surprised, given your performance last night." She smiled lasciviously.

"You want to do that again, don't you?" she breathed, leaning down to whisper in my ear, her lips nearly touching me.

I nodded, though I couldn't recall what she was talking about.

"Good. *So do I.* But you have to eat. Eat, and stay strong."

THINGS WENT dark for what seemed like only a moment, but when I regained awareness of my surroundings, a silver cart sat before me. The cart was the size of a small table, and it bore three enormous platters piled with food. The woman had procured a large, mahogany chair, in which she reclined as she stared at me intently.

"Eat," she said.

I gorged myself, working my way through cuts of beef and pork, a small tureen of soup, a multicolored bevy of steamed and sautéed vegetables, and a small chocolate cake. When I finished, I felt my stomach bulging from within.

I had never before eaten that much food in one sitting. Yet somehow, I was still hungry.

"Excellent," the woman mused.

She clapped her hands, and there was a moment when I almost thought someone had entered the room, coming for the cart. Everything had grown so blurry. The moment passed, and I was still seated on the side of the bed, the woman still before me.

"You need time to digest your food," she said. "I'll take a bath while I wait."

As she slid out of her clothes like a snake shedding its skin, I could think of nothing but going to her.

"Patience," she said with a laugh. "Wait for me here, and rest."

I obliged, lying down in bed. The last thing I heard before everything around me went dark was the sound of her slipping into the water.

Reality returned with a jolt, and the woman was in my arms. She sat astride me, riding me, gasping and sweating. My hands covered her breasts, squeezing so hard that a distant part of me wondered if I'd injure her, but she seemed completely unfazed. As she locked eyes with me, I felt a part of my soul slide into that soft, golden gaze. She was my world. She was *everything*.

David...

The voice trailed through my consciousness like a wisp of smoke, and suddenly a new image bloomed in my mind.

It was Rebecca. My wife's radiant smile jolted me from my stupor.

"Rebecca!" I screamed, thrashing to escape the woman who sat astride me. Her grip was like iron, and she held me easily. Her golden eyes blazed, and the world around me began to lose focus. I willed myself to stay in the moment, to remain conscious.

"*My wife! Where is my wife?*" I screamed.

Another image flashed through my mind, and my surroundings grew more distorted. A young girl, whose smile put the brilliance of the sun to shame.

It was Sarah. My daughter.

"No..." I moaned aloud.

The woman glared at me with terrifying intensity, eyes glowing more brightly by the second. She licked her lips, and I noticed her tongue had somehow grown longer, *sharper*. With inhuman speed, she thrust her head forward and plunged her tongue into my neck.

I gasped with the pain and tried to fight the euphoria that came shortly after.

My last thought was of Rebecca, before everything faded away.

13

I gazed in mild surprise at the latest assortment of food that had appeared in my room, seemingly by itself. As hungry as I was, I didn't think too long on it before ripping the leg off a roasted turkey, tearing into the meat and swallowing it nearly unchewed.

Almost instantly, a violent sickness overtook me. I dropped the meat to the floor, retching and gripping my stomach. A disgusting taste filled my mouth, and the food before me suddenly smelled like a midden heap.

I turned to face the other direction, wanting nothing more than to run as far as I could from the ghastly stench behind me, but my sudden illness had rendered me nearly immobile. I fell to my side, groaning, clenching my stomach and gripping my nose.

Through it all, incredibly, my hunger remained.

I lay there, unmoving, for some time before the door opened and my mistress strode into the room once again. She wore a brilliant red dress, cut low. Her raven hair was tied back with a satin bow that matched the outfit perfectly.

She frowned slightly as she beheld me, and I could not read her expression.

She clapped her hands, and a shape appeared behind her. "Remove those at once," she said, gesturing to the food carts.

The shape entered the room, and everything seemed to grow dim. Though I tried to get a better look at the newcomer, I couldn't seem to *see* them. My mistress knelt before me, further obscuring my view. I closed my eyes, and before long I heard the last of the carts being wheeled out and the hollow thud of the door closing. When I opened my eyes, everything came back into focus.

"You're full of surprises, my pet," the woman murmured, stroking my hair. My entire body thrummed with her touch, and despite my violent nausea, I reached for her.

"You've moved along more quickly than I'd expected. More quickly than I've seen before."

The ever-burning fire in her eyes intensified.

"Your hunger excites me."

Without another word, she slid out of her dress, and I beheld her perfect body.

In an instant, I was upon her. I rained kisses on her face, licking her neck as I entered her with a single, powerful thrust. She closed her eyes and moaned, and again a euphoric warmth filled my body.

She grasped my hair with one hand, pulling me close, as her other hand moved to her neck. She made a single, quick motion that I couldn't quite follow, and the pale flesh of her throat was suddenly awash with a crimson torrent.

She pulled my head closer. "Drink," she whispered.

I salivated, suddenly able to smell the blood, its coppery richness filling my nostrils, making my belly rumble.

Without a moment's thought, I pressed my mouth to her neck, warm liquid flowing over my tongue.

The taste was nearly indescribable. Her blood was like a buttery confection one moment, a robust Cabernet the next. It warmed me like shot of whiskey as it ran down my throat, setting my belly alight with a fire that threatened to consume me. I drank with abandon, feeling my stomach bulge painfully with the sheer volume of it, yet I couldn't stop. A part of me wondered if I would die, and if my stomach would actually rupture.

I found that I didn't care.

Time seemed to stop as my lips remained locked on her throat, and when I felt her hands, impossibly strong, push me away, I howled with disappointment and rage.

How *dare* she stop me!

I bared my teeth, leaning toward her neck. Quick as a viper, she grabbed my head and slammed it into the floor. I heard a sickening, wet sound echo off the chamber walls, and my entire world went red.

Even though the pain that exploded through my skull had turned my entire universe into a jumble, I heard her voice clearly. It came in ragged, panting gasps.

"You...will...*never*...take more...than I offer...*again*!"

I shuddered at the animosity that infused each syllable, and an icy terror clutched me. I got a vague sense of her standing, a feeling of her departing. I felt more than heard the ground-shaking tremor as she slammed the outer door, and my world faded to nothingness.

14

I awoke on the floor, right where she'd left me. The pain in my head had lessened considerably, though a dull ache throbbed near the base of my skull. I tried to stand, but a crushing dizziness forced me back down. I rolled onto my stomach and managed to rise up on all fours. As I slowly opened my eyes, I thought for a moment that my vision was still entirely red.

It didn't take me long to realize that my vision was fine, and the red before me was blood, spread out in a sticky pool over the floor. As I moved, I felt it along my back, crusted and half dried, like a second skin. Slowly I reached a hand around to the back of my head. My hair was a hardened, matted mess. I gently probed about the area where the pain seemed greatest and noticed with surprise that the bone beneath my fingers seemed to bear a strange crease, from the base of my skull all the way up to the top of my head.

Fear gripped me again as the memory of my mistress's rage came flooding back.

What had I done?

I had crossed a line—that was clear. I vividly remembered my desire, my hunger, and my anger toward my mistress for making me stop drinking more of her blood.

How could I have done that? I thought. *After all she's done for me, that's how I repay her? By growing angry at her for not giving me enough?*

A bubble of shame welled up amid my fear. I'd let her down. I was her prized possession, her beloved servant, and I'd been so selfish.

I wondered what would happen if she decided she'd had enough of me.

I fought to push the thought from my head, but I couldn't. It gnawed at my guts, making me shake all over.

I removed my hand from the back of my head and again closed my eyes, sinking back to the floor.

I couldn't go on without her.

I didn't feel myself drifting off. Next thing I knew, I was opening my eyes, feeling the unmistakable murkiness of initial wakefulness. After taking a moment to breathe, I slowly pushed myself up. I was able to sit with no feeling of vertigo. With tremendous effort, I rose to my feet. Surprisingly, the pain was completely gone, as were all traces of dizziness. Again I probed the back of my head. Though my hair was still badly matted, the odd crease that had run through the bone beneath my fingers was mysteriously gone.

I looked again at the floor beneath my feet—congealed blood everywhere. I gazed down at myself and saw that it covered much of my body as well.

I wondered how I was still alive.

The thought evaporated as soon as it formed. I could not recall what I'd just been thinking about, and for whatever reason, it just didn't seem all that important anymore.

I scratched at my neck. The bloody crust that covered

most of my body was starting to itch, so I headed into the bath. The water felt warm and soothing as I sank slowly into the pool. I held my breath and plunged beneath the surface, scrubbing my hair as I sat submerged. When I had removed the last traces of blood, I stood up and washed the rest of my body.

By the time I had finished, the bathwater had turned a pinkish hue. A quick glance at the mirror told me that though the blood was gone, I looked deathly. I pushed the thought from my head, realizing there was no point in dwelling on it. I dried myself with a plush towel and walked back into the main chamber.

When I again saw the pool of blood where I'd lain unconscious, I felt a sense of surprise. It didn't seem possible that all that blood could me mine, but I was having trouble focusing on *why*. As I yet again touched the base of my skull with my fingers, something far back in my consciousness stirred uneasily. Something about what had happened to my head. Something...

The thought was gone. Every time I tried to focus on anything, it was as if my mind just couldn't hang on to it.

I wondered what was wrong with me.

I kicked the bed in frustration, ignoring the pain that bloomed in my foot. Teeth clenched, I lay on the bed, closing my eyes.

If I can't think, I might as well just sleep, I thought.

Unfortunately, sleep didn't come. I stood and walked over to the light switch, flipping it and plunging the room into blackness, hoping to find a bit of peace in the dark.

I was mildly surprised to find that even though I'd extinguished the lights, I could still see everything in the chamber, almost as if the lights were still on. I frowned, reaching over to flip the switch again. With the lights on, the colors were a bit brighter, but that was really the only difference.

It didn't make sense, but before long, thoughts of *why* it didn't make sense just slipped away. I headed back to my bed and covered myself, primarily out of habit. I certainly wasn't cold, even though I was naked.

When was the last time I actually wore clothing? I wondered. *Not since I've been...but I've always been...this is my home.*

Wasn't it?

I was confused again, confused and anxious. I clutched my head, moaning softly.

Why couldn't I think? What was *wrong* with me?

Without warning, the huge outer door creaked open. I sat up quickly and immediately saw her, standing at the threshold. She wore a long, black dress with a high collar. Her lips were pursed, and her eyes blazed.

Instantly I was off the bed and on my knees.

For a moment, she did nothing. Then, she sighed, relaxing. The glow of her eyes softened, and she walked briskly over to me.

"Stand up," she said, gesturing for me to rise.

I did. Though I stood several inches taller than her, I felt like a small child, cowering before the rage of an abusive parent.

"Mistress," I said. "I...I'm sorry. I didn't—"

She silenced me with a look.

"Clearly," she said softly, "you know why you've been punished, so we don't need to revisit it."

I nodded.

"I'm happy to see you're well again." She made a gesture, and some *thing* entered the room.

It looked like a man for the most part, though it was a

great deal taller and proportioned more like a silverback gorilla. Its skin was pasty white and leathery, and it wore soiled rags that appeared to have once been fine livery. The creature crossed the room with a strange, lumbering gait, gazing briefly at me through eyes that seemed far too tiny for such a wide face. It clutched an oversized bucket and a mop that looked as though it had been fashioned from a tree limb.

Somewhere in the back of my head, alarm bells rang loudly, but they were badly muffled by the presence of my mistress.

"So that's who's been cleaning up after me," I said dumbly.

My mistress looked troubled for a moment but regained her composure. "I'm...surprised you're able to see him."

I nodded, not thinking to ask why.

She grasped the sides of my face and pulled my head down gently. "Let me have a look at the back of your head."

I obliged, bending over as far as I could. She probed about with her fingers, every touch sending shivers of pleasure down my back. I grinned, fighting the urge to reach for her.

"Straighten up," she said when she'd finished.

I did, then I stared at her, taking her in, thrilled to be in her presence.

"What am I to do with you?" she said, almost to herself.

Instantly, my stomach did backflips. "Have I displeased you again? Please...tell me what I did, and I'll make it right. I beg you."

Her expression softened, and she smiled ever so slightly, in a manner that never quite touched her eyes. "You haven't displeased me at all."

I grinned, feeling my fear melt away, replaced by an adolescent giddiness.

"In fact, I believe this room has grown too small for you," she said. "You should start reacquainting yourself with the rest of your home."

My grin faltered a bit at that.

Was my home greater than that room?

Something again stirred at the back of my mind, something desperate, something I couldn't ignore.

She touched my cheek gently, turning my head to gaze directly into her eyes.

When I met her stare, all other thought was silenced.

I will care for you, her voice echoed through my mind. *You'll have everything you ever dreamed of, with me. This is your home. I am your family.*

"Yes...mistress," I whispered.

15

A rm in arm, we walked down yet another hallway. I still wore no clothing, but nakedness was the furthest thing from my mind. I was in awe of my home. It was far larger than I realized, crisscrossed with wide passageways and interspersed with many smaller rooms. Some of these rooms were open and boasted plush furniture and fine tapestries. Others were closed off, locked behind doors made of the same heavy wood and iron that stood at the entrance to my own room.

The stone corridors were spacious and lavishly adorned with paintings in ornate frames and sculptures on marble pedestals. The high ceilings of the place gave it an open and airy feel, despite the fact that I had not seen a single window the entire time we'd been about. It was exceedingly quiet everywhere we went, and I began to wonder if the two of us were the place's only inhabitants.

"Soon," my mistress said, "you'll be free to walk these corridors alone, coming and going as you please...when you're ready."

I frowned, my thoughts trying to form amid the haze

that covered my mind every time she was near. "Why am I not ready now?"

"You're ill. It will be some time before you're well enough to be out and about on your own."

I narrowed my eyes. "Am I...defective?"

"Defective?" She laughed delightfully. "No, no, my pet, you're anything but defective." She patted my arm. "No more questions. Just enjoy your time with me." She gave my arm a gentle squeeze, and warmth washed over me. I smiled and said nothing more.

Before long, we were back at the doorway to my room. I tried to hide my disappointment.

"So soon?"

"Yes," she said. "It's time for you to rest. I'll visit you again this evening. And I'll bring you a gift!"

"What kind of gift?"

She smiled coyly. "You'll see."

She released my arm, and I walked slowly toward my bed. As I heard the clunk of the lock turning behind me, I suddenly felt extremely tired.

And hungry.

I could not recall the last time I'd eaten, and thinking about it made my head hurt.

WHEN MY MISTRESS FINALLY RETURNED, the hunger was nearly unbearable. My stomach churned with it, and the pangs were so harsh I could barely stand up straight.

I almost didn't notice the woman my mistress had brought with her.

She was clad in a filthy dress, and her long, brown hair was tousled. She was petite compared to my mistress, standing a head shorter than her. Her wide eyes gazed straight ahead, and her mouth hung open. She stood rigidly, remaining in place as my mistress walked forward.

"Inhale," she whispered into my ear. "Do you smell her?"

I breathed in deeply through my nose, and did smell something. It smelled...*ripe.* "*Delicious*," I muttered, salivating.

"Approach her," my mistress urged. "Inhale her scent more deeply."

I did, breathing in again as I stood inches from her. Each time I breathed in, the aromas I'd originally detected grew stronger. There was a light, airy scent that seemed to suggest a sense of youth. There was also a strong, coppery odor that I immediately knew to be fresh blood, pumping rhythmically just below the surface of her skin. And under it all, nearly masked by everything else, was a dank, musky stink.

Was it fear?

I turned to my mistress, doubling over as another hunger pang speared my guts. Drool ran down my chin, and I gasped at a sudden, strange sensation of discomfort that filled my mouth. My tongue felt as if it were shifting, changing in some manner that I couldn't quite follow. Instinctively I reached up to feel it and noticed a hard, razor-sharp point at the end of it.

At the bottom of my mouth, somewhere within my jaw, I felt a cool sense of emptiness, as if a cavity had opened up and longed to be filled.

"What...what is this? What's happening?"

"You're ready to feed, my pet. Here is your meal. Enjoy it!"

I turned again to face the young woman. She continued to stare at nothing, appearing to not notice me at all. Suddenly I heard her heart. It beat in tandem with my own, throbbing with a cacophony that made my ears vibrate painfully. I grew dizzy with the oppressive sound, and with the scent of her blood, which had suddenly become over-powering.

That's all that's left. The blood. There's only the blood, I thought.

I bent my head toward her neck, toward the pulsating vein next to her throat that seemed to be the source of the violent racket. I drove my pointed tongue into it with all the force I could muster.

Instantly the empty cavity in my jaw filled as I drew her blood in. I felt a small, popping sensation somewhere near the back of my throat as the warm liquid poured down into my stomach. I drew in more, encouraged by this wonderful new sensation, then still more as the excitement of the experience overwhelmed me.

I grasped the woman in my hands, ripping her clothes, tearing her flesh. I drank more and more, my thoughts giving way to horrific abandon as a predatory lust for sustenance consumed me. I wrapped her limp body in my arms, driving her to the floor, drinking more deeply, feeling her deflate beneath my grasp. I gripped her ever harder, snapping bones and ripping cartilage, and still I drank. I drank until nothing remained, until my belly swelled painfully. I disengaged with a gasp, rolling onto my back, unable to stand.

My mistress stood over me, clapping and laughing with great mirth. A strange light danced behind her glowing yellow eyes, and I looked away, unsettled. "Excellent, my pet! You have fed well this evening!"

I rolled onto my side and beheld the woman from which I'd drawn sustenance. She was nearly unrecognizable. Her eyes bulged from their sockets, and her teeth protruded grotesquely from skin that was now stretched impossibly tightly around her skull. Her body was strangely bent, her limbs impossibly askew. I felt a sense of revulsion at the sight, but the feeling quickly faded, replaced by the satisfaction of a good meal.

I heard the door open, and the lumbering, leathery-skinned fellow was back. He picked up the woman's corpse as if it were nothing more than a napkin, tucked it under his arm, and was gone.

"This is a treat for him as well," said my mistress. "Even without the blood and lymph, fresh meat is still fresh meat."

She headed for the door.

"Next time, feed with reservation. Take only the blood. Above all, *never kill your prey*."

She stopped just before grasping the handle.

"You'll hunt on your own, from now on. I won't bring a meal to you again."

Moments later the door closed, and the lock turned.

I lay on the floor, groaning, clutching my stomach. Though it hurt tremendously, a giddy euphoria filled me, making the pain well worth it.

And that pounding...that loud, unbearable pounding, was finally gone.

The woman's heartbeat had nearly driven me mad; there was a point when I'd been convinced that its beating would make my own heart explode. Gently I placed a hand on my chest, just to be sure everything had indeed returned to normal.

I was shocked to find no heartbeat at all.

16

I had no concept of just how long I lay on the floor, waiting for the swelling of my stomach to subside. I spent the time staring off into space until my head finally began to clear. I stood, stretching my arms above me. I felt stronger, more alert now, and acutely aware of my surroundings in a way I hadn't been in what seemed like years.

I wondered where my mistress was.

The thought was almost immediate, accompanied by a sense of panic. I tried breathing deeply, clenching my stomach to keep the butterflies under control. I closed my eyes...and she was there. I could *feel* her in my mind, a small pocket of warmth and desire cradled gently in my consciousness. I instantly relaxed, knowing at that moment that she was aware of me as well.

I sensed that she was moving, heading closer. I sat on the bed, staring at the door to my chamber like a dog awaiting its master. The feeling of her presence in my mind continued to grow, until finally the door opened, and there she stood.

She wore a smart black suit with a blood red blouse, and she smiled radiantly, approaching me. At a gesture from her, the door swung slowly shut, and the lock clicked into place.

"You look well," she said. "Your meal seems to have agreed with you."

I smiled back. "It did. I have no hunger."

"I told you I would take care of you."

I leaned forward a little. "Mistress, may I ask you something?"

"Of course, my pet."

"You said earlier that I'm unwell. What's wrong with me?"

She pursed her lips. "What do you remember of your life?" she asked slowly.

I thought for a long moment and suddenly was horrified: I could recall almost nothing. Beyond patches from the last few days I'd spent in that room, there were only images and emotions. Fear. Loneliness. Hunger. Nothing more concrete than that remained. An impenetrable fog had shrouded my mind, a fog through which there was no hope of navigation.

I slumped on the bed, willing the memories to surface, knowing they were there, somewhere. I gritted my teeth, and my head began to ache.

"Don't strain yourself," she said gently, sitting beside me.

I stopped fighting and turned to look into her bright yellow eyes. "Nothing," I said quietly. "I remember nothing. Nothing except being in this room. And even those memories are dim."

"Not long ago," she said, "you fell horribly ill. You grew delusional and confused. You had difficulty recognizing your surroundings. You even forgot who I was."

Shame lanced my guts, and I couldn't look her in the eye.

"You refused to eat," she continued, "and you grew weaker by the day. I placed you here so you could recover in peace."

"I forgot who *you* were?"

She nodded slowly, bringing her eyes level with mine. "What is my name?" she asked me quietly.

I opened my mouth to respond but was stunned when I couldn't.

"I...don't know."

It seemed impossible. This woman—this wondrous creature of tantalizing beauty and power—meant more to me than my own life, more than the fate of the entire world. I would have done anything for her—died for her, *killed* for her—yet I couldn't even recall her name.

"Do you remember your own name?" she asked.

Again, I was stunned into silence. I shook my head.

"You see," she said, "even now, your memory remains damaged."

Finally I managed a response. "Will it ever return?"

"Perhaps," she said. "Some day. Memories or no, I'm thankful that you're feeding again and that your health appears to be improving."

Shame again dug its claws in deeply, twisting my vocal cords, making me choke on my words. "Mistress...forgive me, but...who are you? Who am *I*?"

She sat silently for a long moment, and I wondered if I had angered her again. Just as I was about to ask if I had offended her, she spoke.

"I am Adalina. Adalina Lacusta, Mistress of the Northeastern Realm. And you...you are Dragos, my most faithful and honored servant."

"Dragos..." I mouthed the word slowly. It felt strange on my tongue.

She nodded. "Dragos. The Dragon. Renowned servant of the House of Lacusta. Your name reflects the power and respect you've earned here, among your family."

The pride that rang clearly in her voice made me sit up straighter. Whoever I was, I'd clearly done much to impress my mistress in the past.

I nodded.

"Dragos," I said again. "My name is Dragos."

"The name suits you," she said softly. "It's a name worthy of one who has served his mistress well."

"When will I be allowed to continue that service?"

"Once your mind has sufficiently recovered, you'll be in a position to rejoin your house. Be patient, Dragos. Your time will come soon enough."

I sighed. "Is there nothing I can do?"

"Oh," she said, smiling devilishly as she undressed, "there is *something*."

She rode me mercilessly, and though pleasure exploded through me time and again, her hands were like steel, and her strength and stamina were boundless. She flung me about like a rag as she had her way with me on the bed, on the floor, in the bath, and somehow, in a manner that I couldn't quite follow, upside down on one of the chamber ceiling's many stout beams.

It was like nothing I'd experienced before. I endured. Besides, this was what gave my mistress joy, and wasn't that my purpose in life?

Several hours later, she finally released me. I lay on the floor where she had left me, lacking the energy to stand.

She dressed very deliberately, and walked slowly and seductively to the door. Even then, devoid of energy and in a great deal of pain, I wanted her again.

"I'll see you soon, dear one. Sleep well."

In an instant she was gone, and the familiar sound of the bolt turning echoed through the chamber.

Every inch of my body was on fire. I felt the swell of countless bruises, many in places I never would have imagined possible. I moaned softly as I tried to push myself to a more comfortable position, but apparently something was wrong with my arms; they gave out at the pressure, shooting white-hot arrows up into my shoulders. I cried out, collapsing back to the floor. I closed my eyes, trying to will the pain away.

The tactic worked better than I would have expected. In a short time, what had been excruciating subsided to a distant, nagging irritation. I knew I was hurt; I could practically sense every injury to my body, no matter how minute —and there were a great deal of them. Nevertheless, the pain stayed where I put it: in a small corner of my consciousness, conveniently out of the way for the time being.

I needed sleep.

Perhaps it was my newfound sense of mental control, or maybe I was utterly exhausted. Whatever the reason, I was sound asleep within moments.

WHEN I AWOKE, the pain was gone. I walked slowly to the bath, and inspected my stark-white naked body in the gilded mirror. Not a single bruise remained. I tentatively moved my arms, pleased when I found them to be pain-free and in perfect working order. I ran my hands over my neck, my ears, my head. No injuries, no swelling.

I also realized I was hungry.

Extremely hungry.

Hunger gnawed at my insides like a starving rat, but I pushed it aside, back into that corner of my mind where I'd contained my pain not long before. The technique worked.

To an extent.

Blood.

I could practically taste its luscious decadence, and its sensuous aroma seemed to hang in the air about me. I closed my eyes tightly.

There were certain ways to control these urges, ways to make the hunger less potent. I somehow knew this. The problem was that I didn't quite have the knack for it, and my thoughts continued to turn to food. I felt my tongue lengthen, its sharp point brushing my lower lip. That hollow, cold spot expanded somewhere within my jaw, begging to be filled. A pressing dryness scratched my throat, one I knew wouldn't go away until I had sated it with a hearty meal.

Focus.

I pushed back as hard as I could against the maddening urge to feed, bringing to bear every ounce of self-control I possessed.

These urges won't consume me, I thought. *Adalina will come. I have to be patient. Patient. Patient...*

17

As time passed, my self-control improved. Though my hunger bothered me less, my boredom was ever-present.

The walls of my chamber seemed to grow smaller by the day, and I began to resent my solitude. The most frustrating part was that I was now perpetually aware of Adalina—her presence had become something almost tangible, taking up residence in a small corner of my mind. I knew of her proximity, her mood, and though I wasn't completely certain, I believed I could tell when she thought of me.

I put my head in my hands. *Why won't she come?* I thought. *Why must I sit here alone?*

Those thoughts were followed by another, darker possibility. What if she left me there? What if I *starved*?

I tried to dismiss the thought. Why would Adalina wish to harm me, her invaluable servant? She loved me, after all, adored me over everything else. Surely, she wouldn't want my life to end or for me to suffer.

Patience, I told myself firmly. *Adalina will return. She'll return, and one day she'll release me from this room and allow me to rejoin her.*

But when would that day come? I felt perfectly fine, if not a bit perplexed from time to time. My memories still hadn't resurfaced; my entire identity was taken purely on faith from what Adalina had told me. Yet I found myself discovering things about myself that I felt, instinctively, I should have known all along.

I found I no longer grew tired, if indeed there had been a point in my life when I *had* grown tired. Sleep served only two purposes for me: to allay boredom and to slow the onset of hunger. Though I could go without sleep, I preferred it to wakefulness, if only because it was something that filled the emptiness that had come to eclipse my existence, and it helped me forget about the growing pit in my belly.

Another oddity was the bath.

Though I knew the water in the pool was heated well beyond the ambient temperature of the room, I felt no difference whether I immersed myself in it or stood sopping wet beside it. Temperature was simply a tidbit of information, idly processed by my brain as I experienced it—not really a sensation.

I couldn't tell why that would seem so strange, nor could I recall whether I had ever experienced it differently, though I did find it odd that such a seemingly innocuous thing would stand out in my mind.

As I pondered this, I felt Adalina's attention suddenly turn to me. My thoughts immediately ceased, and hope swelled in my chest. I sensed her draw nearer. Before long, the chamber door opened, and she strode in, smiling slightly. I'd already stood to greet her and almost didn't notice the small parcel she held.

"For you," she said, holding it out to me.

I accepted the package, which was wrapped in brown paper and bound with twine.

"Open it," she said.

I walked to my bed and placed the package on it, then carefully unwrapped it to reveal several items. A pair of leather shoes and dress socks sat atop a neatly folded oxford shirt and pair of slacks. All of the clothing was the exact same color: black.

"Put them on," she said, a grin curling the corners of her lips.

I regarded her for a moment, then did as instructed.

"You seem confused, pet."

I lifted an eyebrow. "Have I ever worn clothing?"

"You used to prefer it to nakedness. Until you fell ill. Then you refused to wear anything at all. The fact that you're dressing yourself shows that your health has greatly improved."

I finished buttoning the shirt, then sat on the bed to put the shoes on. When I was finished, I stood before her.

"Perfect," she said, giving me an appraising gaze. "That will do nicely."

She turned from me, heading to the chamber door. "Oh," she said, glancing over her shoulder. "If you're hungry, I suggest you follow me."

At her words, I gasped. The mental walls I'd built up to keep my hunger at bay crashed down like a flimsy building in a hurricane. I stared forward, mouth agape, stomach cramping painfully. My mistress was nearly in the hall, and I knew that if I didn't follow, she'd lock me inside again.

I made myself move forward, trying to shore up my defenses. But something blocked me. Some mental force, stalwart as reinforced concrete, thwarted me.

Am I imagining this? Is something really there, or has the hunger deluded me?

Between the pain that racked my body and the foggy sense of pleasure brought on by my mistress's presence, I couldn't tell.

Nevertheless, I managed to keep up with her. I sensed the door closing behind us, and I tried to take note of my surroundings. In the end, it was all I could do to simply move forward and not collapse to the floor.

I followed her through seemingly endless corridors, deserted save for Adalina and me. Everything around me appeared as if I were viewing it through a clouded glass; the hunger made focus nearly impossible. My body ached, my stomach churned, and anxiety gnawed at me.

My mistress slowed her pace, and I shadowed her, frustrated we weren't moving more quickly. I felt my energy might give out at any moment, and I didn't want to suffer the shame of collapsing before her.

She stopped.

I nearly ran into her but caught myself in time. The sudden cessation of forward movement confused me, and I put a hand out to steady myself against the wall. Breathing heavily, I cradled my forehead in my other hand. The anxiousness had moved to the forefront of my thoughts, obscuring everything. Panic seized me.

"Food," I whispered. "I must...I must..." I was unable to finish.

"You have what you need to continue," she said. "You need no help from me."

She sounded amused.

For a moment, that made me angry.

My hostility vanished amid another sudden wave of euphoria. My breathing slowed, and I closed my eyes, trying to think through the mental chaos brought on by my need.

Suddenly something was there: a presence, rich and full, overflowing with life. I inhaled through my nostrils and could almost make out a faint scent in the air.

Blood. Life.

My eyes sprang open as the realization slammed home.

Prey.

The scent of my quarry was so obvious that I was incredulous that I hadn't detected it before. Along with the smell came a distant sensation of life and virility that stood out like a bright-red beacon among the haze of my hunger, and without thinking, I hurried forward, toward a set of intersecting passages.

Left.

I moved without hesitation, the sense of my prey growing stronger. I passed many doors, all of them closed, on either side of the passage. Toward the end, I stopped in front of a door that was indistinguishable from all the others —same dark, heavy wood; same black iron hardware.

Yet this door bore an impression—an esoteric fingerprint. I could almost see the ripples of energy created by the door's recent contact with someone alive and full of blood. I grasped the handle and pulled. The door opened easily, revealing a curved stairway.

Down.

I leapt down the staircase as fast as I could, knowing what I sought was at the bottom. As I descended, signs that I was growing closer began to manifest. The smell of human sweat. The sound of someone—a man, perhaps—whimpering. And the sensation, the psychic imprint of flowing life, seemed to have trebled since I had entered the stairwell.

Suddenly the steps came to an end, and I found myself

in a cramped corridor. The ceiling was nearly low enough to force me to stoop; the top of my head just touched the stonework above. Squat wooden doors, each with a small, barred window, lined either side of the passageway at regular intervals. The sounds, smells, and overall sense of my prey came from behind one of these doors.

I felt my tongue lengthen and sharpen. I felt that cold, hollow space in my jawbone yawn greedily, felt the dryness of my throat and the emptiness in my belly. I smelled musky fear, heard racing blood. I started forward then slowed as I felt my prey retreat.

Probing the prey with my mind, I found a swirl of emotion and racing thoughts, like the tangled strings of a broken violin. I touched those strings, smoothed them, made them hum melodically once again. The tangle of loud thoughts instantly ceased, and the musky scent of fear nearly vanished. I started forward again, but this time my prey didn't retreat.

When I reached the door, I found it locked. I focused on the wood and iron, traced the intricacies of the grain and the composition of the metal with my mind. I saw the latching mechanism, noting the simplicity with which it was constructed. I focused my thoughts on the lock, and it clicked open. I threw the door wide, and before me stood my quarry.

A disheveled, middle-aged man stood before me. He was dressed in a dirty, torn suit, and the odor of his unwashed body nearly eclipsed that of his blood. He hovered near the back corner of the cell, staring forward with unblinking eyes. His mouth hung open slightly. As I approached, the man made no move to escape. When I reached him, I savored the aroma of his lifeblood for an instant before plunging my razor-sharp tongue into the man's throat. The man remained still, slack-jawed and staring blankly ahead.

I drank deeply, and though my state of near insanity begged me to pull in everything I could, I fought back the urge. I remembered Adalina's words. I drank with reservation, feeling my prey with my mind, taking heed of the strength of the man's life-force. When I sensed it was beginning to wane, I pulled back and found, with some surprise, that I was satiated.

Never kill your prey.

The words were etched in my mind, and I whispered them to myself. I backed slowly away, not taking my eyes off the man. My prey remained just as he had been before, staring ahead with eyes that didn't blink.

I slipped out of the cell and shut the door behind me. I mentally probed the lock again and didn't move away until I heard it click. I turned back toward the end of the hallway and jumped slightly when I found Adalina standing just a few inches from me.

"You are a *hunter*," she said, nipping my neck. A shudder of ecstasy flowed through me. "You are *my* hunter."

18

I found myself on the floor of my bedchamber, which confused me, as I couldn't remember entering the room. I remembered Adalina of course. And our time together...I grinned at that.

I walked over to my bed and found another outfit there, identical to the one Adalina had destroyed. I slipped the clothes on, certain my mistress would desire this of me.

Adalina.

I extended my senses, reaching out, seeking her. I found her almost immediately.

Adalina, my love.

My eyes glazed over as I smiled at nothing, relishing the thought of her. I touched that little part of her that was always there, felt it with my mind. If she couldn't be there in person, at least I could take comfort in knowing she was close by.

I did so carefully of course, not wanting to disturb her. I examined her delicately, sniffing at her sweet essence, that special part of her only I could sense. She didn't notice me doing so; I was certain of that. I could tell when she sensed me, could feel the focus of her mind when she had me in view. She was involved in something else, something upon which she was acutely attentive.

I pressed a bit further, focusing on the space where I thought the object of her attention must be. I was surprised to find someone else there. I detected a peculiar hum coming from the person. When I opened himself to it, a shudder of erotic warmth shook me to my toes. I felt my eyes widen as the reality of the situation crashed down upon me. I pushed harder, delved deeper.

Someone was with my mistress. Doing what only *I* should have the right to do!

The other person was unaware of my presence, at least for now. I snarled as I strode to my chamber door. I tried it, knowing at once that I'd find it locked. I pulled harder, straining until the ligaments of my arms stood out in sharp relief, but still the door didn't budge.

I extended my senses into the metal of the door, feeling for the locking mechanism I knew must be there.

I hit a barrier.

I cursed aloud as I shoved against it, but it didn't yield. I pushed harder, but it remained as solid as steel. I gathered every last bit of strength I possessed and roared as I pummeled the obstacle again and again. Nothing changed. The barrier was still there, as impervious as before.

Nearing exhaustion, I stopped. I stood there for a time, breathing deeply, allowing my energy to return.

Focus. Blind rage isn't the answer, I thought.

I probed the barrier delicately this time, forcing myself to be patient, gentle. I used what finesse I could, gliding slowly across it as if it were a lover.

I felt something.

A tiny flaw, almost unnoticeable. I focused on it, dug in deeper.

Then I smiled.

The barrier wasn't as smooth as I'd thought. In that one area alone, I saw thousands—hundreds of thousands, perhaps millions—of ethereal filaments, woven together in a pattern so intricate and tight that it was no wonder I'd initially mistaken the barrier for something solid. I furrowed my brow, honing my senses into as fine a point as I could muster, searching for the smallest chink, the tiniest cranny.

I found it.

I grimaced as I got to work, clenching and unclenching my fists, growing tenser by the second as I felt the other's ecstasy rise to a new pitch. I dug between the tiny strands, testing each one, and then...

Plink.

It wasn't an actual sound I heard but a tiny sensation I felt from within the bowels of the door. I'd severed a fila-ment, and the others were beginning to unwind. I refocused.

Plink. Plink. Plink.

One after another, I snapped more of them, and the barrier that was once so tight became as loose and flimsy as a rotted sack. I wrapped my perceptions around what was left of it, and with a howl of rage and a massive exertion of will, I ripped it asunder. The door exploded outward in a spray of twisted metal and thick splinters. I allowed the dust to settle then stepped over the debris, focusing all my atten-tion on my target.

Something stood before me in the hallway. Something huge, powerful. I nearly didn't notice when it lunged for me, almost didn't see its arms, thick as tree boughs, closing in.

I didn't have to.

My reaction came nearly on its own, instinctive in the manner of breathing, and so fast that the entire world seemed to slow around me. Instantly my adversary came into pristine focus, a hulking, misshapen travesty of a man. I had seen him before. A memory, fleeting yet clear, flashed across my mind of this *thing* removing carts of food from my room.

When had that happened?

The thought scarcely had time to materialize as I slid beneath the beast's grasp as easily and quickly as a viper on the hunt. I struck out in a flurry of incredibly precise blows: one to the side of the creature's head, one to the back of its neck, then a kick to the back of its knee for good measure. I felt the meaty crunch of bone and tissue give way with each strike. I didn't so much as pause my forward movement, even as the creature fell dead to the floor behind me.

I refocused my perceptions on the source of my anger, picking my pace up to a healthy run. I darted through passages, and though I quickly reached an area of my mistress's home with which I was unfamiliar, I somehow knew exactly where to go. I followed my instincts, passing numerous closed doors and encountering no one. Soon I stood before a door that looked identical to the one I'd just destroyed and at the exact opposite end of the building.

As I felt what was going on beyond the door, my eyes rolled in their sockets as a frenzy of jealousy overtook me. Adalina still wasn't aware of my presence; she was completely focused on whoever was in there with her. I thrust my mind into the door, again stymied by the solid presence of another barrier. Though my emotions raged, I gritted my teeth as I pushed my senses into this new obstacle, again looking for a weakness.

I thought my muscles might snap with tension when I

finally found it, and I practically hopped in place with antic-ipation as I severed each filament in turn. When the door collapsed, I propelled myself into the room, shrieking as I brought my rage to bear on the one who dared lay with my mistress.

My target was male, naked, and covered in blood. From the aroma that permeated the room, I knew at once that the blood belonged to Adalina. She stood over the man, half-clothed, a look of utter shock on her face. Her pale neck ran red, and her eyes were unfocused and hazy. In an instant, everything around me slowed. I sprang upon the man, who stared at me in a stupor even as my hands closed around his throat. I tightened my grasp, baring my teeth as sinew and tendons snapped under my forceful grip. The man gurgled weakly, going completely limp as my fingers tore into his flesh. His head lolled to the side, and the man soon stared at nothing.

With a kick like a battering ram, Adalina sent me flying across the room. Landing in a heap, I barely had a chance to stand before she hit me again. I reeled, my vision going black. As fast as I was and as slow as the world around me seemed to move, Adalina was faster, moving like lightning, deftly avoiding my pitiful attempts to defend myself.

One more blow to the head, and I was on the ground. I tried to stand but couldn't. Something was pressing me down; a weight like a boulder seemed to be crushing my entire body.

Adalina stepped into view, directly in front of me. She scowled down at me, her yellow eyes blazing, her raven hair wildly askew. The pressure on my body increased. I heard a snap and realized that one of my ribs had broken.

"You…" she spat, panting. "How…*dare*…you…"

The pressure grew. There was another dull, meaty snap.

Then another. Both of my legs. I was aware of the pain, but it was distant, controlled.

Something slipped into my mind, some psychic tendril that stank of my mistress. It did...*something*...and my barriers were gone. The full force of the pain stole the breath from my lungs; I couldn't even scream. Everything went red.

Just as I thought the pressure would crush the life from me, the redness turned to black.

19

I slipped in and out of consciousness for a time, experiencing only the briefest moments of lucidity. This was a blessing, as I was in complete agony every second my eyes were open. Pain stabbed me deeply from all directions; I felt as though every part of my body were injured.

In these fleeting instants, I realized I was unable to move. My arms and legs were drawn out tightly, secured somehow. This fact barely registered with me, as I spent each moment of hazy awareness struggling to bring my mental defenses back up, futilely trying to block out the pain.

Every time, something stopped me. Some force was there, smooth and impenetrable, preventing me from focusing my mind. It wasn't unlike the barrier on my door I'd destroyed earlier. Only this time, the barrier was in my head.

My moments of consciousness and unconsciousness blended together in a bizarre and terrifying way, imparting the illusion that my entire existence consisted of nothing more than a muddle of half-formed imagery and red-hot pain. The idea of attempting to defeat the barrier became lost in the confusion that was my new reality, and I knew only pain and fear.

That's when Adalina's voice came to me.

Dragos. Come back.

It floated across the void of my mind like a lifeboat in a squall, bringing me back to myself. I opened my eyes slowly and noticed immediately that the pain was back where it belonged—in a far corner of my mind, present but easily ignored. My ability to focus had returned.

I tried to sit up but found once again that I couldn't move. I was in a small stone chamber with a crude wooden door at the far end. The room was devoid of any furniture, save for the straw pallet upon which I lay. I was on my back, and my arms were stretched above my head, fastened at the wrists with some type of silvery, metallic rope. The rope was secured to the wall behind my head with two clasps, seemingly made of the same material. My legs were similarly fastened, secured at the ankles and attached to two squat posts anchored to the stone floor of the chamber. I pulled at my bonds, but they didn't yield in the slightest. I reached my senses out, intent on probing the restraints for the source of their strength, but was shocked when my mental focus suddenly evaporated. I concentrated harder, tried to go deeper, but the same thing happened—the moment I brought so much as a thread of mental energy into contact with the restraints, the thread evaporated like a flash of steam.

"Don't struggle, Dragos. You won't be able to break those bonds. They were forged with your own blood and are quite indestructible, at least to you."

I obeyed, lying still. I didn't try to probe them again.

Adalina gazed down at me. Her eyes had regained their typical, soft yellow glow. The terrifying fire that had burned within them at our last meeting had thankfully abated.

"Why, Dragos? Why did you betray me?"

"Betray *you*?" Even amid the euphoria that had settled upon me at her appearance, a bubble of anger rose to the surface of my thoughts.

"You betrayed *me*, Mistress. Am I not your most prized servant? Have I not been loyal to you and only you? What were you doing with another man?"

A trace of the old fire appeared behind her eyes.

"I shall say this only once: you are *my* servant. Not the other way around. If I choose to enjoy the company of another, that's my business and mine alone. I answer to *no one*."

I glowered back at her but said nothing in return. She turned away and began pacing the length of the room.

"I've tried to instill in you a sense of loyalty and obedience," she continued. "I've given you the comforts of a luxurious home. I've nursed you back to health, taught you to hunt again. I've spent far more time than you realize working to ensure that you fully recover so you can again have free reign of our home.

"You, on the other hand, have rewarded me by behaving like a disobedient child. Do you think I *enjoy* making you suffer? I only do so because it's the only way you'll learn. And you *will* learn. One of these days, I'll get through to you. You'll learn your place, learn who your master is, if it takes a thousand years."

Without warning, some unseen force swept my mental focus away. Pain lanced my body; I howled, writhing at the sudden, unexpected agony.

"You will suffer your injuries without the benefit of your

mental disciplines. I urge you to spend some time thinking about *why* you are suffering. It may save you a worse experience in the future."

Adalina headed toward the door. "And I assure you," she said over her shoulder, "the next time will be *far* worse."

She slammed the door behind her.

———

PAIN WAS EVERYWHERE. It was my world, my universe. Creation itself seemed infused with pain—it erased logical thought, hounding me endlessly. I couldn't sleep. I couldn't think, couldn't escape. I twisted and moaned, stretched taut in my bonds, knowing in a far-off way that I was supposed to be contemplating something, but I was unable to focus on what that might be.

The walls and ceiling of the chamber faded in and out, seeming to move, mirroring my own tortured thrashings. There were times when I wanted to laugh at them, at how silly they looked – moving, shaking, spinning.

As time passed, the walls didn't move so much. I was finally able to focus on a stray thought here and there, and the pain seemed less intense. But a new feeling grew stronger as the pain subsided: a deep emptiness, a hollow sensation that spread out from my belly and made my head swim.

Hunger.

I almost didn't recognize it for what it was; my hunger was profound in a manner I'd never before experienced, every bit as strong as the pain and every bit as mentally taxing. I hungered viciously, struggling fruitlessly against my bonds if only for a chance to catch the faintest scent of blood. I could no more ignore it than I could have ignored the pain, and I shrieked as my desperation for sustenance eclipsed all else.

Something—a sound—snapped me back to reality. For a moment, my hunger was forgotten.

Footsteps.

All of my senses zeroed in on the sound. My will acted of its own accord, assaulting, pressing, and prodding; trying to break in; attempting to penetrate my prey. I sensed something familiar, and I paused, mentally clawing my way through the mush of my thoughts. A face appeared in my mind, kind and beautiful. Flowing dark hair, soft brown eyes, small perky lips.

I knew those lips. Knew those eyes. Knew that warm, inviting smile.

"Rebecca..."

The door opened, and she was there.

I imagined myself floating toward her, reaching for her, wanting nothing more than to embrace her.

"Rebecca, my love," I rasped.

She stood over me, frowning as she produced something from beneath her blouse. Her image wavered.

"Rebecca?"

No. That was wrong. This was someone else, someone different...

The figure bent down and poured something into my mouth.

It was blood.

All thought ceased as I gulped it down, sucking my teeth, trying to make sure every last drop made it down my throat. The woman turned and left, closing the door behind her.

No, not Rebecca. Adalina.

I suddenly remembered my mistress, felt the familiar

euphoria settle over me. I scrambled to remember the face of the woman I'd seen before. I reached for the warmth and kindness her expression had held...and then the memory was gone. I closed my eyes, savoring the sweet taste of blood that remained on my tongue.

Despite the sense of calm my mistress's presence had brought, something disturbing crouched at the edge of my mind, something important, something I must not forget...

And then it was gone.

Closing my eyes, I settled back in as best I could, despite the discomfort of my bonds. I was still hungry, though not so much that I couldn't sleep.

REBECCA KNELT *on the kitchen floor, scrubbing at a stubborn spot. Her dark hair was tied back in a ponytail, and she wore a pair of faded jeans and a green T-shirt. I heard Sarah playing with her dolls in the living room.*

"Finished with the bathroom?" she asked, not looking up.

It was Sunday, cleaning day.

"I..." I started to respond. I choked on my next words as tears ran down my cheeks.

"What is it?" she asked, standing abruptly. "Is everything all right?"

I shook my head, staggering forward. I embraced her tightly. "I don't know. I just...don't know. I love you, Rebecca."

She hugged me back. "I love you too. Did something happen?"

I shook my head. An icy sense of despondency had suddenly clutched my heart, and I had no idea why.

"I don't ever want this to end," I whispered. "I want to be with you always. I want to be with my family. Oh, God, I love you both so much."

She stroked my hair. "We love you too, David. What brought this on?"

"I wish I knew," I said quietly.

Soft footfalls echoed down the hall, and suddenly Sarah was there. Her chestnut-brown eyes shone as she looked up at me. "What's wrong, Daddy?"

I released Rebecca and scooped up my daughter. "I don't know, sweetheart. I'm just...sad for some reason. Very sad."

Sarah threw her arms around my neck and squeezed. "It'll be okay, Daddy. Mommy and me will take care of you."

"I know you will," I whispered. "I know you always will."

Rebecca moved to embrace me as well, and I held my family close.

A FAMILIAR SOUND. The door. I opened my eyes. Hunger slammed me in the guts, made my head fuzzy. I moaned as I twisted in my bonds.

A woman stepped through the door and stood before me.

"Rebecca..." I whispered.

The woman remained silent as she produced a vial and poured the contents into my mouth. I drank the blood greedily, relishing its taste.

"Do you know who I am?" she asked quietly.

Just as the woman's image began to waver and blur, I opened my mouth to respond. I frowned. *No. Not Rebecca.* This woman was different. Colder. I shivered, suddenly frightened.

She frowned deeply, clearly irritated.

"You are...Adalina," I said.

"That's right. Do you know who *you* are?"

I thought long and hard, unable to answer at first. "Dragos," I finally managed.

She sighed, muttering to herself. "What am I to do with you? All my work..."

She stood there for a time, staring off into space.

"There is one thing," she said quietly. "I must be sure."

Without another word, she stalked out, closing the door behind her.

EVERY MOMENT SHE WAS GONE, my hunger grew. At first I was able to sleep, but soon the cold emptiness of starvation wrested slumber from me. The vials of blood she'd provided were barely enough to keep me alive. Again I descended into madness, fighting my bonds with all my strength. I knew no conscious thought; I was an animal, starving, and food was my only priority.

I searched everywhere my senses could reach—every corner of my room and beyond—but I felt nothing except cold emptiness. No signs of life. No blood. No prey. Not that it would have made a difference. My bonds were incredibly strong.

"No blood," I whispered. "No prey."

I reached out again, probing as far as I could, searching for anything that might sustain me, mindless of the fact that my arms and legs were still bound.

There.

Something approached. Warmth. Life.

Blood.

Immediately my will was upon my prey, penetrating, controlling.

Come, I whispered into its mind. *Come to me.*

It continued to approach, its warmth growing stronger. My tongue sharpened. The familiar hollowness, cold and vacant, expanded beneath my mouth, within my jaw.

Closer, I whispered. I could feel my eyes rolling madly. *Come closer.*

The door opened.

Adalina entered, clutching a double-handled apparatus that I didn't bother to try to identify. I wasn't interested in her or her strange tool. My attention was focused behind her, where the sensation of warmth and life originated.

It came into view.

A very old woman, dressed in fuzzy pink slippers and a gray hospital robe, tottered in. Her hair was thin and snow white, and her face bore an incalculable number of wrinkles. Her eyes were glazed, unblinking, as she clasped her tiny, shriveled hands before her.

"Tea," she mumbled. "Is this where we'll take our tea?"

Adalina chuckled. She crossed the room briskly, bending over me.

"I bring you a meal, my love," she whispered, smiling icily.

I felt something cold against my skin, followed by a sudden release. I could move my right arm.

Adalina reached over me, sliding the bolt cutters between my flesh and the next bond. She clipped it, and I pushed myself up, fighting to regain my feet, never taking my eyes off my prey.

"Patience, Dragos. Be still," said Adalina.

I obeyed grudgingly, allowing her to clip the bonds at my ankles.

I stood the moment I was free, not sparing Adalina a second glance. My eyes were no doubt every bit as wide and unblinking as my quarry's, and I gazed at her with the intensity of a stalking cat. Slowly I closed the distance between us, tongue lolling, ready to pounce.

"Tea would be lovely," she said, staring at nothing. "Tea, with two lumps."

I placed one foot in front of the other, growing ever closer, savoring the rich aroma of her life-force. Suddenly her eyes came into focus. She blinked, seeming confused. Then she turned to look at me.

"David," she whispered. She brought a frail, trembling hand to her mouth. "David," she said again. "I knew you would come. I knew it. They said you had gone. Said you'd died. But I knew. I always knew. You can have tea with me again."

Although I heard the words, I didn't understand them. Everything around me had become a jumble of color and sound. The only thing that stood in focus was her essence, the warmth of her lifeblood.

I placed a hand on her cheek and turned her head to the side.

"Oh, David," she said, touching my face. "Sit and have a cup of tea with me."

I speared her throat with my tongue and drank deeply.

She slumped against me, and her breathing grew heavy.

"David..." she whispered.

I pulled everything I could through her, the warmth of her blood filling my belly, infusing me with strength.

"David...I...love you..."

Something about this prey was familiar to me. Something about its energy, its life-force.

Its scent.

In the back of my mind, some lost memory begged to be recalled. It scrabbled against the wall of amnesia that had become a part of me, and I fought to reach it, focusing every ounce of my mental strength to bring it to me.

It came as I pulled the last drop of blood from my victim, came as her shriveled corpse collapsed to the floor. Only it wasn't a single memory. It was a flood of recollections, slamming into the tender recesses of my psyche like a torrent from a burst dam.

I knew my name, knew what I had become, and realized with horror what I had just done.

Rebecca!

The familiarity of my prey—her scent, her life-force—it was hers. It was *Rebecca's*.

And I had killed her.

20

I was paralyzed with revulsion, shocked to my core. I opened my mouth to scream, but nothing came out.

So lost in the moment was I, and so overcome with grief, that I almost didn't see Adalina coming.

I ducked purely on instinct as a blur of motion whistled overhead, slamming into the wall behind me. I spun around just in time to see Adalina pivot, fixing me with golden eyes that blazed in fury.

I returned her glare, snarling, baring my teeth.

This creature. This wretched, inhuman *thing* had taken everything from me. How could anything, even a monster as vile as she, subject someone to something so atrocious?

She will pay. Justice. I must have justice!

The thought exploded through my mind, obscuring all else. With it came a volcanic rage, the likes of which I'd never experienced before. I suddenly felt connected to everything, every granule of dust in the room, every worm and beetle crawling through the earth beneath the floor. The cry for justice thrummed in my veins, sang in my ears.

I sensed Adalina inside and out, felt her frustration, her contempt.

Knew her every move.

A microsecond before she leapt forward, I jumped to the side, striking out as her momentum carried her past me. She dodged and took a few steps back, hands raised like a fighter. I followed closely, throwing a flurry of quick jabs as she continued to move back. She parried the blows easily, and all at once, I felt a tremendous force pressing down upon me. It reeked of her. I staggered backward, fighting to stay upright. I focused my energy, and pushed back against it.

The force dispersed, but the time it took me to regain my footing was all Adalina needed. She struck me squarely in the stomach, sending me back into the wall. I felt several of my ribs break at the impact, and I almost wasn't quick enough to avoid what came next.

Almost.

Adalina went for my head this time, her fist rocketing forward so fast that it sang as it split the air before it. It grazed my face as I juked to the side. Stone exploded outward in a spray of dust and debris as her fist connected with the wall. The unexpected impact stunned her just long enough for me to aim a kick at her knee.

It connected.

Bone shattered, and Adalina cried out as her injured leg faltered under her weight. She handled the fall expertly, rolling cleanly out of the way just as I brought my foot down where her head had been. I continued my assault, springing after her even as she managed to regain her feet. We circled each other for a moment, both injured, cautious. I felt her will gather an instant before she unleashed a blast of energy, and I gathered my own and hurled it forward. The two waves met, crashing together with a cacophony that shook the foundations of the room.

Adalina's eyes blazed in frustration. I felt her gather herself again.

I anticipated.

I lashed out with all my might, bringing the full force of my mental energies to bear upon her. She pushed back. I strained against her, feeling every muscle in my body tighten. Adalina's defenses stood strong.

Sarah...Rebecca...my family. Oh, my beautiful family. Gone. Gone forever.

She had taken everything from me, obscuring my perceptions so completely that I had forgotten myself, forgotten my family, forgotten my God. I hated her. Hated her more passionately than anything imaginable. How could her stench have once seemed so sweet?

"You...will pay...for what you've done to me," I gasped, pushing harder, straining ever more.

Adalina grimaced, matching my power.

"You are...a failure, a *freak*," she spat. "You...aren't worthy to live. You must...be destroyed!"

With a ferocious roar, Adalina charged, battering through my assault. In the instant my attack dissipated, an invisible force slammed into me. Staggering and off-balance, I was vulnerable. Adalina let fly with a vicious kick to my midsection, hurling me clear across the room. I did my best to land gracefully, and Adalina kicked me again as I tried to roll out of the way. I regained my feet, still feeling her thoughts, still sensing her movements. Now, however, I was too damaged to react quickly enough. I did my best to parry, to dodge, backing away as she struck out. Every blow she landed slowed me more. My body was a wreck, and I was losing the ability to react.

She grinned as she came at me again, clearly aware the tide of battle had turned.

Where was the justice in all of this? Was I to be destroyed while this *thing* went unpunished for its horrific deeds? While my wife lay dead at my feet, while my daughter had been forced to grow up without her father?

Justice.

I snarled as the word burned in my mind, infusing my veins with fire. My focus intensified even as Adalina struck me again, even as my arms snapped under the assault; even as I wobbled on my feet, barely able to stand. I felt everything—my broken, damaged body, the tiniest particles of grit and dust beneath me.

The air.

Adalina brought her foot up in a high, arcing kick, directly toward my head. Everything slowed. In an instant, I knew I lacked the speed to move in time. I watched it ascend, even as I focused every last bit of his energy on the air around her. I felt every suspended bit of dust, every tiny invisible organism, every molecule.

I threw all my willpower at those tiny little bits, exhorting them, commanding them.

Move! Faster! FASTER!

Each of them was suddenly in a frenzy, gyrating and vibrating in a manner too erratic for even my heightened senses to perceive.

The air exploded in a blast of heat. Adalina flew backward, shrieking in agony as her skin burst into flames. Her body crashed into the wall on the other side of the room. I felt her focus on the flames, trying to extinguish them, but I lashed out with my own will, disrupting her attempts. Adalina screamed in frustration and leapt for me, her entire body still ablaze.

I pivoted at the last possible moment, striking out just as she moved past me. My fist connected squarely with the side of her head. Despite the damage to my arm, the blow was powerful. I felt bone cave in under the strike; heard the wet, meaty squelching of tissue; and before she even hit the floor, I knew the fight was over.

She lay before me, panting and gasping, as the flames began to die out. I stood and watched her struggle, watched her try to sit.

Watched her fail.

Smiling without feeling any pleasant emotions, I limped over and knelt beside her. The skin of her face was blackened and cracked, and her lips were peeled back from her teeth in a hideous, fixed grin. The fire had gone almost completely out of her eyes. Only a dull, yellow flicker remained.

"I should make you suffer," I said. "I should tear off every limb, every finger and toe, until only your head is left."

Adalina rasped and hacked in a parody of laughter. "You...could never...do that. I am your mistress. You will go back to your room...and you will stay there...until I've healed."

I snorted.

"Whatever you did to my mind—to my memories—it's gone. *Completely*. I'm myself again."

"No. You're not yourself...never yourself...never again. You...are mine now. My...servant. My...*son*."

I reeled as if slapped and gripped her by the throat. "Your *what*? You dare dishonor my mother by claiming me as your *son*?"

Adalina hacked and cackled again, her words distorted by my grasp. "That's...what you are. I...made you. You... belong...to me."

I roared, clutching her neck with both hands, squeezing, pulling, rending tissue, snapping tendons, cracking bone. With one final wrench, her flesh ripped sickeningly apart, and I held her severed head in my hands.

Instantly her head disintegrated. Blackened ash and dust cascaded down my hands and arms. I staggered upright as her body followed suit, crumbling away until nothing but a pile of dust remained.

A sudden rush of energy drove me to my knees. A tremendously powerful force ripped into me, filling my mind to bursting. I cried out as I gripped the sides of my head, certain it would explode outward with the sudden impact of whatever had just bulldozed its way in. For a split second, I detected a second presence that was not my own.

Adalina!

It was there and gone in a flash, and as the presence melted into my thoughts, the energy that had come with it merged with mine.

I felt different. I felt...*powerful.*

I stood slowly, careful not to aggravate my injuries. I focused my mind, applying just a touch of will to the core of my body.

My injuries were better. Not by much, but they were better.

And I was hungry.

I knew that healing myself further would take time— and it would take sustenance.

Dragos. Is that who I really am?

I sat down on the floor as the memories came flooding back.

Rebecca. Sarah. My life...

How long had it been since Adalina had taken me? Time

had lost all meaning when I'd been in her keeping; it seemed like only a week or two had passed, yet Rebecca...

I looked at her wasted corpse, drained of all life, staring sightlessly at the ceiling. Shuddering, I tore my gaze away.

So old. So very old.

I gazed at my own hands and noted the absence of any blemish or wrinkle. My skin was as smooth and clear as the day Adalina had taken me.

I haven't aged a single day. How's that possible?

As soon as the question entered my mind, I knew.

My kind didn't age. My kind didn't die.

It isn't fair. I should be allowed to die. I should have aged with dignity, with Rebecca. I should have been able to watch Sarah grow up.

I buried my face in my hands and wept, though I shed no tears.

My kind had no tears to shed.

21

I hardly noticed the door to my cell open; almost didn't see the hulking, misshapen figure enter. I was lost in thought, in grief; I was mourning the loss of my family and the loss of myself. Rebecca was dead, murdered by my own hand, and David Levin was no more.

Now there was only Dragos.

Dragos. Filthy, blood-drinking Dragos.

I hated that the thought of human blood excited me so much. I hated my predatory nature. Hated my strange mental and physical abilities. Hated that I still lived while Rebecca lay dead at my feet.

The figure stood motionless just inside the door, breathing heavily. Finally, I looked up. The ugliest man I'd ever seen stood before me. The man's face was too wide for his head, and his long hair fell in greasy tendrils down to his absurdly massive shoulders. He stooped as if his spine were curved, and his arms, too long for his frame, hung low like an ape's. His skin was pasty white, as if he'd never been exposed to sunlight. He wore a fine black suit, which made his appearance all the more laughable.

He also smelled *wrong*. Something about the aroma of his life-force seemed tainted, rotten.

This man wouldn't make for good prey.

I swatted the thought down, horrified that one of the first things I'd think about another individual was their potential as prey.

Then, something else occurred to me. *I've seen someone like this before.*

My mind flashed back to the moment I'd battered my way out of my room, when I'd encountered and killed that strange, misshapen man in the hall. Though there were slight differences between that creature and the one that now stood before me, I had no doubt that I was now face to face with the same type of person.

The man ducked his head, clutching a meaty fist to his chest, and addressed me in a deep voice. "My lord," he said, "I am Radu, loyal servant and master of your house. It is my duty to handle the affairs of your estate. I stand ready to serve."

The man stared at me expectantly, his hands clasped nervously before him.

"My what?"

"Your estate, my lord. You have...overcome my former mistress. Her lands, her titles, her power are yours. I am your humble servant."

I smelled the musky odor of fear emanating from the man before me. I sensed the man's uncertainty, saw the tension wracking his body.

The last thing I felt like was reassuring someone else.

"Be at ease," I said nonetheless. "I have no intention of harming you."

Radu relaxed visibly. "I'm at your disposal," he told me.

"I assume you have questions. I can no doubt answer some of them."

I had no desire to engage in conversation. I just wanted to be left alone in my misery. "I wish to know nothing," I said. "Leave me."

The man hesitated for a moment before quickly retreating through the doorway.

Unable to move, I stared at the emptiness where Radu had stood a moment before. My brain was frozen, unwilling to process what had happened. All I could do was recite a single name over and over.

"Rebecca…"

———

I REMAINED WHERE I WAS, on the floor of the cell, curled up next to my wife's decaying body. I wept soundlessly as I gazed at her once-youthful countenance, still shocked that I had killed her.

Immobilized by grief, I had no concept of how long I remained there. Days? Weeks? Time had little meaning for me. What I did know was that Radu's interruptions were growing tiresome.

Three more times, the stunted half-man had pestered me about the "affairs of my estate." Each time, I'd sent Radu off, telling him in no uncertain terms that I wanted to be left alone.

"It isn't my place to say," Radu had said in a quiet, trembling voice the last time he'd shown up, "but you can't remain here forever. You have a household to run."

I had nearly exploded at that, and it was all I could do to send the man away without decapitating him.

It isn't his fault, I told myself, my anger still simmering.

He isn't the monster. I am. And he's right about one thing: I can't stay here forever. Rebecca must be laid to rest.

Although her body had begun to decompose, neither the sight of her putrefying flesh nor the stench bothered me in the slightest. Whatever part of my brain had once reeled in disgust at such things seemed to have been altered along with everything else.

The next time Radu, positively reeking with fear, poked his head into the chamber, I slowly pushed myself up off the floor.

"I need your help with something," I said quietly, before Radu even had a chance to speak. "This woman needs to be properly buried. There are others like you here, correct?"

Radu nodded his head. "You have a great many servants, my lord."

"Really?" I said. "Each time I've been through these halls, they've been empty. Where are the others?"

"They've always been here, though out of sight. Lady Adalina did not like her children to have too much interaction with us."

"Children? You mean there are more like me here?"

"There *were* more like you. None of them survived Lady Adalina's passing. Except you."

"What do you mean?"

Radu nervously ran an oversized hand through his greasy hair. "I am not completely clear on the particulars my lord, but it's my understanding that until maturity, children are quite dependent on their parents. The death of a lord or lady means the death, or madness, of their offspring."

I felt my rage threaten to return.

More of us. More helpless victims for her to twist and torture. How many were there?

Though I figured that Radu would know the answer, I was too disgusted to ask.

RADU LED me out of the dungeons, up the narrow staircase that I had once descended in search of prey. A quick scan with my senses told me that all of the cells below were now thankfully empty.

When Radu opened the door on the narrow landing at the top of the stairs, I was flabbergasted to see that the corridor before me bustled with activity. Servants—just like Radu—moved to and fro, lumbering about their business.

They were all shapes and sizes; some broad and tall like Radu, some shorter and more petite. All of them wore ragged finery, and though there were subtle differences between each of them, they all bore the same distinctive hallmarks—exceedingly pale, leathery skin, wide faces, and long, greasy black hair. It took me a moment to realize that there were females present as well. They were nearly identical to the males, except that they were generally smaller.

The fact that there were so many of these...*things*...led me to wonder if I might be looking upon some type of previously unknown subspecies of human.

I held my tongue as I followed Radu through the grand hall before me, in awe yet again at the works of art that adorned nearly every wall. Striking paintings, immaculately crafted sculptures, and brightly colored tapestries were everywhere. The chamber doors on either side of the hallway were now open, and I could see the scores of lavishly decorated bedrooms that had once hidden behind them.

I again noted the lack of any window; the entire place

was lit with electric bulbs, cleverly fashioned to resemble candle flames, that shined dimly from countless wall sconces and ancient chandeliers.

"Where are the windows?" I muttered to myself.

"I beg your pardon?" Radu said, glancing over his shoulder as he turned left into a narrow passageway.

"The windows," I said, more loudly as I followed. "Why are there no windows here?"

"Because there would be nothing to view but dirt. Nearly a dozen feet of earth separates these ceilings from the ground above. We have every comfort money can buy, the most modern technology at our fingertips, and the world above is none the wiser."

I raised my eyebrows. "All of this? Underground?"

Radu nodded. "We 'borrow' our electricity from the grid of the populace above. We have running water, a sewer connection, and we're networked via a dedicated fiber optic cable."

"But how has all of this been kept a secret? Doesn't anyone ever wonder where the extra power goes? Is there no municipal service that could discover your sewer connection?"

"Those threats do exist," said Radu, "Which is why certain powerful locals receive a handsome stipend for their continued silence on the matter."

"Unbelievable," I breathed.

"You have no idea," said Radu.

The narrow passageway abruptly opened to another large hallway, and Radu led me to a massive set of double doors that towered at the end. The doors were intricately gilded with gold and silver, and the figure of a massive dragon with rubies for eyes and emeralds for scales spanned them from end to end. The doors were incredibly well constructed, with only the slightest seam running between them, such that at first glance the dragon appeared to be a single, solid shape.

"Your quarters," said Radu. "Lady Adalina had them especially prepared for you."

I furrowed my brow. "Why would she have done that?"

"I believe her intention was for you to remain here for a time once your transformation was complete."

My transformation.

I glowered at the dragon, and it took every bit of restraint to keep from smashing the figure to splinters. "Thank you," I said through gritted teeth. "I'll wait here until you're ready. Gather what you need and get me right away. I won't have my wife lying on the floor of that rotten dungeon a second longer."

"Immediately, my lord. There are but two ways to the surface. Shall I show them to you now?"

"Later, please," I said, never taking my eyes from the dragon.

I heard Radu depart behind me, the odor of the man's fear suddenly strong again.

I wondered why Radu had suddenly grown so frightened. Then I noticed a frenetic light, like the illumination cast by a raging fire, which made the gilding seem to come alive. A quick glance behind me dispelled the notion that the hall was aflame.

It wasn't long before I realized that the light blazed from my own enraged eyes.

22

Several hours later, I stood beneath a sky full of stars, bright with the waxing moon. Piles of rubble—ancient cut stone—lay all around, half covered in dirt and vegetation. The two hidden entrances of which Radu had spoken were cleverly concealed within the surrounding ruins. A swath of freshly turned earth lay at my feet, and several creatures, all of them strikingly similar to Radu, stood not far from me with shovels in hand.

I was amazed at how quickly Radu had been able to execute his requests. Per Jewish law, I'd required a simple pine coffin in which to bury my wife. Radu had procured one within hours, as well as the labor necessary to carry it to the surface and bury it, with my wife inside, properly. The man had come through surprisingly well.

"Thank you all for your help," I said to the gathered individuals. "You may return underground."

Silently they turned to leave, heading toward one of the larger piles of rubble.

"Radu," I said. "Stay here for a moment. I have a few questions I'd like you to answer."

Radu nodded, remaining where he was, as the rest of his kind disappeared into an opening at the foot of the pile.

"Where is this place?"

Radu looked puzzled. "How do you mean?"

"What country?"

"Moldova, My Lord."

Moldova.

Adalina had whisked me clear across the globe to Eastern Europe.

"And how long have I been here?"

"I'm not certain the exact date when Mistress Adalina first brought you to us, but I believe it was a little more than fifty years ago."

"Fifty *years?*"

I'd known it had been a long time, simply by how much Rebecca had aged. To hear it actually confirmed by someone else made the reality of it that much more shocking.

"A small period of time for one such as you," said Radu. "Mistress Adalina reigned here for more than six hundred years before you...ah...took her place."

I was silent.

Six hundred years, and she didn't look a day over thirty.

"What...am I?" I whispered, almost to myself.

Radu looked perplexed. "Surely you know better than I, my lord. You and those like you run the great houses. We servants are meant to do only one thing: serve."

Strange as it seemed, on an instinctual level I had a rudimentary understanding of the nature of my being. Now that Adalina's glamour was gone and I could think clearly, I found that my lack of aging and strange new abilities seemed almost natural.

Almost as if I'd been born with them.

I thought back to what Adalina had said as she lay dying on the floor of my cell, about how she had called me "son." I shuddered, electing not to think on the matter further.

"Thank you," I said. "That will be all. You may go back with the others."

Radu turned to leave, and before long, I heard the soft scraping sound of a large piece of stone being dragged into place. Then all was silent.

I stared at the earth before me, feeling I should say something, but unable to find the words. What could I possibly say that could make up for my long absence? For the fact that I'd killed her?

"I'm...sorry..." I choked on the words as I said them, surprised I was able to utter anything at all. My head swam from the all the recent events, and I could barely hang on to a cogent thought.

One thing I did know was that I was hungry.

Severely, painfully hungry.

Without thinking, I stretched out my thoughts, probing as far as I could in every direction. Almost instantly, I found what seemed to be several nearby villages: four little enclaves, all roughly equidistant from where I stood, each one teeming with life.

With food.

"No," I said. "I won't harm those people. I *won't*."

I didn't care how hungry I was or how physically or emotionally distressing my hunger would become. I was no monster. I wouldn't feed on the weak and helpless, wouldn't stalk and devour innocent people.

I'm an abomination. I don't deserve to live.

I sat on the ground before Rebecca's grave, cradling my face in my hands. I was determined to starve before I harmed another living person.

The skin on the back of my neck began to tingle. The eastern sky had grown slightly brighter. I was suddenly filled with a fear I didn't understand, an animalistic instinct to run and cower in the shadows. Refusing to move, I fought the feeling down.

I won't leave Rebecca, I thought.

I turned to face the sky, my fear mounting as the light grew brighter. I closed my eyes tightly. I felt like a child, lying in bed in a dark room, convinced a monster would spring forth from the closet. Pure, illogical terror gripped me, and I rose to my feet and moved toward the entrance to my subterranean domain.

I fought it. I used every bit of mental power to force myself to return to the graveside, to sit upon the damp earth.

I won't leave her side!

I struggled with my fear until the first rays of light exploded over the horizon. Instantly my skin was ablaze with searing pain. I screamed as I inhaled the acrid odor of smoke, writhed as my hands cracked and blackened. I lost all focus, all power. Finally, I collapsed to the ground.

The pain. Oh, the pain!

My mental defenses were gone, and I suffered silently, lacking the strength to even cry out. I was paralyzed, defenseless, and all I could do was watch the sun break free of the horizon, beginning its inevitable ascent in the sky.

Though my skin had ceased smoking, the pain was as strong as ever, washing my sanity away. I lost all sense of time as the sun beat down on me, lost all conscious thought as it devoured my strength.

I remained unable to move, unable to think, until the sky darkened with the approaching dusk, and the sun began its descent beyond the western horizon. I blinked my eyes, tried to sit. I managed to struggle weakly, my feet scrabbling against the soil.

It was still too bright.

I closed my eyes, waiting for night to fall.

When it did, when the stars and moon had returned, and the sun had vanished completely, my full strength returned with it. I thrust my barriers into place, forcing the pain of my decimated skin out of my mind while gingerly pushing myself up onto my knees.

I grunted, trying to ignore the crackling sounds my charred skin made as I rose to my feet. As it had before, violent hunger replaced the pain, and once again my mind began to slip away.

No, I thought. *I won't feed. I will die. I* must *die.*

Again I closed my eyes, trying to focus, to keep my mind clear.

I will not feed.

My mind extended outward of its own accord, seeking the villages, seeking life.

I will not feed!

Blackness.

I AWOKE FEELING FULL, whole. My lucidity had returned, and most of my pain had vanished. I looked at my hands and noticed that my flesh appeared almost normal. Though my skin looked a bit grayer than usual, the dead, cracked blackness of scorched flesh had disappeared.

Then I noticed the bodies. There were two of them. A man and a woman, both young, laying at the foot of a massive oak tree. Right away I saw how sunken their flesh was, as if every bit of fluid had been sucked from them.

Their eyes bulged sightlessly from skin that clung too tightly to their skulls, and their teeth protruded from thin, shrunken lips. I glanced behind me and saw the lights of a small town off in the distance.

More death on my conscience!

I fell to my knees, tearing at my hair. What had I become? Had free will abandoned me? Did I lack the ability to choose *not* to kill?

A part of me knew the answer. Knew it by instinct.

Free will is the province of humanity. But I'm not human. Not anymore.

There was a puddle of water, clear and still, on the ground beside me. I gazed into it, seeing for the first time my deathly pale skin, my glowing yellow eyes, and my jet-black hair.

I barely even looked human. I looked like Adalina.

It wasn't fair. It wasn't *right*. My humanity had been my greatest God-given asset, and it was gone, taken from me by a creature that valued her own pleasures and amusement above all else. Justice didn't seem served by her death alone. Adalina was gone, yet there I was—forever changed, forever twisted.

I wish she were still alive, I thought. *I'd kill her again. And again. I'd kill her every moment of every day, in the most painful ways imaginable. I'd...*

I stopped that line of thought, appalled at my sudden lust for violence.

What is wrong with me?

I forced myself to stand and move away from the two innocents who lay before me.

"I'm sorry," I whispered. "I'm so sorry."

I began the long trek back to the only place I knew I'd be welcome, the only place I could now call home.

23

Moments after I'd dragged the stone slab back into place, heavy footsteps approached from below, echoing up the spiraling staircase that descended into the darkness. I instinctively reached out with my senses.

Radu.

The man smelled worried.

Moments later, Radu's hideous, stooped form emerged from around the bend.

"My lord," he rasped, clearly out of breath. "I've been anxiously awaiting your return. You have a visitor."

"A visitor? Who?"

"Lord Arsenios Cabesellius. Lady Adalina's father."

"Her *father?*"

"Yes," replied Radu. "He's been here since yesterday."

I frowned as anger rose in my chest; I forced it down, maintaining control.

So her father has come to see me, I thought. *Perhaps he's seeking vengeance against me.*

I gathered my will, scanned myself for injuries.

Although I hadn't yet fully recovered from my confrontation with Adalina, I was confident I possessed enough power to defend myself, should it become necessary.

"Bring me to him."

Nodding, Radu hurried off down the stairs. Once we reached the bottom, Radu led me out of the passageway, down another flight of stairs, and through several corridors that eventually opened to a large chamber. The ceiling was at least two stories high, lit with four chandeliers that looked like the one in my room. Several tapestries depicting great horned beasts surrounded by countless fallen men at arms adorned the walls; although I did not appreciate their subject matter, I paused for a moment to admire their workmanship.

Plush antique furniture was arrayed around the room in what seemed like conversational groupings, with the two largest couches flanking a low table of dark, glossy wood. This arrangement stood directly before an immense hearth in which a fire blazed.

A man sat on the farthest couch. He rose when we entered the room. His black hair was closely cropped, and he had a neatly trimmed beard and pointed mustache. He wore an elaborately patterned, billowing silk tunic that hung almost to his feet. Strange pointed shoes, similarly patterned, poked out from beneath it. His skin was exceedingly pale, and his eyes glowed with a subtle yellow light.

"Dragos, I presume?" said the man, in an accent I couldn't place. "You look a bit worse for wear."

I glanced down at myself, noting again just how gray and damaged my skin had become from my recent experience with the sun. I crossed the room slowly, probing the man with my senses. I detected a well of power and age within him that went far deeper than anything I'd felt from

Adalina. I resolved to act with caution, knowing this man was an order of magnitude stronger than my former mistress had been.

Radu kept pace beside me as we approached the man. "My lord," Radu said, "may I present Lord Aresnios Cabasillius, father of Lady Adalina Lacusta."

Lord Aresnios inclined his head, and I returned the gesture.

"Thank you, Radu," said Arsenios. "Please leave us. Lord Dragos and I have much to discuss."

Radu glanced at me. I nodded, and with a deep bow, Radu departed.

Arsenios sat back down and gestured for me to join him.

I hesitated, then walked slowly to the opposite couch and took a seat.

"As Radu has indicated, I'm Arsenios Cabasillius, Adalina's father. I'm your grandfather, Dragos."

I frowned, remembering how Adalina had referred to me as her son. Rage swelled in my chest, but I fought it down, masking and controlling it.

Either Arsenios didn't notice, or he didn't care. "So," he said casually, "as Adalina is no longer with us, the remainder of your care falls to me."

I didn't respond at first. In truth, I could think of nothing to say. The statement seemed laughable.

"If I may ask," I finally said, "what do you mean by that?"

Arsenios leaned back on the couch and folded his pale hands in his lap. "There's still much for you to learn. Normally Adalina would have passed this knowledge on to you herself, as any parent would. Circumstances being what they are, the responsibility is mine."

I leaned forward, gazing into the man's pale yellow eyes. I detected no trace of deception from Arsenios, but I remained ready, muscles tight, in case I should need to make a quick escape.

"What knowledge would she have wanted me to obtain?"

"Much," Arsenios said, casually resting his feet on the table, the tips of his pointed shoes aiming skyward. "You probably know very little of our ways, and undoubtedly you have many questions. As my daughter is...unavailable, I'm here to instruct you and to make sure your questions are answered."

I relaxed just a hair. Nothing about the man's tone or mannerisms suggested that he was there to seek revenge. On the contrary, he seemed completely at ease.

"So," Arsenios continued, "ask me anything. I assume by now you have some idea of who and what you are."

"Barely."

"You are a Nobleman," Arsenios said, steepling his fingers. "You are the embodiment of power, as is everyone else like you. Our kind shares a common legacy: to rule the lesser species of this planet. You yourself are the ruler of a vast estate, lands, wealth, and prey in abundance. Adalina was a shrewd woman, and her dealings were most lucrative. Radu is probably better suited to bringing you up to speed on the affairs of your house, but I can tell you that her influence in this part of the world was quite remarkable."

"I'm a bit confused," I said. "How exactly did she manage to influence anything at all from down here? She would have only been able to go out at night, and judging from the way we appear, most people would probably react with alarm or fear if they saw one of us."

"That's definitely true," said Arsenios. "Our species differs quite a bit from theirs. Fortunately, their minds are rather easy to influence. A simple glamour, and suddenly we don't appear nearly as frightening. You'd be surprised at the level of influence we've gained around the world. Our kind has always had a knack for obtaining the covert support of whatever humans happen to be in power. They're simple creatures, really. Throw enough money their way, and they'll do almost anything."

I grunted. I hated to admit it, but that was probably true.

"We've always been discreet," Arsenios went on. "Though it's true that legends and folklore have sprung up regarding our kind over the centuries, the stories remain ridiculously far from the truth. Our true nature and purpose remain secret, while the humans who fancy themselves in positions of power do *our* bidding. Over time, we've learned a great deal about shaping the world around us. We've also learned an important fact: humanity is fragile. It must be protected, at all costs."

Arsenios sighed, absently smoothing his beard.

"And let me tell you, protecting a species that seems bent on self-annihilation is no easy task. Though a smattering of bloody conflicts throughout history can be traced back to an overambitious Lord or Lady throwing a tantrum, the vast majority of devastating wars have been the humans' doing. In fact, more than a few major world conflicts have been *avoided* simply because of our involvement."

"But why?" I said. "Why bother protecting humans? Aren't they inferior creatures, unworthy of our attention?"

"The reason is simple: with no humans, we all die. Even so, I have always believed that it is proper to have respect for one's source of life. Not many others agree with me, but I always try to remember that I would not be alive were it not for the existence of humans. The least I can do is help them avert a war every now and then."

I was stunned. The last thing I'd expected to hear from

this man was anything resembling altruism; Adalina certainly would not have regarded the humans nearly as highly.

Maybe this Arsenios isn't so bad, I thought. *He certainly doesn't seem to share his daughter's viciousness.*

"Why humans, though?" I asked. "Can't we consume animal blood just as easily?"

Arsenios chuckled. "Try it sometime."

"I don't understand. What can the harm be?"

"In addition to violent illness—which will happen the moment you've fed on an animal—you'll eventually starve. We derive no sustenance from animal blood. Humans are the only living creatures capable of sustaining us. The next time you're near an animal, smell it. You'll immediately see what I'm talking about."

I thought on that for a moment and recalled the odor I'd sensed from Radu and the others like him. I also remembered the reaction I'd had after eating meat the last time Adalina had brought it to me.

"Does that have anything to do with why Radu smells...wrong?"

"The two issues are certainly related," Arsenios explained. "Radu—and the other Servants like him—are no longer strictly human. They're genetically modified individuals that have been bred specifically to exist in our company and serve us in our homes."

"But how is such a thing possible? The technology to engage in genetic engineering at that level doesn't even exist."

Arsenios smiled, and I felt a sudden chill.

"Perhaps humans lack that technology, but we don't. Knowledge outside the bounds of human understanding has been passed down through our ranks for countless millennia. Radu is stronger, smarter, and more adaptable than any human alive. He's been bred to be completely loyal to his master. He—and the others like him—are quite literally bound to us. I'm not sure how it's done; the sciences have never been my province, but his mind is structured in such a way that a...tether, of sorts, exists between him and the master her serves. He also requires a fraction of the water and nourishment that your average human needs. His kind might not be much to look at, but they're incredibly useful and easy to keep."

I felt sick. I hid it well, fighting hard to mask my anger and shock at learning that humans had been subject to genetic alteration and who knew what kinds of medical experiments. I could almost picture darkened laboratories, secret dungeons, screaming victims...

I tore my thoughts away from such things, afraid my barriers would break, worried I'd lose my composure in front of Arsenios.

"As your existing Servants die off, you'll be allocated more from the Council. Take care that you treat them well. For all their superiorities, they're every bit as fragile as humans. It wouldn't do for you to eliminate your supply before others are made ready for you."

"I'll bear that in mind," I said quietly. "Also...what is this Council?"

"An administrative body, responsible for allocating resources, organizing the Convocation, and performing other tasks that require any sort of centralized leadership."

"So they're like a government?"

Arsenios shook his head. "Not in the slightest. For one, they're made up of Servants, like Radu. It was agreed that granting leadership—even in merely an administrative capacity—to any single group of Nobles would be disastrous. The Council merely manages our affairs, but on a grander scale than what Radu does for your own household."

"From what you've said, it seems there's a desire to keep the peace among our kind."

"Of course," said Arsenios. "Peace and civility lay at the heart of our society. For our kind to thrive, petty squabbles and power grabs must be avoided. There's very little infighting among the Nobility, and absolutely no murder— except under very particular circumstances."

"Such as?" I prompted.

Arsenios cocked and eyebrow and looked me squarely in the eyes.

"But...how is that considered a special circumstance? Aren't you upset that I killed your daughter?"

"No," said Arsenios. "One of parenting's greatest challenges is to know when to let go. Adalina crossed that line with you, and she paid dearly for that misstep." He shrugged. "This sort of thing happens from time to time. Let that be a lesson to you, when the time comes for you to choose a son or daughter."

"When the time comes...for what?" I said, staring forward intently.

Smiling, Arsenios leaned back. "Our drive to procreate might not be as strong as it is in some of the lesser species, but it does rear its head occasionally. When the time comes, you'll know."

I didn't respond, *couldn't* respond.

Everything Adalina did to me—the lies, the punishments, the torture—was just to parent *me?*

A new loathing for the creature I had become churned in my guts.

Arsenios must have taken my silence for confusion.

"When you reach a certain age—it could be three hundred or three thousand, everyone is different—you'll yearn to pass on your gifts and knowledge. This urge will grow until it surpasses the realm of obsession. It'll dominate your thoughts, consume your life, and it won't abate until you choose an offspring."

I tried not to cringe. I understood all too well the drives my kind experienced. If what Arsenios had said was true, and I'd one day be in a position where I'd *want* to control, dominate, and twist a human being into some type of horrible creature...

That won't happen. I won't give in. No matter the temptation, I won't do to anyone else what Adalina did to me.

"Why me?" I said quietly. "Out of everyone on earth, why would Adalina choose me?"

"Something about you drew her attention," said Arsenios. "Consider yourself lucky. I believe she was doing business in America around the time you came here. She no doubt saw you at some point, and developed a fascination with you."

My mind immediately went back to the last thing I'd been doing before Adalina had taken me.

Working. On a contracted project, for a foreign client.

Could it be that my old company's overseas client was somehow connected to Adalina? Might she have even been at one of our meetings? I strained to remember if anyone who had been present reminded me of her, but came up blank.

With her powers, she could have easily disguised herself as anyone. There's no point trying to pick her out of that crowd.

"So," I mused, "we were all born the same way. Brought in, changed."

"Yes," said Arsenios. "Sexual reproduction is the practice

of baser life forms. Direct genetic alteration of lesser species is how we survive."

Genetic alteration...so that's what has been done with me. I'm no different than those Servants—an experiment, twisted into a monstrosity.

Suddenly something else occurred to me. Perhaps I wasn't alone in the way I felt. Perhaps there were others who resented their transformations, who remembered what it was to be human. Maybe Arsenios was just such a person.

"Do you remember anything from your former life? Before you became what you are now?"

Arsenios regarded me strangely for a few moments. "I remember nothing," he finally said. "Why do you ask?"

"I have...memories," I said, suddenly sensing I was treading on potentially dangerous ground. I chose my words carefully and used every discipline I could muster to mask my true feelings behind them. "They're fragmented. Broken. I want to know more about what they are."

Arsenios smiled reassuringly. Something about his expression, about the way his eyes softened, reminded me of my *real* grandfather. "Try not to worry about them," Arsenios said. "They'll fade over time. Whoever you were is no more. You'll forget and know only who you are now. I promise you, these memory fragments won't trouble you for long."

I tried to calm myself, though not for the reasons Arsenios would have guessed.

I do not want my memories to fade. I want to remember, always.

"Has anyone ever...not forgotten?"

"There have been stories, gossip, about children who remembered their former lives. This is a touchy area for some, as to produce such a child would be a great shame for any house. To my knowledge, these offspring are routinely and quietly terminated."

My eyes grew wide.

"Don't worry. I'm sure you aren't one of *them*. The others were anomalies, impure. Something went wrong during their gestation. As the stories go, their powers never fully developed, and those individuals were easily destroyed. You overcame Adalina, a woman nearly six hundred years your senior. She was far too strong to have been killed by some freak offspring."

"That's good to know," I said, trying to keep my emotions under tight control.

"Is there anything else you'd like to ask me?"

I paused for a moment. Though I felt it would be wisest to keep this meeting short, I could not contain my curiosity.

"What of your own transformation? Where do you come from? Is your father still alive?"

Arsenios sighed, a pained expression briefly creasing his brow.

"My father was a Roman Lord. From what I understand, I was taken from a small stock of Byzantine humans, who my father had been carefully cultivating over a period of generations after the Western Roman Empire fell. Regrettably, he is not alive today."

I was astounded to hear of the death of such a seemingly immortal being. My surprise apparently showed, for Arsenios chuckled quietly.

"Yes, we can be killed. I don't really wish to relive what happened, but I'll leave you with this: there are definitive reasons why murder has been forbidden among our people. It occurred far too frequently in the past, with petty duels and vengeance killings extinguishing irreplaceable chunks of our population."

Unsure of how to respond, I remained silent. Shockingly, I rather liked Arsenios, and did not wish to cause him any further pain.

"Anything else?"

I shook my head. My mind whirled from all I had learned, and I could think of nothing more to say.

"Should anything else occur to you—and I'm sure something will—don't hesitate to visit me in my home. You're always welcome."

I nodded. "Thank you, but how will I find you?"

"I will show you momentarily. Before I do, there's one other thing I must mention: the Convocation. The Convocation is a function held every two hundred years in which the Nobility gathers to socialize and conduct business. You'll be expected to attend, to represent your house. That brings me to another point: you'll need to decide on a name for yourself."

"But I have a name."

Arsenios waved his hand dismissively. "You have a pet's title, given to you by your mistress before she had a chance to release you. Such 'names' dissolve the moment a child leaves the nest. It's up to you to choose what to call yourself. Personally, I chose a name that, to me, conferred a sense of distinction and was common in the time period in which I was born. You'll want to think carefully regarding your name, as you'll be stuck with your decision for eternity. Pick something honorable that will bring distinction to your house."

"I'll think on it," I said.

"The Convocation will take place in a mere ten years," said Arsenios, standing. "The only way in is by Shadow Travel."

"Shadow Travel?" I said, rising as well. "What's that?"

"The quickest, easiest way for us to traverse great distances. Observe. *Feel* what I do. Follow with your senses, to see where I go. I won't shield my essence from you; you should be able to follow. This is the means by which you can visit me in my home."

Arsenios walked to the corner of the room, to a shadowy spot cast by the fire that the candlelight overhead didn't touch. Reaching out with my senses, I felt Arsenios extend a small part of himself into that shadow. Without warning, the man blinked out of sight, seemingly swallowed up by the darkness.

I walked slowly to where he'd been standing, probing the shadows. There was something there, a psychic cord of some kind. I followed it and found that it expanded into thousands of individual filaments, each with its own set of branches. These filaments and branches shot off in every conceivable direction. Along one of those branches, far in the distance, I sensed Arsenios, moving away at a rapid pace. I was suddenly certain that were I to follow the same branch, I'd wind up wherever Arsenios went.

I chose another at random, following it with my mind. I sensed complete darkness, coldness, the absence of life, and a great, yawning distance. I chose a different path. This one was more vibrant. I smelled something on the other end, something delightful.

Blood. Life.

I extended myself a bit farther and saw dim shapes moving about a brightly lit room.

Brightly lit, save for a single shadowy area, under a chair in a corner.

I immediately knew I had only to thrust myself into this filament, and I'd be there, in the room with those shapes.

But I withdrew, not wishing to be seen. The room in which I stood came back into focus.

Such a skill will prove to be incredibly useful.

I turned to stare at the fire. I wondered for a moment at the *need* for a fire—my kind certainly didn't require them, for light or heat. Clearly ambiance still meant something, even to creatures such as me. I gazed at the flames for a moment longer, calmed by their movements, before slowly heading back to my chamber.

24

I sat behind a monstrous mahogany desk, situated at the end of a vast chamber that housed row upon row of filing cabinets, along with an impressive array of computer equipment. Radu sat in a chair beside me, meticulously detailing every mind-numbing aspect of the estate's financials. I was stunned at how much wealth Adalina had accrued over the centuries; Arsenios hadn't exaggerated when he'd mentioned her business acumen. She'd been worth billions. Adalina had owned property all over the world, from villas in Italy to penthouses in Tokyo, and had a personal stake in more businesses than I could keep track of. She sat on the board at a major software company in Germany, was a majority stakeholder for a large bank in the U.S., and held a plethora of other important positions elsewhere around the world. It seemed to me that Adalina had somehow developed the ability to be in a thousand places at once. I was also surprised to learn I was legally listed as her next of kin and had inherited everything she possessed. Apparently, Radu—and whatever human network he employed—was quite skilled at fabricating and manipulating legal documents.

I also learned about Adalina's many aliases, which she had needed over the years to conceal the fact that she was more than six hundred years old. I realized that if I wished to have any contact with the human world over the coming centuries, I'd need to do the same.

Radu had then led me to a wing of the compound that seemed to contain nothing but clothing—rooms upon rooms of every fashion type imaginable, from every corner of the world.

"You will need to fill a variety of roles to effectively run your businesses," Radu told me. "It will be necessary to look the part in each of them."

I SHOOK MY HEAD.

"Why is any of this necessary? With a glamour, I could appear to wear anything I want."

Radu shrugged. "I often heard Adalina complain of how fatigued she'd become after maintaining a glamour for an extended period of time. Perhaps it's less tiring to simply hide one's eyes or pallor than to create and hold the image of an entire outfit."

I considered that for a moment; though I had not yet had occasion to try my hand at such illusions, I supposed that line of logic made sense.

It was at that point, with a veritable treasure trove of clothing before me, that I decided to shed the outfit that Adalina had given me. Instead, I chose something simple and comfortable that reminded me of what I might have once worn on a cozy fall weekend: blue jeans, tennis shoes, and a black turtleneck.

I suddenly felt tired, which surprised me, as I didn't require sleep. I excused myself, then headed back to my chamber. I sat in bed—an immense overstuffed mattress with enough brilliantly patterned linens and tasseled pillows to make my head hurt—and pondered my exhaustion for a moment. For the first time, I explored that far-off part of my mind, where my pain and discomfort had been sequestered. I hissed as I felt the true depth of the injuries from my recent battle with Adalina, realizing I still bore quite a bit of damage.

I lay on my back and closed my eyes. I focused on my injuries: on knitting flesh, on mending bone, and I felt better...*much* better. As I sat up, hunger slammed me in the gut, doubling me over. For a terrifying moment, I thought my sanity would flee yet again.

I need to feed. Now. Before I lose myself and kill someone else.

The room was pitch-black, enveloped in shadow, so finding a spot for Shadow Travel was an easy task. I thought of the nearby villages, found the necessary filaments, and followed one that led straight to the bedchamber of a reclining woman. The room was modestly furnished, with a stout set of drawers on the opposite wall from the bed. The woman looked to be about forty years old, with dark hair interspersed with bits of grey. She was alone, and sound asleep. In an instant, I was by her side. I thrust my consciousness into her mind, soothing her, lulling her into an even deeper sleep. I bent slowly over her, not making a sound, and inserted my sharp, elongated tongue into her neck. I drank slowly and deliberately, careful not to take too much.

I tried to ignore the ecstasy that flowed through me as I consumed her life force, tried to convince myself that the rapturous taste of her blood wasn't as good as the food I used to consume as a human.

I do not enjoy this. I eat only because I must.

When I felt the slightest ebb in her life-force, I withdrew and retreated into the shadows. I followed another filament, to another darkened room, where a young man lay, snoring softly. I fed again, careful not to take too much, stopping at the earliest sign of danger.

I was still hungry. Whatever I'd done to quicken my healing, it had sapped a great deal of my energy.

I fed three more times that evening, careful to extract only what I needed. When I'd grown bulbous and giddy with blood, I returned to my chamber and sat in bed.

How could I have just done that? Taken blood from so many without a second thought? What have I become?

I closed my eyes, too horrified to think about it further.

MONTHS WENT BY, and I recovered. Once I'd completely healed, I found I didn't need to feed nearly as often, for which a part of me was thankful. Since I spent less of my time hunting, I busied myself in conversations with Radu, learning everything I could about the business dealings of my former mistress.

I was both amazed and disgusted at Adalina's ability to make money seemingly anywhere, from legitimate enterprises to the most terrible criminal schemes. She'd had a hand in everything, from the dealings of back-alley organ traffickers to well-known international businesses. Her involvement in each enterprise was cleverly hidden behind two or three intermediaries—all of whom were very well paid and none of whom knew her true name or nature.

Adalina had stashed her liquid assets in banks all over the world. She'd worked out a system whereby every several decades, her accounts would be closed and all related monies would be transferred to other institutions, under different names. Radu was well versed in the system and assured me that he would handle all transfers when the time came.

I found myself growing to like Radu more and more as the days went by. The man was singularly focused on his tasks, he was quick to respond to my every request, and he never judged me based on what I was. I had learned that Radu was the only Servant in my house to bear a name; such an honor was bestowed only upon the worthiest of Servants, and apparently Adalina had also seen something special in him.

He is a hard worker, but I enjoy his company for a different reason. He treats me as any employee would treat their boss, not as a terrified human would treat a monster.

"How long will you live?" I found myself asking during one of our meetings at my enormous desk. "You've clearly handled this sort of thing before. Surely you couldn't have been with her since the beginning, over six hundred years ago?"

Radu chuckled, his too-wide mouth curling into a toothy grin. "True enough, my lord. I've been bred to live a very long life by human standards—they tell me I'll live to be about two hundred. But I wasn't the one who originally dealt with Adalina's holdings. I've had three predecessors. All of their instructions, records, and documents have been meticulously maintained. When I start nearing the end of my life, I'll pass on what I've learned to whoever arrives to replace me."

"This system seems to work very well," I said. "I have no desire to change it."

"Very good, my lord."

"Tell me something else, Radu. How did Adalina conduct business with her intermediaries? Was she required to meet with them face-to-face?"

"Yes, my lord. And there are times when you'll most likely need to be present at similar meetings. In fact," he said, reaching for a sheaf of papers, "next year she was slated to meet with one of her primary intermediaries to discuss certain offshore accounts. It would be a good idea if you went in her place. I will, of course, notify this individual of her untimely demise and inform him that his former business associate's next of kin has taken over the family business."

"Excellent," I said. "We should sit down sometime soon and discuss any other upcoming meetings. I also have some ideas about what can be done with some of this excess wealth Adalina has been amassing for so many years."

"Your ideas are always most welcome, my lord."

I nodded and excused myself.

Millions of starving people, and Adalina had more money squirreled away than some nations. No longer. If I'm forced to live this god-awful life, at least some good will come of it.

I would keep some of the assets for myself, as I'd undoubtedly need them to fund my efforts at concealment over the coming centuries, but the amount I now possessed was grotesque. I'd have nothing to do with hoarding so much wealth, even though my very name brought to mind a creature that does nothing but hoard.

Dragos. The Dragon.

In spite of the name's connotations, I rather liked it. The name had grown on me, even though I hated that my former mistress had given it to me. It wasn't as grand and self-important as her name or Arsenios's, but it was *mine*. I neither wanted nor liked the power and wealth I now possessed, and I had no desire to choose some haughty name or title for myself. "Dragos" would do just fine.

And I can never go back to my old name. David Levin is dead.

I wouldn't disgrace my family, or the memory of the man I had been, by reclaiming that name now. Inevitably, thoughts of my name brought thoughts of my family with them.

Sarah.

More likely than not, she was still alive. My heart ached when I thought of the life she must have lead and how she must be suffering now.

Her father disappeared when she was a girl. Her mother disappeared when she was grown. Both parents gone from her world.

I had spent many a night pacing my room, sobbing silently, thinking about the little girl I never saw grow up, thinking about the family from which I'd been torn. There were times when my rage exploded uncontrollably, and a piece of priceless antique furniture in my chamber would suddenly burst into flames.

My Servants always cleaned up the mess, always replaced the furniture, and never asked questions.

Sarah. My little girl, my baby.

I yearned to go to her, but I knew I couldn't.

What would I say to her? How would she react, seeing me as I am now? A yellow-eyed, pale-skinned monster?

She would be terrified. Even if I employed a glamour to erase those features, as Adalina had done at our first meeting, what would I say to her? Would I appear in the guise of an old man, reveal myself to be her father, and claim I'd suffered amnesia? Would I appear young, as I looked the day I had vanished, and tell her the truth?

No. None of those things would work. I won't lie to her, and I won't try to make her understand the truth of what happened to me. She'd never believe it anyway.

"But...what if..." I mused, allowing my thoughts to trail off.

Yes. That was it.

I stood abruptly, and headed down the hall to find Radu.

25

When darkness fell on Tipton Street, misty rain fell with it. The pavement shone in the glow of the streetlights as I made my way down the sidewalk, past several cozy-looking homes, all with well-kept landscaping. I stopped before the fourth home from the corner, a charming little bungalow with neatly trimmed hedges and a sensible car parked in the driveway. I wore a fine, dark suit and carried a black leather briefcase. The glamour I had employed gave me the appearance of a fifty-something man with a touch of gray in my hair.

Despite being an all-powerful life-form, I was nervous. Radu had managed to track Sarah down more quickly than I would have imagined, employing whatever network he used to handle such things. I had carefully rehearsed my spiel, worked with Radu repeatedly to get my stories straight, but the thought of seeing her again filled me with so many conflicting emotions that I was on the verge of panic.

What would I do when she came to the door? Would I

cry and embrace her? Would I fall to my knees, the truth cascading from my lips despite my better judgment?

No. I have to maintain control. I can't frighten her, and she can't know who I truly am.

As God did to pharaoh, I hardened my heart, and I clamped down on my emotions with the full force of my will. I strode to the door and rang the bell. Moments later, a man appeared at the door. He had neatly trimmed thinning hair and wore a loose-fitting sweater and jeans. I smiled and extended a hand.

"Mr. Miller?"

The man took it, returning my smile. His grip was solid and firm.

"I'm Jacob Goodman of Goodman and Summers. We spoke over the phone."

"Eli Miller. Pleasure to meet you. Come on in," he said, standing aside.

I entered, wiping my feet on a mat that sat just inside the entryway.

"Should I remove my shoes?" I asked.

"You can keep them on," said Eli. "The floor needs to be washed anyway."

I glanced around as Eli closed the door. The home was clean and bore the standard clutter associated with an active family. A coffee table in the living room was stacked high with what looked to be school text books, and a family portrait that I passed by depicted a man, a woman, and a teenage boy.

A grandson. I have a grandson.

I briefly squeezed my eyes shut to hold back the tears.

"My wife's in the kitchen," Eli said, heading toward the back of the house. "Our son is out with friends, so we should have some peace and quiet for a while."

I inclined my head toward the portrait.

"Looks like a fine young man," I said. "What's his name?"

"David," said Eli. "We named him after Sarah's father."

No amount of mental control could contain the wave of bittersweet sorrow that washed over me, and I staggered slightly as I followed Eli into the kitchen, clutching a hand to my breast.

Maybe this was a bad idea. Too many emotions.

I redoubled my efforts, and managed to keep my feelings in check until I entered the kitchen. Then, I felt the world around me go dim as I saw her, seated at the kitchen table.

My God, she looks so much like Rebecca.

Though her hair had gone almost completely gray, and she bore quite a few more wrinkles than Rebecca had when I had been taken, she was practically a clone of my wife. Same high cheekbones, same strong chin, same dimples when she smiled.

Be strong. Remember your purpose here.

Sarah rose when I entered. She smiled, extending a hand, and I took it.

Pain exploded up my arm and into my shoulder, washing over my body. My eyes grew wide as I felt my mental control on the precipice of collapse. If not for the fact that I already had my emotions under tight control, I would have fainted from the intensity. I groaned softly, straining to maintain eye contact, to keep smiling.

She withdrew her hand, her brow creased with concern, and the pain immediately stopped.

"Mr. Goodman, are you all right?"

"Yes," I said, trying to recover. "It's just...my knee gives me a bit of trouble whenever it gets too damp out. Old injury."

"I completely understand," she said, returning to the table. "Please have a seat. Get off your feet for a while."

I nodded appreciatively and sat next to her, careful not to touch her gain. Eli took the seat across from me.

What the hell just happened?

I extended my senses toward her, hoping to ascertain the cause of my reaction, and was shocked when my perceptions simply evaporated. I tried again but felt absolutely nothing from her; it was as if an invisible barrier shielded her from the force of my will.

I knitted my brow, wondering what could cause such a thing to occur, and then I noticed it: a brightly polished silver Star of David dangling from a thin chain around her neck.

My star!

There was no doubt about it—the star was mine, or at the very least, it was an exact replica.

"That's a very striking piece of jewelry," I said. "Where did you get it?"

"Oh, this?" She cradled the star in her hand, smiling faintly, a faraway look in her eyes. "It was my father's."

I gazed at its brilliant sheen, unable to believe my good fortune.

Someone must have recovered it after the thief dropped it near the car.

I was ecstatic that it had been found and that my daughter now wore it. She must have cared for it a great deal, for it shone so brilliantly that it nearly hurt my eyes. Suddenly uneasy, I looked away.

"Over the years, I've bought her more necklaces and pendants than I can count," said Eli, "but she's always favored that piece."

"It suits her," I said quietly.

Rebecca looked down at the table, her expression unreadable.

Eli reached over and placed a hand on her arm. "You okay?" he asked quietly.

She nodded. "Yes...I will be."

I busied myself with my briefcase, placing it on the table and digging through papers. I felt that if I looked at my daughter at that moment, I'd lose the little control I had left.

"Will you please excuse me for a moment?" Sarah stood quickly and hurried out of the kitchen. A moment later, I heard the faint sound of a door closing.

"The past few years haven't been easy on her," Eli said. "She'd been healing, but now...now that seven years have passed, and her mother's finally been declared legally dead...all of the old wounds are back."

"I understand," I said. "This sort of thing is never easy."

"Especially considering the circumstances," Eli sighed. "I can't imagine what she must be going through. She lost her father at a very young age, and then her mother just...*disappeared*. Right out of the home."

I shook my head. "So I've heard. That is truly awful."

Eli nodded.

"She suffered from dementia. We'd placed her in an assisted living community because we were afraid of what might happen if she lived with us. Our home is safe, but it doesn't have the security we'd thought would be present in a facility designed to house people with mental issues. We thought if she lived here, she might walk out one night, and we'd get a call saying she'd been hit by a car or was found frozen to death.

"Sarah blames herself. She thinks we should have had her move in with us, that we would have been able to protect her better than the home did. And you know what?

My guilt is...tremendous. I'm the one who recommended that place. I'd heard great things about the care and the staff. Who knew they'd be totally incompetent, letting a patient wander off like that?"

I nodded. I wanted to tell him what had really happened, wanted to do anything to assuage Sarah and Eli's guilt. My jaw clenched in frustration; I felt so helpless. I could reveal the truth with just a few words.

But I knew the truth would be even more damaging. How would it sound?

'Her mother didn't wander off. She was abducted by an immortal creature. Oh, and by the way, I'm Sarah's father.'

It would sound absurd.

I shook my head. "I can't imagine your family's suffering. I'm very sorry."

Eli sighed. "Sometimes I just don't know what to do. Her father vanished too, you know. When she was very young."

"I knew that her father had passed away some time ago, but I wasn't aware of what happened to him."

"They think it was a robbery gone wrong, and the assailant made off with the body to cover his tracks. He didn't come home from work one night, and the police found traces of his blood near his car, along with that Star of David. The chain was broken, as if it had been torn off."

"And the police never found the body?" I asked, knowing the answer and feeling cruel and foolish for posing the question.

The conversation has to appear natural. I had to ask that question.

"No," said Eli. "They never did." He chuckled lightly. "Don't take this the wrong way, but I don't know why I'm telling you this. I don't even know you. But for some reason —and please, don't think I'm crazy—I feel like I *do* know you. And I...oh, I don't know. I feel like I can tell you these things."

"It's not crazy at all," I said. "These are things you clearly needed to get off your chest. And I'm always willing to listen. I only hope you feel better now."

Eli stared at me for a moment. "You know what? I do."

The two of us grew silent as we heard Sarah's footsteps approaching. She sat back down at the table. Her eyes were red and slightly puffy.

"I apologize," she said. "I just...needed a moment."

"No apology needed. I'll try to make this as quick as possible. I understand how painful this is," I said, placing a sheaf of documents on the table before them. "As I explained over the phone, your parents had a number of offshore investments that did very well for them over the years."

"I still don't understand," said Sarah. "I don't remember Mom ever talking about any offshore investments."

"I've seen this sort of thing more than you might imagine," I said. "Quite often, there are assets that have been forgotten or that the heirs simply were never made aware of, for whatever reason. From what I've observed, your parents started investing aggressively shortly after marrying, and their portfolio grew to quite an impressive degree over the years."

I opened the sheaf of papers and produced a small packet.

"This is a summary of their current holdings. Cash only. Your mother and father had documents drafted that stated, upon their deaths, that their assets were to be liquidated and split equally among all their children. As you're their only child, all those assets go to you."

I handed the papers to Sarah. Eli scooted his chair over

and scanned them with her. Her hands trembled as she read, and she and Eli looked shocked. She dropped the documents as she tried to turn the page with a hand that was anything but steady. At last, she reached the final document.

"But this...this is..."

"Is this *right?*" asked Eli.

I nodded.

"But how...I don't understand. I don't think Dad made a lot of money before he disappeared, and Mom certainly didn't earn anything near enough to save this much."

"They invested very wisely. Their portfolio spans almost seven decades. Seventy years of growth can turn even a modest sum into a fortune."

"But nearly *thirty million dollars?*" Sarah said. "I...I don't get it. What did they invest in? And why wasn't any of this included in their will? The probate attorney we spoke with didn't mention this."

I shook my head. "I don't know why they chose two different legal firms to handle different assets after their deaths. Perhaps they wanted to be doubly sure that these funds remained separated from the rest."

"But why would they do that?" said Eli.

"You don't suppose..." said Sarah. "Could any of this money have been obtained illegally?"

I laughed. "Not at all. All the information about the investment firm they used is in those documents. I'm sure you'll recognize the name. A legitimate and well-respected company."

"I still...I just can't get my head around this," said Sarah.

"It's a little like winning the lottery, isn't it?" I said with a slight smile. "Hard to grasp when it happens. Not that I have any personal experience with that, but I can certainly imagine."

"Is there anything we need to do?" Eli asked.

"Sign a few documents," I said, "acknowledging receipt of the funds. Then do whatever you want. Keep the money where it is, wire it to another institution, buy a mansion in Paris. It's totally up to you."

I removed a few more papers from the folder and set them before Eli and Sarah. I withdrew a pen from my brief-case and passed it to Sarah, careful not to touch her.

She accepted it with a hand that still trembled, and signed her name. Eli followed suit.

This is more taxing than I would have imagined.

Though I relished every moment I was in Sarah's pres-ence, maintaining composure while trying to answer her and her husband's questions was exhausting.

"Wonderful," I said, pushing my feelings down. I collected the documents from them and placed them in my briefcase. "Would you like me to send you copies of these documents in the mail, or e-mail them to you?"

"E-mail, please," said Sarah.

I finished packing up my briefcase and was about to stand when pain lanced my arm, stealing my breath. Sarah had placed her hand upon my shoulder and was gazing into my eyes. I drew forth every iota of mental control I could, trying to shove the pain off to a distant place.

I almost didn't succeed.

Something was different about this pain. It didn't merely hurt—it was debilitating, and repulsive in a manner that I couldn't explain. Every instinct in my body told me to pull back from her and flee as far and fast as I could.

I stood my ground, maintaining my cool and meeting

her gaze while trying to keep my eyes off the Star of David around her neck.

It shone with a light so bright it was painful to behold. I couldn't understand why Sarah and Eli weren't shielding their eyes.

Maybe they can't see it.

The thought both intrigued and horrified me.

"Thank you," Sarah said softly. "Thank you so much. I wish we could have met under better circumstances. You seem so kind, almost familiar in a way. If I didn't know better, I could swear I've met you somewhere before."

I managed a smile. "I'm sure I would have remembered meeting a person as lovely as yourself."

Sarah returned my smile and released her hand from my shoulder.

The pain vanished instantly, and I nearly collapsed with relief. I stood quickly and took a step back from her, not far enough to seem odd, yet not close enough for her to readily grasp me again.

"Mr. Goodman..." Eli stood as well, extending a hand. I shook it vigorously. "It was a pleasure to meet you."

"The pleasure was mine," I said. "Now if you'll excuse me, it's getting late, and I'd like to get back to the office to make sure these documents are processed as soon as possible."

"Of course," said Sarah. "I'll show you out."

The moment the door closed behind me, the full weight of my despair crashed down upon me. My shoulders slumped as I walked slowly toward the street, and I wept silently, knowing I'd most likely never see Sarah again.

You did it, I told myself. *You went through with it, and you got to see her one last time.*

I turned and walked back the way I had come. Even after

I was out of sight, with absolutely no danger of detection should I choose to employ Shadow Travel, I didn't return to my home. I kept my glamour up, kept heading down the street. Despair was my companion, walking the lonely streets with me, reminding me of everything I had lost.

I never got to see her grow up. Never saw her first day at school. Never saw her drive a car for the first time or get married. Never saw my grandson as a baby, or as a young boy. Everything...gone.

In the past, it was times like these that turned me to God, to my faith. I found solace in reading the psalms; found comfort in those words, passed down through so many generations. Now I feared that such succor would never be mine again.

The Star of David...could that mugging have been staged? Could Adalina have set the whole thing up to get rid of the star and get close to me?

In light of everything I'd experienced, it seemed plausible. I mulled that over for a while, continuing to walk the cold, rainy streets alone. I glanced at the homes that lined each side of the suburban road. Most of them were older, though every so often a rebuild thrust itself out of its surroundings like a weed in a flower patch. I didn't care very much for the newer homes' architecture—too many curves for my taste.

After a few more miles, I found myself standing beside the wrought-iron fence of a cemetery. I gazed at the headstones, crouched like mischievous imps within the rain and darkness. Further down the sidewalk, I noticed a pair of gates beneath a stone archway. A tall, silver cross stood atop the arch.

I wonder...

I made my way slowly toward the gates. Like the star of

David, the cross appeared to gleam in the night, hurting my eyes. By the time I reached the archway, the cross's luminescence had grown to a point where I could no longer look directly at it. Slowly, hands trembling, I reached toward the gate's iron bars. I gently closed my fingers around one of them.

With a howl of pain, I leapt back, shaking my hand. Again, my instincts told me to flee, and I was filled with a terror not unlike what I'd experienced during my first sunrise. I forced myself to remain calm, to walk away slowly. Panic wouldn't do anyone any favors.

Religion doesn't matter. Faith is what hurts.

That much, at least, seemed clear—faith was the bane of my species; love and kindness their kryptonite. I wondered if I'd react the same way to a mosque or a Buddhist temple. My gut told me either of those things would prove just as painful.

But why? Why does faith, or the energy produced by faith, harm us? Is it somehow at odds with the energy we're capable of harnessing?

Thoughts of good and evil, light and dark, began swirling through my mind, and a new loathing for the thing I'd become twisted my insides. Rage boiled to the surface of my thoughts. Never again could I enter a synagogue, never again could I read or even touch the Torah.

It finally settled in that everything—*everything*—had been taken from me. David Levin was truly dead.

26

Radu couldn't understand why I did the things I did—that much was clear in how the man looked at me and the hesitation he sometimes showed when carrying out my instructions.

I really don't care, I thought, *as long as he remains faithful and does his job.*

Radu always did, unfailingly. Despite my strange financial requests, despite behavior that was no doubt completely at odds with everything Radu knew about my species, the man responded to my every whim without question.

So far, I had liquidated nearly 25 percent of my total assets, donating the money to charity. Radu had helped me without protest, making all the necessary arrangements.

I'm not done yet. I can still do more good, still help more people. All I need is time. Time to find the right causes, time to sell off the next batch of investments.

Time was something of which I had a great deal.

I was often reminded of this fact when the day's business had been concluded, when I'd fed, and when I had an endless expanse of *nothing* with which to occupy myself.

How do these creatures do it? How does the boredom of ever-lasting life not drive them insane?

Perhaps that was why Adalina had spent so much time amassing wealth and priceless treasures—it gave her something to do.

Couldn't I do something similar but in reverse? Couldn't I use my remaining assets to create charitable foundations? Homeless shelters? Organizations for the poor?

The notion intrigued me. Perhaps I was going about this all wrong. Perhaps rather than simply throwing money at charities, I could create my own self-funded charitable organizations.

As I pondered this, I felt Radu approaching.

"Yes, Radu?" I said, before the man even had a chance to knock. "You may enter."

"My lord," Radu said, stepping into the room and bowing low. "Lord Arsenios has arrived and wishes to see you at once."

Arsenios? What on earth could he be doing here?

"Please take me to him," I said.

As before, Arsenios waited for me in the receiving chamber, seated in the exact same spot, in front of the too-large fireplace.

"Lord Arsenios," I said, nodding. "Welcome back. What brings you to visit?"

Arsenios nodded in return, rising to his feet. He wore the same outfit as before—multicolored tunic and pointed shoes. His clothing rustled as he stood. "I've come to begin your preparations for the Convocation."

"I thought the Convocation was some time away yet."

Arsenios raised an eyebrow. "My boy, it's in less than a month."

Less than a month?

It seemed as if the two of us had just met in this room days ago. Had ten years really passed so quickly?

"Forgive me," I said. "Time has become...strange to me. It didn't seem like so much had passed since our last meeting."

Arsenios waved his hand nonchalantly. "Think nothing of it. The passage of time will take some getting used to. Your lifespan is now measured in millennia, not years. You could close your eyes and sleep for a century, and hardly notice it.

"Now, we need to talk a bit about what to expect." Arsenios walked toward the fireplace, admiring the large painting that hung above it. It was of an incredibly detailed forest, and was painted in deep greens and browns. I had always found that particular work to be quite calming. "You've had some time to get accustomed to your environment and to your new self," Arsenios continued, "but as yet, you haven't been expected to socialize with others of our kind. As you might imagine, decorum is quite important, and I won't have my grandchild making an ass of himself in the presence of the other Nobles."

"I'd appreciate any advice you can give me," I said.

"Politeness is key," said Arsenios, turning to face me. "Make eye contact. Be respectful. Shake their hands during introductions. Above all, keep the conversation light. Many will be curious about you and about the circumstances that led to Adalina's death. That's a family affair and no one else's business. Give no one any fuel for gossip.

"Your primary goal is to observe and to learn. You'll be the youngest there by far, and the others will know that. Make no suggestions, even when the Council opens the floor for discussion. Age carries great weight in our society, and one as young as you won't be taken seriously."

"Will the others be hostile toward me?"

"No, not hostile. But they'll regard you as a child, and they'll expect you to know your place. Let the adults lead the discussion, let them make whatever plans they see fit. It's seen as distasteful for the young and untested to try to take over the reins of leadership and planning."

A child? I'm nearly a century old! How old will I have to be to become an adult in their eyes?

"What exactly do you mean by 'untested'?" I asked, choosing to keep my thoughts to myself.

"I mean," said Arsenios, "that no one has had a chance to see how you'll lead your house. What feats will you accomplish? Will you be a titan of business like Adalina, or will you excel at the sciences, like some of our esteemed brethren? Or will your victories be more militaristic and political in nature, as mine have been?"

I was intrigued. "What kind of military victories are you talking about?"

Arsenios smiled, and I swore that his chest puffed out just a bit.

"I've evened the odds of many battles in which there would have been great bloodshed, and stopped some conflicts before they started. Without me, the Cuban missile crisis would have resulted in World War III. I've also influenced the lives and decisions of more government officials than I can count. I've helped preserve humanity through the channel that serves as the race's primary means of expression: violence."

I frowned. "I'm confused. How does violence help *preserve* the lives of humans?"

"Humans are like any other animal," Arsenios explained. "They fight among themselves, quite brutally, at the slightest provocation. Military action among their species in inevitable. There will be wars, some of them cataclysmic. I mitigate the losses by ensuring no one side ever becomes powerful enough to do significant damage."

"But there have been countless wars where one side dominates the other."

"Yes," said Arsenios, "but look at the end result. The human population is now at roughly thirteen billion, and will continue to grow."

I felt my eyes grow wide. "Thirteen *billion?*"

Arsenios tossed his head back and laughed. "You really must pay more attention to current events! I know it's easy to become absorbed in one's household duties, but you need to avoid becoming a hermit. Take some time to follow what's going on in the outside world."

"I suppose I should," I said.

"At any rate," Arsenios continued, "you have to strike a balance with their kind—they're inherently vicious creatures who would go insane if they couldn't fight their silly wars. I help ensure the conflicts are measured—never resulting in enough casualties to threaten the race but allowing a clear victor to emerge. Without my aid, I imagine the humans would have incinerated the entire planet by now."

"Has your influence really been that profound?" I asked.

"It most certainly has."

"Why not use it to end the conflicts entirely? Wouldn't we be best served if the humans didn't kill each other at all?"

Arsenios shook his head. "My boy, didn't you hear what I just said? These creatures *need* violence. They thrive on it. When you're caring for livestock, you need to make sure their most base needs are met, while still ensuring the health of the herd. Eliminating their ability to kill one another would be psychologically damaging to the species and could have far-reaching consequences."

I couldn't believe what I was hearing.

Is that really how these creatures view humans? I thought. *As nothing more than livestock? And they have the* audacity *to accuse humans of barbarism and violence when their very act of "parenting" involves horrific torture?*

"We've developed systems over time," Arsenios continued, pacing slowly before the fireplace, "that have allowed the humans' petty conflicts to play out while still maintaining a healthy population."

"I see," I said, trying not to let my anger show. "Quite impressive."

Arsenios beamed. "I'm proud of what I've been able to do in order to aid in our race's survival. You'll no doubt experience a similar sense of pride once you find your own calling."

"I can only hope that when that day comes, I'm half as successful as you have been," I said.

"I don't doubt you will be. You are my grandson, after all."

"Tell me," I said, "what else should I expect from this Convocation? Should I prepare for an assault or violence of any kind—perhaps from a former friend of Adalina's?"

"As I said earlier," said Arsenios, "we don't kill our own. Murder among our kind is a ghastly offense and simply isn't tolerated. The only exception is when a parent loses their way and doesn't heed the direction in which their offspring is headed."

"That, or when an offspring fails to develop properly," I said quietly.

Arsenios nodded. "That too."

Maybe I should give these creatures a little credit. As

wretched as they are, at least they've figured out how to eliminate murder among their own kind.

"You've hinted in the past that murder was once an issue among the Nobles," I said. "How big of an issue was it? Did murder really happen all that often?"

Arsenios nodded. "Long ago, in my youth, it was a plague among us. In those days, Lords and Ladies fought for power and prestige, engaging in petty duels over matters of little consequence. Eventually we realized that for our race to survive, such ridiculous skirmishes needed to be stamped out. And so they were. Too many Nobles—my father included—fell victim to such nonsense."

"Have Nobles ever been responsible for human wars?"

Arsenios sighed. "A few unsavory types have deliberately stirred up conflict in a rival's territory, but this sort of behavior is frowned upon and doesn't happen often. There is no prohibition against it, however, as the Nobles involved never actually harm one another."

Of course not, I thought. *Only the poor humans, who had nothing to do with the original dispute, are the ones who wind up suffering and dying.*

"Enough of such matters," said Arsenios. "I must ask—have you chosen a name for yourself? It seems unfitting that I continue to address you by the name Adalina gave you."

"I have chosen," I said. "My choice is to keep the name I've been given."

Arsenios frowned. "I'm confused. Given by whom?"

"By Adalina. I've chosen to keep the name Dragos."

Arsenios abruptly stopped pacing, and looked as if he'd just swallowed animal blood. "You can't be serious. Dragos is your *pet* name. Such names are given to children without land or titles. You're the head of a great house, master of the Northeastern Realm, not some half-formed whelp."

"I'm quite serious," I said. "That's my choice. Dragos is all I've ever been, all I've ever known. Pet name or not, it suits me. Particularly considering my mother's desire to hoard wealth, a pursuit I'm inclined to follow in my own way."

"I see," said Arsenios. "But there are many names that convey a sense of wealth."

"I can think of none better than 'Dragon.' Power. Hunger. Wealth. All embodied in a single name: Dragos."

Arsenios seemed thoughtful. "I suppose...I can see the allure. If only Adalina hadn't given you that name."

"That doesn't concern me. I'm happy with the name. Why should anything else matter?"

"It will stir up controversy and gossip," said Arsenios. "A race that lives for eternity has ample time to spread rumors and talk behind one another's backs."

"Again," I said, "such things don't concern me. I merely wish to live here quietly, to feed when I'm hungry, and to acquire more wealth."

"Noble goals, all. I just wish you'd reconsider the name."

"I'm very sorry, but the matter is closed," I said as gently as I could manage. "I'm keeping the name."

Arsenios remained silent, staring at me. "Your resolution is strong," he said at last. "It emanates from you, filling this entire room to the brim. It's as strong a will as I've ever felt. Adalina..." He chuckled. "She wouldn't have stood a chance. Foolish woman."

He was quiet for a moment longer, still gazing at me. "Keep the name," he said. "You'll get no more argument from me."

I was a bit surprised to hear him relent. "Thank you, Arsenios. I appreciate your understanding."

"When someone believes in something as strongly as

you do," Arsenios said with a slight grin, "it's futile to argue with them." He clapped me on the shoulder. "You'll do fine at the Convocation. Just fine. Some of the other Nobles..." He laughed. "Let's just say there are a few haughty gossip-mongers that I'd *dearly* like for you to meet."

I caught a slightly sadistic glint in Arsenios's eye, and I grinned in return.

"I won't disappoint," I said.

27

The rest of the month passed quickly. I fed when needed, and attended a few meetings that Radu had on my agenda, one with a squirrelly little man who served as my liaison with the board of directors at a large telecoms company, and one with a snobby and abrasive woman who represented my interests in an international law firm. Above all, I tried to spend less time pacing and incinerating furniture.

I slid into a finely tailored black suit—one that Radu had selected especially for the Convocation. Arsenios would arrive soon, as the two of us planned to attend the Convocation together. As I gazed at myself in the mirror, my thoughts turned to my daughter yet again. I took solace in the fact that Sarah and Eli would spend their remaining years on earth in lavish comfort. Though it was better than nothing, it couldn't erase my pain at having been torn away from my daughter.

I could have given her so much. I could have given her everything I have.

Even before, when my emotions regarding the matter

had run nearly out of control, I knew that to have given more would have been folly. Thirty million dollars was more than enough to arouse suspicion and cause a host of potential problems for Sarah and her husband. Had I given more, I would have risked exposing myself or having the wrong people interested in where all that money really came from.

You gave what you could, and Sarah can live a life befitting the meaning of her name – princess - for the rest of her days.

I knew I should feel relief at that, but in my present state of mind, relief seemed impossible. Worst of all, I had nowhere to turn. Although Radu was a wonderful administrator, I couldn't imagine him understanding the hell I was going through.

And Arsenios? Completely out of the question. He can never know that I remember my former life. No one can.

My memories of who I had been remained strong. Deep down, I knew they'd never fade the same way they did with Arsenios and the rest of our kind. A part of me would remain forever ensconced in humanity.

And that's my greatest strength. At least I still remember who I was. At least I still feel compassion and love.

I often wondered why my memories didn't fade, while the memories of all the others did. Arsenios had referred to those who remembered their pasts as freaks, crippled in a way that would render them useless as additions to the species. I wished that I could ask Arsenios about what it might mean that my memories remained intact, but I knew that would be suicide. Arsenios had made it perfectly clear that those who remembered were systematically terminated.

Clearly I'm far from crippled, though. I may remember who I was, but I'm still strong.

Was my condition a fluke? Or were there others who remembered their pasts and also possessed great strength?

Perhaps others like me have existed before and exist now. Perhaps, even with their strength, they still couldn't overcome their masters.

I came back to that notion often. How would I have fared if a creature as old and powerful as Arsenios had been my master? Adalina had been strong; there was no mistaking that. Arsenios was significantly stronger, though, and I would have wagered there were others of our kind who were even more powerful than him. I had barely beaten Adalina. If Arsenios had been the one, instead of her...

I preferred not to follow that line of thinking.

Whatever the reason, I was there, as powerful as any my age, yet in full possession of my human faculties. Though I hated what I was, I was forever grateful that I hadn't lost the ability to recall the joy of my former life. That alone kept insanity at bay.

"My lord," came Radu's voice, snapping me out of my reverie. "It's time."

I nodded, following him down the hall. Arsenios was in the audience chamber, waiting for us.

"Shall we?" he said when I entered.

"Lead the way."

Arsenios faced the same shadowy corner he'd used on the first day he'd come to visit, and in an instant he was gone. I reached out with my senses, thrusting myself into the shadows. I felt Arsenios's distinctive psychic imprint among the filaments and easily tracked him to the one he'd used. I pushed myself further, entering the pathway, and suddenly I no longer stood in my audience chamber.

The place where I now stood was far grander, lavish on a scale that would have put Adalina to shame. The room was high and airy, with marble columns supporting a domed ceiling that bore a striking fresco of the heavens as seen from deep space. Spiral galaxies and celestial bodies peppered the ceiling from one end to the other, imparting the illusion that the room was open to the night sky.

The walls were filled with priceless works of art, and I recognized more than a few of them.

The Mona Lisa. The Starry Night. The Birth of Venus. They're all here.

I touched Arsenios's arm, and the older man regarded me.

"Are all of these paintings *real*?"

Arsenios grinned. "They are."

"I thought all of these were in museums."

"The museums own only fabrications, very cleverly replicated," said Arsenios. "The Nobility possesses the most priceless treasures on earth. Works of art, original literature, technology beyond the understanding of humans—these things belong to us, just like everything else on this planet."

"But why collect human art? Doesn't the Nobility have any artists of its own?"

"The creation of art is not something we excel at," Arsenios said, walking slowly forward. "It's seen as a baser practice, one best left to the humans. For all of their imperfections, no one can argue with the fact that humans are capable of creating great beauty, on rare occasions."

I was silent, and I could hear the faint sounds of a classical orchestra and the distant hum of conversation.

A Servant in fine livery greeted us almost immediately. He looked much as Radu and the other Servants did—disproportionate, strangely twisted, barely human. He inclined his head.

"I bid you welcome and good evening, my masters," he said in a strangely high voice. "Please come this way."

The Servant strode toward a grand hallway, lined on both sides with paintings and statuary. Arsenios and I followed. Arsenios seemed perfectly at ease, looking straight ahead, not varying his gait in the slightest. I, on the other hand, was spellbound. The artistry that surrounded me had, in my time, been regarded as some of the greatest on earth, and it took tremendous effort not to stop every few steps to admire some new masterpiece.

The hall curved to the left and eventually opened into yet another high-ceilinged chamber. Every bit as opulently appointed as the first, this room was also quite a bit larger— at least two or three times the size.

And it was filled with pale-skinned, yellow-eyed creatures. Some of them turned to peer at us as we entered. I was overwhelmed. I *felt* their power; felt the force of their combined will, of their probing, grasping perceptions—so many minds slithering over and under one another like vipers in a pit. I gritted my teeth and strengthened my resolve.

Too much...it's too much.

The air hummed with psychic activity, and I did everything I could to turn my perceptions inward.

Arsenios glanced at me. "You'll get used to it," he said. "Your mind will learn to filter it all out."

I feel like an overstimulated toddler in a crowded room, I thought.

I pushed my discomfort aside, trying instead to focus on the physical. Right away I noticed that every creature before me looked remarkably similar: pale skin, dark hair, yellow eyes. Despite this, there were subtle differences between them. For one, their skin tones encompassed a wide *range* of pale, a concept that would have been unthinkable to me before that moment.

And there was no rhyme or reason to the clothing most of them wore. In my entire life, I had never seen such a variation in fashion within a single group of people. It wasn't simply that each individual seemed to prefer their own distinct style; it was as if each creature present seemed to prefer a distinct *time period*. There was me, wearing a sleek and modern black suit. There was Arsenios, wearing the clothing of a Byzantine Noble. Across the room was a small group, dressed in what appeared to be the frilly costumes and powdered wigs of sixteenth-century European aristocrats. Not far from us, a bearded man stood alone, dressed in a simple white toga and leather sandals. Everywhere I looked, I saw outfits from a different period in human history.

"They're all dressed so differently from each other," I murmured.

Arsenios shrugged. "Everyone has their own particular tastes. For the most part, we tend to stick with what we know best."

Before I could respond, I felt a new presence approach.

I must be getting better at this, if I picked that out among everything else.

Moments later, a tall man stood before us. He was bald and wore a striking apricot-colored robe, embroidered with elaborate dragon patterns. He held a thin, silver leash in his left hand.

A bewildered-looking woman—a human woman—stood beside him, dressed in the rags of what appeared to have once been a fine evening gown. She was quite a bit shorter than the man, and her long, black hair was tousled and matted. The leash was fastened to a black leather collar secured tightly around her neck. I frowned and chanced a brief extension of my perceptions. What I felt from the woman puzzled me—there was a certain power there beyond what I would expect from a human, but it seemed somehow incomplete. I also smelled her blood—her heart was still beating; blood still ran in her veins.

And she was afraid. *Terrified* would have been an even better description. Her consciousness was obscured by a thick cloud of fear, one that I was surprised I hadn't smelled right away. Immediately, I felt a deep pity for the woman before me.

"Lord Chin," said Arsenios, nodding.

"Lord Arsenios."

Lord Chin gave me a somewhat disinterested glance before returning his gaze to Arsenios. "I see we have a newcomer. Your lineage?"

"Of course," said Arsenios. "He belonged to Adalina."

"And where is Lady Adalina this evening? I wouldn't have thought she'd miss the opportunity to show off a new creation."

"Dead," said Arsenios.

Lord Chin raised his eyebrows. His gaze returned to me, more appraising this time. The hair on my arms suddenly stood at attention as a foreign presence slipped past my defenses, probing me in a way that was wholly unpleasant. I grimaced slightly as I refocused my efforts, gathering my will. I seized the invasive presence and cast it out, re-forging my mental defenses in a way I felt would be effective in repelling another such invasion.

Although Lord Chin's expression was unreadable, I caught a brief whiff of something in the air.

Uneasiness?

"He's very young still," said Lord Chin.

"Indeed," said Arsenios, with a mild twinkle in his eyes. "But I believe he'll mature quickly."

I noticed that the leashed woman now gazed at me with an intensity bordering on hysteria. Now there was no mistaking the odor of her fear. It radiated from her in a way that made me uneasy. I averted my eyes, not wanting to cause her any more discomfort.

Lord Chin harshly jerked the leash, eliciting a yelp from the woman.

"It's impolite to stare, Gou."

The woman shrank away from him, staring at the floor.

"You'll have to excuse her," said Lord Chin, addressing Arsenios. "She's untrained yet. I considered not bringing her along, but...what can I say? I do so *love* my pets."

A spark of rage kindled in my breast. How could this *thing* treat a human being as if she were an animal?

Because to him, she is an animal. She's a pet, to be enjoyed or tormented on a whim. And one day, perhaps she'll destroy him.

That thought gave me a tremendous sense of satisfaction, and I couldn't stop a grin from spreading across my face.

"What are you smirking at, boy?" Lord Chin said. "Do I amuse you?"

"Not at all," I said, meeting his steely gaze.

"Perhaps your mother never had a chance to teach you manners. It's impolite to leer at your superiors."

"Lord Arsenios has done well in teaching me how to give proper respect when it's due."

"It seems Lord Arsenios is a poor mentor," Lord Chin said. "Perhaps he's too involved in his usual petty political scheming to see to your tutelage."

"What Lord Arsenios does in his spare time is none of my business," I said. "I have found him to be an apt teacher where matters of court and courtesy are concerned."

I glanced sidelong at Arsenios, and could have sworn from the apparent tightness of his shoulders that he was fighting to contain laughter.

Lord Chin sniffed. "I do so miss the days when duels weren't frowned upon. It gave the better members of our society the chance to teach respect to those who needed the lesson."

"Sounds like hell," I said. "It seems to me that things are better off now."

Lord Chin glared at me, saying nothing. He turned to Arsenios. "It has been...pleasant, Lord Arsenios. Unfortunately, there are some *important* Nobles with whom I must discuss some urgent business. I bid you good evening."

Arsenios inclined his head ever so slightly.

Lord Chin sauntered away, and I glared after him.

"That went well. Very, *very* well," said Arsenios.

I gazed at him. A wide grin had spread across his face, and there was no mistaking the twinkling in those pale-yellow eyes.

"Was he one of the Nobles you wanted me to meet?"

"*The* Noble I wanted you to meet."

My anger rose again as Lord Chin snaked his way through groups of conversing lords and ladies while pulling the woman, Gou, behind him.

"I take it that man has some sort of personal problem with you," I said.

"He and I had a rather unpleasant disagreement a few centuries ago, and Lord Chin has always been the type to bear grudges."

I leaned in closer to Arsenios. "What happened, if you don't mind my asking?"

"I'd spent decades trying to ease tensions between the Ming and Qing dynasties of China. Lord Chin, who'd grown displeased with a Noble whose lands and business interests were closely tied with the Ming, decided to undo years of careful planning and stir up a war. The result was the Manchu conquest of China, in which tens of millions of humans died."

"I see," said Dragos. "Frowned upon, but not prohibited."

Arsenios nodded. "In that particular case, though, too many human lives were lost. I brought the attention of what he'd done to the council, and so many of the others agreed with me that Lord Chin's standing among us suffered considerably. He's never forgiven me for that."

I continued to peer around the room, allowing just a bit of the mental chaos around me to sneak in through my barriers. I was beginning to see what Arsenios had meant and could almost separate out individual patterns of thought within the swirling miasma. Underneath it all was a great humming, an undercurrent of sorts that pervaded the entire collection of individual voices. For a moment, I assumed it was simply background noise, echoes of all the personalities that were present.

No. It's not background noise. This is...unique.

I frowned as I studied it, daring to open my perceptions a bit wider, trying to ascertain its source. I traced it to the far end of the room, to a point that was obscured beyond the masses of Nobles.

"Arsenios," I said, "would you walk with me?"

Arsenios nodded, following me across the room. The man paused here and there, exchanging brief pleasantries as we traversed the space. As we moved, I made out individual snatches of conversation here and there.

"...cut their tongues out. They always regrow them when they're fully turned, and it reduces back talk..."

"I've always preferred women. Their bodies are more flexible. Human males break far too easily..."

Every step I took—every moment in that place—made me more disgusted, stoking the fires of my rage.

"...mutilated the whole family. My father always told me not to play with my food, but the woman's screams were so amusing that I just couldn't..."

I gnashed my teeth, trying, unsuccessfully, to tune out the voices around me. Seemingly every conversation that floated my way dealt with the sickest horrors imaginable, wrought from imaginations so unabashedly sinister that it turned my insides to ice.

These creatures...these repulsive things. My God, this is my family now. My race. I'm one of them.

I was so distressed by the thought that I almost didn't notice the crowd thinning out near the edge of the room. As I forced my emotions down, trying desperately to maintain calm, I noticed several figures seated against the wall. They were all silent and sat perfectly still. Though there were six of them all told, my attention immediately zeroed in on the one at the center.

His dark hair and beard were long—both were cut to roughly the same length, trailing down to his chest. He wore what appeared to be animal hides, and his feet were bare, covered with coarse black hair. Though his manner of dress was surprising, the man's aura was shocking.

The deep undercurrent of power that coursed throughout our surroundings unquestionably came from him. So great was the force of will behind his presence that it could have easily eclipsed all others in the room. There was power there, to be sure, but there was also incalculable age. I felt insignificant, like a mosquito before a tornado.

I averted my eyes, not wishing to offend the man by staring.

"Who is *that*?" I asked quietly.

"The Progenitor," said Arsenios, with an unmistakable tone of reverence. "The first."

"The first...like us?"

Arsenios nodded. "All of us—you, me, Lord Chin, everyone here—are of his lineage."

I pondered that for a moment. I supposed that all species could be traced back *somewhere*; I'd just never fathomed the possibility that my kind's origin was alive and well, sitting in a corner at the very event we now attended.

"How old, I wonder..." I trailed off.

"Older than humanity," said Arsenios. "At least, that's the general consensus. It's rumored that he came from the stars."

"The stars?" I asked, incredulous. "You mean to tell me that he's some kind of extraterrestrial?"

Arsenios shrugged. "The eldest among us insist that he came from...someplace else. Another planet, most likely, or perhaps from an entirely different dimension. It's rumored that his human appearance is just a glamour, but if it is, it's not one that I've ever been able to detect. No one knows exactly what he is, and no one that I know of has ever had the courage to ask him. I've personally never heard him speak at all."

If he's not human—and never was—what does that make all of us?

I pondered the implications of that as I glanced back at the six men. All of them were dressed like the Progenitor, though none of the others bore the same hallmarks of age and power. That wasn't to say there was no power there—indeed, some of the individuals with whom the man sat emitted an aura that greatly rivaled that of Arsenios.

"What about the others?" I said.

"His children. Some of them are quite old as well, though none nearly as old as he."

"Why does he have so many?"

Arsenios shrugged. "It's always been that way. The Progenitor deigns to keep multiple children close at hand. Though I recognize most of them, there are a few new faces."

"I see. Why do his children remain with him, while others of our kind go off on their own?"

"Things are...different with the Progenitor. He doesn't always follow the same societal norms as the rest of us, nor should he have to. At his age, and with his power, he can do as he pleases."

The Progenitor. All of this—the cruelty, the unfairness, the torture—it all started with him.

I pushed my anger down. I knew there would be deadly consequences if this man had any inkling as to my true nature—of my memories, of my self-hatred, of my desire to return to humanity.

Keep calm. Stay silent. Your rage can wait.

"I feel his power," I said. "It's hard to believe that kind of force can come from one man."

"It's rather impressive, isn't it?" said Arsenios. "Now come. There's someone else I'd like you to meet."

Before Arsenios had taken a step, I noticed the nearby lords and ladies glancing in my direction, nudging one another, speaking in hushed tones.

A sudden movement caught my eye, and I spun about.

The Progenitor had stood and was walking slowly forward.

Toward Arsenios and me.

The room fell eerily silent. Not a single person moved, and no one uttered a word. Only the music continued, piped in from some cleverly hidden sound system.

I felt, more than saw, the man walking. The foundations of the earth beneath him seemed to rumble, as if a mountain trundled forward. Although terror threatened to rise up and take over, I forced it down.

Calm. Remain calm.

The Progenitor continued forward until he stood an arm's length in front of me. He ignored Arsenios and all others in the room, staring directly at me with deep, golden eyes.

The man spoke, and his voice alone seemed to carry the weight of eons behind it.

"You smell wrong."

His accent was unlike anything I had ever heard, and I almost didn't understand what the man had said. Before I had a chance to respond or question the words, the Progenitor slowly turned and headed back the way he'd come. He resumed sitting, gazing straight ahead.

Instantly the room was abuzz with the hiss of uneasy conversation. Even Arsenios seemed tense.

"Well," Arsenios said quietly, "that was a first. Why don't we just head in the opposite direction?"

I quickly nodded, and we crossed the room, going back the way we'd come. Before, it had been somewhat difficult to traverse through the tight groups of lords and ladies that spanned the chamber from one end to the other. Now, however, it was easy; no one seemed to want to get too close to either of us, and we were granted a fairly wide berth.

We stopped when we were back near the entrance.

"What was that about?" I said.

"No idea," said Arsenios. "I always thought the earth would end before that man ever uttered a word."

"What did he mean when he said I smell wrong?"

"One can only guess. You smell fine to me."

I grunted. "His opinion doesn't concern me. Nor does Lord Chin's or anyone else's. Except perhaps yours."

I was surprised to hear myself speak the words, but I'd found that somehow, Arsenios had grown on me. Perhaps it was the result of loneliness and the fact that he was the closest thing I had to family. Maybe it was because I was genuinely beginning to appreciate the guidance he was providing me.

Arsenios smiled gently. "Once this night is over, their opinions won't matter. Not until the next Convocation, two hundred years from now. You don't ever need to interact with any of them before then, if you so choose."

I sighed. "I don't wish to dishonor you or cause rumors that your lineage is somehow flawed."

Arsenios waved the comment away. "My detractors will hate me no matter what happens. As for the others, time will bring them around. Run your house as Adalina did, and a millennium from now, no one will even remember the Progenitor's words. Remember, in their eyes you're still a child. You may not have their respect yet, but you'll also be given more leeway than a fully mature Noble."

"Thank you, Arsenios," I said. "Your advice brings me comfort."

"I always do what I can for my line."

For the rest of the night, the two of us avoided conversation with others—or rather, conversation avoided us. Arsenios did engage the occasional lord or lady in small talk, though the exchange was always brief and was typically terminated by the other party. I remained silent, trying to tune out the Nobles' remarks about their gruesome deeds and wishing to return home before my anger got the better of me.

Sometime later, the music abruptly ceased. As the music died, so did the conversation.

"What's happening?" I whispered.

"The conclusion of the Convocation," Arsenios explained. "The Council will appear and bring to light any new business. Then the floor will open for discussion and debate."

I sensed them coming before I heard their footfalls. Seven individuals, all bearing the distinct mental imprint of a Servant. I smelled their tainted blood as they entered, and I stepped aside along with the other Lords and Ladies as the creatures walked slowly past.

Other Servants appeared on either side of the chamber, rolling several large, flat structures to the far side of the room. The structures fit together to form an elevated stage, roughly five feet off the ground. One by one, the council members climbed up and stood to face the chamber. The tallest one, a stoop-shouldered male with facial features so distorted he seemed more animal than man, stepped forward and raised his arms before addressing the room.

"We bid you welcome to the two hundred ninety-first Convocation." His voice was quite clear and articulate, considering the way he looked. "The Council will discuss each business matter then open the floor for input on each item."

I listened as each council member rattled off issue after issue for the Lords and Ladies to discuss. Funding for scientific experiments to enhance the longevity of Servants.

Concerns about parts of the world where major conflict seemed imminent. Whether or not to increase the ration of Servants for each house. Each of these points brought opposing views from different quarters, and at times the discussion grew heated. There was one thing, however, that I found surprising: in all cases, a consensus was eventually reached. The Lords and Ladies who had something to say made their cases, debated, and conceded when it became clear which path would best service their race. Then they simply moved on to the next issue, with none of the grumbling or posturing I would have expected.

If humans possessed a tenth of this ability to resolve their own differences...

I stopped that thought before it had a chance to go any further. I would *not* give these creatures that kind of credit.

After several hours, the final council member, a petite female with overly large teeth—even for a Servant—brought up the last item of business: human cultivation. Should the Nobles covertly introduce genetic enhancements in unborn fetuses to increase blood production and bolster their immune systems, or should humanity be left to develop on its own?

The debate for this item was especially heated, and I gleaned that it was an issue that had arisen before. From what the people around me said, this was one of the rare items that had never before gained consensus among the Nobility. As the debate continued, I grew more horrified by the minute. These *things* were discussing the natural evolutionary process of humanity as if it were nothing more than some kind of agricultural cycle. And there also was serious consideration of secretly invading the bodies of countless pregnant women in order to perform these experiments on them.

My rage, so tightly controlled, blossomed anew. It tested me to my limits, straining the bonds of my mental discipline. My jaw tightened to the point where I thought my teeth might shatter, and I felt the familiar fire racing through my dead, dry veins.

Arsenios raised his arm, signaling he wished to take the floor.

"My brothers and sisters," he said, "this issue has been discussed at length many times before. We reach the same conclusion each time. I move for final dismissal of this issue."

I saw another hand shoot up abruptly at that. Lord Chin weaved his way through the crowd, dragging a terrified Gou behind him.

"Rebuttal," he barked, lowering his hand and fixing Arsenios with an unwavering gaze. "This issue has still not been fully debated. Many of us still want this plan to move forward."

Arsenios frowned. "Tell me, Lord Chin, what you have to say that hasn't already been addressed? There is no scientific proof that these proposed enhancements are warranted. Under our guidance humanity has thrived. Frankly, we have more food than we know what to do with."

"Some would argue that humanity has thrived too well," said Chin, his golden eyes flashing. "At this rate, humans will soon be too numerous for the planet to support. We must prepare ourselves for the possibility of a mass extinction, when every remaining human will need to be optimized to meet our needs."

Arsenios laughed. "Extinction? You speak of extinction at a time when humanity has entered its golden age. War is nearly nonexistent. The environment has begun to recover. Human medical science has reached levels never before seen. There is no basis for your position that a mass extinction is a concern."

Chin glowered at Arsenios, hands on his hips, reminding me of an angry child. "You mark my words, Arsenios. One day you'll be wrong, and I plan to see that we don't all die because of it."

Arsenios waved the comment away. "I move again that we dismiss the issue. This argument is going nowhere. Provide me with compelling evidence, and you might change my mind."

Another Noble raised her hand, at which point Arsenios and Chin yielded the floor. Chin never took his gaze from Arsenios, and his eyes shined with rage.

As the debate carried on, my anger grew beyond my control. Though grateful that Arsenios had taken a position against this abhorrent idea, I could not get past the fact that many present seriously considered the plan to be valid. I abruptly turned and began to leave the room.

"Dragos!" Arsenios whispered, catching up to me. "What are you doing?"

"I've heard enough," I said, trying to keep the venom from my voice. "My opinion means nothing here anyway, and I refuse to listen to a conversation in which I have no say."

"I know this is a contentious issue," said Arsenios. "And I'm certain you have an opinion on it. But you're violating decorum. No one leaves before business is concluded. I can forgive you for everything that's happened so far tonight, but not this. Leaving now would be viewed as a tremendous sign of disrespect."

I stopped at that, forcing my bitterness down and meeting Arsenios's gaze. "I'm sorry, my friend. I never meant you any harm or dishonor. But I simply can't stay here any longer."

I continued through the crowd and out into the hall, leaving Arsenios behind. A tiny part of me felt bad about putting Arsenios in such an awkward position, but I knew that in the end such things wouldn't matter in the slightest.

Because I'm going to kill them all.

This would be my life's sole purpose. Thoughts of the Nobility's destruction would drive me, keeping the insanity of eternal boredom at bay. I would cleanse the earth of their kind, eliminating their stain from the world forever.

And I'll start with that bastard Chin.

28

Years passed as if they were days. No one came to visit—Arsenios hadn't appeared since the night of the Convocation, yet I was far too busy to grow bored or lonely. I filled my days with study and research, trying to conceive of a way to find and kill a noble. No clear strategy emerged, despite my best efforts. I had no idea how to track them; they all seemed incredibly adept at concealment, and every lead I followed turned up blank.

Frustrated, I put my pursuit of vengeance on hold, and turned my attention to the management of my ever-growing charitable enterprises.

So far I had set up three self-funding organizations; all profits from my various businesses went straight to causes I deemed worthy—aid for the homeless, assistance for struggling families, and cancer research were among my favorite endeavors. Gone were the underground dealings with human traffickers and the blood money of organized crime. I'd given Radu explicit instructions to phase out all illegal, corrupt, or unethical business dealings.

Ever the faithful servant, Radu had complied.

When I wasn't managing my money, I was experimenting with my abilities. Shadow Travel in particular fascinated me, and I spent days at a time Traveling all over the world, testing new filaments, sniffing at the void from which each road spun. Today, I'd visited Venice, walking about St. Mark's square, nearly silent in the dead of night. I was amazed at how little had changed since the last time I'd visited on a trip with my parents in high school.

Technology hasn't touched this place at all, I'd thought.

New York had been a different story. I'd gone the previous evening to admire the Statue of Liberty, and was shocked to see just how much the skyline had changed. Several new buildings had sprung up, bearing the distinctive curved lines of modern architecture. Covered in solar cells from top to bottom, they reflected the moonlight brilliantly, and I was loath to admit that I spent more time gazing at them than at the statue I'd originally gone to see.

It was during another of my trips abroad that I made a discovery that changed my life.

"RADU," I said.

Radu inclined his head, standing just inside the door to my bedchamber, awaiting my words.

"I'm departing to travel abroad. I'm not sure how long I'll be gone."

Radu nodded. "As always, my lord, I'll keep your house in good order until you return."

"I'll be back before the next board meeting with the Cancer Society of the Americas," I said. "Please instruct my contact to take greater care when timing his visits with me. The last one lasted nearly until sunrise."

"I will inform him."

"Thank you, Radu. I'm off then."

Without another word, I peered into the deep shadows in the corner of the chamber and plunged in. I had no particular destination in mind. I followed the longest filament I could find, stretching out my perceptions, getting a sense of where it went.

Lots of snow. And cold.

Though I no longer truly experienced the cold, I was in no mood for snow that night, so I chose another route.

Warmer but rainy. Foggy and misty.

Not quite what I had in mind. Besides, with the way the end of that path blazed before me, almost painfully, I knew it was midday wherever it led.

Another, then.

I extended my mind, feeling for something...clearer. And darker.

I found it.

As I entered the filament, I was instantly aware of a very strange sensation; the psychic cord upon which I Traveled seemed to vibrate with an unseen power. It reminded me of the filament I'd followed when Arsenios had first shown me how to Travel.

Can it be?

I followed it to its end, emerging in a dark field. The sky was clear, and the stars shined brightly. I sensed humanity off in the distance, and...something else. Strong energy, totally different from that of a human or animal.

A Lord or a Lady.

The creature wasn't far off and wasn't yet aware of me.

How was I able to sense them?

There was no mistaking it—the strange psychic vibration I'd felt had been the imprint of this creature, left over from their Travel. Never before had I felt another Noble's energy while traversing the filaments.

Why now?

Perhaps my abilities were still maturing, and my strength had increased to a point where detecting another traveler was now possible. Whatever the reason, I tried to contain my excitement as I quietly folded myself back into the shadows.

As I headed home, a new possibility bloomed in my consciousness. What if each of us had our own unique signature, our own resonance, like a fingerprint?

If that were the case, no Noble on earth would be safe from me.

———————

I STUDIED the pool of shadow that sat in the corner of my audience chamber. It was the very same spot Arsenios had used to initiate Shadow Travel both times he'd come to visit. I extended my perceptions, probing about the shadows, peeking into the darkness at the filaments that lay beyond. I could sense myself quite strongly, and...

There it was.

Another energy signature, extremely faint, that wasn't my own.

I focused on it, wrapping my senses around it, forming a picture of Arsenios in my mind all the while, trying to recall exactly how the man's energy had felt to me.

Moments later, I had it. The trail was indeed Arsenios's; I knew it beyond a doubt. I withdrew from the shadows and headed to my personal chambers.

I need time to experiment. To plan. No one can know what I'm doing—not even Radu.

The murder of another Noble seemed to be the only thing—besides the discovery that I remembered my past—that would garner a severe punishment from my peers. If I meant to go through with it, I'd need to be cautious. I would have to figure out a way to cover my tracks, to erase every trace of myself from not only the filaments but also whatever surroundings I happened to frequent during my travels.

It had to be possible. I knew it in my gut. Besides, something Arsenios had said the first time we'd met, when he had first shown me how to Travel, suggested that such a thing could be done: *I won't shield my essence from you.*

There *had* to be a way to conceal my energy, to stop it from rubbing off on whatever I touched. Whatever the technique was, it continued to elude me. I at first attempted to contain my energy through strict concentration, but I quickly found that one could no more meditate their fingerprints away than they could focus away their psychic imprint.

Exasperated, I turned to researching and planning. I'd need to know everything I could about Lord Chin—where the man lived, how many Servants he had, and if he had any fully formed children living with him who might be strong enough to pose a threat. I also needed a backup plan, a means to disappear quickly, if my assassination attempt failed.

If my acts are discovered, every lord and lady in existence will be after me.

Though I trusted Radu completely, I knew there were steps Nobles could take to extract information from Servants. To keep everything as quiet as possible, I acquired several pieces of property around the globe—vast acreage in the American Midwest, several miles of forested land in northern Canada, and an isolated, private island in the

Caribbean—from funds in an account I'd secretly set up. Radu's record keeping was meticulous to the point of insanity, and it had taken quite a bit of time to figure out a way to gradually funnel assets into the account without the man's knowledge.

Once the properties had been secured, I set about preparing each of them for my arrival. Every improvement I made needed to be personally arranged, lest Radu or another of my Servants catch wind of what I was planning.

As difficult as these preparations are, they're all completely necessary.

Though I hadn't managed to get an exact head count at the Convocation, I estimated that there had been hundreds of Nobles present. Tracking and eliminating them all was going to take a very long time, and I needed to be sure I always had someplace to go, no matter how far into the future my quest took me.

Once each piece of property was prepared to my satisfaction, only one thing stopped me from moving forward.

My damned energy signature.

It wasn't until roughly halfway through the following year, amid countless frustrations and failed attempts, that I realized that I'd been approaching the problem all wrong. I recalled how I had managed to block some of Adalina's assaults by applying a psychic shield of sorts. Could that shield work in reverse, blocking my own energy like a glove would block fingerprints?

It took more practice and concentration than I would have imagined. It was one thing to lash out with a blast of energy to disrupt someone else's attack. Doing the reverse, in a carefully-controlled shape, was exceedingly difficult. Nevertheless, I spent weeks perfecting the technique, until I was able to walk about freely with the shield intact. Another few weeks, and I was able to tighten the shield so that it practically clung to me.

Now for the true test.

I spent about fifteen minutes standing in the door of my chamber, reaching my senses into the hall just beyond, eradicating every last bit of my own energy. When I was certain none remained, I closed my eyes, shielding myself. It was shaky, but if I walked slowly enough, I was able to keep the shape trim and tight. I entered the hallway, and spent about five minutes pacing slowly back and forth. When I was finished, I returned to my chamber entrance and dropped the shield. I stretched my senses out.

Nothing. It's as if I was never there.

A huge grin spread across my face, and I laughed aloud. The sound was strange to my ears as it echoed through the hall, as I hadn't laughed in a very long time.

I can finally begin.

29

I sat quietly, holding an image of Lord Chin in my mind, focusing my thoughts on every last detail—his apricot robes, his shiny bald head, the thin silver leash he held. I pushed my concentration deeper, focusing on Chin's energy, his psychic imprint. I felt the resonance— the silent hum of power—tickle the back of my memory.

I held on to the sensation as I pushed myself into the shadows, extending my senses as far as possible. At first I felt nothing. There didn't seem to be a pathway in existence that held an iota of Chin's essence. Then, suddenly, I caught a whiff of something distant, a tiny trace of the power I was looking for.

In an instant I was at a new filament, and there was no mistaking it—this one held the imprint I wanted. I plunged in, racing through the pathway at a dizzying speed, until I emerged in a large chamber that was illuminated by a great number of electric chandeliers. I instantly understood why Lord Chin wanted the room so bright—countless glittering statues of dragons festooned the space, from one end to the other. Some stood on pedestals, some squatted in alcoves, and some were elevated, mounted high on the room's stone walls. They were made of onyx, jade, and gold, and they sparkled in a manner that was dazzling to behold.

I realized at once that I wasn't alone. Though I'd learned that Lord Chin currently had a number of children—nearly a hundred, by some accounts, and none of them fully formed—I did not expect so many to be present in Chin's main audience chamber. Ten women reclined on couches and chaise lounges that were scattered about the room. Some of the women were naked, while others were clothed only partially, in silk robes that never succeeded in covering them completely. Though all of them bore the ripe complexion typical of humans, none of them smelled *right*.

I reached my senses out and felt dozens more of them somewhere nearby, all half-turned, just like the women who shared the room with me.

My God how many people has this beast taken over the centuries?

Almost immediately, a Servant—dressed in embroidered robes that were nearly as fine as Chin's—appeared. Though he wasn't terribly broad, he was quite tall, standing nearly a foot above me.

"My Lord," the man said, inclining his head. "Forgive me, but I was unaware that Lord Chin was expecting a visitor."

"He wasn't," I said.

The servant seemed a bit taken aback, but didn't miss a beat. "Whom shall I tell him has arrived?"

"Let him know Lord Dragos is here to see him."

The servant bowed low and departed at once.

I waited in silence, surprised at the lack of conversation from the women present. They appeared to be half asleep; none of them moved save for a minor adjustment here or there. I didn't need to probe them to know that Lord Chin had placed a haze on each of them, much the same as Adalina had done with me.

I felt the servant and his master approaching. I knew Lord Chin was old and most likely quite powerful, and surprise would be my most effective weapon.

Appear calm, I told myself. *Mask your emotions. Strike when he least expects it. And if you fail, at least you'll no longer have to go on living as one of these...things. If he destroys you, at least you'll find rest.*

My rage bloomed anew when the man entered the chamber. Instantly, Chin fixed me with the haughtiest of glares. Gou trailed behind him, though she was thankfully no longer leashed.

"Dragos," he said. "I might have expected such an egregious breach of decorum from an immature child such as you."

"Lord Chin," I said, lowering my head.

Maintain pleasantries. Do nothing to put him on guard.

"I really must do something to keep rabble like you and Arsenios out of here. Perhaps a ward on these premises. Yet even he wouldn't dare barge in here without an invitation or an appointment."

He turned and glared at Gou, and she yelped as she quickened her pace behind him. Chin stopped in front of me, scowling and unblinking. I felt the man's annoyance, as well as his disdain. And there was a force of will behind the emotions that I found chilling.

Remember the Convocation, I told myself. *Remember how you had the strength to resist him. You can win this fight.*

"Well?" Lord Chin said. "Out with it, boy. Why have you polluted my home with your presence?"

My anger toward Chin grew more heated by the

moment. I let it erupt. I dropped my defenses, allowing Chin to feel what I felt. The man's eyes grew wide just as a fire born of hatred and rage rushed through my veins. A wall of heat exploded from me, knocking Lord Chin from his feet and incinerating his robes. In an instant, Gou simply wasn't there, no doubt vaporized by the sheer heat of the blaze.

The other women in the chamber suddenly snapped out of their stupor as half of them—along with the furniture upon which they sat—burst into flames. Those who remained unscathed screamed in terror, fleeing for the exit.

I felt a deep pang of guilt, but quickly suppressed it.

There will be time for remorse when this battle is over.

Lord Chin leapt to his feet. Though his clothing was in ruins, his body was unscathed. His eyes blazed a deep yellow as he bared his teeth in a ferocious snarl. I slammed yet another wall of flames into his hateful visage.

Chin sliced through the energies easily, sending gouts of flame parting to either side. The inferno crashed into the wall behind him, melting one of the golden statues and charring another to a crisp. As Chin leapt forward, I felt him gather his energy a split second before the assault came.

I brought my defenses to bear just before the wave hit. The energy behind the attack was as strong as a typhoon, its sheer force driving me to my knees. I felt another coming as Chin quickly closed the distance between us, and I gathered my own energy and clumsily knocked it aside.

I regained my feet just as Chin came at me, leaping back as Chin aimed a kick at my midsection. The man was extremely fast—faster than Adalina. I dodged and parried as best I could as he rained a flurry of blows upon me. I struck out for his head, but he deftly avoided me, clubbing my arm in the process. I felt my wrist snap, but I pushed the pain down as I lashed out again, scoring a solid hit to Chin's temple. I felt his skull crack, and he leapt to the side, cursing as he clutched his head.

I pushed the pain of my broken bone as far back in my mind as I could, barely having a chance to do so before he was on me again. This time, every punch and kick was accompanied by a perfectly timed burst of energy; I reeled as I attempted to defend myself against both the psychic and physical onslaughts. His strength was overwhelming, and I began to feel fatigued. Every attack was just a hair too fast—I tried to anticipate Chin's moves but continued to fail. Pain bloomed in my cheek as his fist connected, and then again in my side as his foot sunk in deeply, doubling me over. I pushed the pain of each wound back and noted with horror that my body was starting to slow down under the strain of so many injuries.

I flailed with my mind, sending another burst of heat and energy at Chin, but he batted it aside.

How is he able to do that? It's like my attacks have no power at all. How is he mustering so much strength?

Perhaps I'd been wrong about Lord Chin's power. Perhaps my ability to resist him at the Convocation had been nothing but a fluke. Perhaps Chin hadn't really been trying all that hard in the first place, wanting to keep his true strength a secret.

The next assault was the strongest by far. He charged forward amid a whirlwind of punches and kicks, hurling wave after wave of violent energy at me. The attack battered my mental defenses and smashed my body to near uselessness. Unable to continue, I sank to my knees.

Lord Chin glowered down at me, the fire in his golden eyes blazing to a point that was nearly blinding. "Pathetic," he said. "But quite satisfying. I had a feeling that one day I'd destroy you. It's most fortunate that you decided to attack me first. My actions were done in self-defense; no crime has been committed, at least not on my part."

I extended my perceptions toward him, determined to at least find the source of his strength before my own life was snuffed out. I was shocked to discover that the resonance of power I'd felt from him was no longer there.

How can this be?

Lord Chin had clearly demonstrated his awesome abilities, yet to me, his energy signature seemed no more potent than that of any of his half-turned pets.

Chin squatted next to me.

"You've killed my children, damaged my home, destroyed my treasures. You shall pay dearly for that."

He wrapped his long, thin fingers around my neck and began to squeeze.

At the man's touch, I could feel Chin much more intensely, and I knew immediately that I hadn't been mistaken—he felt nearly dead, his power almost nonexistent. I didn't waste time trying to figure out how or why such a thing had happened; I simply reacted.

"I...will...not...*yield!*"

With a scream of desperation, I gathered every bit of strength I had left and hurled it all at Chin. He released his grip as it slammed into him. He flew backward, landing in a heap on the other side of the room.

"Your energy is gone," I said, panting. My voice was scratchy and nearly inaudible; the force of Chin's grip had nearly crushed my larynx. "That's why...that's why you appeared so strong. You put your literal *soul* into those attacks."

He gnashed his teeth, growling like a cornered animal. His strategy had been a gamble. He'd known he was no match for me after our encounter at the convocation. Sacri-

ficing his very life force was the only way he might
have won.

And it nearly paid off.

Chin staggered to his feet. I felt him try to gather his
energy, but nothing happened. His entire body sagged, and
he collapsed to the floor.

"How *stupid* of you," I croaked, limping closer. "You've
exhausted everything. Every last ounce of your life energy.
How long would it have taken you to recover from this?
Months? *Years?*"

Chin remained silent, glaring at me defiantly.

"Stuck-up and self-assured to the end," I said. "And how
weak for someone of your age. Arsenios would have crushed
you in an instant."

I lurched forward, gripping Chin by the neck. He struggled weakly as I twisted and pulled. The man's eyes bulged
from their sockets and his mouth twisted into an agonized
grimace as his vertebrae gave way with a sickening snap,
and I tore his head from his shoulders. Blood ran down my
arms, and bits of tattered flesh hung in gore-soaked
strands from the stump of Chin's neck. Almost instantly,
Chin's body—and severed head—crumbled away to nothingness.

For a moment, he was inside me. I felt his lust, his
corruption, his terror, and his overwhelming feelings of
inadequacy, as if they were my own. Then they were gone,
absorbed into my consciousness as what remained of Chin's
power became one with me.

I stood slowly, relishing the feeling. Though what I'd
gotten from him paled in comparison from what I had taken
from Adalina, the feeling was remarkably similar.

Once I kill enough Nobles, I'll be a match for anyone at court.
None them will escape my wrath.

I focused my perceptions on my body, taking stock of my many injuries.

Three broken ribs. Broken arm. Sprained ankle. Cracked vertebrae.

I closed my eyes and breathed deeply, pinpointing each injury separately, knitting bone and mending tissue. I left the smaller scrapes and bumps alone, wishing to preserve as much energy as possible. I still had work to do at Lord Chin's manor.

Better. Much better.

I took a few steps, testing my legs. I felt nearly perfect, aside from some minor aches, which I easily pushed to the back of my mind.

I have to be quick and thorough. There can be no witnesses. The servants must be eliminated. The children...perhaps something can be done to save them.

I was loathe to take any more lives, but there was no way of telling which of the Servants might have witnessed the battle. The only safe way to proceed was to ensure none of them lived to tell the other Nobles about what had happened.

I stretched my senses out as far as they would reach, feeling for any signs of life. I found a multitude of servants, along with a number of Chin's half-formed children. I headed for the nearest one—a Servant, by the feel of it—and encountered the tall, robed man I'd first seen.

"What on earth has—"

I cut him off with a blow to the head that caved his skull in. The servant collapsed, lifeless. I proceeded to the next Servant, taking her by surprise. A kick to the stomach and a strike to the back of the neck ended her life almost instantly. Another Servant saw what had happened and lunged for me, screeching. I easily slid under his grasp and doubled him over with a strike to the solar plexus. I kicked him in the side of the head, sending half of the man's brain and pulverized skull spewing across the room. When I happened upon a roomful of them, I obliterated them all in a similar fashion, one after the other, despite their feeble attempts to defend themselves.

When I'd eliminated every last Servant, I turned my attention to the half-formed humans. The first woman I found crouched in the corner of a lavishly appointed bedchamber, shaking and gibbering uncontrollably. She was young, of medium height and build, with long, tousled blonde hair. Her skin was light, and she wore a red and black silk robe that hung open, revealing her breasts. Smelling the stench of insanity almost instantly, I probed her mind, hoping there was something I could do.

There wasn't. In her half-formed state, she'd been completely dependent on Chin. With his death, a part of her had died as well.

Is this what would have happened to me if someone had killed Adalina?

The thought made me shudder.

"Don't fear," I whispered. "I'll set you free."

I focused for a moment, then unleashed a wave of searing heat that instantly turned her to ash.

Now for the others.

Though I was exhausted, I dealt with each of the women the same way. Instant incineration seemed far more merciful than bludgeoning them to death, and I was deter-mined to end them as quickly and painlessly as possible, regardless of how tired I was.

When the last one lay in ashes, I sat on the floor, cross-legged, and closed my eyes. I carefully crafted a shield that clung as tightly to my skin as I could manage. When I was satisfied, I retraced my steps, destroying any mental signature I'd left behind. The process took hours—I'd been all over Chin's keep, and had left my imprint from one end to the other. Though I figured I could have shielded myself prior to seeking out Chin's Servants and children, I still didn't have enough confidence in my technique to engage in fighting and killing while trying to keep such an intricate shield in place.

Finally, my task was complete. Not a trace of my energy signature remained.

I trudged back to the same pool of shadow I'd used to enter Lord Chin's audience chamber. I plunged in, seeking a corner of the earth where night had fallen and prey could be had.

30

"My Lord," said Radu. "Lord Arsenios has arrived, and wishes to see you at once."

How long has it been since I've spoken with him?

I took a moment to think.

Perhaps it's been a few months since the battle with Chin, but since the convocation...years. Perhaps he's no longer angry with me.

"Please," I said. "Take me to him."

We found Arsenios in the audience chamber, pacing before the fireplace.

"Arsenios," I said. "It's good—"

"Lord Chin is dead," Arsenios interrupted me.

I feigned surprise. "Dead? How is that possible?"

"Simple. Someone killed him."

"Was it one of his progeny?"

"No one knows," said Arsenios. He stared directly into my eyes, unblinking. "What was left of him was found yesterday, when Lady Aster arrived at his home to discuss business."

"This is...shocking," I said. "I thought murder was unheard of among our kind."

"It is," said Arsenios, his gaze unwavering. "I thought I made that perfectly clear."

I stared back at him, my expression carefully blank. "You did, which is why I find this situation so surprising."

Arsenios stared at me for a moment longer, then sighed, pacing again. "The council has ordered a full investigation. It's thought that the Progenitor himself will be present."

"I'm sure they'll find the killer," I said. "With the entire community after him—or her—how can there be any hope of escape?"

"There won't be," said Arsenios. He again brought his gaze to bear upon me. He paused for a few moments then added, "Some believe you're responsible."

"That's absurd."

"More than a few Nobles witnessed your disagreement with Lord Chin at the Convocation," he said, "and there are some who believe you might be flawed in some way."

"Flawed? How so?"

The older man sighed. "There were the Progenitor's words. And the fact that you're a relative unknown, the newest member at court. I'm sure you can imagine the speculation." Arsenios was silent for a moment. "I was there myself," he said, "at Lord Chin's home. I detected nothing. No trace of anyone, save for Chin himself. Whoever did this has a great gift for covering their tracks. Well beyond what your abilities should be, as young as you are. That, I think, is what might vindicate you with the others."

Arsenios clasped his hands behind his back and walked slowly forward.

"But they don't know you as I do," he continued. "I know how skilled you are. You killed Adalina, a woman who should have possessed many times your strength. Only a Noble of exceptional innate ability could have managed that while barely formed. I know what you are capable of."

"Are you saying you suspect me of this crime?" I asked quietly.

Arsenios narrowed his eyes. "Did you do it?"

"So you *do* suspect me."

"Did you do it?" he repeated.

"Of course not!"

Arsenios held my gaze for a moment longer, then sighed as he stalked back toward the fireplace.

"I want to believe you, Dragos. Truly, I do. But there's something you're not telling me. You have remarkable control; not a single emotion leaks out. *Why?* Why do you conceal your true self from me, if not to cover something up?"

I shrugged. "Perhaps I don't enjoy being read. I'm not a book."

"Damn it, man!" Arsenios slammed his fist against the mantel, leaving a sizable crack. "Do you realize how this seems to me, Dragos? If you're innocent, prove it. Open yourself to me."

"No."

"Then you must have something to hide."

I took a seat in one of the armchairs and crossed my arms over my chest. "I don't. I simply don't want to be violated. My emotions are private."

"You sound just like a human."

"Is that meant to offend me?" I asked.

"It's meant to demonstrate how foolishly you're acting."

I shook my head. "I won't have my private thoughts or emotions read by anyone, not even you. I'm sorry, my friend."

Arsenios stared at me for a long while, and I returned his gaze. He sighed and dropped his eyes. "Just so you realize," he said quietly, "if you're found to be the culprit, I'll kill you myself."

Without another word, he walked toward the shadowy corner of the audience chamber.

"Arsenios," I said.

He stopped, still facing away from me.

"You speak of secrets, and hiding one's thoughts. Yet you've withheld information from me, from the very beginning."

There was something that had been bothering me since the night of the convocation, something I hadn't had much time to focus on due to my recent exploits. I guessed that I would never get another chance to ask any of the Nobles about it.

Arsenios slowly turned to face me, his eyebrows raised.

"Where are all the other Nobles?" I asked.

"What do you mean?"

"You told me the Progenitor is older than humanity itself. Judging from the power I felt from him, I certainly believe it. It also stands to reason that he's been on earth for a very long time. However, at the Convocation, the eldest among all the others present couldn't have been much older than you. If all of us are of the Progenitor's line, where are the rest? Where are your grandparents, your great-grandparents?"

Arsenios pursed his lips. "We don't speak of that."

"Of what?" I pressed. "There should have been hundreds more. *Thousands* more. If our lines extend back as far as I think, why are there so few, and why are they all so young?"

"I'll say this once more, and only once: we don't speak of

it. The past *shall not* repeat itself. We vowed long ago never to let that happen again."

"Let *what* happen? You're not making any sense!"

Arsenios placed his hands on his hips, his yellow eyes flashing. "There is a reason murder is strictly outlawed. Several thousand years ago, someone young and very powerful—like you—went on a rampage. Her lust for power only grew the more she killed, and she reached a point where she had gained such strength that only the Progenitor himself was capable of stopping her. That woman alone wiped out nearly our entire population, save for the most cunning, who were able to conceal themselves from her."

I stood dumb, unable to answer.

History repeats itself. Human or monster, it seems no one is safe from the past.

Arsenios turned to leave, stopping briefly before the pool of shadows. "You could have a very bright future among the Nobility, Dragos. I sincerely hope you haven't destroyed your opportunity to do so."

An instant later, he was gone.

Caution. Patience. Act slowly and arouse as little suspicion as possible.

The thought had become something that I endlessly recited. Since the death of Lord Chin, two other Nobles had met their end at my hands.

Lady Aster was the next logical choice, as she'd been present at Chin's not long after I had killed him. I'd briefly—and ever so cautiously—returned to the scene of the crime to try and get a sense of her aura, then I'd personally dug up every detail I could about her. When I was certain I knew all

I could of her home, her compliment of Servants and her children, I struck. She'd been nearly as powerful as Adalina, but had fallen after a short battle. Clearly she was unwilling or unable to use the same tactic Chin had used, and her life force had been fully intact when I ended her.

Her home was a foreboding place, a French country manor that looked from the outside to be completely abandoned; every window was boarded over, the landscaping had given way to wilderness, and thick vines covered nearly half of the building's exterior. I was only mildly surprised to find that the interior of the house was every bit as posh as the other Nobles' homes. I walked the halls of the manor the same way I had at Chin's residence, systematically eliminating all of her Servants. Regrettably, her two children—a middle-aged man and a teenage girl—had been as damaged as Chin's had been, and I had no choice but to destroy them.

As I was busy removing the traces of the aura I'd left in the wake of my assault, I sensed the imprint of another Noble about the place—perhaps a friend, or frequent visitor of Aster's. When I had finished at the manor, I immediately returned home to begin investigating this new presence.

It turned out to be that of a Lord Hawk, of England. Unlike the other Nobility I had so far encountered, who lived in out-of-the-way places where the casual observer was unlikely to tread, Lord Hawk's home—an immense, Tudor-style mansion—was right on the outskirts of London.

Though I knew exactly where to find him, I had waited nearly a decade to strike, afraid that Lady Aster's killing was still too recent. I instead filled my days with as much charitable work as I could. When I felt that enough time had passed to lull the other Nobles into a false sense of security, I went to pay this new lord a visit.

Lord Hawk was the most powerful Noble I faced yet. Our

battle had lasted far longer than the others, and left the interior of the mansion a complete ruin. Flames had at some point engulfed part of the home's roof, eliciting a response from the local fire department. I had to rush through my cleanup tasks more quickly than usual, and I hoped I hadn't missed any of my imprints along the way.

Years passed, and Arsenios maintained his silence. At no point since our last meeting had he tried to contact me, and I worried about what might happen I paid him a visit. I knew beyond doubt that Arsenios suspected me of the murders, and I wondered just how far he would go, even without definitive proof.

Arsenios's lack of communication, though bothersome, was not the thing that concerned me the most. Lately, I had begun to notice strange psychic disturbances in the countryside surrounding my home. When I went out to investigate, I was astounded to discover the residual energy traces of no less than thirty Nobles.

They suspect me, and they're watching. The longer I stay here, the more danger I'm in.

I needed a new home, where the Nobility couldn't find me.

I've been so careful about covering my tracks. I've left no evidence behind.

Clearly I had slipped up somewhere along the way. Perhaps I'd left something of my energy behind at Lord Hawk's.

"Radu," I said, seated beside my monstrous desk, where most of my and Radu's meetings took place.

"My lord?"

"Begin preparations to move the estate. I want everything packed up and ready to go. Divert as many Servants as you need from their usual tasks; this needs to be done as quickly as possible. I've acquired a sizable parcel in the American Midwest, and it's been made ready for our arrival. I want everything prepared in two weeks' time—and when I say everything, I mean *everything*. Not just documents and papers, but all my furniture, artwork, and tapestries. I want this place completely barren, with not even a speck remaining by the time we leave. I want no evidence that anyone has ever been here."

Radu blinked several times. For a man who rarely let any emotion show, such cues from him were quite extraordinary. "I was unaware of any new land acquisitions," he said.

"I did all this in secret. It was better for everyone that you had no knowledge of this, for your protection and mine."

"I see," he said. He regarded me with his beady brown eyes, looking as if he'd say something more, but he remained silent.

"Well?" I said. "Do you have something to add?"

Radu stayed quiet for a moment longer. "If I may be so bold," he finally said, "you are the one who has been killing the Nobles, aren't you?"

I grew rigid, my gaze locked on Radu's eyes.

How could he know that?

Radu squirmed uncomfortably, dropping his gaze.

"I meant no disrespect, my lord," he said. "I apologize for mentioning it. What you do is your own business, and I—"

"Yes," I said quietly, cutting him off. "Yes. I'm the one."

Slowly Radu raised his head, meeting my eyes again.

"I should have known you were too intelligent not to figure that out," I said. "Does what I've done surprise you?"

Radu shook his head. "No. If it were any other Noble, it might, but you're different."

"How so?"

"You are more like me. You don't think that all others are beneath you. You don't mistreat your Servants the way the other Nobles do."

"Does it disturb you that I've killed other Nobles?" I asked.

"It does not."

From what I could read of the man, there wasn't a shred of evidence to suggest he was lying.

"But why?" I said. "I thought Servants were bred to be totally loyal to the Nobles."

"That doesn't mean that we don't have the ability to think on our own. I served Adalina because my instincts drove me to do so. That did not stop me from despising her."

My mouth fell open. I closed it quickly, not wishing to appear shocked. "I never...I see. I just thought that all of the breeding and conditioning would have forced you to like us."

Radu folded his large hands in his lap. "The ability to like and dislike others is fortunately something they haven't managed to breed out of us yet. We like *you*. The others, on the other hand..."

"I understand," I said. "Honestly, I wondered how it was possible for any Servant to actually *like* one of those creatures."

Radu made a strange snuffling sound, placing a hand over his mouth. It took a moment for me to realize that he was laughing.

"Maybe you and I have more in common than I thought," I mused. "You're closer to human than any of the Nobles, and me...well, let's just say that I'm closer to human than anyone realizes."

Radu nodded. "We all knew there was something different about you."

"What I am doing is dangerous," I said. "It could get me, and all of you, killed. I aim to destroy the Nobility completely. The humans deserve to live their own lives, make their own choices, from outside the shadow of the Nobility. I'm telling you this because I want to give you a choice: stay with me and help fight, or leave. I will not force you to possibly face death because of decisions I've made."

"I have already decided," said Radu, fixing me with an intense gaze. "And so have the others. We will serve you until we die."

"That's not the conditioning talking, is it?"

"No. The others like and respect you, as do I. None of us ever thought we'd meet a Noble we didn't hate. What's more, I believe that you can make a difference in this world."

"Thank you, Radu. You don't know how much that means to me. I will certainly try. I won't rest until this world is cleansed of their filth. You have my word."

Radu grinned. "All of us will be here to help. And as for the preparations, I'll begin coordinating our efforts at once. Not a single item shall be left behind. Also—if I may be so bold—additional Servants would be most helpful. We've lost a handful to old age in the decades since you became master of this house; you would be well within your rights to request more from the Council."

I sighed. "I think the Council might suspect me. I've sensed the presence of other Nobles—many other Nobles—around this place lately. I'm starting to think if I show my face anywhere, I'll wind up dead. I know this will make your job more difficult, but it's for the best. For all of us."

"I understand, my lord," Radu said.

"Do whatever you need to do. If you require any assistance from me, you have only to ask."

Radu stood and bowed deeply, excusing himself.

I never expected to count my Servants among my allies. I always thought they'd need to be kept in the dark.

I sat there for a moment longer, pondering this new development, before snapping myself back to reality.

Time to get to work.

I knew that to single-handedly move so many Servants and possessions via Shadow Travel would be an exhausting feat and could take several days, even if I worked nonstop. Nonetheless, it was absolutely necessary. I wanted nothing of myself to remain in the underground complex; any object left behind that carried even the slightest trace of my energy might fall into the hands of someone who could potentially use it to track me.

I knew I'd be better off simply destroying everything, but as much as I hated to admit it, I had come to enjoy the artwork and antiques in my home. I had grown to love my collection of paintings most of all, particularly the piece depicting the forest that hung above the mantel in my audience chamber.

When we settle in, I thought, *I'll have Radu begin severing my ties to any businesses with which I'm still affiliated. I'll resign from every board, and liquidate all of my holdings. The money will be deposited in new institutions. My charitable enterprises, I'll turn over to the humans who've already been running them. I need to lay low for a while, perhaps for many years.*

I gazed off into space, allowing the enormity of what I was doing to sink in.

Whatever happens, I'll see this to its end. Either the Nobility will die, or I will.

31

United States, Kansas, 2274 CE

The surrounding countryside was breathtaking, even when blanketed in the darkness of night. I had always loved peering at the vast swathes of grassy meadows and farmland that stretched endlessly in all directions. It seemed that where I stood was one of the last places in the country where there was so much space, uninterrupted by urban sprawl.

That's only because I've never sold to developers.

I owned just about everything as far as one could see, though I continued to allow farmers to rent my acreage. Something about the straight lines of the crops stretching into the distance brought me comfort, particularly in a world that had changed so drastically from the one I'd known as a human.

Farming was more or less obsolete. Only the privileged few could afford food grown on traditional farmland. Most of society's crops came from huge industrial greenhouses, twice the size of the skyscrapers I remembered from my younger years.

This land is truly calm and beautiful—a fitting resting place for an old friend.

I stood alone, before a mound of freshly turned earth. Many similar mounds surrounded me, though most of them were covered in tall grass and wildflowers.

"Radu, you were a true friend. May your memory be a blessing."

The words felt strange on my lips, a tie to a faith I hadn't been able to observe for centuries. Yet uttering them gave me comfort.

Radu deserves more than my casting him into the earth, forgotten. He's always been there for me, ever faithful. I'll miss him so much.

The man had lived far beyond his life expectancy, continuing to stand by my side for more than two hundred years after the death of my former mistress. He was one of the last Servants to remain, and I knew the rest would be gone before too much longer.

I'll be completely alone.

I felt a deep pang at that. Radu and the others had become so much more than mere Servants; they were my friends, my confidants, helping me stay one step ahead of the Nobles. I'd grown close to Radu in particular, whose wisdom, advice, and companionship I had come to treasure.

I look forward to the day when I too am allowed to pass into oblivion. One day my loneliness will end. But not yet.

The Nobles were still too great a threat to be ignored. Despite my ever-growing power and my increasing efficiency at dispatching them, many still remained. They'd grown ever-more cautious over time, well aware that an

assassin was stalking them from the shadows. Their movements had grown far less in recent years. Gone were the days
when their auras touched nearly every corner of the earth.
Sometimes, it would be years before I picked up a new trail.
Worse still, all of the information I'd gathered about their
whereabouts was now useless. It seemed as if every Noble
had picked up and moved; far too often, all I found when I
followed one of my old leads was an empty mansion.

*No matter. Wherever they are, they won't remain safe for
long. I'll find them. I'll find them all.*

I took another moment to relish my surroundings, then
abruptly winked out of sight as I returned to the silent walls
of my home.

32

Western Empire (North American Continent), 2632 CE

I closed my eyes and concentrated, focusing my power. After many years, I'd finally picked up another lead, this one disturbingly close to my newest stronghold, in the ancient woodlands to the north of the newly minted Western Empire.

It's more of an alliance than an empire, I thought. *At least the consolidation was done peacefully.*

Gone were the individual countries that had once comprised most of the globe. The two remaining North American territories had at last reached an agreement, and were now governed by a single body.

Such change. The United States hasn't existed for nearly three hundred years. Canada is a distant memory, along with Mexico and everything to the south.

The land and people were still there, of course, but the countries had changed names, merged, divided and re-merged so many times that I had lost track of it all. Now, there were only two major governing entities on earth: the Eastern Federation and the Western Empire.

And the only reason there is a Western Empire is because everyone in the west is afraid.

The eastern part of the world had unified long ago, with the countries of Europe first becoming a single body, only to later be joined by those of the Middle East, Africa and what had once been Russia and China. Australia had remained on its own the longest, but for reasons of trade had eventually petitioned to join the Eastern Federation.

The west had experienced no such consolidation, at least not on that scale. The Northern and Southern territories had remained staunchly independent, until fear of the unification on the other side of the world had driven them together.

There was nothing to be afraid of in the first place. Not once has the east ever threatened the west. Paranoid idiots.

The east had, on many occasions, invited the west to join with their government, but the Northern and Southern Territories had always refused. The whole thing made no sense to me. In a world that was becoming increasingly global, what was the advantage of stubbornly remaining alone?

Politics are none of my concern, I thought, pushing my musings to the side. *What matters is finding the Noble that has been traipsing around my forest.*

I renewed my concentration, carefully tracking the foreign presence to its source. I gazed into the shadows of my bedchamber, and in an instant I was in the middle of the woods, right where the Noble's trail ended.

The Noble Traveled from this spot. I should not have too much trouble finding them.

I peered into the shadows, easily locating the filament

that the Lord or Lady had used. I felt it all the way to its end, surprised to find no wards present. I'd be able to Travel directly wherever the Noble had gone, with no interference.

Either this isn't the Noble's home, or this individual is a complete fool.

I gathered my strength and plunged in, Traveling a distance that seemed to take me clear across the globe.

I emerged in what appeared to be an ancient Roman bath, with marble pools of fragrant, steaming water arranged in a semicircle around the room. Tall columns held up a white stone ceiling, and statuary towered among them.

I barely had time to register anything else when a blast of energy smashed into me from behind. I gasped as I parried, just able to avert the majority of the flow. The smell of charred cloth and my own burnt flesh stung my nostrils, and I whirled about just as another wave crashed into me.

This time, I was ready. I sliced the wave in two, reaching out with my senses, searching the chamber for my assailant. I found the Lord quickly, crouched behind a massive statue of Jupiter. With a furious roar, I slammed a wall of searing flame into the statue; it exploded with a concussion that reverberated off the chamber walls, its pieces flying in every direction. The Lord scampered from his hiding spot, sending yet another blast of energy in my direction.

I leapt to the side as the force of the onslaught tore a hole in the marble floor, and bits of shrapnel peppered my face. I pursued the Noble, attacking and parrying, laying waste to any sculpture or piece of furniture that got in my way. In spite of several direct hits, the creature was remarkably resilient, hopping back on his feet each time I knocked him down, always managing to stay just ahead of me. A white blur is all that was visible of the Lord; I could not even tell what he wore, or what the man looked like.

All I can sense is that it's a man, and that he's powerful.

The thought barely registered when I suddenly felt another presence, then another, then *another*, blink into existence not far behind me. My belly turned to ice as I felt the Nobles gather their energy, and I just managed to throw a shield up as the combined force of their attack drove me to the floor.

I panted as I willed myself to stand, vaguely able to make out the three newcomers through the smoke and dust of the chamber. Two appeared to be women, and seemed to be wearing oversized, frilly dresses. The other was a man, but I couldn't make out any of his features.

I felt another attack coming from my rear, knowing that the Noble I'd originally come to find had rejoined the fight. I gathered my will and slapped the man's attack aside, only to have three concurrent heat waves roar toward me. My shield, already weakening, could not withstand the assault. It shattered, and I screamed as my flesh crackled and blackened.

On legs that were nearly too weak to hold me, I staggered toward the nearest pool of shadow and threw myself in. I took the most roundabout way I could, jumping from filament to filament, into and out of the physical world, certain the others would be behind me. With exhaustion threatening to overwhelm me, my shielding was clumsy, and I knew I was shedding my essence everywhere. I tried my best to destroy my residual energy as I went, but was completely uncertain how effective the technique was. After over an hour of darting through a network of pathways, I emerged on a moonlit hilltop. I lurched toward a shadow cast by some shrubbery when I felt the others emerge right behind me. I cursed as I dove for the blackness, feeling the power of their assault scour the earth to my rear.

This time I was far more cautious. I focused as hard as I could, raising a shield in spite of my exhaustion, knowing that the chase would never end as long as my energy was detectable. I felt them growing closer and I started to panic, convinced that I'd never have the strength to sustain a shield as I Traveled. Then, very gradually, I sensed the others falling behind.

It's working.

I kept it up until I was certain I'd confounded their efforts, then immediately headed home. When I emerged in my chamber, the acrid smell of burning flesh immediately coated the back of my throat. The fact that it was my own flesh that I smelled did nothing to put me at ease. I collapsed to the floor, my clothing in tatters, my skin seared black. I gasped as I shifted positions, trying to force the pain to the back of my mind, directing the little energy I had left to healing my legs enough so I could stand.

I barely managed it.

I staggered to my feet, hunger burning a hole in my stomach. If I didn't feed soon, I would lose myself.

How could I have been so stupid?

The setup had been perfect, the bait too tempting for me to resist. Somehow the others had found me; no doubt I'd gotten careless during one of my many trips around the world in search of the remaining Nobility. They must have known that the energy from one of their own, plainly visible in the woods surrounding my home, would draw me like a hawk to a mouse.

This is a new tactic, one I didn't expect and one I have to prepare to face in the future.

Never before had I witnessed such cooperation among

the Nobility. In hundreds of years spent hunting and killing them, I'd never needed to face more than one at a time. They were solitary creatures, loathe to include others in their schemes, and incredibly secretive, even among themselves.

That seems to have changed. Now they're on the offensive, and they're helping each other.

I'd need to be even quicker, even more cautious, than ever before. The Nobles were adapting, and as powerful as I was, it was brutally apparent that when working together they possessed the strength to destroy me.

Even though I felt incredibly weak, I took a few moments to test the wards around my stronghold. They remained strong.

No one besides me will be able to Travel here, at least.

Carefully, I reached out my senses and found a dark part of the earth teeming with prey. I Traveled as quickly as I could, vowing to exercise more caution the next time I dared strike a Noble.

33

Caput Mundi, Western Empire, 2893 CE

The city of Caput Mundi was well named. Though the Empire had co-opted the name from countless ancient cities before it, I felt that if any city could be considered the capital of the world, it was none other than the main trading hub and capital of the Western Empire.

It stood in a massive valley on the eastern edge of the Rocky Mountains, and its size was awe inspiring. It spanned the entirety of the valley floor, extending well up into the hills and mountains that surrounded it on all sides. Its endless, silvery spires gleamed brightly even in the moonlight, and I could only imagine what they looked like in the glare of the sun.

The buildings were some of the tallest in the world, extending well into the lower atmosphere, and were built to house a population that numbered over a hundred million. I remembered a time, seemingly not that long ago, when entire nations carried smaller populations than the single city before me.

This is what happens when the Nobility is too weak to restrain humanity. People build wonders, and the population booms.

I felt a tremendous sense of pride whenever I beheld the city. It was tangible proof that humans were capable of anything.

They're even poised to explore the galaxy.

Both the East and West were in a race to see who could venture the furthest from the solar system, and the Western Empire had a narrow lead. According to the latest news reports, the most recent generation of the Empire's space-craft could travel at 98.7% of the speed of light, enabling neighboring solar systems to be reached in a matter of years.

Space exploration had always fascinated me, even more so due to the fact that Shadow Travel was limited to the planet earth. In all of my journeys over hundreds of years, I had never found—or sensed—a filament that led anywhere beyond the confines of my home planet.

Each time a manned expedition reached a new planet, I always eagerly awaited the holographic images of the places they discovered. The last ones I'd seen featured a lush land-scape, completely covered in dark purple vegetation—the product of absorbing light from the planet's red dwarf star.

One day, when I've killed the rest of the Nobles, perhaps I'll sneak aboard one of their ships and see these distant worlds for myself.

I hoped that day would come soon, but I knew that I still had much to do before I could even entertain such thoughts. I shook my head, turning my attention back to Caput Mundi.

Even at this late hour, the city overflowed with life.

There was movement everywhere as antigravity transports and ground vehicles alike shuttled workers, tourists, and off-duty citizens to every corner of the city and beyond. Though there was much to take in, and I could have easily stared at the scene before me for hours, it was the tallest building, situated at the city's central point, that held my attention.

The building was heavily warded.

I'd detected the ward not long ago, on one of my many trips around the world in my never-ending search for the remnants of the Nobility. The ones who still lived were the strongest, most cunning, and the best at concealment. Those who resided at the center of the city had exercised the most brilliant tactic yet, for which I grudgingly gave them credit.

Typically, the Nobles lived in the least-populated areas they could find, always careful not to draw the attention of humans to their activities. This group, however, had set themselves up in the heart of one of the largest cities on the planet.

It'll be exceedingly difficult to dislodge them without killing innocents.

I abhorred the notion of involving humans in my conflicts with the Nobility, and always took it hard on the rare occasions when I killed innocent bystanders.

Blood on my hands. Blood of the people I'm supposed to protect.

This was, no doubt, why this particular group had chosen the Central Spire, the seat of government for the entire Empire, in which to conceal themselves. That area of the city was the most active, and the Nobles were undoubtedly well aware of my affinity for humans. Any assault on them would have to take place within the building itself, with the utmost caution, to avoid spilling human blood. Razing the entire structure and picking through the rubble for my targets wasn't an option this time.

I can't Travel directly into the building, due to the ward. I'll need to enter physically.

I didn't like the idea of entering without Traveling, nor did I like the fact that I couldn't read the inside of the building through the protections the nobles had implemented. There was also a good possibility that humans would be inside, even in the night. I'd need to employ a glamour to keep my true nature hidden, and there was always a chance that my adversaries would detect it.

I have to enter that building, regardless of the risk. I'll try to avoid collateral damage, but that might not be possible. And if a human happens to see me as I truly am...well, so be it.

A series of distant shouts drew my attention to a small wooded preserve behind me. The shouts were followed by a series of loud, sharp hissing noises, each accompanied by a brilliant green flash that lit up the trees. The sounds and lights abated, and I could just make out the pale glow of personal illumination devices bobbing about someplace deeper within the darkened trunks. I didn't need to see the people to whom the devices belonged to know who they were, or what they were doing.

Security detail. Hunting ferals.

One of the unfortunate sacrifices I had been required to make over the years, in the interest of both safety and efficiency, was to leave most of my victims' Servants alive. With the tactics the Nobles had developed to counteract my assaults, there was simply no time to traverse my targets' strongholds and kill all of the creatures off.

The result was an entire race of mutated humans that, without the guidance and control of their masters, had escaped their homes, running wild in the scant wilderness that remained on earth. The creatures had bred like rabbits and had come to both intrigue and appall the modern scientific community. The greatest minds on earth had long been trying to discern where these mutations had originated. Many ferals had been rounded up and put through who knows what kinds of medical tests and experiments. Even with all of their accumulated knowledge about them, doctors and scientists still argued vehemently about whether ferals constituted a drastic evolution—or devolution—of humanity.

However the humans regarded them, one thing was clear: without the force of will imposed by their masters, they were mindlessly violent creatures who thought nothing of murdering anyone unfortunate enough to get close to them. Though attempts had been made to keep their populations down, their numbers always seemed to bounce back.

Though I had always regretted unleashing such a threat, a part of me took satisfaction in the fact that yet another of the Nobles' horrific deeds was exposed for the world to see.

As the lights in the nearby woods grew brighter, I threw up a glamour to avoid detection.

This won't get any easier, no matter how long I procrastinate.

Knowing well that Travel into a crowded city ran the risk of someone seeing me appear out of nowhere, I turned from the woods and began the long walk to the Central Spire. I wound my way through the countless streets and alleyways of Caput Mundi, taking in the sights around me. The glamour I'd spun up showed me to be a twenty-something man with brown skin and bright purple hair, dressed in a tight plaid jumpsuit with knee-high, electric blue boots—a relatively common look for the young these days.

No one looked at me twice as I made my way through the streets, and after a few hours of brisk walking, I finally arrived at my destination. There was but one entrance to the spire, a rather breathtaking pair of translucent doors, two stories high, that typically stood open during the day. They were closed now, but there was a normal-sized entrance, tiny by comparison, carved into the lower portion of the right-hand door. This point of ingress was meant to accommodate the small amount of people who had business in the building after hours.

A cadre of four guards stood before it. They wore full body armor, black as the night sky, with matching helmets that sported opaque, black visors. Each of them held a metallic gray molecular disruptor—a devastating weapon that, though it bore a vague appearance to the ancient guns of my former life, was an order of magnitude stronger.

Distasteful. I would have thought that by now, people would know better than to manufacture such weapons.

I slipped into an alleyway beside the building and, when I was certain no one was watching, replaced my previous glamour with one that mimicked the appearance of the guards—same body armor, same opaque helmet. I crept to the entrance of the alley, reaching out with my senses, finding the presence of each guard. As I'd done with countless prey, I wrapped myself around their conscious minds, lulling them into a state of dazed calm. When I finished, I stepped out of the alleyway and walked toward them. Each of the guards appeared as they had before, standing and facing forward, but their arms now hung at their sides, and I knew that if I could see their eyes, they'd be staring forward blankly. One guard had dropped his disruptor to the ground.

I continued forward, slipping right between them and passing through the entrance. I knew from experience that there was most likely a biometric field in place, set up to scan any who entered the building, that would trip an alarm if an unauthorized person were to enter. I didn't even slow my pace.

Those fields don't even recognize me as a living thing.

The atrium of the building was easily five stories high, with several full-sized trees sprouting from an open, grassy area in the center of the chamber. A series of light orbs hovered about a story up, giving the place a soft, pleasant glow. A lone guard, dressed similarly to those out front, lounged at the front desk with their feet up, appearing to not even notice me as I moved out of the atrium to the rear hall of the structure.

When I'd turned the corner and was out of sight, I stopped moving and, ever so cautiously, reached out with my senses.

The others are here somewhere, and are surely aware of me by now. But where?

I focused harder, probed deeper, and was so absorbed in my search that I very nearly didn't feel the sudden swell of energy from the floor beneath me.

"No!" I spat, throwing up a shield just as the ground erupted, hurling me into the air. I held my shield tightly, only able to see a blinding white glare surrounding me on all sides. I hit the ground hard, and the earth trembled violently beneath me. With mounting horror, I sensed the Spire above rocking dangerously.

Those bastards...they rigged the building with explosives!

I regained my feet, stumbling as a chunk of falling material smashed into my shield. The ground heaved, and a cascade of rubble poured down on me, pinning me underneath. I sensed the pressure above me mount as more debris fell on top of the pile.

I thrust myself into the surrounding darkness, instantly

Traveling to a point just down the road. I saw a thick plume of dust and smoke billowing from the base of the spire, completely obscuring the first few stories. The gut-wrenching groan of twisting metal reverberated through the city, and the portion of the Spire that was visible above the rising plume of smoke began a slow and deadly descent. Screams pierced the air from all directions, and people scrambled madly in the streets.

I gaped as I watched it fall, realizing with grim certainty that many, many people would die. I stood tall, clenching my teeth as I drew in every scrap of power I could. The air around me crackled with energy and the earth beneath my feet trembled. I felt pressure building in my skull, felt my sanity begin to reel at the sweetness, at the *awesomeness*, of the power I held. Then with a roar that shook the buildings around me, I threw it all at the Spire. For a moment, its fall slowed.

"I have it," I grunted. *"I have it!"*

I cradled the titanic structure in the force of my will, and my vision began to go dark as I slowly, *carefully*, began to lower it.

Can't...hold it...for long, but at least people will...

The Spire shattered with a thunderous boom. Innumerable fragments sparkled like stars among the dazzling lights of Caput Mundi, hovering but for a moment before raining to earth in a hail of destruction. I collapsed to my knees, barely able to raise a shield in time as a cloud of metal fragments crashed down atop me. I tried to ignore the screams of those around me as the debris ripped through them, and I staggered to my feet, shield somehow still raised.

Without warning, a blast of energy sent me crashing into the building across the street, destroying what was left of my shield. I struggled to my knees, trying to gather my strength. Though I could not see the Noble, I could feel her.

She's strong as hell. Wonderful.

I felt her slowly approaching, seeming to take her time. I suddenly felt others like her as well, scattered about the city.

Lying in wait. In case I escaped the building. And they're not even bothering to hide themselves from me.

My mind raced, and in an instant, I decided to do something I knew I'd regret.

The needs of the many outweigh the needs of the few, I thought. *I'm sorry, my people. I'm sorry...*

I gritted my teeth as I focused my mind, homing in on her presence. She was just down the street, at the foot of a large, squat building. I moved my focus to the building, finding its foundation, analyzing its construction. I hesitated for a moment, then with an exertion of will, I vaporized its support structure.

I heard the Noble shriek as the entire building crashed down on top of her. Before she could regain her wits enough to raise a shield, I focused on the tiny pocket of rubble where she lay trapped. I threw all of the energy I had at it, turning it into a blast furnace.

I felt her agony as the heat scorched her to ash.

Instantly a presence filled me. Anguish, shock, fear—I felt the Lady's emotions as if they were my own, as her power became one with mine. Refreshed by yet another addition to my vast well of strength, I stood, scanning the area.

Not a trace of another noble.

Perhaps they'd retreated, or maybe they'd sensed their companion's defeat, and were merely hiding. I gnashed my teeth in frustration.

Whatever the reason, I can't feel them anymore. But I'll find them. I'll find them, and make them pay for the lives that ended today.

As much as I wanted to stay and try to help those who suffered around me, I knew that nothing good would come of it.

There are too many hurt, too many injured. And the other Nobles could be nearby, waiting to attack. I need to get out of here.

I plunged in to a patch of shadow near the foot of a building, feeling a pang of regret as I left the screams of the dying and injured behind me.

It was called the worst terrorist attack in human history. The day the Central Spire fell was the event that heralded the greatest war, the Final War, between the East and the West.

Those who held power in the West blamed government-backed radicals from the East for the destruction. The East accused the West of staging the entire thing, destroying the building themselves as an excuse to go to war. It did not take long for the situation to escalate out of control, and humanity paid the ultimate price.

Chaos. Pure chaos.

Those were the only words that came to mind when I beheld the state of the world. Billions of people dead. The biological agents the opposing sides had used to wage war on one another had spread much farther than the radius of their initial targets. Not a corner of the earth remained unaffected by their taint; so potent were the toxins that even plant life had been decimated at ground zero of each impact site.

The world has gone mad. What is the point of a war where neither side survives?

I wept for humanity and beat my hands upon the floor of my chamber in frustration that everything I had done—and all that I had become—had been for nothing.

I've been fighting to save a species that has almost completely destroyed itself.

I also could not help but blame myself for the part I'd played.

If I had just left the Nobles alone, none of this would have happened.

The thought regularly came to me, wreaking havoc on my sanity. Had I been doing the wrong thing all along? Humanity had been living and thriving, even with the Nobles present. Maybe Arsenios was right. Maybe the humans needed the Nobles just as much as the Nobles needed the humans. Maybe I was single-handedly responsible for destroying the planet's natural order.

Aside from my endless remorse was a purely instinctual concern: survival. With no humans, there would be no food.

No prey. No blood. No life.

I could only imagine the panic that must be erupting among the small circle of Nobles that still survived. How long before they turned on one another and fought among themselves over the scant prey that still lived?

And how long will that prey remain? How long before all humans, even the few that have somehow made it this long, are dead?

I had gotten used to hunger. It was my constant companion, a reminder that the world would never be the same. Sensing prey had grown more difficult since the toxic agent had infected the population; although I had no idea what changes it had wrought on the surviving humans' DNA, it had fundamentally altered the way in which they appeared to my senses.

Most days I simply wandered, trying to find a stable food source. The threat of madness was ever present, and it regularly took every bit of my energy to stave it off. Worse yet, whenever I did seem to find a wayward human upon which to feed, my prey inevitably didn't survive the feeding.

They've all grown so weak. There's no life, no will to survive, left in any of them.

Thoughts of finding the last few Nobles dwindled and faded. My instinct to survive became my sole driving force, and I prowled the wasteland of earth like a starving jungle cat.

34

North American Continent, 3402 C.E.

Civilization had died. The great cities had emptied long ago, and all that remained were ruins. Some humans had survived the cataclysm of the Final War, and their descendants had grown stronger, free from the taint that had suffused those feeble remnants of humanity when the war had first decimated the planet.

For that, at least, I was thankful. The endless days of madness and near starvation were finally gone, and prey had become much easier to track. There was no sign, however, of the remaining Nobles. I knew several still lived, but centuries of fruitless searching had left me frustrated. My adversaries were so well concealed that I wondered if I'd ever be able to find them.

I had tirelessly searched every filament I could find, Traveled everywhere I detected the faintest trace of energy that could be attributed to a Noble, but came up empty each time. I had resorted to slowly wandering the world, mile by endless mile, probing with my senses, hoping that if I grew close enough to their hiding spot, I'd detect something.

My travels again brought me to Caput Mundi, a city so changed by the ravages of time that it was nearly unrecognizable. The spires that had once nearly reached the heavens had toppled ages ago, leaving destruction in their wake. No vehicles moved in the vast, empty streets, and nothing green grew anywhere in the valley. The small cluster of preserved forest that had once stood at the valley's eastern edge, however, had blossomed into a vast woodland, in which a variety of wildlife now thrived.

I began the tiresome process that had become routine over the years: I stretched my perceptions as far as I could, treating each area within reach as part of a grid. I thoroughly probed each section, then moved on to the next.

I delved deeply into the ruins of Caput Mundi, then into the areas beyond the valley.

Nothing.

Finally, I turned my attention to the eastern wood.

I hit a wall.

I knew from my last visit that another valley lay just beyond the edge of the woods, but the entire area was blank.

Puzzled, I extended my senses again, feeling for something, *anything*, but it was as if a great void had opened up and swallowed the entire valley.

I should be able to feel something, even if all that's left of the valley is a chasm. Something isn't right.

I gathered my energy to Travel to the far edge of the woods, but something stopped me. A sudden intuition told me to move slowly, to be cautious.

What if...

I didn't allow the thought to continue. False hope wouldn't do me any good.

Instead I marched forward, toward the woods. I threw up the slightest hint of a glamour, just enough to distort me should any prying eyes be about. The trek took most of the night, and just as I was becoming concerned that I'd have to abandon my journey before the sun rose, the woods thinned out, and I beheld the neighboring valley.

As it was far smaller than the valley of Caput Mundi, it didn't take long for me to make out a stretch of well-maintained buildings—probably close to a hundred in all—and roadways directly at the valley's center. Although the buildings were nothing more than small cottages, primitive by the standards to which I had become accustomed, they were well organized and, upon closer inspection, inhabited.

Humans! An entire village of humans!

I could scarcely contain my elation. All this time, I'd assumed that all traces of civilization had become extinct. The humans I regularly encountered had primarily reverted to a hunter-gatherer existence. Not since the Final War had I witnessed such a large community of humans living together, in *buildings* no less.

I tried my best to reign in my excitement as a nagging question popped into my mind: why hadn't I been able to sense any of what lay in the valley? I finally managed to tear my gaze away from the village as I pondered this, and instantly, I became aware of what stood to the north and south of the settlement.

Two massive black fortresses, nearly identical in construction, towered on opposite hilltops like fierce sentinels. Cursing under my breath, I quickly made my way back through the woods.

It was blatantly obvious that I'd found the last of the Nobles.

The entire valley must have been warded; that was the

only explanation for why my senses had failed to detect anything beyond the woods. A ward would have been the only thing capable of obscuring my perceptions to such a degree.

But warding an entire *valley*? This feat was new to me, and I knew that to accomplish something so unprecedented had to have taken a great deal of power. And the wards that were in place—I'd *never* seen anything so complex, so immune to detection. Even while standing right on top of them, I'd failed to sense their presence. The only evidence that they were there was that I couldn't sense what my eyes could plainly see.

The amount of power it must have taken to generate those wards is unfathomable. Whoever did this was strong—stronger even than I am.

I resolved to move forward with extreme caution, knowing that whoever resided in that valley most likely had the power to destroy me. I didn't stop walking until I reached Caput Mundi, where I quickly Traveled back to my home.

I need time to think. Time to plan.

My mind whirled with possibilities, and I felt nearly giddy as I tried to slow a suddenly endless tide of thoughts. There was hope yet for humanity, and hope yet for my own salvation.

PART III

CHANGES

35

J endar and Mathias felt enraptured by Dragos's every word, and when he finally finished his tale and settled back into his chair, neither of them could speak. The telling had taken hours, and the brothers had barely moved the entire time. Not once did they interrupt him with questions or comments.

This is too much...far too much.

Jendar could hardly process what he'd heard. The world from which the creature in front of him had come was beyond anything he could have imagined, as was the true nature of the Nobles who ruled over the valley.

And they're the last two who are left, other than Dragos. Thank the skies.

Jendar didn't think he'd be able to live in a world where potentially hundreds of Nobles roamed.

"I'm...speechless," said Mathias.

"It's a lot to digest," said Dragos. "What I've told you undoubtedly contradicts everything you believed about the lord and lady of your valley. But I told you the truth—they're not gods. They're living beings, just like you, though 'life' has a distinctly different meaning for them. There's nothing magical or fantastical about them. They're simply different."

"But their powers," said Jendar. "*Your* power. You can call fire forth from nothingness. You can see in the dark; you never need to sleep; and you can never die. You've lived for a span of time that I can hardly understand, but you appear to be nearly as young as we are. I believe you when you say the Nobles aren't gods, but to combat that kind of power doesn't seem possible."

"I *can* die," said Dragos, "and so can they. We can be killed, just as you can. As for combating their power and bringing them to a final end—that's why I'm here. Though it's true that no human can stand against them, there are ways to keep them at bay."

"The necklace you mentioned, the one with the silver star," said Mathias.

"Exactly," said Dragos.

"I still don't understand how these objects have such power," said Mathias. "You spoke of faith, but what does that mean? I have faith that my spade will dig a hole, but does that make it a tool capable of fighting the lord and lady?"

"That isn't the kind of faith I was talking about," said Dragos. "What I referred to is a far deeper, more spiritual sense of belief. You have no concept of a spiritual life, no understanding of what it means to have true faith in anything. You even lack faith in yourselves. The Nobility eliminated religious faith from your kind by destroying any trace of ancient spiritual practices. They set themselves up as gods to prevent you from deciding for yourselves whether there's a power higher than them. They've eradicated any meaningful sense of faith in yourselves—you can't read or write; you're not allowed to study, learn, or grow; and your lives are cut short well before your time. With all these limitations, how can you get a true sense of your accomplishments as a species? How can you realize how unique and wonderful you are when the Nobles decide everything for you, and you have no chance to succeed at anything?"

Neither Jendar nor Mathias said a word. To Jendar, the things the lord spoke of were completely foreign concepts. He could sew, and he knew how to mend a roof and tend a garden. Weren't these worthy accomplishments? What exactly did this creature mean?

"Think of it this way," Dragos continued. "You've done something no one from your village has ever done. You've crossed into the forbidden zone, in the company of armed servants, and met face-to-face with a member of the race that's imprisoned you. You have come to realize that you *are* prisoners—prisoners confined to a single valley to be raised as cattle. You've seen beyond what has been fed to you your entire lives. Doesn't this stir some sense of accomplishment within your souls? Do you feel no pride whatsoever at what you have done?"

Jendar was quiet for a moment. "I suppose I do," he said.

Dragos smiled for the first time, surprising the brothers. "As well you should. Your bravery and unconventional thinking are traits that will save humanity and allow your race to flourish again. They're your greatest weapons against the persecution of the Nobles, and they'll carry you into the future for untold years to come."

"But what good are these things to us?" said Mathias. "Surely such accomplishments alone can't harm the lord and lady. How do we fight back?"

Dragos's lips curled into a smile again, his pale-yellow eyes twinkling. "I have a plan," he said.

THE LARGE MALFORM that had escorted Jendar and Mathias to their audience with Dragos took them down another passageway, this one lined with plain metallic doors. Dragos had insisted that the two of them retire for the evening and enjoy a large meal before the three of them met the next morning to plan their strategy.

They stopped at the last door in the hall. A small black panel was positioned in the wall next to the door, about halfway up. The malform waved its hand in front of the panel, and the door slid open.

The chamber was quite large—twice the size of their cottage—and smelled better than Endreach at the fall harvest festival; the smell of freshly cooked meats and breads, along with other aromas Jendar couldn't even identify, wafted through the air. Immediately they noticed the large table, not far from the entrance, arrayed with plates full of food.

"Eat," their guide grunted. "Sleep." It turned and walked back down the hall.

The moment Jendar and Mathias had fully entered the room, the door slid shut behind them. The walls of the chamber were the same as every other wall in the structure —fashioned from a smooth, dull-gray metal. The difference here was that the room was brightly decorated, portraits of flowers and sunny outdoor scenes hanging every few hands. A large deep-red woven rug spanned nearly the entire floor, and there were two beds at the far end, piled high with fluffy, brightly colored blankets and pillows.

Jendar had never seen so much food. The amount of meat was staggering, greatly eclipsing their monthly ration.

There were cuts of what looked to be beef, but also other meats that were foreign to Jendar.

"What do you suppose this is?" Mathias said, eyes wide, as he grabbed a large chop and put it on his plate. "Or this?" he speared a slice of some type of fragrant, pinkish meat with a serving fork and added it to his growing pile of food.

Jendar merely shook his head, grabbing a plate for himself. He took a handful of small green, round fruits from a bowl, as well as a slice of bread and one of the strange meat chops.

"This is outstanding!" Mathias exclaimed, taking a bite of the pink meat.

Jendar paused and grabbed some of it for himself. The moment he bit down, the meat seemed to melt on his tongue, filling his mouth with a luscious, smoky flavor. He gobbled down some of the green fruits next; they burst in his mouth when he bit into him, their sweet juices offsetting the savory meat in a manner that was absolutely lovely. Until that moment, he hadn't realized how hungry he was.

There was more to choose from besides meat and fruit; a whole assortment of vegetables and nuts lay atop the table, most of which Jendar didn't recognize. He sampled everything, delighting in the food's exotic flavors.

When they had eaten as much as they could hold, they sat back in their chairs, neither of them speaking. Jendar had no idea what to say. He could barely process what Dragos had told them, and his head swirled with the day's events.

Driven from our home, from our village. We can never return to the cottage where we were born, where our parents died. And Bershon...poor, poor Bershon.

He wiped his eyes.

"What's wrong, brother?" asked Mathias.

"Bershon," Jendar said.

Mathias stood and placed an arm around his brother's shoulders. "I miss him too," he said. "I can't believe he's gone. Just yesterday...he was with us. Alive and well."

"Everything has changed," said Jendar. "In the space of a single day—everything."

"We have to hang on to hope that all these changes will be for the better. Even the unpleasant ones."

Jendar picked up a cloth napkin from the table and blew his nose. "You're right, of course. Thank you, brother. We'll mourn Bershon properly when all this is over."

Mathias sat back down. "I wonder what kind of a plan this Dragos has in mind."

"No idea," said Jendar. "I suppose we'll find out in the morning."

"Do you trust him?"

Jendar nodded. "We're still alive. I suppose that's reason enough to trust him."

"I don't know how I'll sleep here, in this place, with a lord under the same roof. Aren't you afraid he'll feed on us?"

Jendar shrugged. "We're probably safer here than we are at home. How many times do you suppose the lord and lady have fed on us in our lifetimes while we were sleeping? It could have been any number of times, and we never would have known. The feedings don't leave a wound unless the victim is ready to die."

Mathias sighed. "I guess you're right. Nothing we can really do. We'll just have to hope he won't bleed us dry."

"I don't think that'll be an issue," said Jendar. "He seems to hate the fact that he needs to feed on humans to survive. I'd find it hard to accept that such a man would kill a human being so thoughtlessly."

Mathias lifted an eyebrow. "Interesting. You just called him a man."

Jendar paused for a moment. "I suppose I did."

"Talking with him like that, listening to his story—it did make him seem almost human."

"I agree," said Jendar. "If I took anything away from that meeting, it's the distinct impression that there's more human in him than monster."

"I just hope he's as intelligent as he is powerful," said Mathias, "or else any plan he has could kill all three of us."

"I guess we'll just have to see what he has in mind. For now, I think we should get as much rest as we can."

Jendar stood, stripping off his shirt as he headed for one of the beds. "Tomorrow we'll find out."

"Tomorrow," Mathias agreed.

———————

THE BOYS AWOKE to find a hot breakfast of meat and eggs awaiting them. When they'd finished eating, they met in the same room as the night before. When Jendar and Mathias entered, the first thing they noticed was a large map laid out across the table. As they drew closer, they realized it was a map of the valley, along with the nearby surrounding areas.

"Good morning, gentleman," said Dragos.

Jendar and Mathias nodded in response.

"I trust you slept well?"

"We did, all things considered," said Jendar. "Those beds are a lot more comfortable than our straw pallets up in the loft."

Dragos smiled. "Good. Then let's get started." He sat and gestured for the brothers to sit as well.

"My goal is to keep you and the humans in the village

out of danger," he began. "To that end, I need someone the villagers know and trust to help facilitate their escape from the valley. I can think of no one better than the two of you."

"But what can we do?" said Mathias.

"You can help with the villagers. For this plan to work, everyone will need to stay calm and move quickly. I will send a few of my servants in to clear the village. They'll act as if the lord and lady sent them, so no one should question their orders. You will need to be present as well, to help reassure everyone that there is nothing to fear, particularly when the fighting breaks out."

"Fighting?" said Jendar.

Dragos nodded. "By moving the humans out of the valley, I'll be confiscating the lord and lady's sole food source. They'll do everything in their power to prevent that from happening. That's why our actions need to be swift and decisive, and why I've already prepared my forces for combat."

"You mentioned before that you have the ability to travel to any point where a shadow is cast," said Jendar. "Why not get the villagers out that way?"

"The wards on the valley make Shadow Travel in or out impossible for me. I've spent the past few years attempting to devise a way past the wards, and I nearly succeeded once, when I attempted to contact the two of you."

Jendar suddenly remembered their terrifying visit from the Noble in their cottage. "That was you?"

Dragos nodded. "I originally planned to appear to you directly, in your home. I thought our conversation would be less intimidating for you if it took place in familiar surroundings. I wanted to see if I could break through to your location, as appearing in the flesh at that time of day would have been most dangerous for me. I thought I had succeeded, but something—some force—pushed me back. Afraid I'd be discovered, I retreated.

"I suspect that's when the lord and lady first became aware of my presence. That's why I had to act quickly and bring you both here as soon as possible."

"The lord and lady probably figured out who you were trying to visit," Mathias said quietly. "That's how we were discovered. That's why Bershon was taken and why Jendar and I were targeted next."

Dragos gazed off for a moment, his expression unreadable. "The thought occurred to me as well. I can't tell you how sorry I am that I put you in danger and that your friend was taken because of me." He shook his head. "Another senseless death on my conscience."

The brothers remained silent for a moment, until Jendar finally found his voice. "What's done is done," he said. "You weren't the one who took Bershon, nor were you the one who drove us from our home. The creatures responsible for that are the ones we have to worry about now."

Mathias nodded slowly. "I agree. Let's stick to planning."

"Thank you for understanding," said Dragos. He paused a moment before continuing. "My servants won't attack the lord and lady directly. They'll provide a distraction and keep *their* servants from taking the field. We'll attack here..." He tapped the north fortress. "...and here." He tapped the south fortress. "All the while, my servants will be clearing the village, directing the villagers to exit to the west, via the village's central road. You two will be at the outskirts, waiting for them."

"What do you want us to do when they reach us?" asked Jendar.

"You'll keep them calm, and you'll reiterate what my servants have already told them. The few among my servants who can speak clearly have memorized an edict, supposedly issued by the lord and lady themselves. The villagers will be told that a hostile force has invaded the valley, and they're being evacuated beyond the forbidden woods until the threat has been dealt with. Tell them you're in the lord and lady's service, but mention nothing about me. If any of the villagers are curious about what happened to you, tell them you've been punished for travel beyond the Line of Demarcation by permanent removal from the village, to live out the rest of your days as the lord and lady's servants. That explanation should be adequate."

Mathias nodded. "No one knows what happens to those who are taken from the village. I guess that'll be believable enough."

"Once everyone has been gathered," Dragos continued, "my servants will lead you all through the woods, back here. This building has been warded against Shadow Travel—no one but I may enter or leave using that method—and the doors are quite strong. This building has more than enough space to accommodate several hundred people. They'll be safe here."

"But what if we're attacked on our way back?" Jendar asked.

"It's unlikely that you will be. I've taken measures to ensure that my servants will be a powerful force. Our enemies will have a difficult time penetrating our defenses. Even if they manage it, there should be enough time to get everyone here safely before the Nobles' servants catch up to the villagers."

"How can you be so sure that your servants will be superior to theirs?" asked Mathias.

Dragos grinned. "I've spent several hundred years hoarding every piece of functional weaponry I could find.

I've amassed enough arms to equip every one of my servants, with more to spare."

"But what about the lord and lady?" Mathias pressed. "Will these weapons work against them?"

Dragos shook his head. "If they joined the battle, my forces wouldn't stand a chance. But there's a simple way to prevent them from getting involved: sunlight. The rescue operation will be carried out first thing in the morning, on a day filled with sunshine. I've also taken another precaution. In addition to weaponry, I've traveled the earth with a few trusted servants in search of something else that will be quite useful, something I couldn't search for myself."

Jendar raised his eyebrows.

"Objects of faith," said Dragos, "that were cherished at a time when faith still existed."

"Where did they find such objects?" asked Mathias.

"The dead," said Dragos. "Ancient burial grounds. Sites where great battles were fought. Places, like this city, where hundreds died in the streets. I had them collected and preserved. I've never laid eyes on them myself, but I've been told it's quite a collection. Most of the servants who go to battle, as well as every villager, will wear one around their neck. These objects, plus the sunlight, should be enough to prevent the Nobles from getting involved."

"But what about you?" asked Jendar. "Won't you be prevented from joining in too?"

Dragos nodded. "I'll be forced to remain here to coordinate our efforts. I have devices that will enable me to communicate with my servants over long distances. That will have to be enough. Once the humans have been secured in this building, it'll only be a matter of time before the lord and lady come to retrieve them. My guess is they'll be here the moment night falls. That's when I intend to destroy them."

"But how can you be sure they'll come? And how will they get through if everyone around them is wearing a talisman?" asked Jendar.

"My servants will be sequestered in the building by that time; the lord and lady will have free reign to move about outside as they please. I'll also provide them with a convenient means of entry: a door with a faulty locking mechanism. This will, of course, lead to corridors laden with deadly traps.

"Before you ask, the lord and lady will unfortunately be immune to any trap or snare I can deploy. But their servants won't be. More likely than not, they'll send their forces in first, then follow when they feel that any outside interference has been minimized. I intend to whittle down their forces to a minimum before I enter the fray."

"What happens if they defeat you?" Mathias asked.

"They won't. I will be victorious. I *must* be victorious."

Jendar remained silent. He preferred not to think of what would happen if Dragos fell to the lord and lady. Besides, he was actually starting to like the man, and he didn't want to see another decent person lose his life.

"So what's next?" asked Mathias.

"We wait. Recent days have been nearly cloudless, and I expect that to continue. If the weather cooperates, we'll be able to make our move first thing tomorrow."

Jendar tried to swallow, but his throat had gone dry. *He really means to do this. And Mathias and I will be in the thick of it.*

"We're ready," he managed. "We will see this through to the end."

36

J endar peered through the trees, toward the village, basking in the early-morning sunlight. Everything appeared serene as people began to awaken and go about their business. Mathias stood beside him while the hulking shapes of malforms loomed around them. Each of the beasts held a long, cylindrical item with a flat, tapered end. Though the objects looked tiny in their massive hands, they would have been just right for either Jendar or Mathias to hold.

Dragos had explained what the objects were right before their departure.

Matter disruptors. Designed for only one thing—for humans to kill other humans.

Jendar shuddered at the prospect of a time in history when such weapons were commonly used and when killing had occurred on such a grand scale.

He fingered the strange amulet that hung around his neck. It was a dull, copper-colored piece of jewelry comprised of two short segments intersecting at right angles. Each of them wore something similar—Jendar noticed that many bore objects that looked almost identical to his, though many other designs and shapes present were quite different.

They'd left Dragos's stronghold just as the first rays of sunlight peeked over the eastern horizon. Their force was three hundred strong, arrayed in three columns. The lines had marched through the winding streets of the abandoned village together but had split up when the woods came into view. One group headed south, the other north, while Jendar and Mathias's group had gone straight ahead. Their instructions were to make their way to the edge of the woods nearest the village and to remain hidden until Dragos gave the signal.

Vomit rose at the back of Jendar's throat. Would they have enough time to get everyone out? Would people even listen to them once the servants brought them to the outskirts of the village?

He clutched the leather satchel Dragos had given him, feeling the weight of dozens of talismans inside. He glanced at Mathias. His brother, carrying a similar satchel, stared ahead intently, unblinking.

The night before, they'd spent hours preparing the talismans. They had affixed a thin chain to each, then carefully wound the chain around each object. The last thing either of them wanted was to deal with a tangled mess.

Sweat trickled down Jendar's brow, and his heart raced. When would the signal come?

The malforms seemed unconcerned, even relaxed. If they felt any nervousness at all at the prospect of facing battle, none of them showed it.

I envy them, thought Jendar. *To be able to remain so calm in the face of something so terrifying.*

His thoughts were interrupted by a series of faint pops—

hundreds of them—echoing across the valley. A concussion like a distant thunderclap suddenly rang out, and Jendar jumped.

"There!" said Mathias, pointing to the northern end of the valley, toward the distant shape of the fortress.

Darkness still shrouded the structure, but there was something more now: faint-green flashes of light erupted continually from different points on the hilltop surrounding the building.

As Jendar turned to the south, the same scene unfolded on the opposite hilltop. "There as well," he said, pointing.

His heart raced faster.

A sudden, faint crackling sound came from somewhere nearby. The lead malform lifted its arm, to which a strange device had been strapped.

"Move forward." A voice suddenly cut through the noise, and the device grew silent.

Dragos's voice, thought Jendar.

The lead malform turned and grunted loudly, waving the others ahead. Jendar gritted his teeth and followed, stepping out into the open, leaving the safety of concealment behind. Mathias accompanied him, along with twenty other malforms.

Per the plan, the rest remained behind. Dragos didn't want the villagers to be greeted with the sight of so many of the creatures right away, nor did he want the lord and lady to know just how many of his servants there were. When Jendar had asked him how he intended to prevent the Nobles from using rats and blackjays as spies, Dragos had simply told them he'd exterminate all such creatures from the valley on the morning of the rescue. Jendar had asked him how he intended to accomplish such a feat.

Dragos had merely grinned wryly and said "one thing my race is good at is killing."

Whatever he did, it worked. I haven't seen a single blackjay since we left the city.

They drew closer, and half the malforms split off from the main group when they reached the village's edge. As Jendar's group stopped, he watched the others walk up the main road, each heading in a different direction.

"Attention!" a chorus of slurred, half-intelligible voices carried across the morning air, growing fainter as the malforms moved farther away. "The lord and lady have declared a state of emergency and have ordered the evacuation of all villagers! Proceed to the west side of the village! Exit on the main road! Attention!" They repeated the message again and again. Eventually they were so far away that Jendar could no longer make out the words.

He approached the road, unfastening his satchel as he went. It didn't take long for the first group of harried villagers to approach him. "Jendar?" It was Astra, the apprentice pyre builder, and several others with whom Jendar was also acquainted. "I haven't seen you around the village the last couple of days. Karmen stopped by your cottage to check on you, but no one was there. Is everything all right?"

"Yes, Astra, everything is fine. Please hurry—we don't have much time."

Astra hurried over, followed by the others. Jendar and Mathias handed each of them a talisman, instructing them to put them on. The villagers complied.

"What are these for?" asked one of the women.

"For protection," said Jendar. "Protection from the invaders."

"What is all this about?" asked Astra. "And where have

the two of you been?"

"We were punished," said Mathias, "for venturing too far into the woods. We're to live out the rest of our lives as servants of the lord and lady."

Astra shuddered. "I'm...so sorry," he muttered.

More villagers began to arrive.

"Why are we being evacuated?" Jone Weaver pressed. "What's happening at the ends of the valley?"

"We're told it's a foreign invader," said Mathias. "We've been sent here to get all of you out and take you someplace safe."

"Astra," said Jendar, "if you would, head out into the field. Go and stand near that group of malforms. They're with us—they won't harm you. The rest of you, please join him."

Although Astra didn't look pleased, he nodded and did as asked. The other villagers followed him.

Jendar and Mathias spent the better part of the next hour fielding similar questions from nearly everyone they saw. They did their best to answer quickly, while being as reassuring about the situation as possible. They also made sure that every single person wore a talisman.

The steady stream of villagers shrank to a trickle, and then the trickle faded to nothing. One of the malforms returned; the others weren't far behind.

"Is that everyone?" Jendar asked. The last malform nodded. Jendar and Mathias trotted over to where the rest of the villagers stood.

"All right!" Jendar called out. "Listen up, everyone! We're to be escorted through the woods by the lord and lady's servants." There were more than a few murmurs at this, as well as sounds of panicked conversation. The noise from the crowd soon grew too loud for Jendar to speak over.

"Please!" he shouted. "Please be calm!" The villagers quieted down a bit, enough for him to keep talking. "There's a secret village on the other side of the woods, where the lord and lady have a stronghold waiting for us. We'll be safe there. But we have to move quickly!"

He gestured toward the woods and headed forward at a brisk pace.

What if they don't follow? What if they don't believe any of this and decide to stay behind?

He glanced behind him and was relieved when he saw the crowd moving slowly forward.

As they neared the woods, the malforms within the trees moved to the side to allow them to enter. There were more than a few gasps and whispers when people caught sight of the remainder of their escort, and the flow of people began to slow.

"Keep moving!" shouted Mathias. "The malforms are here for our protection! They won't harm you! Keep moving!"

Eventually the words got through to everyone, and the forward momentum continued. Jendar kept on through the woods, right beside Mathias and several of the malforms. He glanced behind him every few feet and sighed in relief when the last of the villagers had made it into the woods. Though the rear of the column was difficult to make out, he knew the malforms would be closing ranks behind the villagers, just in case an assault came from that direction.

We're actually going to pull this off.

He allowed himself a slight smile as he picked up his pace, and tried not to jump when the occasional boom of a distant explosion echoed through the air. Every so often, he turned his head and offered words of encouragement.

"Doing great, everyone! The journey isn't long. Keep up the pace!"

Mathias joined in, calling out occasionally, trying to keep everyone's spirits up.

They'd been moving for nearly an hour when the air began to grow cooler, and the light filtering in through the overhead boughs started to dim. At first Jendar thought it must be a large cloud passing between them and the sun, but he stopped moving when the sunlight continued to fade and the darkness of twilight enveloped the surrounding woods.

As he peered up through a crack in the canopy, his breath froze when he realized a thick gray haze stretched across the sky. As he watched, the haze grew increasingly opaque, darkening to complete blackness. The woods were plunged into darkness, and more than a few villagers cried out in fear. The group halted, as seeing ahead was impossible.

"Remain calm!" shouted Jendar, though nervous sweat poured down his forehead. "Please keep moving! Go slowly! Allow your eyes to adjust!"

"What is it?" whispered Mathias. "Why has the sky grown dark?"

Jendar had no answer to his brother's question.

THE TOP FLOOR of Dragos's stronghold was completely transparent—the walls and ceiling had been built with a metallic substance that offered a perfectly unimpeded view of the outdoors to anyone standing inside, while obscuring the interior from those outside the structure. Whatever the substance was, it was also effective at blocking out the sun's rays. The room in which he stood was the only place on earth where he could still enjoy the brightness of the sun without the threat of absolute agony. He had a clear view in every direction, though his attention was now focused on the eastern wood.

A black fog was creeping over the treetops, completely blocking out the bright-blue sky above. It continued to spread, covering the woods, moving slowly across the ruined city. The line of shadow, nearly perfectly straight, advanced across the remnants of buildings and streets, growing ever closer to Dragos's stronghold.

He cursed under his breath. He hadn't expected this, hadn't even considered that the Nobles had the resources or the ability to expand their own personal twilight across such a broad area.

Somehow they've figured out a way.

Abruptly he turned, heading for the stairway at the center of the room. The floor below was completely dark. He plunged himself into the shadows and emerged a moment later at the edge of the wood near the northern hill. He sprinted toward the fortress, cursing the wards that prevented him from Traveling directly there.

By the time he reached the hilltop, battle raged all around him. His servants fired wildly at the waves of malforms that poured from the gateway of the fortress, green flashes lighting up the landscape time and again. Their adversaries exploded into flames as the blasts from the matter disruptors connected, yet still they came. Dead servants, most of them still clutching oversized clubs or swords, littered the barren rocky soil surrounding him. Every one of the fallen was horribly charred and mangled. In an instant, he saw that his own forces had pushed the others back nearly to the walls of the fortress.

Dragos moved forward to get a better look. He was pleased that his assumption about his foes' armaments had been correct—the lord and lady's forces bore only crude weapons. They hadn't possessed the foresight to properly arm their troops.

He laughed softly. *It's a slaughter. They don't stand a chance.*

As soon as the thought crossed his mind, he felt a new presence on the field. Dragos paused for a moment, baffled at what his perceptions told him.

A Noble. And another. And another!

He sprinted toward the front lines, not believing what he felt. More and more Nobles emerged. He tried to catch a glimpse of the barely visible newcomers as they flitted back and forth in front of the fortress's walls. Suddenly one of his servants exploded in a spray of gore, reduced to nothing but a pair of legs with jagged, bloody stumps where its torso had been.

Another met the same end, and soon his servants were dying all around him, violently eradicated by some unseen force. Dragos focused his perceptions but didn't sense any energies involved. He brought his attention to the newcomers. Roughly twenty Nobles had joined the battle.

None of them possess the strength it would take to make someone explode. *What is going on?*

He lay flat on the ground, using his eyesight instead. As one of the Nobles dove behind a rock, Dragos noticed something in its hands. It popped up from behind its cover a moment later, pointing what appeared to be an improvised matter disruptor in his direction. There was a muted flash from its tip, then came the gut-wrenching sounds of another servant being ripped to shreds.

Dragos raced back in the other direction. All at once, he

sensed a group of about a dozen Nobles break off, heading toward the woods at a dead run. He hesitated, trying to think quickly. These lords and ladies were incredibly weak and seemed very young.

And all of them are dressed in the brown woolen garb of an Endreach villager.

Dragos was horrified at the implications; apparently the lord and lady had not stopped at using the villagers for food. They'd been building an army, abducting villagers and turning them into Nobles. The eldest present couldn't have been more than a hundred years old; he knew that he could destroy them with relative ease, but doing so would take time, and would leave his servants at the fortress vulnerable.

Either way, one of these groups of Nobles is going to get to the villagers.

"Damn it," he spat, furious for not anticipating this possibility. He swiftly gathered his energy.

"Fall back!" his voice boomed across the battlefield. "Regroup at Point A!"

Instantly, his servants shouldered their weapons and ran for the woods. Dragos plunged into the shadows then reappeared at the edge of the woods nearest the southern hilltop. A frenzied sprint brought him quickly to within sight of the battle.

The scene was the same—newly formed Nobles, roughly twenty strong. Half of them were at the fortress, ripping his forces to shreds. The other half were well into the woods already, moving quickly.

He again shouted the order to fall back and Traveled to where he knew he'd be needed—the column of nearly defenseless villagers, slowly making their way through the pitch-black woods.

37

"Jendar!"

Jendar jumped at the voice, spinning around, and was shocked to see a man sprinting out of the underbrush nearby. The man wore the exact same outfit as Dragos, but had rosy skin, brown eyes and blonde hair. Several of the villagers gasped at his sudden appearance.

"Dragos?" he said. "Is that you? How did you—"

"It's a glamour," he said quietly. "I did not want to alarm anyone. But that isn't important. You're in grave peril. More Nobles have entered the fray."

"What do you mean, 'more Nobles'?" Mathias whispered, his eyes wide.

"The lord and lady have been busy," said Dragos. "There are forty or fifty very young Nobles out there, converging on this location. I'm shocked I wasn't able to sense them before; the lord and lady must have somehow obscured them from detection. Looks like they're all former villagers. I don't think I can stop all of them quickly enough to guarantee your safety. You have to move faster. There's still time, but only if you hurry. I'll slow them down as best as I can."

"Former villagers?" said Mathias. "You don't mean—"

Dragos nodded. "They've been turned. All of them. To be used as soldiers."

Jendar felt as if he'd be sick. *So that's what happened to all those who disappeared over the years.*

"Wait!" he said. "What about the talismans? Can't they protect us?"

"The talismans can prevent the Nobles from touching you or exerting their power upon you. But that won't stop their servants. If all my own servants are killed, there'll be no one to stop the Nobles' servants from removing the talismans."

Jendar swallowed a lump in his throat. "So what do we do?"

"Move faster."

Without another word, Dragos darted back into the woods.

"All right, everyone—we need to pick up the pace!" Jendar yelled. "Let's move! *Move!*"

Although his eyes had adjusted a bit to the darkness, he was nervous about jogging through the woods when visibility was less than ideal. Even so, he trotted forward, signaling for the others to follow.

"At this pace, it shouldn't take long," said Mathias.

"I just hope the villagers can maintain it. Some of them aren't as young as we are."

Mathias nodded and kept moving forward.

DRAGOS DIDN'T KNOW how much of his original force had survived, if any at all. The young Nobles had wielded their weapons with deadly precision; Dragos hoped his servants had at least been able to slow them.

Every so often, the sound of weapons fire carried through the air.

Not much of it, though—there should be more. Every one of my troops is armed.

He feared the worst and wondered whether his plan could possibly succeed.

The northern group was closest; he felt them moving, not far off. He paused for a moment to get his bearings then plunged into the shadows and appeared directly in their midst. He took a quick tally.

Eleven.

Each of them was armed with those strange modified disruptors, weapons with which Dragos was unfamiliar. They cried out in unison as he fell upon the nearest Noble, crippling him with a few well-placed blows to the neck and face. The others turned just as the first one fell to the earth. One quickly raised her weapon and fired a round. As Dragos focused, the air before him coalesced, sending the energy burst fizzling off into the woods. A split second later, he'd closed the distance between them. He struck out swiftly, caving the creature's entire face in.

Four of them reached him at once, striking out in concert, coordinating their efforts perfectly so as not to impede one another.

Someone has trained these creatures to fight.

For an instant Dragos was on the defensive, parrying and dodging four sets of fists and feet. He drew upon his power, lending speed to his limbs, and suddenly the young Nobles seemed to move as slowly as snails. He snaked easily between their assaults, landing solid hits on every one of them, dropping each in succession. As soon as they fell, he turned his attention to the rest.

They were no longer there. They had fled into the woods, and he felt that each one was traveling in a different direction.

I'll never get them all.

He turned his attention to the group that lay prone at his feet. As he focused a minor effort of will, each of them instantly burst into flames. He felt their combined consciousness enter him as their bodies crumbled to ash. He felt their confusion, their youth.

Their devotion to their masters.

Enthralled. Completely enthralled. All of them.

The fog that typically existed upon the mind of a half-turned child covered them all. Dragos was shocked to see it present on a group of fully grown, fully formed Nobles.

I never knew such a thing was even possible.

As disturbing as it was, he had to admire the lord and lady's ingenuity.

Such creatures would make a nearly perfect fighting force.

Since chasing down the members of the first group was fruitless, he reached his senses out toward the group he knew was coming from the south. He zeroed in on them, Traveling there instantly. He fell upon them in the same manner as he had the first group, and they responded in the same way: some of them fell; the rest of them scattered.

At least they'll need to regroup before they reach the villagers. That might give us the time we need.

Dragos Traveled back to the woods near the head of the main column, throwing up a glamour and trying to approach slowly, so as not to startle the villagers.

"Commander," Dragos said, addressing the lead

malform. The creature turned to regard its master. "Take the other servants and fan out through the woods. There are young Nobles about, armed with some type of matter disruptors. Lie in wait for them, and open fire as soon as you see them. Relay the instructions to the others."

The creature nodded and fell out of step. It grunted loudly and gestured at the others. The rest of the malforms began to slow, as did the villagers.

"Tell them to keep moving!" Dragos said.

"Everyone keep going!" shouted Jendar. "Our escort will remain here. Mathias and I will lead you the rest of the way!"

Though Dragos could have imagined it, he thought he heard a few sighs of relief from the villagers behind him. He reached out, sensing, probing. Although the younger Nobles were scattered all over the woods, they were beginning to converge on the villagers. He chose the nearest one and Traveled there instantly.

Dragos took him completely off guard and, with a swift blow to the head, ended his unnatural life instantly. He prepared to Travel to the next one, gaining hope that maybe he was wrong. Maybe he *could* stop all of them, if he moved fast enough.

His thoughts crashed to a halt as he felt the energy of the battle abruptly change.

No.

Two new presences—incredibly old, incredibly strong— had appeared in the woods.

Right near the humans.

My entire plan is falling to pieces.

Everything had hinged on the sunlight and the fact that the lord and lady would be trapped in their fortresses. Their being able to move about freely changed everything.

The talismans will protect the villagers. At least I have that.

Dragos Traveled to where he knew they were waiting. It wasn't the time or the place he'd wanted this conflict to take place, but he had run out of options.

JENDAR URGED THE VILLAGERS ON, telling them to hurry, lest the invading force catch up to them. They moved as quickly as a large group traveling through a darkened wood possibly could—which was to say not very quickly at all.

We're so close, thought Jendar. *The woods are beginning to thin. If we had just a bit more time...*

Instantly, two figures blinked into existence in front of him. He hissed as his body froze, and his heart hammered against his rib cage. A similar exclamation came from Mathias.

Someone bumped him from behind, cursing loudly. A confused murmur suffused the group as everyone stopped suddenly, jostling their neighbors, some of them falling to the ground.

The lord and lady, Jendar thought. *Right here. Right in front of us.*

Their strange dress—the man, wearing a multi-colored outfit with pointed shoes; the woman, wearing a long, apricot robe; their pale skin; their gleaming yellow eyes—there was no mistaking them.

Jendar clutched the talisman that hung about his neck. Feeling its slight weight in his hand made him feel a bit better somehow.

"Silence!" The lord's voice boomed through the woods, and every villager instantly grew quiet. "Return to your village at once! You're on forbidden ground!"

This will ruin everything! thought Jendar as a chorus of confused voices erupted from behind him.

"I thought the lord and lady wanted us here..."

"What do they mean? Didn't they tell us to..."

"Jendar and Mathias said they were working for them..."

He had to do something and do it quickly.

"They're impostors!" he screamed as loudly as he could. "Invaders!"

Everyone behind him grew quiet again.

Jendar walked slowly forward, brandishing his talisman. "You have no power over us! Leave this place at once or suffer our masters' wrath!"

The eyes of the lord and lady blazed. The lady stepped forward menacingly. "You insolent little—"

Her voice was cut off as a black shape slammed into her. She grunted loudly as she flew through the air and crashed to the ground moments later. The lord was suddenly a blur, and he and the strange shape circled and danced in a dizzying manner, too quickly for the eye to behold. In an instant, they were both gone.

Dragos! It must be!

Just then, hundreds of crackling pops erupted from the woods behind them. Staccato flashes of green light madly lit the treetops off in the distance.

"Run for your lives!" screamed Jendar.

Without even bothering to see who followed, he sprinted forward. Mathias followed suit, and from the sound of it, the rest of the villagers did as well. Branches snapped and leaves rustled as the thundering footfalls of hundreds of terrified people echoed through the woods. Jendar finally chanced a glance behind him and noted with relief that the villagers were following.

The brothers dodged branches and leapt over scrub,

hearing the occasional cry of pain as someone behind them turned an ankle or tripped and fell. The canopy overhead started to thin noticeably, and Jendar's lungs burned as the ground sloped upward. He also saw the first signs that the ruined city was growing nearer—immense metallic shapes jutted from the earth.

If the villagers noticed these new sights, none of them stopped to stare. Everyone was on the move, running pell-mell through the woods, crying out as the sounds of battle drew closer.

Almost there, Jendar thought. *We're almost there.*

The woods grew thinner, until Jendar burst forth from the last of the trees as the ground leveled off and the valley spread before him. He allowed himself a moment to stop, to make sure the villagers were following.

"Keep going!" he shouted to his brother. "Lead them all back!"

Mathias nodded as he continued on.

Not a single villager managed to keep up his or her pace as the sights of the valley unfolded before them. Some stopped moving entirely, despite the growing battle behind them.

Jendar urged them on. "I know it's strange. I know it's magnificent, but you've got to keep going!"

Again and again, he shouted those words, and thankfully the people listened. Jendar stayed where he was until the last person emerged. Glancing back into the woods, he cried out as he saw just how close the battle had drawn.

Dragos's servants were right behind them, running as they fired their weapons into the woods to their rear. Every so often, one of them collapsed in a spray of gore, seemingly brought down by weapons fire from the opposing side.

They're right on top of us!

Jendar turned and followed the crowd down the hill, onto the road that eventually would lead them to Dragos's stronghold.

THE LORD AND LADY TRAVELED, and Dragos followed. They fled to the grounds near their fortresses, to the village, to the eastern bog. They never stopped long enough to engage him, always remaining just out of reach.

They're toying with me.

In reality, he knew it was much more than that—they were keeping him occupied, keeping him out of the battle between their young thralls and Dragos's servants. They knew he had the power to end that battle, if he only had the chance to join the fight alongside his forces. Twice already, he'd tried to intervene. Both times, the lord and lady had promptly Traveled to points right beside the mass of fleeing humans. They moved fast—so fast he couldn't get a good look at either of them.

They want me to know that if I get involved in that conflict, they'll close in on the villagers.

He had no choice but to indulge them in their game of cat and mouse, at least taking solace in the fact that by keeping him occupied, they kept themselves out of the conflict as well. That was perhaps Dragos's greatest advantage—he knew that, on their own, neither Noble was a match for him. Only with their combined strength did they stand a chance of overcoming him.

Yet they're not attacking me. They're leading me on a chase, all over the valley, never standing still long enough to strike a blow. Why?

As he sensed them again move near the humans, he

Traveled to their location, only to witness them vanish back across the valley. Clenching his teeth in frustration, he prepared to go after them again.

No. They're playing you for a fool. Stop and think.

What did they have to gain by distracting him? Why not simply attack as a pair and put an end to the struggle?

Then it clicked.

The thralls!

What if the purpose of these new Nobles wasn't really to provide a fighting force? What if they were meant for something more important?

Like a final confrontation.

Dragos Traveled back to the rear of the column of villagers, right behind Jendar. He kept pace with him, glancing behind. He clearly saw the battle moving to a close and watched the last of his servants fall.

They're meant for me. The lord and lady must lack confidence in their ability to stop me on their own. But forty or fifty young Nobles, plus the added might of the lord and lady?

Dragos doubted that even he was strong enough to beat those odds. He stopped running, facing the woods just as the first of the Nobles burst from the tree line. He felt the rest of them closing in, nearing the edge of the woods, like ants scenting a picnic. Then he felt a sudden swell of power as two other forces—older and far more powerful—joined them.

This is it. This is how they mean to end it.

He extended his senses farther, feeling for humans.

Fifteen. Fifteen injured, still in the woods.

He shook his head. "I'm sorry," he said, "but there's no other way."

Dragos dropped every mental defense he had. Every fetter on his emotions fell away, and he felt nothing but rage. Rage at the lord and lady, rage at the new thralls. Rage at himself, at what he'd become. Rage at everything he'd lost.

He roared as the fire of his anger raced through him. The earth shuddered as a wave of searing heat burst from his body, expanding as it slammed into the tree line. Instantly the woods were ablaze. Dragos pushed harder, adding more rage, more fire. The inferno raced back toward Endreach, consuming everything it touched.

He stopped when he heard the screams, when he felt the thralls dying. Only three had made it out of the woods. He focused his will upon them, and in seconds, they were ash. A sudden blackness enveloped him, obscuring his vision, but a moment later everything became clear again.

A man and a woman stood before him. The woman wore an apricot-colored silk robe, strikingly embroidered with dragons. Her midnight-black hair was pulled back in a tight ponytail, and her ash-gray skin glowed in the light of her golden eyes. The man had close-cropped black hair and wore a tunic identical to the one he'd worn when Dragos had first met him so many years ago.

Dragos tilted his head. "Arsenios," he said. "It's been a long time."

38

Jendar's lungs ached, and his heart felt as if it would explode. Nevertheless, he ran as fast as he could, trying to keep pace with the villagers in front of him. They'd made it halfway up the road. If they kept up their current speed, Mathias and the first villagers would arrive at the stronghold in minutes.

All at once, the entire valley was awash with reddish light. Dumbfounded, Jendar stopped, glancing behind him. He froze when he saw the entire wood had burst into flames.

What happened?

Despite the heat from the blaze, he felt chilled to the bone.

Is this some new weapon? Have our forces been defeated?

Other villagers also stopped and stared, and the group's forward progress slowed.

Despite his worry and his doubt, Jendar tore his gaze away from the conflagration. "Don't stop now! We're nearly there!"

He grabbed the nearest villager and shoved him forward. The man stumbled, eyes wide, but started moving again. That seemed to snap the rest of the nearby villagers out of their stupors. They turned and once again fled for their lives.

———

Arsenios and his companion regarded Dragos darkly, their eyes blazing so brightly that they cast a subtle light over the area in which they stood. Dragos maintained a careful distance, keeping his senses honed and locked on both of them.

"I always felt it would come to this," said Arsenios. "Ever since we last spoke, I knew I would need to put you down."

"An obligation to your lineage?" asked Dragos.

"An obligation to us all," said Arsenios. "You pose the single greatest threat to our continued existence. I've waited a very long time for you to finally show yourself."

"And who is your companion?" said Dragos, gesturing to the lady. "I don't recall seeing her before."

"We've met," she said. "Long ago, in the presence of my former master."

Something about her bearing, about her distinctly Asian features, dredged something up from the deepest corners of his memory. But...no. It couldn't be.

"Gou?"

"My name," she said, "is Liu. Gou was merely a pet name."

"How did you survive?"

She grinned, revealing perfectly straight, white teeth. "Lord Chin sent me to safety just as you attacked. I was badly burned, but I was alive. It took me months to heal."

Dragos shook his head. "I sincerely regret that it came to that. I would have saved you if I could have."

"No matter," said Arsenios. "I found her a day later, near death and half insane from the loss of her master. I took her as my own. I nursed her back to health, and I oversaw the rest of her development. She was a better offspring to me than you ever were."

The corners of Dragos's lips turned down. "You mean you continued to twist her, rather than allow her to die?"

"He saved my life! I was lost and alone because of you," said Liu, venom bubbling beneath the surface of her words. "Lord Arsenios restored me and raised me as his own daughter. He taught me to be strong. I owe everything I am to him."

"You've violated every tenant we hold dear," Arsenios said, his tone biting. "You've decimated our species. The damage you've done is irreparable and unquestionable. What I find curious is your reasoning. Why have you done this? For power?"

"No," said Dragos. "Power holds no interest for me, although the more of it I possess, the more Nobles I can kill."

Arsenios took a cautious step forward. "But *why*? Why have you dedicated your existence to destroying your own kind?"

"I might ask you the same thing," said Dragos. "I can feel your power. You're far stronger than you should be, even at your age. How many Nobles died to give you this strength?"

"I had no choice!" The older Noble's eyes blazed. "How else was I to survive against someone who broke our most sacred rule? I did not *want* to kill my brothers and sisters! I've become a monster...because of you!"

Dragos shook his head. "You were already a monster. All of you were. That's why I decided long ago that every Noble must be exterminated."

"You're mad," said Arsenios. "That's the only explanation."

"No, Arsenios. Madness isn't what drives me. My humanity does," Dragos said quietly, his throat clenching as his sense of loss bloomed anew. "I *remember*. I recall everything from before I was corrupted. I know who I was before my humanity was robbed from me. I watched my daughter —my *real* daughter—grow old and die. *I bled my own wife dry.* What your kind does is reprehensible. You take the righteous, and you twist and destroy them. You prey on humans as if they're animals, and you use them as tools to further your own species."

"The Progenitor was right," said Arsenios. "You *are* flawed. Perhaps I was too conceited to see it. I thought no one of my lineage could ever turn out the way you did; I thought my line would always be pure."

"I'm not the one who is flawed," said Dragos. "You are. All of you. Anyone who would enslave another, anyone who would seek to subjugate an entire race is—"

"We kept the humans alive," Arsenios said, shaking his head. "Your slaughter disrupted our control, destroyed all our efforts at peacekeeping. Our networks fell apart, and the governments of the world ran wild. What do you think caused the Final War? It was *your* actions at the spire, and the fact that we were too weak to stop you!"

Dragos sighed. "I refuse to believe that. Whatever the humans did, they would have done regardless of anyone's involvement. If not the spire, something else would have been the catalyst for war."

"You're a fool. All this time you've been exterminating Nobles, trying to save humanity, while it was your own actions that nearly destroyed it."

"No," said Dragos.

Despite his doubts, he felt the seed that Arsenios had planted begin to bloom. What if there was some truth to what the man had said? What if humanity really *had* needed to be restrained, to prevent such a calamity from occurring?

His thoughts immediately went to Caput Mundi, hundreds of years ago, to the spire. Perhaps the nobles had ensconced themselves in the building that housed the seat of the Western Empire's government not as a tactic to keep Dragos at bay, but to stay close to the humans who had the power to destroy the earth. If that were the case, could it really be that the world was in its current state because of his actions?

The thought of it made him sick.

I can't change what's already happened. Fixating on this now will only get me killed.

With a great deal of effort, he pushed his doubts down as far as they would go.

"You don't understand," said Liu. "Even after all this time, you haven't learned how primitive and base humans are."

"They needed us," said Arsenios, "just as we needed them."

"There's no solid proof of that," said Dragos. "You've said nothing to convince me that such a calamity wouldn't have happened anyway."

Arsenios sighed. "Then you'll die a fool."

Without a hint of warning, Arsenios and Liu lunged forward. They moved as two skilled dancers, simultaneously lashing out with a flurry of punches and kicks that sent Dragos skittering backward. He reeled from the assault, trying his best to dodge and counter. Every blow he aimed they deftly avoided or parried, responding with a series of strikes that were impossibly fast.

Growing frustrated, Dragos abandoned his attempts at a physical onslaught, lashing out with a barrage of heat and energy. Together Liu and Arsenios easily parried the flow, retorting with a force of even greater strength. Dragos cursed as he leapt to the side, desperately slicing at the wave with all the power he could muster. The Nobles' combined energy smashed into the earth where he'd been moments before, hurling chunks of dirt and stone in all directions.

As Dragos rolled beneath the cloud of debris, Liu suddenly appeared before him. She brought her foot down, grazing the side of his head as he propelled himself away. Arsenios followed with a kick that was so swift it was a blur. His foot connected with Dragos's gut, sending him sprawling to the ground. Desperately, he lashed out with another burst of energy. The mild effort it took them to parry it gave him just enough time to regain his feet before both Nobles were on him again.

The power they'd absorbed from other Nobles over the centuries put each of them alone at nearly the same strength as Dragos. Never would he have expected that tactic from anyone else, a fact that Arsenios obviously had used to his advantage. Without question, Dragos had been outmaneuvered, and he knew he would pay for it.

Liu and Arsenios circled wide, keeping him in their sights. He tried to focus on them both, tried his best to anticipate what would come next. In an instant they lunged with a speed that made each of them blur, even to his sharp eyes. He leapt back, snarling as he parried a rapid barrage of strikes and blasts of energy.

His energy waned as each new wave hit him. They struck in tandem, fusing their power in a way that Dragos couldn't follow. The attacks were relentless, never slowing, even as exhaustion overtook him. They gathered themselves again, and his response was a hair too slow. They smashed through his defenses, sending him to the earth in a heap. Dragos staggered upright, swaying as he fought to maintain his balance.

Broken ribs. My left arm is fractured in three places. Dislocated shoulder. Cracked skull.

Nevertheless, he pushed the pain of his injuries down as Arsenios lunged for him. Dragos pivoted, lashing out with his good arm. Arsenios cried out as Dragos's fist connected with his temple, leaping back as Liu came to his defense. She aimed a kick at Dragos's head, and he barely ducked in time. He countered with a kick of his own, only to have Arsenios reappear at her side and bat his foot away.

Pain lanced up his leg as the force of the block cracked his ankle. Dragos hobbled back, raising a shield just as Liu and Arsenios threw another combined blast of energy at him. Dragos's shield shattered, and he collapsed to the earth.

He had lost.

"That little stunt with the woods tired you out," said Arsenios, his eyes flashing. "You shouldn't have used so much of your power. I expected more from you, Dragos. You were supposed to be stronger than this."

Dragos debated fleeing to his stronghold; it was warded, and the two of them would be unable to enter.

I could try again. I could study them, analyze what went wrong.

He discarded the thought. The outcome of any such conflict between him and the two of them would be the same, regardless of the precautions he took.

And what about the villagers?

If the Arsenios and Liu managed to pen him in, there would be no way for him to provide food for the people who, hopefully, were taking refuge in his stronghold. His food stores were limited, and neither he nor his servants would be able to get past the Nobles' forces to gather more. Everyone would starve.

"Our kind will be safe once again," said Liu.

Dragos felt them gather their energies, combine them into a staggeringly powerful force of will that he knew would have the power to scour him from the earth.

Then, like a light in the darkness, it came to him. It was a radical solution—one that would very likely kill him—but he had to try.

I have nothing left to lose. I'll be dead either way.

Dragos plunged his senses deep within himself, past the core of his being, to a part of him that existed beyond the bounds of thought or consciousness. The essence there was pure, shining with a light more brilliant than anything he'd ever beheld. For a moment, he was stunned at its beauty, shocked that a creature such as he could possess something so wondrous, concealed just below the surface.

My soul. My life-force.

This was the same tactic Chin had used all those years ago. In all his battles, no matter how desperate, Dragos had avoided tapping this source of power. There'd always been another way, a different means to achieve victory or escape. Now, however, his options had run out. Although he risked destroying the very fabric of his own existence, it was his only option.

This must end now.

Without a second thought, Dragos plunged into the light, redirecting it, infusing the force of his will with every last speck he could hold. Just as his two adversaries were on the brink of hitting him with everything they had, he unleashed it.

His surroundings exploded with white-hot fire, and the earth beneath them glowed red as the heat melted every last particle of dirt and rock. Liu and Arsenios screamed as their flesh burst into flames. As Dragos's own skin crackled with the heat, he did his best to fight through the agony, to keep the onslaught going for as long as he could. Arsenios tried to leap beyond the radius of the inferno, but Dragos snapped him back with an exertion of will. Liu had collapsed to the earth, writhing as she became a living torch. Arsenios beat hopelessly at the flames that consumed his body, his features melting into a horrifying mask, all the while pummeling the force that Dragos employed, trying to break through and disperse the heat. It was no use—he might as well have tried to quell a star.

With the last of his strength, Dragos lunged forward, thrusting his hands into the flames that blazed from Arsenios's body, gripping him by the neck. He wrenched with every last bit of strength he possessed, and with a final roar, he tore the head off the older man's body. Dragos sagged to his knees as Arsenios's bewildered consciousness entered his mind.

Sadness. Loneliness. Such torment...

He felt tremendous pity for Arsenios, even as everything that was left of him faded to nothingness. All this time, the man had been permanently twisted, forgetting his humanity completely. Yet there had been a sort of kindness within him, a desire to help others, even if that desire was a bit misguided.

He could have been a great man, if only he hadn't been a Noble.

All at once, the light and the heat vanished. Arsenios was gone, his ashes scattered in the wind. Dragos's world faded around him. That wellspring of power, his soul, flickered like a guttering candle. Liu lay sprawled upon the earth, her clothes burned completely away, her naked skin blackened from top to bottom. Her head was nothing more than a charred skull, and her once white teeth had turned a dark shade of grey. They grinned maddeningly from beneath deep eye sockets where only the faintest yellow glow remained. Somehow, she slowly pushed herself to her knees, bits of ashy skin flaking off of her body.

I hope I have enough power left to destroy her.

Determined to end her before death could take him, Dragos crawled forward as he felt the last of his life-force ebb away.

In an instant, she was gone, enveloped by the shadows, and Dragos was alone.

She still...had the strength...to Travel?

The thought unraveled like a ruined garment, and Dragos collapsed into darkness.

39

Jendar and Mathias had barely gotten everyone inside Dragos's stronghold, with the doors sealed behind them, when the eastern edge of the valley erupted in a flash of blinding light.

"What was that?" asked Mathias, peering out a window.

Jendar knit his brows together. "I have no idea, but it can't be good."

The villagers noticed it too and were whispering excitedly as they pointed toward the light. Though it didn't last long, it left Jendar dazzled. Futilely he tried to blink the afterimage out of his eyes.

"Where's Dragos?" he said.

"I'm not sure. He hasn't come back," said Mathias.

Jendar fidgeted with the talisman around his neck, gazing out the window at the spot where the light had seemed to originate. The woods were still ablaze, bathing half of the ruined village in a madly dancing reddish glare.

"He might be in trouble," said Jendar. "I don't like this one bit."

"He can handle himself," Mathias assured him.

Jendar fingered his amulet again. Just knowing it was there filled him hope and courage. "I'm going out there to find him," he said. "He might need help."

"But there's a *battle* going on! And the lord and lady are probably out there somewhere too."

"That's why I have to find him!"

Jendar headed for the doors. He had a terrible feeling; there was no way he'd be able to sit still and wait to see what unfolded.

"Don't open these doors, no matter what happens," he told Mathias. "Keep everyone calm. I'll be back as soon as I can."

He waved his hand in front of the access panel, and the doors slid open.

Mathias grabbed his arm.

"Don't do this. It's suicide. Dragos can handle himself. Why are you putting yourself at risk?"

Jendar threw off Mathias's grasp.

"Because I *have* to."

He darted out, ignoring Mathias's stunned expression.

DRAGOS FLOATED in a lake of unconsciousness, drifting soundlessly in darkness. The sensation was bizarre yet somehow peaceful. He could vaguely sense the world around him, could just feel his body. His mind seemed attached to it by a single thread, ready to snap and send him to...

Freedom.

That was what awaited him beyond the void. Freedom from his hideous existence. Freedom from loneliness, escape from eternal torture.

Rebecca. Sarah.

He could almost hear the voices of his wife and daughter, could nearly smell them in the stillness of this place. He knew they were nearby, waiting for him.

I'm coming. Be patient...I'm coming...

Suddenly there was someone else. A familiar presence.

A living human.

The scent of blood filled his nostrils, enraptured his senses. The tie to his body felt stronger, and the voices of his wife and daughter died away.

Rebecca! Sarah!

Hollowness. Cold, empty. Another void, this one just beneath his mouth. It begged to be filled with warmth, with sustenance. His mouth opened, and his tongue sharpened and grew. There was flesh nearby. He sought it out, groping blindly.

There!

He plunged his tongue into the ripe meat of fresh prey. He drank deeply, pulling everything he could, mindless with hunger and fatigue. As the connection grew stronger, the void fell away. He was in his body again; he felt his injuries, sensed his surroundings. He clutched something in his arms.

Prey.

His eyes opened, his senses probed, and he recoiled in horror.

Jendar!

He withdrew instantly, dropping the prone, pale figure to the ground.

What have I done?

Jendar was ashen, cold, and smelled of death.

No! Damn it all, no!

THE SUN WAS EXCEEDINGLY BRIGHT, making even the dull metal of the surrounding walls appear resplendent. Jendar raised his arm to shield his eyes but found he could barely manage it; it was as heavy as iron.

He dropped it to his side and closed his eyes again.

"Jendar?"

Mathias's voice, someplace close by.

He tried to speak but could only groan softly.

"Jendar! You're awake!"

"What...where...?" he sputtered.

"Hush," said Mathias. "Don't try to talk. Just rest."

With great effort, Jendar opened his eyes. He was in the same bed he'd slept in the first night he and Mathias had come to the stronghold. "Dragos carried you back here, several days ago, after we saved the village. Do you remember?"

Jendar frowned. Suddenly his head hurt. He remembered leaving, heading for the spot where he'd seen the light, and finding Dragos unconscious and badly burned. He'd gone to him, and then...

He fed on me. And I...I let him. I removed my talisman so he could get close to me.

With tremendous effort, he reached a hand up and touched his neck. He felt the puncture wound.

"Don't try to move. You almost didn't survive."

"Is Dragos...alive?"

Mathias nodded. "You saved his life."

Jendar closed his eyes and settled back down. "Good."

"He really regrets what happened. Called you a fool more than once. He's been in here a lot. Standing and watching over you."

"Where is he now?"

"Resting. Recovering. He was in pretty bad shape too."

Jendar said nothing more. The knowledge that Dragos was safe put him at ease, and he fell into a deep slumber.

When Jendar opened his eyes again, it was night. The room was softly illuminated by a dim globe that hung overhead. He sat up slowly, noting that he felt much better. He glanced down to see a strange device—like a thick bracelet —fastened to his left wrist. He fingered it, trying to find the clasp.

"You should leave that alone."

Jendar glanced up and saw Dragos standing by the windows at the far side of the room. His yellow eyes glowed faintly.

"That device has been feeding you for the past week," he said, walking toward the bed. He looked far better than he had the last time Jendar had seen him, though his eyes lacked their usual deep intensity, and he favored his right leg.

"Feeding me?" Jendar frowned, rotating his arm to get a better look at the object.

"It's an intravenous clamp," he said. "Inside is a tiny nutrient pouch. The nutrients are released, over time, into your bloodstream. It's as if you've had three square meals a day, complete with water."

"Amazing," said Jendar.

"You're looking stronger. Soon I think you'll be ready for some real food."

Jendar stretched, surprised at how stiff his muscles were.

"Do you remember what happened?" asked Dragos.

Jendar nodded. "I remember everything, up until the point where you started feeding."

"Why would you put yourself in such danger?" Dragos

asked quietly. He walked over and took a seat next to the bed. "You could have resisted, could have fled. I was in no condition to pursue you."

Because you're like no man I've ever met, and I couldn't just let you die.

"I...I felt I owed you," he said instead. "I couldn't let your life end. Not after everything you did for us."

"I nearly killed you," said Dragos. "In my dying state, I had no control over my actions. Only after I'd bled you nearly dry did my sanity return enough for me to pull back."

"But you *did* pull back. I knew you would. I had...faith."

Dragos smiled. "It seems the Nobles never quite managed to breed out the best traits of humanity." He sighed, glancing toward the window. "Your village can live in peace, free to develop naturally. No more restrictions, no more forced marriages or untimely deaths. You can develop your own laws, live your own lives, as free people."

Jendar grinned at that. "Speaking of the village," he said, "where are the villagers? Are they still here?"

"I sent them back."

"Is that safe? Are the lord and lady truly dead?"

"The lord is dead. The lady escaped. I haven't been able to trace her. She obscured her trail."

Jendar heaved a sigh. "What if she comes back?"

"We'll make sure your people are armed and educated against the threat her kind pose. A knowledgeable population is a dangerous one. She'll seek easier prey elsewhere."

"Elsewhere? Do you mean there are other people out there?"

Dragos nodded. "There are."

"Are they free, like we are now?"

"In a manner of speaking," said Dragos. "The remaining humans are different than you. The lady won't find them nearly as satisfying as what she's grown used to these past several hundred years. They are, however, far easier quarry.

"Yours was the last true settlement. The others live as nomads, traveling in small groups, huddling in animal-skin tents for warmth. Humanity has changed much these past six hundred years or so. I sincerely hope it'll change again, for the better."

"Are the remaining humans so different from us?"

Dragos leaned in closer to Jendar. "Fundamentally, no. But where the Nobles are concerned, yes. For generations, the people of your village have been bred for a specific purpose: to feed the lord and lady. Your yearly inoculations contained drugs designed to alter your blood chemistry, and make you more satisfying and potent when fed upon. I'm not certain just how lasting these effects will be; perhaps after another generation or two, the changes will have worked their way out of your system."

"Even if they don't," he continued, "there's nothing to fear. I don't believe the changes will be harmful in the long term; in fact, quite the opposite. You and the rest of your villagers may live very long lives—longer than a human would have under normal circumstances."

"I'd be interested to see how long we're capable of living, now that our lives won't end at a prescribed time."

"So would I," said Dragos.

He was silent for a moment, gazing toward the windows again, before speaking.

"Please stay here as long as you like. When you feel strong enough, we can remove the clamp and try some actual food. You can return to the village whenever you're ready."

He turned to leave.

"Dragos?"

He paused, turning toward Jendar. For the first time, Jendar met the gaze of his golden eyes without flinching. "What will you do now? Will you remain here, in your stronghold?"

"For now," said Dragos. "I'll need time to recover. What I did to defeat the lord and lady cost me more than you can imagine. I'd also like to help you, while I heal—there's so much that humanity has lost, so much that I can teach you. I'll pass on what I can, and I'll keep an eye out for Lady Liu. If she doesn't return, then I eventually must seek her out. She's far too dangerous to be left alive."

He turned and left. Almost as soon as the door closed behind him, Jendar was asleep again.

40

J endar breathed the morning air deeply. The faint smell of manure wafted in from the fields, and the sun reflected brightly off the windows of the nearby cottages. He and Mathias had begun work on a second home, just down the road, for Mathias and his new bride, Mathilda Thatcher.

The village had changed much over the past three years. It had begun to expand into what had once been the western wood, and many new buildings were under construction. These structures were far different from the squat wooden edifices the villagers had become accustomed to. Using new techniques gleaned from the trove of cylinders that Dragos had left them, structures could now be built larger and taller than anything seen in the village before.

We've learned so much in such a short time, Jendar thought.

There was more to learn still. Dragos had done his best to provide basic instruction in the sciences, engineering, and medicine. Such a feat hadn't been easy at first. The villagers had been terrified of him, and had not allowed him to enter Endreach. It had taken weeks of countless meetings on the village square convince the others that Dragos had been responsible for saving them all, and that he could be trusted.

In the end he'd taught the villagers to read and write, had instructed them on history and culture, and had introduced literature. After over a thousand years of life, the man had developed a wealth of knowledge on a dizzying array of subjects. The people of Endreach quickly came to appreciate him, and welcomed his guidance.

The villagers had converted the largest building in the village—an old warehouse—into a place of learning, where people could gather in numbers to listen to Dragos speak. At the back of the structure, they'd added a spacious room where all the cylinders Dragos had collected over the years now resided. Players were available to anyone who wished to use them, and the waiting list to get a hold of one stretched into months.

Jendar headed down the street, calling out greetings to those he passed. Endreach was changing rapidly; there was no doubt about that. Wooden roofs were being replaced with a thin pounded alloy the villagers had scavenged from Caput Mundi. By and large, people no longer kept personal gardens, opting to instead use their outdoor spaces for self-drilling wells.

Water right out of our own backyards. Who would have thought?

Light sticks and light orbs were also common sights within peoples' homes, and several of the largest light orbs scavenged from Caput Mundi had been placed on tall posts beside the streets of Endreach, providing illumination even on the darkest nights.

Food was more abundant than ever; fields stretched

endlessly in every direction, and the villagers were raising cattle in far greater numbers. The lord and lady's fortresses still stood at either end of the valley, though perpetual darkness no longer shrouded them. Dragos had dispatched his malforms to each structure after the fighting was over to clear out the remnants of the lord and lady's forces, and had gone through each structure himself more than once just to be sure no more threats remained. When he was satisfied that all was safe, the villagers had begun exploring the buildings themselves, scavenging raw materials and medical supplies.

The weapons they'd found remained in each respective fortress. Everyone regarded the matter disruptors the same way Jendar and Mathias did, with shock and horror. No one could fathom turning one of those devices on another human being. Dragos had convinced them not to throw them all into the bog as Jendar had originally proposed, in case Lady Liu should ever return with more malforms. In the end they were placed in locked store rooms, under a rotating guard of volunteers from Endreach.

Aside from the volunteers, the fortresses remained empty. There was talk of using one of them as the seat of the new Village Council, though Jendar figured that most of his fellow residents were still too frightened of the buildings to conduct business there.

Someday, they won't be so scared. When it really sinks in that the Nobles are gone, we'll put those buildings to good use.

Jendar stopped when he came to a half-built structure where a group of men and women congregated. Mathias emerged from the group, smiling widely.

"Up early again?" asked Jendar.

"I've been up for hours," said Mathias. "I wanted to get

down here to make sure the job site was clean before the day's work began."

Jendar laughed. "You cleaned the site last night! Just admit it—you're excited."

Mathias shrugged, grinning even more broadly. "What's not to be excited about? A new home and a new life. Mathilda is every bit as excited as I am."

Jendar glanced at the crowd, where a stout woman with delicate features and fiery-red hair stood. Her belly swelled with child. She waved when she spotted Jendar, and he waved and smiled in return.

"Your wife looks as lovely as ever," said Jendar.

"I just hope we finish our home in time," said Mathias. "It'll be very cramped if we have to live with her mother and father once the baby is born."

"You can always come back home," said Jendar.

"You know her parents won't hear of it. They insist on taking care of us until we have a place of our own. The last thing I want to do is disrespect them by leaving, especially when they've been so generous and kind."

"I figured as much," Jendar said. "But remember, the two of you are always welcome."

The brothers watched as the rest of the workers arrived.

"Looks like we'll be getting started soon," said Jendar.

Mathias nodded. "This is quite a project. The biggest house in the village!"

"For now," said Jendar. "Imagine what we'll be building in a decade, thanks to everything Dragos has taught us."

"I suppose you're right," said Mathias. "Still, I'm incredibly happy with it. It's going to be a wonderful home."

They were silent for a moment.

"Do you suppose we'll ever see him again?" said Mathias.

"You mean Dragos?"

Mathias nodded.

"I hope we do," Jendar said quietly.

Mathias placed a hand on his shoulder.

"Though you never discuss it, I know how you feel about him," he said. "This can't be easy on you."

Jendar smiled sadly, and gave his brother's hand a gentle squeeze. It had been nearly a year since Dragos had announced his departure, and no one had seen him since the night they'd all said their farewells.

"I hope he's all right," said Jendar.

"I'm sure he is. If we've learned anything about him, it's that he knows how to handle himself."

"Do you think he'll ever find Lady Liu?"

Mathias nodded. "I'm certain."

In addition to everything else, Dragos had taught the villagers everything he knew about his own species—their strengths, their weaknesses, how they hunted, how they thought. He had his malforms give talismans to every one of them, and no villager was ever without one of the tiny objects hanging around his or her neck.

Jendar fingered the star he was wearing—a gift Dragos had instructed his malforms to give specifically to him.

"If Lady Liu ever makes her way back here," he said, "she's going to get more than she bargained for."

One of the men broke away from the group and approached the brothers. "Ready to get started?"

Mathias smiled and clapped Jendar on the back. Jendar grinned in return, and the brothers walked toward the unfinished building. Jendar was determined to help make it the best home the village had ever seen.

ABOUT THE AUTHOR

Kevin Pines was born and raised in the Chicago suburbs. He lives with his family and many animals, including two dogs, four cats, five chickens, and an aquarium full of Platies (in which a number of new fry seem to appear each day). He enjoys coffee a bit too much.

Visit him on the web: www.kevinpines.com.